LEGENDS

OF
THE *Outback*

Books in this miniseries are:

#3595 *A Wife at Kimbara*
#3607 *The Bridesmaid's Wedding*
#3619 *The English Bride*

Each story can be read independently, but together they create an intimate family saga.

LEGENDS OF THE *Outback*

MARGARET WAY

MILLS & BOON

CONTENTS

A WIFE AT KIMBARA   7

THE BIDESMAID'S WEDDING   167

THE ENGLISH BRIDE   327

A Wife At Kimbara

CHAPTER ONE

BROD STRODE FROM the blinding light of the compound into the welcoming gloom of the old homestead's hallway. His whole body was sheened with sweat and his denim shirt covered in dust and grass stains. He and his men had been up since dawn driving a herd of uncooperative cattle from drying Egret Creek to Three Moons, a chain of billabongs some miles off.

It had been a long hot slog filled with plenty of curses and frustration as several beasts in turn tried to break away from the herd. Dumber than dumb in some situations cattle had a decided ability to hold their own in the bush.

He could do with a good scrub but there was scant time for that. His schedule was as hectic as ever. He'd almost forgotten, the station vet was flying in this afternoon to give another section of the herd a general check over. That was about three o'clock. He had time to grab a sandwich and a cup of tea and return to the holding yard they'd set up under the gum trees.

Now he focused on the stack of mail neatly piled on top of the rough pine bench that served as a console. No Kimbara this he thought with bleak humour. Definitely not the splendid historic homestead of his birth.

His father resided on Kimbara. Stewart Kinross. Lord of the Desert. Leaving his only son to slave his guts out running the cattle chain while he claimed all the glory. Not that there weren't quite a few people in the know. Not that it bothered him all that much he thought swivelling to throw his black Akubra onto a peg on the wall. It landed unerringly on the target as it always did but he paid no attention. His day would come. He and Ally together had quite a stake in the diverse Kinross enterprises with ancestral Kimbara, the flagship of the Kinross cattle empire the jewel in the crown.

Grandad Kinross, legendary hero, had seen to that, never blind to his son Stewart's true nature. Andrew Kinross was long gone while his grandson lived a near outcast on Marlu for the past five years. In fact it had been since Alison, hiding her heartache over the breakup of her passionate romance with Rafe Cameron, left home for the Big Smoke, the name the Outback bestowed on big bustling cosmopolitan Sydney.

Alison said then she wanted to try her hand at acting like their celebrated Aunt Fee who had taken off at eighteen full of wild dreams of making a brilliant career for herself on the London stage. And wonder of wonders Fee had actually succeeded despite a well publicised out of control love life. Now she was back on Kimbara writing her sensational memoirs.

Fee was quite a character, too famous to qualify for black sheep of the family but with two big-time broken marriages behind her and the legacy of an exquisite English rose of a daughter. Lady Francesca de Lyle, no less. His and Ally's cousin and from what they'd seen of her as good as she was beautiful. Couldn't have been easy with the arty oversexed Fee for a mother.

Now Fee was telling all, convinced her biography would be a huge success in the hands of one Rebecca Hunt, an award-winning young journalist from Sydney with another well received biography of a retired Australian diva under her belt.

Just to think of Rebecca Hunt lit a dangerous flame somewhere inside him. Such was the power of a woman's beauty he thought disgustedly when he distrusted her like hell. He had no difficulty summoning up her image. Satiny black hair framing a lily cool face, but with one hell of a seductive mouth. The mouth was a dead give-away. Yet she was so utterly immaculate and self-possessed she was darn near mysterious. He could never imagine someone like him for instance mussing that sleek hair or laying a finger on her magnolia flesh. She was way too perfect for him. Brod gave an involuntary laugh the fall of light in the hall giving his lean handsome features a brooding hawklike quality. In reality the patrician Miss Hunt was just another mightily ambitious woman.

It wasn't his father that had her in thrall. No way would he accept that. Not that his father wasn't a big handsome guy, assured, cultivated, filthy rich, fifty-five and looking a good ten years younger. Forget the meanness there. No it was the wild splendour of Kimbara that interested Miss Hunt, of the large ravishing grey eyes. Eyes like the still crystal waters of a hidden rock pool, yet he had divined instantly Miss Hunt would discard her promising little career any day to become mistress of Kimbara. From a fledgling career to riches beyond her imaginings. Only one catch: She could only have it all while his father lived. After that it was his turn.

The Kinross tradition had never been broken. Kimbara, the Kinross's ancestral home was passed directly from father to firstborn son. No one had ever abdicated in favour of a brother though Andrew Kinross had been a second son, surviving the Second World War when his elder brother James hadn't. James had died in his brother's arms in a far distant desert, very different from their own. One of the countless terrible tragedies of war.

Shaking his head sadly, Brod moved to pick up the mail riffling through it. It had been flown in that day while he was far out on the run. Wally his loyal, part aboriginal ex-stockman had brought it up. Since he had badly smashed his leg in a fall from his horse, Wally's duties revolved around the small homestead and the homestead's vegetable garden, which was currently thriving. Wally wasn't turning into a bad cook, either. At any rate better than him.

Only one piece of correspondence really caught his eye and somehow he had been expecting it. He ripped it open smiling grimly at the contents. Why would the old man contact him directly when he was so good at letters? He took a harsh breath. No "Dear Brod." Nothing like that. No enquires as to his health. It appeared his father had arranged a gala event to impress and entertain Miss Hunt. A polo weekend at the end of the month. In other words ten days' time. Matches starting Saturday morning with the main event 3:00 p.m. Usual gala ball in the Great Hall Saturday night.

His father would naturally captain the main team, read, hand-pick the best players. His son Brod would be allowed to captain the other. His father hated like hell that his son was so damned good if a bit on the wild side. God pity him, his father seemed to hate everything he did even as the chain thrived. If the truth be known his father didn't look on him as a son at all. Since he had grown to manhood his father had treated him more like a rival. An enemy at the gate. It was all so bloody bizarre. Small wonder he and Ally were emotionally scarred, but both of them had confronted it.

Their mother had run off when he was only nine and Ally a vulnerable little four-year-old. How could she have done it? Not that he and Ally didn't come to understand it in time. Getting to know their father so well, his black moods, the colossal arrogance, the coldness and the biting tongue they reckoned their mother had been driven to it. Maybe she would have fought for their custody as she swore she would but then she had gotten herself killed in a car smash less than a year later. He vividly remembered the day his father had called him into his study to tell him about the accident.

"No one gets away from me," Stewart Kinross had said with a chilling smile on his face.

That was Brod's father.

He shook his head in despair. At least he and Ally, the closest of siblings, had had Grandfather Kinross to turn to. For a
while. A finer man had never been born. The best thing that
had ever been said to him had come from one of his grandfather's closest friends, Sir Jock McTavish.

"You have all your Granddaddy's great fighting heart and
spirit, Broderick. I know you're going to live up to the legend!"

Jock McTavish knew how to size a man up. In the many
shattering confrontations Brod had had with his father over the
years he tried to hold fast to Sir Jock's words. It hadn't been easy
when his father had never ceased trying to grind him down.

Brod sighed and thrust his father's letter into the pocket of his
jeans. He had no desire to travel so far, he told himself. It was
one hell of an overland trek from Marlu to the Kinross stronghold in the Channel Country in the far south west of the giant
state of Queensland. Plus he was too damned busy. If he went
at all he would have to fly. His father sure hadn't offered to
pick him up in the Beech Baron. He'd have to call up the Camerons as he did frequently even after Ally's breakup with Rafe.

He'd grown up with the Cameron brothers, Rafe and Grant.
The history of the Kinross and Cameron families was the history of the Outback. It was their Scottish ancestors themselves,
close friends from childhood who had pioneered the fabled region in the process turning themselves into cattle barons. Both
dynasties had survived. Not only survived, flourished.

Sudden frustration seized him. He remembered as vividly
as yesterday the time Ally had come to tell him she couldn't
marry Rafe. She was going away. A journey of self-discovery
she called it. Her romance with Rafe was simply too overwhelming for comfort.

"But hell, Ally, you love him!" He could hear his own disbe-
lieving voice. "And he sure as hell is crazy about you."

"I love him with every breath that's in me," Ally had responded passionately, fiercely wiping tears from her face. "But
you don't know what it's like, Brod. All the girls fall for you,

but not a one of them has touched your heart. Rafe squeezes the heart out of me, do you see? I'm sick of him and sick with him. He's more than I can take on."

Bewildered he had ploughed on. "So he's forceful? A man's man. He's not in the least like our father. There's nothing dark and frightening about Rafe, if that's what you're worried about. He's one hell of a guy. What's got into you, Ally? Rafe is my best friend. The Kinross'es and the Camerons are damned near related. We all thought your marriage to Rafe would finally unite our two families. Even the old man is all for it going ahead. Marvellous choice and all that. Couldn't be more suitable." He aped his father's deep, polished tones.

"I can't do it, Brod," Ally had insisted. "Not yet. I have to learn a lot more about myself before I take on Rafe. I'm terribly sorry to disappoint you. Father will be furious." Her beautiful clear green eyes darkened at the prospect.

He had taken her in his arms then, hugging her to him. "You could never disappoint me, Ally," he told her. "My love for you is too great. My respect for your wisdom and spirit. Maybe its because you're so young. Barely twenty. You have your whole life in front of you. Go with my blessing but for God's sake come back to Rafe."

"If he'll have me." Ally had tried to smile through her tears.

It hadn't happened. Rafe had never seriously been drawn to another woman but the one person they never talked about was Alison. That subject was taboo. Tough, self-sufficient as he was giving no sign of hurting, Brod knew. Ally had dealt his friend a near mortal blow.

Momentarily disconsolate he stared sightless through the open doorway. Five years later and Ally still hadn't returned home. Ally like Fee had developed quite a talent for acting. Something in the genes. Ally had just won a Logie for best actress in a TV series drama playing a young doctor in a country town. She was enormously popular for her beauty and charm, the way she gave such life and conviction to her frequently affecting role. He was full of admiration for her but he really missed her; the comfort and humour of her company. God knows how Rafe, being Rafe, coped with the bitterness of rejection that must have accumulated in his heart? He didn't take it out on him though Grant, the younger brother had been known to fire off a few salvos. Rafe and Grant were as close as he and Ally. To hurt one was to hurt the other. Both brothers would be certain starters in the main polo match the coming Saturday afternoon. Both excellent players though Rafe had the edge. But neither was going to faze him.

He liked the going tough and dangerous and he didn't think he'd have too much trouble persuading one or both to join his team despite his father and he'd need their help getting to Kimbara.

The Cameron's historic station Opal Plains bordered Kimbara on its north-northeast border. Grant ran a helicopter service from Opal that covered their part of Outback while Rafe was master of the vast station. Aristocrats of the Outback, the press called all three of them. They presented a polished front to the world, but there had been plenty of sadness and tragedy in their lives.

No, even if he could cadge a ride with Rafe and Grant he had no desire to confront either his father or the magnolia skinned Rebecca. If the truth be told he couldn't bear to see them together. His father showing that seemingly flawless young woman all the exquisite care and consideration he had never accorded his daughter, let alone his wife.

Often to amuse as much as torment himself he conjured up the ridiculous picture of Stewart Kinross down on his knees before the luminous eyed Miss Hunt begging for her hand in marriage. His father so rich and powerful he thought he was invincible. So sure of his virility, he thought he possessed such sexual magnetism he could easily attract a woman half his age. If it weren't so damned likely it would be funny. Women couldn't resist power and money. Especially not adventuresses.

He'd have to find out a little bit more about Miss Rebecca Hunt, he decided. She was remarkably close lipped about her past though he knew from the blurb on the back of the recent biography she'd been born in Sydney in 1973. That made her twenty-seven. Three years younger than he. The rest went on to list the not inconsiderable achievements of her short career.

She had been named Young Journalist of the year at the age of twenty-four. She'd worked with the Australian Broadcasting Commission, SBS and Channel 9. Two years with the British Press. A book of interviews with the rich and famous. The diva's biography. Now Aunt Fee.

Next to nothing about her private life, though. It might have been as blank as a nun's only Miss Rebecca Hunt behind the cool facade was so absolutely fascinating she couldn't have escaped at least a few sexual encounters. If she was footloose it had to be by choice. Was she waiting for the right man? Charming, clever, rich and powerful.

Most people thought Stewart Kinross was just that, until little bits of him occasionally seeped out. The ego, the self-centeredness, the caustic tongue. But when he set out to, Brod had to admit, his father could be dazzling. A young woman like Miss Rebecca Hunt was bound to be socially ambitious. If she took on his father she would get more than she bargained for, the conniving little witch. He almost felt a stab of pity.

No, he didn't want to go, he told himself, suddenly realising he wanted to go very much.

CHAPTER TWO

REBECCA WAS STANDING on the upstairs balcony looking out over Kimbara's magnificent home gardens when Stewart Kinross finally tracked her down, as purposefully as a hunter tracks his quarry.

"Ah, there you are, my dear," he smiled indulgently, as he moved to join her at the balustrade. "A bit of news I thought you might like to hear."

She swung to face him, so lovely he couldn't take his eyes off her.

"Then let's hear it!" Rebecca responded brightly, shying away from the thought her host had taken quite a fancy to her. A thought too embarrassing to pursue. For all his wealth, suavity and charm, Stewart Kinross was of an age with her father. Not that a man as rich and handsome as that couldn't get just about any woman he wanted. But not *her*. Involvement, even with a man her own age wasn't an option. Peace of body, mind and heart were too important. Yet Stewart Kinross was looking at her delightedly out of grey-green eyes.

"I've organised one of my famous polo weekends for your enjoyment," he told her, realising she was making him feel younger with every passing day. "The Matches will be followed by a gala ball, Saturday night with a big breakfast cum brunch in the garden Sunday morning through to noon. After that our guests like to get off home. Most fly, some make the overland trek.

"It sounds exciting." Rebecca struggled a little to sound enthusiastic. In truth her heart was thumping though none of her disquiet showed in her face. "I've never actually attended a polo match."

"Why do you think I've organised this weekend?" he chuffed, his handsome mouth curving beneath a full, beautifully clipped moustache. "I overheard you telling Fee."

She felt a sudden loss of safety. Stewart Kinross for all his charm was a man who was used to getting what he wanted. It would be a disaster if he wanted something from her she couldn't possibly provide. "You're very kind to me, Stewart," she managed to say. "You *and* Fiona," she stressed. "I do appreciate it."

"You're very easy to be kind to, my dear." He tried to keep the feeling out of his voice but failed. "And you're making Fee so happy with what you're doing with her book."

"Fee has a fascinating story to tell." Rebecca turned slightly away from him, leaning her slender body against the white wrought-iron balustrade. "She knows everyone who's anyone in the English theatre as well as so many powerful international figures. There's just so much subject matter. An abundance of it."

"Fee has lived a full life," he agreed somewhat dryly. "She's a born actress as is my daughter, Alison."

His voice was surprisingly cool for a proud father.

"Yes, I've seen her many times on television," Rebecca said admiringly. "Some of the episodes have been remarkably affecting because of the wonderful quality of her acting. She brings her character, the country doctor, to such life. I'd love to meet her."

"I don't think you'll see Alison back here." He sighed with evident regret. "She's well and truly settled in Sydney. She rarely comes home on a visit. Then, I sometimes think, it's only to see Brod not the father she's almost forgotten."

Rebecca looked at him more sympathetically.

"How can that be? I'm sure she misses you. Being the star of a top rating television series must put a lot of pressure on her. I imagine she has very little free time."

"Alison was raised in the Outback," Stewart Kinross said his expression judgemental. "On Kimbara which if I say so myself is a magnificent inheritance. She has no need to work."

"You can't mean you'd deny her a career?" Rebecca was taken aback.

"Of course not." He took his cue from her tone. "But Alison made a lot of people unhappy when she left. Not the least the man who loved and trusted her. Rafe Cameron."

"Ah the Camerons." Rebecca remembered all the stories she'd heard. "I researched their family history at the same time I was researching yours. Two great pioneering families. Legends of the Outback."

He accepted her accolade as though she were speaking directly about him. "Our families have always been very close. It was my dearest wish Alison would marry Rafe. A splendid young man. But she chose an acting career just like Fee. I'm telling you because you'll be meeting Rafe at the polo. I've scheduled it for the weekend after next.

"Rafe will never forgive, never forget what Alison did to him and even as Alison's father I don't blame him. Rafe is Brod's best friend, I think a good steadying influence on him. Brod is a rebel, which you might have gathered. Has been since his childhood. A pity because it makes for a lot of friction between us."

"I'm sorry," Rebecca responded. "Will he be coming for your weekend?"

"He's certainly been invited." Stewart Kinross looked away over her head. "But Brod likes to keep me begging. The thing is he's needed to captain the opposing team. At least he inherited his prowess from me. I expect I'll hear from him at his leisure. I'm very keen for this to go well, Rebecca. I want you to enjoy your time out here as much as possible."

"It's wonderful to be here, Stewart," Rebecca said, her heart sinking at the look in his eyes.

"What would you say to a ride this afternoon." He put his hand on her arm leading her back into the house lest she escape him.

"That would be lovely, Stewart," she responded, careful to inject a note of regret, "but Fiona has need of me. We're really moving along with the book."

He bowed his handsome head powerfully, protectively over her. "My dear, you can't refuse me. I can do some persuading when I have to. I'll set it straight with Fee and you and I can take the horses out. It's wonderful you ride so well. I want you to look on your time with us as part work part vacation."

"Thank you, Stewart," Rebecca murmured, feeling trapped and somehow ungrateful as well. Stewart Kinross had been the kindest and most considerate of hosts. Perhaps her early experiences had left her a bit paranoid.

In the early evening Broderick Kinross rang. As it happened Rebecca was passing through the hallway so she backtracked to answer the call.

"Kinross homestead."

Whoever was at the other end said nothing for a moment then a male voice so vibrant, so unforgettable, it gave her a shock responded. "Miss Hunt, I presume."

"That's right." She felt proud of her calmness.

"Brod Kinross here."

As if she didn't know. "How are you, Mr. Kinross?"

"Just wonderful and such a tonic to hear your voice."

"I expect you want to speak to your father," she said quickly, feeling the sharp edge to the black velvet delivery.

"I expect he's enjoying his pre-dinner drink," he drawled,

"No, don't disturb him, Miss Hunt. Instead could you please tell him I'll be at Kimbara....

Not *home?* She listened.

"For the polo weekend. Grant Cameron is giving me a lift should my father decide to send the Beech for me. Dad's pretty devoted you know."

Sarcasm without a doubt. "I'll tell him, Mr. Kinross."

"I trust in time you'll be able to call me Brod." Again the ghost of mockery.

"My friends call me Rebecca," Rebecca finally said.

"It suits you beautifully."

"Why must you sound mocking?" She brought it out into the open.

"That's very good, Miss Hunt." He applauded. "You know how to pick up nuances."

A sparkle of anger lit Rebecca's eyes. She was glad he couldn't see it. "Let's say I know how to pick up warning signals."

"Quite sure of that?" he responded just as coolly.

"You don't have to tell me you don't like me." He could scarcely deny it after that first time.

"Why in the world wouldn't I," he answered and rang off with nothing resolved.

What *was* he getting at? Rebecca let out a short pent-up breath, replacing the receiver rather shakily. Their one and only meeting had been brief but disturbing. She remembered it vividly. It was late last month and he had flown in to Kimbara unexpectedly...

She had put on her large straw hat before venturing out into the heat of the day. Fee had had a slight headache so they had taken a break. Every chance she had she liked to explore this fantastic environment that was Kimbara. The sculptural effects of the trees, the shrubs and rocks, the undulating red dunes on the station's south-southwestern borders. It truly was another world, the distances so immense, the light so dazzling, the colours more sun-seared than anywhere else. She loved all the burnt ochres the deep purples the glowing violets and amethysts, the grape-blues that made such a wonderful contrast to the fiery terracottas.

Stewart had promised her a trip into the desert when the worst of the heat was over and she was greatly looking forward to it. It would be too much to expect she would be granted the privilege of seeing the wild heart burst into bloom. No rains had fallen for many long months but she had seen Stewart's collection of magnificent photographs of Kimbara under a brilliant carpet of wildflowers and marvelled at the phenomenon. Not that localised rain was even needed to make the desert bloom, he had told her. Once the floods started in the tropical far north sending waters coursing southward, thousands of square miles of the Channel Country could be irrigated. Swollen streams ran fifty miles across the plains they were so flat. It was such a fascinating land and a fascinating life. Stewart Kinross had to live like a feudal lord within his desert stronghold.

She had just reached the stables complex, which housed some wonderful horses, when she heard the clash of voices. Men's voices not dissimilar in timbre and tone. Angry voices that made her go quiet.

"I'm not here to take orders from you," Stewart Kinross was saying in a rasping voice.

"That's exactly what you're going to do unless you want to scuttle the whole project," the other younger voice answered none too deferentially. "Face it, Dad, not everyone likes the way you operate. Jack Knowles for one and we need Jack if this enterprise is going to succeed."

"That's *your* gut feeling is it?" There was such a sneer in it Rebecca recoiled.

"You should have some," Stewart Kinross's son quipped, sounding to Rebecca's ears convincingly tough.

"Don't lecture me," his father came back thunderously. "Your day is not yet and don't you forget it."

"Not with you on about it all the time," the son retorted. "An argument, Dad. That's the best reward I ever get. But hell, I no longer care. In case you've forgotten I do most of the work while you sit around enjoying the benefits."

At that Stewart Kinross exploded but Rebecca waited for no more. She turned abruptly shocked by the palpable bitterness of the exchange. She had heard Stewart Kinross and his son weren't close but she hadn't been prepared for the depth of that disaffection. She had heard as well Broderick Kinross at the age of thirty ran the Kinross cattle empire from distant Marlu. Something he seemed to have confirmed. It was all very disturbing. Even as an outsider she felt the emnity. It was a new insight into Stewart Kinross as well. Fee had assured her her nephew and niece, Brod and Alison, were wonderful young people. Not that Fee had seen a great deal of them with a life based in London. But she spoke of them both with great affection.

It occurred to Rebecca for the first time, though Fee was a great talker, she was remarkably reticent about her only brother. Certainly Rebecca felt appalled by the cold venom of Stewart Kinross's tone. She would have thought he would be immensely proud of his son.

Troubled by what she had overheard Rebecca walked quickly away. The last thing she wanted was to be seen but her efforts were doomed to failure. Both men must have moved off in her direction because a few moments later Stewart Kinross's commanding voice required her to stop.

"Rebecca," he called in a nice mix of authoritarian and genial host.

She turned watching them emerge from the stables complex, probably on their way back to the house.

"Stewart!" Even with her large shady hat she had to put a hand to her eyes against the brilliant sunlight.

Two men in silhouette. Both very tall, a couple of inches

over six feet, one with the full substance of maturity, the other a whipcord rangy young man, both wearing the standard Akubra, the younger man with a decidedly rakish tilt. He had a great walk, she thought, putting her in mind of some actor, a kind of graceful lope.

She felt little tears in her eyes at the near unendurable light and wondered why she hadn't brought her sunglasses.

They caught up with her easily and she had her first sight of Broderick Kinross, heir to the Kinross cattle and business empire.

She didn't know how she had pictured him. Handsome certainly, given the family good looks but not *this*. He literally blazed. The blue eyes so vivid they trapped her gaze. For an instant she had the extraordinary sensation something had cut off her breath.

"Rebecca, may I introduce my son, Broderick." Stewart Kinross looked down at her, sounding as though he preferred not to. "He's here for an interim report to me." He continued more briskly. "Brod, this is the very clever young woman who is writing Fee's biography as I'm sure you've heard. Rebecca Hunt."

Rebecca gave Broderick Kinross her hand perturbed by the adrenaline that was pouring into her body. She looked up into a lean, striking face, beautiful glittering blue eyes. For someone who had laboured long and hard to maintain a fail-safe cool facade she now felt bathed in heat.

"How do you do, Miss Hunt." He was perfectly courteous, on the formal side, yet she felt the shock and hostility that was in him. Why? "When I last spoke to Fee she was very happy with the start you've made on the book. Obviously she has confidence in you."

"I'm very grateful that she thought of me at all," Rebecca said, subdued by the tingling in her hand. "I'm not terribly well-known."

"Don't be so modest, my dear," Stewart Kinross responded

in a voice like warmed syrup. He draped a proprietorial arm around her shoulder. Something he had never done before. "I read your biography and thoroughly enjoyed it." Very gently he turned her around, enchanted by the way the large straw brim of her hat shadowed her face. "You really shouldn't go wandering around in the heat. For all that charming hat you risk burning that lovely skin."

Why the hell don't you hug her, Brod thought with black humour.

He never thought he would live to see adoration in his father's eyes, but this was coming mighty close. Fee had confided to him on the side "your father is quite taken with Rebecca." More like infatuated.

Brod felt a bit shell-shocked himself and he'd had more than his share of girlfriends.

She was lovely in a way that didn't appeal to him at all. The hot-house flower. Good bones, but delicate like a dancer. A little scrap of a thing. No more than five-three. Big light-filled grey eyes, satin near-black hair that fell almost to her shoulders and curved in under her chin and that fabulous skin. All the girls he knew had a golden tan, were tall and athletic and they didn't wear beautiful silly hats with brims that dipped and flowers and ribbons for a trim. Miss Rebecca Hunt was no wildflower. She was an exotic. A vision of cool beauty.

"I take it we've finished our business for the day, Brod." Stewart Kinross turned his handsome head with its immaculate cream Akubra to address his son.

Brod took his eyes off Miss Hunt for a moment to answer. "Please, Dad, give me a break. I can't go away without speaking to Fee." The words were said with gentle irony, but Rebecca could see he had no intention of going.

"Well then, come along," Stewart Kinross answered pleasantly, but with a certain glint in his eye. "I'm sure Mrs Matthews—" he referred to Kimbara's long time housekeeper "—can provide you with some afternoon tea."

"So have you had sufficient time to form an opinion about our world, Miss Hunt?" Brod asked, falling back into line with the petite Miss Hunt in the middle. He was glad his father had at last removed his arm from her delicate shoulders. He felt like flinging it off himself.

"I love it." Her charming voice was filled with sincerity. "It may seem strange but I don't know my own country as well as I know some places overseas."

"There is the fact Australia is so big," he offered dryly, indicating the vastness around them.

"And you can't be all that long out of university?" He glanced down at her meaningfully.

"I'm twenty-seven." She gave him a shimmering cool glance.

"My dear, in that hat you look seventeen," Stewart Kinross complimented her.

"Scarlet O'Hara," Broderick Kinross murmured, sounding none too impressed. "You didn't once travel Outback?"

"As I say, oddly no." Rebecca gathered her defences around her. "My work kept me in Sydney for the most part. I spent two wonderful years overseas, based in London, though I never got to meet Fee. I've visited all the state capitals, tropical North Queensland many times. I love it. I've holidayed on the Great Barrier Reef, but this is another world after the lushness of the coastline. Almost surreal with the vast, empty landscape, the monolithic rocks, and the extraordinary changing colours. Stewart is going to take me on a trip out into the desert."

"Really?" Broderick Kinross shot a glance at his father, his cleanly cut mouth compressed. "When is this?"

"When the worst of the heat dies down a little," Stewart Kinross said with almost a bluster.

"Magnolias wilt in the heat," Broderick Kinross lowered his head to peer at the curve of Rebecca's cheek.

"Trust me, Mr. Kinross." Rebecca's head shot up as she gave the sardonic Broderick a brief sidelong glance. "I don't wilt."

"I'm holding my breath until you tell me more about yourself," he retorted, a faint catch of laughter in his voice. "I'm sure any young woman as beautiful as yourself has a boyfriend somewhere."

"Actually, no." She wanted to cry out, "Please leave me alone." He was getting to her as he obviously meant to.

"What is this, Brod, an interrogation?" his father asked, drawing his thick black eyebrows together.

"Not at all. If it seemed like that I apologise," he said. "I'm always interested in your visitors, Dad. Miss Hunt seems more interesting than most."

Interesting wasn't the word. A true femme fatale.

They had just reached the main gate of the compound, a massive wrought-iron affair that fronted the surrounding white-washed walls when a nesting magpie shot out of a tree, diving so low over their heads Rebecca gave an involuntary cry. She was well aware magpies could be a menace when they thought the nest was under threat. The bird wheeled with incredible speed clearly on the attack but this time Broderick Kinross, with a muffled exclamation, pulled her against him with one arm and made a swipe at the offending bird with his black Akubra.

"Go on, get!" he cried, with the voice of authority.

The bird did, keeping just out of range.

To Rebecca's searing shame her whole body reacted to being clamped to his. It was a dreadful weakness that she thought long buried.

"It can't hurt you." He released her almost immediately, staring up at the peacock-blue sky. "They're a damned nuisance when they're nesting."

"You're all right aren't you, Rebecca?" Stewart Kinross asked, genuinely solicitous. "You've gone rather pale."

"It was nothing, nothing," she began to laugh the moment off. "It's not my first magpie attack."

"And you've told us you're pretty brave." Broderick Kinross caught her gaze. A moment that spun out too long.

"I told you I don't wilt," she corrected, a tiny blue pulse beating in her throat.

"No." A ripple of something like sexuality moved like a breeze across his face. "Wasn't she magnificent, Dad?" he teased.

"You must understand that Broderick likes a little joke, Rebecca," Stewart Kinross said, a crack appearing in his grand manner.

"Then I generously forgive him," Rebecca spoke sweetly even though her breath still shook in her chest.

What she wanted out of life was peace. That she intended to guard fiercely even against a cyclonic force. Broderick Kinross had the dark, dangerous power to sweep a woman away.

On the Saturday morning of the polo match, Fee woke late, still feeling weary from insufficient sleep. She turned on her back easing the satin pads from her eyes. Living so long in England she had all but forgotten the brilliant light of her homeland. Now she had these eye pads on hand for the moment when the all powerful sun threw golden fingers of light across the wide verandah and into her bedroom.

She was a chronic insomniac these days. Nothing seemed to cure it. She'd tried knock out pills—get up in the morning and have a good strong cup of coffee advice from her doctor—but she hated drugs, preferring herbal cures, or relaxation techniques, not that she had ever been a great one to relax. Too much adrenaline in the blood. Too many late, late nights. Too many lovers. Too many after performance parties. Too many social events crammed into her calendar. She thought she might be able to unwind once she returned home but it wasn't happening.

Of course she and Stewart never did get on, as children and adolescents. Stewart so absolutely full of himself. Since birth. Fiona had taken herself out of the jarring environment of playing second fiddle to her swaggering brother, The Heir, by setting sail for England. Of course her beloved dad, Sir Andy, shocked out of his mind at the prospect of losing his little princess had tried to stop her but in the end when faced with her shrieking virago acts sent her off with enough money to keep her in great style while she studied drama in preparation for her brilliant career. She'd managed this through a combination of beauty— let's face it, even at sixty she could still make heads swivel— lots of luck, the Kinross self-confidence and a good resonant speaking voice, possibly from all that yelling outdoors. She had the lung capacity to fill a theatre like her good friend La Stupenda. And the Gods be praised, native talent. If you didn't have that you had nothing.

The thing that was really niggling away at her was this new potentially destructive situation with Stewart and Rebecca. God knows she'd seen enough of ageing men wearing pretty things young enough to be their daughters even granddaughters on their sleeves, but she wasn't at all happy about Stewart's interest in this particular young woman she'd become so fond of. Apart from the big age difference, part of her wanted badly to warn Rebecca against her brother's practised charm. How could any young person, a near stranger, know what lay beneath the superbly self-assured manner? No wonder little Lucille, her dead sister-in-law had run off. Lucille so gentle a spirit would have fared badly trying to withstand Stewart's harsh nature. In the end she'd shrunk from it.

And there was the way Stewart had treated his children, especially Broderick, who had his mother's glorious eyes although he was clearly a Kinross. Sir Andy had written to her often about his concerns and she had seen for herself Stewart's coldness towards his children whenever she returned home. Those were the years when her darling Sir Andy was still alive. She wouldn't be here now much as she loved the place of her birth only for the fact Stewart was trying to talk her into selling her shares in several Kinross enterprises. There were many family interests to discuss. No need for her to run off. This was the home of her ancestors.

Oddly enough it had been Stewart who had begun all the talk about her writing her biography. He had even suggested a possible candidate for the job. A young award-winning journalist called Rebecca Hunt, already the author of a successful biography about another family friend, opera singer Judy Thomas. *Dame* Judy lest any of us forget. Stewart had read Judy's autographed book and been impressed. He'd also seen the young Hunt woman being interviewed on one of those Sunday afternoon programs about the Arts.

"Ask her out here, Fee," Stewart had urged her, laying a compelling hand on her shoulder. "If only to see if the two of you could get along. After all, my dear, you've had a dazzling career. You have something to *say.*"

She'd fallen for it hook, line and sinker, closing her eyes to the past, gratified by his interest, thinking Stewart could be very charming now that he'd mellowed. Clever, clever, Stewart.

She'd done what he wanted. Lured Rebecca into his trap. Stewart had obviously fallen in love with her. On sight. She was just the sort of patrician creature he had always liked with her pure face and haunted eyes. Oh, yes, they were haunted for all Stewart thought they were cool as lakes. Rebecca had a past. Behind the immaculate exterior, Fee suspected Rebecca had her own story to tell. A story involving some very bitter experience. One that lay hidden but not buried. Fee knew all about the wilderness of love.

She threw back the silk coverlet, putting her still pretty bare feet to the floor. Much as she adored the company of her nephew, secretly revelled in watching him outplay his father in all departments on the polo field, she just knew this weekend was going to bring plenty of tension and heartache.

Why had Stewart invited Brod in the first place? He had to know by now Brod outstripped him as a polo player. Then there was the tantalising presence of the beautiful, unusual Rebecca. What middle-aged man, however wealthy, would set out to woo a young woman then expose her to the likes of Brod for good-

ness' sake. It didn't make a scrap of sense unless Stewart was
applying yet another test.

Stewart was a great one for putting people through hoops.
Such an arrogant man. Perhaps if the seemingly perfect Rebecca
didn't pass the test she would fall from her golden pedestal and
be made so uncomfortable she would be forced to leave. Fee
was now certain her brother had marriage on his mind and it
wasn't out of the question. Even after all these years. Not that
they had been womanless. Stewart had had his affairs from time
to time but he had obviously never found the woman he wanted
to keep for himself. The prize possession. Lucille lovely as a
summer's day had been that for a time but somehow Lucille
had found the courage to run away. The next one wouldn't be
given the opportunity.

Fee didn't like to think it could be Rebecca. She was worried Rebecca might be someone who'd been hurt so badly she
could settle for security. An older man, rich, social, establishment, grounded in the conventions. Rebecca could easily mistake an impressive facade for safety.

CHAPTER THREE

HOURS LATER, in the golden heat of mid-afternoon, Rebecca found herself watching the main polo match of the day with her heart in her throat. She'd enjoyed the morning matches played with such high spirits and comradeship but this was another league again.

All the players were exceptionally fast and focused, the ponies superbly trained especially with all those clubs swinging near their heads and the competition it seemed to her anxious, dazzled eyes exceptionally fierce.

Once she thought Stewart charging at full tilt would come off his horse trying to prevent his son driving the ball through the goal posts. He didn't succeed but it appeared to Rebecca to be too dangerous an effort. For all his fitness and splendid physique, Stewart was in his mid-fifties. No match really for the turning, twisting, speeding Broderick, the most dashing player on the field, though the commanding Cameron brothers ran him close. But for sheer daring, Brod Kinross had the added edge if only to beat his father. They certainly acted as if they were engaged in a highly stylised joust.

"That was close," Rebecca, a little frightened, murmured to Fee who was lounging in a deck chair beside her. "I thought Stewart would be flung out of the saddle."

Trying to impress you, my dear, Fee thought. "It's a dangerous game, darling. I had a dear friend, Tommy Fairchild, killed on the polo field. That was some years ago in England but I think of him almost every other day. Brod's a dare devil. I think it's important to him to even up a few scores."

"Meaning?" Rebecca turned her head to stare into Fee's eyes, finding them covered by very expensive sunglasses.

"Good Lord, Rebecca, I know how perceptive you are," Fee said. "Didn't it strike you that afternoon you met Stewart and Brod that they don't get on."

"Perhaps a little." She kept the fact she'd overheard them quarrelling to herself.

"Darling, you can't fool me. You've noticed, all right. Both of them were trying but it's just something they have to live with."

"But you said Brod has to even up the score?" Just to speak his name gave her a peculiar thrill.

"Brod has been on the receiving end for a long time," Fee confided. "I dote on him as you know. And Alison. I'm going to make sure you meet her. Stewart became very withdrawn after the children's mother left. Brod, despite the fact he's a Kinross through and through, has his mother's beautiful eyes. Perhaps looking into them brings up too many painful memories for Stewart." After all it wasn't inconceivable.

"Do you really think that?" Even Rebecca sounded sceptical.

"No." Fee delicately grimaced. "The truth is Stewart wasn't cut out to be a father. Not every man is."

"Then Brod and his sister must have suffered?" Rebecca rested back in the recliner prepared to listen.

"Assuredly, my dear," Fee agreed. "Money can't bring everything to life, not that I've ever been without it," she had the grace to admit. "But so far as Brod is concerned his upbringing has only made him tougher. Unlike his little mother. Petite, like you. Lucille was her name. Pretty as a picture." Fee's mind instantly conjured up a vision of Lucille on her wedding day. Young, radiant, madly in love with her Stewart. She'd flown home to be Lucille's chief bridesmaid. Her little pal from their schooldays but she'd never been around to lend Lucille her support. She'd been too busy becoming a celebrity.

"She didn't last long," Rebecca observed sadly, echoing Fee's own thoughts.

"No. It was all quite dreadful. You can't imagine how shocked I was when I got the news. Sir Andy rang me. I always called my father that. He was knighted by the Queen for his services to the pastoral industry."

Something Rebecca already knew. "Stewart didn't ring you?" she interrupted gently.

"No," Fee answered rather grimly, then remained silent for a time.

Sensitive to her pain Rebecca changed the subject. "I have to say I'll be relieved when the match ends," she confessed with a wry laugh—Brod's team had scored another goal. "I can't really enjoy it with my heart in my throat."

"You're a tender little thing." Fee moved to pat her hand. "Though at this level I agree it's pretty lethal and Stewart and Brod are going at it hammer and tongs. Half-time coming up. Ten minutes usually. Stewart is bound to want to know if you're enjoying yourself. If I were you, my dear, I'd tell him you're finding it all terribly exciting."

"But I am." Rebecca twisted to smile at Fee, marvelling as ever at her glamorous appearance. "I just don't want anyone to get hurt."

"Ah, look at Brod," Fee broke in gleefully. "Isn't he luver-ly," she cried, Eliza Doolittle style. He was indeed. On the other side of the field Broderick Kinross was stripping off his polo shirt to exchange it for another. His jet-black hair, thick and waving, gleamed in the sunlight with a matt of dark hair spreading across his darkly tanned chest then narrowing down to his close fitting jodhpurs.

He was an incredibly handsome man. So much so Rebecca felt a sudden uprush of desire that alarmed her. Not that he was flaunting his splendid body or paying any attention to the heated glances of the female spectators enjoying the spectacle from around the field. He was too busy sharing a joke with his friend, Rafe Cameron.

Rebecca wished for a moment she had a camera. She'd like to photograph these two magnificent young men together. Of a height, wonderfully fit, perfect foils. Brod for all his brilliant blue eyes was dark, deeply tanned by the sun whereas his friend had a thick mane of pure gold hair that was quite stunning. The other brother, Grant, busy chatting up a pretty girl, shared the family fairness, but his hair was more tawny with a touch of red. Both she had remarked when introduced had hazel-gold flecked eyes.

"Quite something aren't they?" Fee hooted, following Rebecca's gaze. "A pride of lions only Brod is the panther among them."

"They're all very handsome," Rebecca agreed. "I'm surprised they're not all married."

Fee shook her beautifully coiffured head. As dark as Rebecca's until her fifties she was now close to blond. "But surely you know?"

"Know what?" Rebecca stared directly at her. More revelations?

"I thought Stewart might have mentioned it," Fee said. He certainly spent enough time chatting to Rebecca. "At one time we all hoped Rafe and Alison would tie the knot. They were very much in love but somehow Alison got cold feet. Product of a broken home perhaps. She ran off to Sydney much as I ran off to London, though I left no great love behind.

"As we know she's become highly successful. So life goes on. Wild horses wouldn't get it out of him but I believe Rafe was devastated. At any rate he won't allow Alison back into his life.

"As for Brod. He's a hot favourite. Always has been. But Brod will make darn sure he picks the right woman. Grant is a couple of years younger than both of them. He's been working terribly hard establishing his helicopter business. All three are big catches for the girls."

"I'll bet!" Rebecca smiled. "Stewart did tell me a little about Alison's broken romance."

"So are you interested?" Fee pulled herself up to capture Rebecca's luminous gaze.

"My career is important to me, Fee," Rebecca answered lightly.

"A woman can't do without love in her life."

"So I'm learning from your biography," Rebecca quipped instantly.

"Cheeky." Fee smacked at Rebecca's slender arm playfully. "Don't leave it too late, darling. That's all." She spread a beringed hand. "Here comes Stewart. He doesn't look quite as enthusiastic as he did at the start of the match."

"Brod didn't exactly give him any quarter," Rebecca pointed out dryly.

"Each man for himself on the polo field, my chick," Fee drawled in her distinctive voice, which still had so much sex appeal in it. "How's it going, Stewie?" she called a little tauntingly, entirely on her nephew's side.

Stewart Kinross studied his sister rather stonily for a moment then said with slight indignance. "We're doing fairly well. Anything can happen in the second half." He switched his glance to Rebecca, dressed like Fee in a silk shirt and narrow cut linen pants only her outfit was pristine white whereas Fee was a kaleidoscope of colours and patterns with a lot of glitter he didn't find attractive. "You're loving it aren't you, Rebecca." He smiled at her, a remarkably handsome, mature man.

"I'm a little worried for you, Stewart," Rebecca admitted truthfully. "It's a dangerous game."

As a response it was a disaster. "I like to think I keep up, my dear," he answered, looking a bit huffed.

"Oh, Stewart, you do know what I mean," Rebecca protested softly.

He looked deep into her eyes seeing God knows what. "That's fine then, my dear. It's Brod who's putting himself at risk. Maybe you could tell him to his face." He looked back towards the field. "Though I must have done something right... I taught him all he knows. Sometimes I wish I hadn't. Ah well." He glanced back to smile at Rebecca. "I must be off. Time's up."

Rebecca realised she shouldn't say, "Take care." Instead she gave a little encouraging wave while Fee, enjoying every moment, bit back a laugh. "Darling, were you really suggesting Stewie is over the hill?"

A soft little cushion was to hand. Rebecca used it.

"Hey, hey." Fee leaned forward and caught it. "Stewie doesn't like to think he's settling into the twilight zone. For that matter neither do I."

In the end Brod's team won and Rebecca watched as a tall, good-looking blonde in skin-tight jeans and a blue T-shirt that showed off her shapely breasts, went up to him, threw her arms around his neck and kissed him with much relish.

"Liz Carrol," Fee said with a grin. "She likes him. Can't you tell? Then again, why hide it?"

"Is she his girlfriend?" Rebecca found herself asking, though she hadn't intended to.

"What do you think? Brod sees a few others but most of the time he's just too darned busy. He's got a big job—for life. When he picks a wife he'd better pick well."

Eventually it was Rebecca's turn to congratulate the winning team, standing before the captain wondering why she felt so terribly perturbed by a pair of brilliant blue eyes. Had anyone ever looked at her like that? What kind of look was it? Whatever it was it acted like a magnet.

"Fee told me you were a little anxious at the action," he said leaning back against a rail, looking down at her. Oh, yes, she was beautiful.

Rebecca nodded unapologetically. "Today was my first experience of polo. I have to admit some of it scared me. I thought

Stewart would be thrown from his horse at one stage during the first half."

"You were concerned."

She stared up at him, revealing nothing. "Why not?"

He shrugged and flung an arm up to rest on the rail. "He's been thrown before and survived. We all have. I'm curious to know, what do you think of my father?"

"I'm sure I'm not supposed to say I hate him," she said coolly. "I think he's many things. As are you."

"Include yourself in that, Miss Hunt," he answered sardonically, studying the way her dark satiny hair curved around her face. What did she do? Polish it with a silk scarf? "Even Fee knows remarkably little about you."

"Have you asked?" she challenged, her rain coloured eyes widening.

"Indeed I have."

"I can't imagine why you'd be interested in me."

Yet she bit her lovely full lower lip. "I'm sure you have many a dramatic revelation to divulge," he drawled. "I'm just blunt enough to point out you're turning my father's head. It's not often I see him take such glowing pleasure in a young woman's company."

"I think you're exaggerating." Perhaps she, too, would have made an actress.

He laughed. "Then why is that magnolia skin stained with colour?"

"It could be your lack of discretion," she countered.

"Actually I'm trying to be frank. You've only been on Kimbara a short time yet you've made a considerable impact on my father and Fee."

"Obviously not *you*." She was still managing to speak with perfect calm even if she couldn't control the fire in her blood.

A taut smile crossed his striking face. "I'm not as susceptible as Dad or as trusting as Fee."

"Goodness you ought to set yourself up in the detective business." She kept her voice low in case anyone was watching. They were.

"Come on, all I'm suggesting is you tell me a little more about yourself."

"You won't find my face in a rogue's gallery if that's what you're thinking." She stared back at him.

"How about an art gallery?" he suggested. "Your style of looks is incredibly romantic. In fact they ought to name a flower after you."

"No artist has offered to paint me so far," she told him. "What exactly is it you suspect me of, Mr. Kinross?"

Her face was still flushed, her eyes as lustrous as silver. "You're angry with me and quite rightly." He dropped his hand off the rail and stood straight. Another foot and their bodies would be brushing.

"*I* think so."

"But from where I'm standing I think you might be trying to steal my father's heart."

She felt so affronted she tossed her silky mane in the air. "Part of it might be because *you're* screwed up."

He stared back at her for a moment then threw back his handsome head and gave a genuine peal of laughter. A warm seductive sound. "I'm not hearing this," he groaned. "You think *I'm* screwed up."

"It must be a very heavy load to carry," she said without sympathy.

He laughed again, white teeth dazzling against dark copper skin. "Actually you might be right."

"We've all got our hang-ups to disengage," she pointed out with clinical cool.

"I can hardly wait to hears yours."

"You're not going to hear them, Mr. Kinross."

"*Pleez,*" he mocked. "If we're going to have these conversations you'd better call me Brod."

It was a mystery to her she was keeping her cool. "Thank

you for that. I'd love it if you called me Rebecca. All I'm asking, *Brod,* is you give me the benefit of the doubt before starting to label me 'adventuress.' From what I've seen, your father
is perfectly charming to women in general."

"Isn't that the truth," he answered, his voice dangerously
gentle. "Charming, yes. Possessive, no."

"Is that how you read it?" She kept the worry out of her tone.

"Most women can't resist being the object of desire."

She felt as if they were engaged in some ritual dance, circling, circling. "That's something I know nothing about." She'd
been determined to play it cool but her simmering temper was
making her eyes sparkle.

"Quite impossible, Rebecca." His lips curved. "If you put
on your dowdiest dress and cut off that waterfall of hair, men
would still want you."

She had the disturbing sensation he had reached out and
touched her, run his fingers over her skin. "I don't think you've
reckoned on whether I want them," she answered, too sharply,
as her heart did a double take.

His blue eyes filled with amused mockery. "Now where is
this leading us?"

"Probably nowhere." She managed a shrug. "The whole conversation was your idea."

"Only because I'm trying to learn as much about you as I
can." He realised he was getting an undeniable charge out of
what amounted to their confrontation. It was like being exposed to live wires.

"I'm thoroughly aware of that," Rebecca said, "but I do hope
you're not going to start checking on me. I might have to mention it to your father."

Ah, an admission of power. Why had he ever had one minute's doubt? His eyes narrowed, lean body tensing. "I'll be
damned, a threat."

She shook her head. "No threat at all. I'm not going to allow
you to spoil things for me, that's all."

"I can do that by checking you out?"

"That's not what I meant at all." Her voice went very quiet. "I'm here in one capacity only. To write your aunt's biography. Both of us want it done. It's a pity you've made up your mind I've more on the agenda. It's almost like you're waging war."

"Isn't it," he agreed.

"Perhaps you've got nothing to win." She threw out the challenge, suddenly wanting to hurt him as he was hurting her.

"Well we can't say the same for you then."

The sapphire eyes gleamed.

Both of them were so involved in the cut and thrust, neither noticed Stewart Kinross approach until he was only a few yards away. "I was trying to make out what you two were talking about?" He smiled, though it never quite reached his eyes.

"Why don't I let Rebecca tell you," Brod drawled.

"Clearly it was something serious," his father said. "Everybody else seems to be laughing and relaxed."

"Brod was taking me through the technicalities of the match." Rebecca was worried her voice might tremble but it didn't. It sounded very normal. "I'm hoping to understand the game better."

"But, my dear, I could have explained all that," Stewart Kinross assured her warmly. "Sure it wasn't something more interesting?"

Rebecca twisted round to look at Brod. "Nothing except a few words about my work."

"I'm sure it will be so good you'll have people dying to read it," Brod said suavely. "Ah well, I'd better circulate. Some of my friends I haven't seen for a long time."

This caused Stewart to frown. "You can see them anytime you want to, Brod."

"I guess I'm too damned busy, Dad. Especially since you promoted me. See you later, Rebecca." He lifted a hand, moving off before his father could say another word.

Stewart Kinross's skin reddened. "I must apologise for my son, Rebecca," he rasped.

"Whatever for?" She was anxious not to become involved.

"His manner," Stewart replied. "It worries me sometimes. I've had to deal with a lot of rivalry from Brod."

"I suppose it's not that unusual," Rebecca tried to soothe. "powerful father, powerful son. It must make for clashes from time to time."

"None of them, I assure you, initiated by me," Stewart protested. "Brod takes after my father. He was combative by nature."

"And generally regarded as a great man?" Rebecca murmured gently just to let him know she had read up extensively on Sir Andrew Kinross and liked what she had learned.

"Yes, there's that," Stewart agreed a little grudgingly. "He positively doted on Fee. Denied her nothing that's why she's so terribly spoiled. But he expected a great deal of me. Anyway, enough of that. What I really wanted to know is did you enjoy the day? I organised the whole thing for you."

"I realise that, Stewart. It's something I'll always remember." Rebecca tasted a certain bitterness on her tongue. Remember? But for wrong reasons. Most of the time her eyes had been glued to Broderick Kinross's dashing figure. She could still feel the rush of adrenaline through her body.

"You know, sometimes I get the feeling I've known you forever," Stewart Kinross announced, resting a hand on her shoulder and staring down into her eyes. "Don't you get that feeling, too?"

What on earth do I say? Rebecca thought, suffused with embarrassment. Whatever I say he seems to misinterpret it. She allowed her long thick lashes to feather down onto her cheeks. "Maybe we're kindred spirits, Stewart," she said. "Fee says the same thing."

It was far from being the response Stewart Kinross wanted, but he knew damned well he would never give up. Many good years remained of his life. Maybe Rebecca was a little young. It didn't strike him as *too* young. In their conversations she sounded remarkably mature, in control. Besides, as his wife she would be well compensated. He was definitely a very rich man and if that had to do increasingly more with Brod's managerial skills he wasn't about to admit it.

Meanwhile half-way across the field Brod, the centre of an admiring circle, continued to observe this disturbing tableau. They could have been father and daughter, he thought with the cold wings of anger. Only he could read his father's body language from a mile. Her dark head so thick and glossy reached just about to his father's heart as it would his. Her face was up-tilted. She looked very slender and delicate in her outfit, boyish except for the swell of her breasts. His father's hand had come up to rest on one of her fine-boned shoulders. He was staring down into her eyes. God, the utter impossibility of it but it was happening. His father had fallen in love. The thought shocked him profoundly. He turned away abruptly, grateful that his friend, Rafe, was approaching with a cold can of beer. A black fairy story this.

Rebecca stood before the mirror holding two dresses in front of her in turn. One was lotus-pink, the other a beaded silk chiffon in a dusky green. Both were expensive, hanging from shoe-string straps and coming just past the knee rather like the tea dresses of the early 1930s when women looked like hot-house blooms. It was the sort of look she liked and one that suited her petite figure. Fee had told her much earlier their guests liked to dress up so now she studied her reflection trying to decide which dress looked best. She was glad she'd packed them, though again Fee had advised her at the outset to bring a couple of pretty evening dresses.

"Stewart likes to entertain whenever the opportunity presents itself."

Hence the polo weekend. And all for her. Only a couple of

weeks ago it would have given her the greatest pleasure. Now the fact that Stewart Kinross had somehow become infatuated with her raised a lot of anxieties. Not the least of them Broderick Kinross's attitude.

Knowing his father better than anyone else he had immediately divined the exact quality of Stewart's interest. She would bet every penny she had Brod believed she had gone along with the situation. Even encouraged it.

Becoming involved with a much older man was one thing. Becoming involved with a *very rich* older man was another. It happened all the time and society accepted powerful influential men could get anything they wanted. Lots of money, it seemed, made a deep impression on everyone.

Stewart Kinross, if he suddenly remarried, could even father another family, increasing the number of heirs to the family fortune. It all left Rebecca feeling freezing cold. Life had been terrible when she had had a man in her life. She'd been so young and she had had no idea what jealousy and obsession meant. But she had learned. How she had learned!

Rebecca stared at her haunted eyes in the mirror. She was standing absolutely still, holding the lovely dusky green dress in front of her like a shield. She told herself she didn't care what Broderick Kinross thought. His suspicions understandable maybe were absolutely groundless. From her first day at Kimbara she had considered Stewart Kinross to be an exceptionally charming and generous man. Now she saw that might not be the case. The only thing that was becoming increasingly clear was he was smitten. She had seen that look of possession in a man's eyes before. She didn't want to see it again.

Abruptly Rebecca turned away from the mirror. The green dress would do. It even lent some of its colour to her eyes. She wasn't afraid of Broderick Kinross, either, though she half dreaded seeing him tonight. If she really were an adventuress looking to snaffle his rich father she couldn't have made more of an enemy. In a way she understood. A new wife would automatically become part heiress to the Kinross fortune. Perhaps gain a controlling interest. She was probably right at this moment news. A few of the women guests hadn't been able to hide their speculation. Thank God Fee was on her side. She had come out here simply to write a celebrity's biography, never thinking she could be catapulted into a Situation.

Almost an hour later, when Rebecca was ready to go downstairs and mingle with the guests, a knock came at her door. She went to it expecting to see Fee resplendent in one of her stunning outfits only Stewart Kinross stood outside the door holding a long velvet box in his hand.

Rebecca moved forward a little blindly not wanting to invite him into the bedroom.

"My dear girl, you look absolutely beautiful," he said, his strongly boned face softening into undisguised admiration. "I love your dress. It's perfect."

"And you look very distinguished, Stewart," she said, edging a little along the painting hung in the hallway. Indeed he did. Commanding, fastidious with the physical presence of someone much younger. Only the eyes were a shade predatory, she thought out of sheer nervousness. What on earth was in that navy velvet box? Not a present surely. She was far from enraptured. She was dismayed.

"Perhaps we could go back into your room for a moment," he said in his now familiar richly modulated tones. "More private with guests in the house. I couldn't be more pleased with your choice of dress, the colour, the style. I have something here I thought you might like to wear tonight. A family heirloom I must of course take back but I notice you didn't bring much jewellery with you…probably not expecting a do like this."

She hadn't the slightest intention of accepting. "Stewart, I really feel…" she began, watching him raise a heavy black eyebrow.

"You can't refuse a simple request, my dear. I want to show you off."

"Whatever for, Stewart?" She tried the wide-eyed look. "They must know I'm only here to write Fee's biography."

"I wonder if you realise you've found your way into our hearts, Rebecca. I'm sure you'll be gracious, my dear. Especially when you see this."

Somehow he had compelled her to move backwards into the lovely cream-and-gold room with its antique French bedroom suite, its fine paintings and porcelain objects. She'd never been in such a bedroom in all her life.

A few feet into the room she turned to face her host. He was wearing a white dinner jacket and a white shirt with his black evening trousers, black tie, his thick dark hair deeply waving like his son's winged with silver. "This hasn't seen the light of day for some time," he said, lifting an exquisite necklace from its container before turning to set the container down on a cabinet.

"Stewart, that looks very important." She just managed to keep her voice from wavering. Appended from a gold chain was a truly magnificent large oval opal flashing a beautiful play of colours, the legendary gem stone surrounded by full cut glittering diamonds.

"Important to our family, yes." He smiled, his large tanned hands undoing the delicate catch. "There's quite a story attached to this opal," he said. "When I have the time I'll tell you but our guests will be waiting."

She tried once more to refuse, knowing the sort of man he was, knowing she might offend him. "Stewart, if you don't mind, I can't wear such an obviously valuable thing. Besides in some quarters opals are said to be unlucky."

"Rubbish!" He banished that idea with a snort. "The Greeks and the Romans valued opals very highly as well they might. Queen Victoria loved the opals that were sent to her from her Australian colonies. The royal jewellers made her up many magnificent pieces. A big opal strike made the Kinross and Cameron fortunes. So no more talk of that, my dear. This will complement the lovely green of your dress. It's almost as though you knew what I had in mind. Be a good girl now," he said cajolingly, "Hold up your hair."

Short of an argument Rebecca thought she had little option. She held her long hair away from her neck while Stewart placed the necklace around it and did up the catch.

"There, what did I tell you?" He took infinite pleasure in her appearance. She was sheer perfection from her gleaming head to her pretty narrow feet in evening shoes whose colour exactly matched her silvery beaded dress.

She thought she'd find herself bright pink with embarrassment when she turned around swiftly to face the long pier mirror. She of all people knew how dangerous it was to court obsession. How much it could devastate a life.

But the necklace was beautiful. So beautiful lying against her bare skin.

"My God you're lovely," she heard Stewart say, his voice surprisingly harsh. "Lovely in just the way I like."

Why hadn't she seen what this could lead to? Was she a fool? Did she think she was protected by the big age difference?

"I think after all I'll take it off, Stewart," she said quite strongly.

"No." He sensed immediately he was giving too much away. He urged caution on himself. He always took getting what he wanted for granted but this young woman was different—very special.

"Rebecca, Stewart?" Fee, looking every inch the star of the theatre surprised them by appearing in the open doorway, her shrewd glance going from one to the other. "What's the problem?"

"Good God, what are you talking about. There's no problem, Fee," her brother responded testily. "You seem to be wearing a billion dollars around your neck. I thought Rebecca might like the loan of a necklace."

Now Rebecca turned full into the light looking back at Fee, her beautiful eyes so lambent they might have been fighting back tears. Fee made an instinctive clutch at the doorjamb, feeling shocked, appalled and astounded all at once. She had been waiting for something to happen, she'd been getting little intimations right through Rebecca's stay—now it was literally before her.

Rebecca was wearing Cecilia's Necklace against her creamy breast. The last time Fee had seen it, Lucille had been wearing it. As was her right. Cecilia's Necklace had been handed down through the generations to each successive mistress of Kimbara. Fee remembered it on her own mother when Fee was a girl. It took her some moments to straighten, superb actress though she was, her inner disturbance detectable in her marvellous green eyes.

"Don't you think I'm right, Fee?" Stewart knowing her reaction, tried to circumvent a rash answer.

What do I do? Fee thought, looking back at her brother. Make a scene? In that instant she knew she couldn't, scenting danger. Kimbara and everything on it was Stewart's while he lived and he was given to considerable hauteur. Rebecca's slender figure seemed to be quivering. It was obvious she, too, was shocked by Stewart's gesture even without knowing anything of the opal's history. Unless Stewart had told her?

"I haven't seen that in a long time," Fee managed to remark with her nephew's trademark irony.

"It deserves an airing." Stewart was uncomfortably aware Rebecca's face was looking flushed, when he knew he had to treat her like a piece of priceless china.

"It looks absolutely wonderful on you, Rebecca," Fee said enmeshed in a dilemma. Weren't men fools? "And it goes beautifully with your dress." Rebecca would writhe in shame if she advised her to take it off and she was much too fond of the younger woman to do that. From the beginning they had fallen into a warm, easy camaraderie.

"I was concerned it was too valuable," Rebecca said, grateful beyond belief for Fee's comforting presence. The sheer awfulness of it! She just knew in her bones wearing the necklace wasn't right.

"You're amongst family and friends, my dear," Stewart assured her with a sudden shift to the avuncular. "There's no question of its becoming lost or stolen."

No, but it was going to cause a great many surprises, Fee thought wretchedly. For Brod above all...

Downstairs in the homestead's huge drawing room with its striped silk walls and splendid curtains at the sets of French doors, the oriental and European furnishings, the guests were assembled enjoying drinks before they all wandered over to the Great Hall where there would be dancing and a sumptuous buffet. The band had been flown in along with a well-known TV personality to act as compere, and the caterers had spent most of the weekend labouring to make everything a great success. Stewart Kinross always paid well but he expected everything to be first-rate and was furious when it wasn't. The owner of one catering firm had once hinted, "Ugly".

Living in isolation for so much of the time Outback people revelled in these occasions and as Rebecca accompanied Stewart and Fee down the sweeping staircase she could hear the steady hum of conversation and banter, the sound of music and laughter. Partying was what it was all about. She was acutely aware she was being treated like family of some sort. Certainly not the journalist who had been hired to write Fiona Kinross's biography.

As they reached the parquet floor of the Front Hall, which was what the family called the spacious entrance, several guests flowed out to meet them, Broderick Kinross among them such a blaze in his eyes Rebecca felt herself vibrating like a plucked string. She had the impression something about her had transfixed him. He was certainly staring at her, his gaze so sizzling she felt she might melt like wax. Maybe he objected violently to her wearing a valuable family necklace.

Other people on the verge of calling out appeared to fall silent, a gap Fee instantly filled with great self-assurance.

"Now, my darlings, what say we all have another glass of champagne, then it will be time to adjourn to the Great Hall. We can't have the band sitting around entertaining themselves now, can we?"

The blonde, Liz Carrol, in a slinky Armani red jersey, said something into Broderick Kinross's ear, something that deepened the fire in his eyes. Something Rebecca was convinced was about *her*.

They all went back into the drawing room, Rebecca accepting her first glass of champagne of the night, though some of the guests appeared to have had a good many already. One of the young men who had played on Stewart's team, Stephen Mellor, turned to her smiling, telling her how lovely she looked. He'd heard it from Brod the young woman who was writing Fee's biography was as "stylised as an orchid" something indefinable about Brod indicating she didn't appeal, but Rebecca Hunt was really something. He started to ask her to save some dances for him when Rebecca caught Broderick Kinross's eyes across the room. He gave her a salute with his crystal flute of such mockery Rebecca felt it bordered more on contempt, then turned back to his companion, Liz Carrol.

"I think we might all walk across now," Stewart announced after about ten minutes, taking Rebecca's arm in a courtly sort of way. "You're going to love what they've done to the Hall, Rebecca. This new firm I got in knows how to rise to the occasion."

The black velvet sky was ablaze with stars, the breeze that blew in from the desert surprisingly cool.

Leaving Liz with their friends, Brod caught up with his aunt, drawing her a little to one side. "Damn it, Fee, what's Dad up to?" he asked in a deep growl.

"I've never known him to act like this," Fee confessed. "Not since the early days when he was courting your mother."

"And the necklace! What in hell are we supposed to make of her wearing it?"

Fee lifted a graceful hand and hunched her shoulders. "Darling, I'm as frantic as you are. I had absolutely no idea this was going to happen." Which at least was the truth.

"But why? And why tonight?" Brod groaned. "You can bet your life everyone will be talking about it. It sure made Rafe and Grant sit up and take notice."

"I'll bet!" Fee agreed wryly. "Darling, we can't talk about this now." The breeze made the long skirt of her black chiffon gown swirl around her and she held it down. "We have guests. All of them with big ears."

"They're not taking any notice of us," Brod pointed out crisply. "Most of them have gone ahead. Dad must have told her the story?"

"I really don't know." Fee shook her head worriedly. "I'm absolutely sure Rebecca wasn't expecting it. I suspect Stewart is entirely responsible for her wearing it."

Brod reacted explosively. "God she looks like Rose White in the fairy tale and she's a miserable little gold-digger."

Fee had never known him so coldly angry. "Darling, you're wrong, so wrong. Rebecca is a fine young woman. I think I'm a good judge of character."

"How can I be wrong, Fee," he said, shaking his head, "when it's as clear as crystal. I remember vividly my mother wearing that opal with her beautiful hair drawn back. This isn't a break with tradition. I'm starting to believe Dad intends to marry your Miss Hunt."

Fee gave a deep sigh. "I'm afraid he might be thinking along those lines, but he'll have a job trying to convince Rebecca to marry him."

"What do you really know about this girl?" Brod retaliated. "Some women love money. Maybe she didn't come here with anything in mind, then again maybe she did?" Along with his feelings of outrage Brod felt almost as though he'd been doubly betrayed.

"That isn't quite how it happened," Fee decided to confide. "Your father set it all up."

"Wha-t?" He sounded stunned.

"Stewart saw Rebecca on television when she was being interviewed about Judith's book. He liked what he saw and persuaded me to approach her."

"Dad did?" Brod started to move like a restive thoroughbred.

"Darling, at that time a biography hadn't entered my head." Fee put a soothing hand on his white jacketed arm. "I was home for a visit, half pleasure, half business. Your father was trying to talk me into selling a lot of my company shares. He has the right to buy me out as you know."

"Don't do it, Fee," Brod warned. "There are all sorts of issues involved."

"I told you I wouldn't." She shook her head. "Stewart persuaded me I had a story to tell. I fell for it hook, line and sinker, vain creature that I am."

"Dad would do that?" He was amazed.

"He must be lonely, Brod. Rattling round in a mansion all by himself," Fee offered by way of explanation.

"He's had a dozen opportunities to remarry over the years. Roz Bennet was a nice woman."

"Indeed she was. And is. But she doesn't fill the role of object of desire. Stewart doesn't find it easy to love, Brod. We all know that. You and Ally especially."

"This is infatuation, Fee," Brod told her grimly. "Obsession if you like and you know what they say, obsession blurs the vision. This girl is only a bit older than Ally. In other words she's young enough to be his daughter."

"It happens, Brod," Fee said in deep wry tones.

He shook his head, scrapped his chiselled chin. "I have to tell you I'm shocked."

"I'm finding it a bit unseemly myself and I've seen everything," Fee agreed dryly.

"Miss Hunt must really fancy herself as a femme fatale."

"Darling, is it bothering you a great deal?" Fee said gently, putting a hand on him arm and urging him to walk on towards the brilliant lights of the Great Hall.

"Believe me, it sure as hell is."

It seemed to Rebecca she and Broderick Kinross spent most of the night trading loaded glances but so far he hadn't come near her. What was there to talk about anyway? It couldn't be more obvious he didn't like or approve of her but she received an inordinate amount of attention from his father who repeatedly asked her to sit out dances with him.

"I never did like dancing," Stewart said.

"Really, you manage very well." Rebecca smiled, keeping her tone light.

He looked pleased. "Thank you, my dear, but I'd much prefer it if you could just sit here with me and talk. Well hello there, Michael." He looked up pointedly as a sandy-haired very attractive young man who could never quite get to dance with Rebecca, suddenly marched right up to them.

"Good evening, sir." Michael gave a little bow. "Marvellous party." His snapping brown eyes settled on Rebecca. "How about it, Rebecca? I'd love it if you'd dance with me." He smiled into her eyes.

"Rebecca is a little tired…she's been so much in demand." Stewart Kinross went to shake his leonine head but Rebecca returned the young man's smile warmly and stood up.

"Not at all, Stewart," she said lightly, "I seem to have been sitting most of the night."

Oh well hell, she thought as she moved off. Stewart deserved that.

Thrilled, Michael, nicknamed Sandy for obvious reasons, manoeuvred her onto the floor. "Arrogant old devil isn't he?" he chuckled.

"He isn't old," Rebecca said. "He's a very handsome man."

"Heck the lot of them are," Sandy snorted. "Fee's still a knockout. Ally's a dream. Brod of course is Brod. A knock 'em dead kind of guy. I think Liz has got her pretty little talons into him."

"They're an item are they?" Rebecca wasn't sure she liked that.

"Could be, but Brod's not an easy man to read. Then again we hardly see anything of him nowadays. He's got big responsibilities. They keep him busy. One of these days his dad is going to push him too far."

"Meaning?" Rebecca glanced up quickly.

Michael backed off. "I don't want to explain, Rebecca. I want to have fun. But take my word for it. And what the heck are you doing with that gorgeous chunk of opal around your neck?" He looked down at the glowing opal within its glittery setting.

"Why do you ask?" Rebecca said, she hoped pleasantly.

"Miss Rebecca, it's been causing an incredible amount of interest," Sandy drawled.

"Did it cost a million dollars? Actually I didn't want to wear it," she confided, "but Stewart insisted. I didn't bring much in the way of jewellery with me and he was being kind. I thought it was a family piece not the Crown jewels."

Sandy raised an eyebrow. "Ma'am, in this part of the world it darn near is. You know its story?"

She felt a chill pass through her. "No, I'm afraid not."

For a moment he looked surprised. "It's not as though I'm initiating you into a big secret."

"I love secrets," Rebecca said when in actual fact dismay was creeping over her.

"Then we can't disappoint you," a familiar voice said from just behind her shoulder.

"Ah hell, Brod, you're not going to steal Rebecca away?" Sandy asked with a mixture of disgust and resignation in his voice.

"I really have to speak to her, Sandy. You'll get your turn."

Sandy stared into Rebecca's eyes. "Promise?"

"I promise, Michael," she said, feeling herself tense all over at the thought of being in Broderick Kinross's arms.

"Gosh, I didn't know my name sounded so good," Sandy relinquished her to Brod and moved off, catching another girl around the waist without missing a beat.

"You've created a sensation tonight." Brod was shocked by how natural it seemed to hold her. So natural he had the mad notion to abruptly pull back.

"So it appears," she answered dryly. She tilted her head to look up at him, letting her gaze linger on him. Knowing she was a fool. The sapphire eyes were flashing danger signals, his handsome face taut within its Byronic frame of dark hair. She couldn't imagine a man looking more stunning. Or more elegant for that matter. He showed his breeding. Even in his everyday denim work clothes.

"That's a beautiful dress." He traced a searing glance down her face, her throat, to the lilac shadowed cleft of her breast.

"Thank you." She tossed it off very coolly, though she had trouble catching her breath.

"One needs a beautiful dress if you're going to wear important jewellery."

"You're dancing with me for a reason." She threw down the challenge.

"I think we understand each other." He nodded.

"So it's the necklace?"

"You betcha." He moved her closer as another couple threatened to bump into them.

"So do you want to tell me all about it?" she invited.

"You mean Dad didn't?" He gave her a twisted smile, scepticism pricking his eyes.

"He told me he'd tell me about its history some time." She tried to hide her fluster.

Her ethereal appearance was deceptive, he thought. She really handled herself well under fire. "Its not as though it's a closely guarded secret."

"You'd be doing me a big favour if you'd get on with it," she flared, very slightly.

He stared back at her through appraising eyes. "The necklace you're wearing has been presented to every Kinross bride for generations. *No one* else wears it. Not Fee. Not my sister. I last saw it adorning my mother's neck. You'll know already the Kinross Cameron fortunes were largely built on a big opal strike in 1860?"

"Yes, I've read all about that," she confirmed, shock pouring into her. "Fee has told me a great deal more."

"Yet no one mentioned Cecilia's Necklace?"

His cynicism was intolerable. "That's what I'm wearing?"

"The magnolia image is just right for it. How smart of Dad to realise."

"I didn't want to wear it," she answered him, her voice like cut glass.

"But you have such a sense of style."

"Your father insisted." She tried to swallow a tide of feelings. "I didn't like to offend him."

"Would you have worn whatever dress he wanted as well?"

The music momentarily stopped. All the guests applauded wildly. It was her moment to escape but he kept a light hold of her arm, trapping her like a fluttering bird in a cage.

"I really don't have to put up with this," she said after a stricken minute. Every pulse in her body was jumping.

"You really do." He glanced over her satin sheened dark head at the swirling dancers. "You're free to go back and sit beside Dad as soon as I've done."

"I can walk off right now." Yet his magnetism was a powerful thing.

"Try it," he said very quietly, a warning in his eyes.

"Bullies don't appeal to me." Her mind and her senses were furiously at war.

"I wouldn't dream of bullying you." His touch gentled. "By the same token, devious little Scarlett O'Hara types don't appeal to me."

"You're talking nonsense."

God wasn't he? He felt incredibly mixed up but his voice was hard. "Not after what's happened tonight. Every last person here witnessed it. They'll all go off to spread the news."

"Which is?" Her heart was beating so swiftly she hated him.

"You have considerable standing in my father's eyes. Not to say power."

"Perhaps he was just being kind." She knew he wasn't.

Brod laughed. "Being kind isn't quite Dad's style. Hell, Miss Hunt, he might as well have given you a great big engagement ring. I know my mother's was a flawless four carat solitaire. It's still in the safe."

She broke clear of him suddenly but he caught her hand, drawing her off the floor towards a stand of golden canes that had been brought in for decoration.

"I'm genuinely shocked at what you're saying." She swung to face him. In fact a kind of fear tore through her.

"Out of what? Guilty you've been sprung?"

"How charming you are." She wanted desperately to abandon herself to rage but it wasn't her way.

"I want you to take me very seriously." Out of the corner of his eye he could see his father stalking towards them. His father. Almost his enemy.

"Oh, I do." She shrank away a little, her beautiful eyes darkening with intensity.

"Obviously you're hugely concerned your father might remarry. It's even possible you might no longer be heir." She yielded into giving this taunt.

He stared down at her, discovering he wanted to kiss that

mouth. Crush it. "Sorry to disappoint you," he said with sleek humour. "My inheritance is all tied up. Even Dad can't change it. But keep talking, Rebecca, I want to know your plans."

"What would be the point," she answered with cool scorn, shrugging a delicate shoulder. "You've made up your mind about me."

"Well, you've been able to do something Ally and I could never manage," he pointed out very dryly. "You have my father eating out of your hand." Brod turned his dark head. "Ah, here Dad comes. In which case I'll excuse myself. I'm sure he'll take care of you, Miss Hunt."

Rebecca didn't think she could get through the night, though outwardly she acted with considerable panache. It was, she realised, her training. She had to meet fear with calm. She wasn't going to have the opal around her neck, either. She intended to take it off as soon as she decently could. The fact that Stewart had insisted she wear it upset her profoundly and she didn't blame his son for challenging her so keenly. But why hadn't Fee warned her? Though now she came to think if it, Fee had acted oddly when they were in the bedroom. Fee could have said," I don't think it's a good idea for Rebecca to wear it," but on reflection Rebecca knew why. Stewart Kinross was a man of considerable hauteur. There was probably no one with the exception of his rebel son who dared to tell him what to do.

The buffet was as sumptuous as promised, the long tables with their floor-length starched cloths, hydrangea pink and blue, groaning under so much delicious food it was a wonder they didn't snap with the load. Hams, turkey, chicken dishes, big platters of smoked salmon, seafood airlifted from the Gulf of Carpentaria in far North Queensland, prawns, lobsters, whole baked barramundi, an endless variety of salads, rice and pasta dishes. Hired bartenders handled the drinks, two young waiters circling constantly, the high emotion of the band and its lead singer occasionally drowning all other sound. Couples wandered back and forth between dances enjoying everything that was offered.

Rebecca ate little, though. She was too upset. Instead she spent some time speaking to the Cameron brothers who clearly were too gentlemanly to embarrass her by mentioning the Necklace. Flashes were now going off constantly as most of the guests posed for their photographs to be taken.

Across the room Rebecca saw Broderick Kinross the epicentre of a small group with Liz Carrol holding his hand and smiling brilliantly into his face. Fee was having a great time, too, moving freely from one group to the other, leaving them laughing exuberantly with one of her endless flow of anecdotes.

Eventually she found her way over to Rebecca's side while nice Michael went off to fetch Rebecca a sparkling mineral water. No way was Rebecca going to drink too much. Her whole life was control.

"How's it going?" Fee asked with a warm smile.

Rebecca turned her fawnlike neck, and looked Fee straight in the eye.

"Fee, why didn't you tell me this necklace is never worn by anyone except the Kinross wives?" she demanded.

"Oh Lord!" Fee murmured under her breath, dropping abruptly into a beribboned chair, one of a great many scattered about the beautifully decorated hall. "I really thought Stewart might have told you."

"Come off it, Fee." Rebecca glinted at her. "Would I have worn it had I known?"

"No." Fee shook her head sadly. "Not a nice girl like you."

"Why couldn't you have said something. I really hate being made a fool of."

Fee winced. "I deserve this, I know. But I don't think I have to remind you Stewart is absolutely master in his own home. He wouldn't have taken too kindly to my intervention. Besides I blush to admit it I had the teeniest little doubt you might have known. You and Stewart have grown quite close."

"Good grief!" Rebecca could hardly believe it. "The only feeling I have for Stewart is respect for his position. Goodness, Fee, I'm half his age."

"I know that, darling, but you forget I've seen a great deal. Plenty of young women respond to money."

"Not me," Rebecca said flatly.

"All right, all right." Fee reached over to Rebecca's hand placatingly. "But I'm worldly enough to divine you've suffered a rather bad experience in the past. A broken romance. A sensitive young woman like you might then settle for other things. Security. Safety. You do see what I mean?"

"I still can't believe it. I'm not settling for anything, Fee. I'm quite happy the way I am." She chose to think so anyway.

"So if Stewart didn't tell you, who did?" Fee enquired.

"Your nephew, of course." Rebecca shot her a shimmering glance. "And he didn't pull any punches. Boy doesn't he love to sit in judgement!"

"You can't blame him, I suppose," Fee said loyally. She had barely recovered herself.

"Actually I don't," Rebecca said wryly, "but I've never met anyone so…so…downright hateful in my life."

"He's upset you." Fee's heavily mascared green eyes looked remorseful.

"It kills me to admit it, yes. He actually believes I'm after his father."

"Gracious, darling, is that so unusual? Look around you. Half the women in this room and that includes the young ones would jump at the chance of becoming Stewart's second wife. He's still a very handsome man and he's megarich. You know what they say…"

"Power is the greatest aphrodisiac."

"Exactly, darling."

"Well it isn't for me. Not for a moment," Rebecca said straightening the gold chain on the opal necklace, the centre of all the fuss. "As soon as the moment presents itself I'll go back to the house and lock it away."

"Good. I'll try and join you," Fee said. "Not that I know the combination to the safe. Perhaps Brod does."

"Leave *him* out of it." Rebecca's eyes flashed like sun on ice and Fee had to laugh.

"You and he have made the sparks fly between you. I've never seen you furious."

"I've no desire to be, Fee," Rebecca countered earnestly. "I've loved being here on Kimbara. I love working with you on our book but I'm not happy with this…situation that seems to have developed."

"Let me talk to Brod," Fee offered, looking anxiously into Rebecca's serious eyes. "The last thing I want is to lose you. We work so well together and having you in the house brings my daughter a little nearer."

"Of course you miss Francesca." Rebecca was getting to know all about Fee's marriage to her English Earl. How she had one child from it, her only child, Lady Francesca de Lyle, a young woman around Rebecca's own age.

"Of course I do," Fee sighed.

"She still lives with her father?"

"Not any more. She has a place of her own in London. She works in public relations. Rupert bought it for her. He was alway a wonderful father but Fran visits Ormond House often. Takes her friends. Working on the biography has brought it all back. It grieves me now to think I was never there for my little girl when she needed me. All through her schooldays. I wanted to be but somehow I let her down. I had a brilliant career but it made a great many demands on me and my time. Really it ended my marriage. No wonder Fran worships her father. He was both mother and father to her."

"But the three of you are all at peace now, Fee?" Very gently Rebecca reached out a sympathetic hand.

"Oh, yes, darling." Fee blinked her amazingly long eyelashes.

"Rupert has long since remarried. Happily, I'm glad to say. Francesca rings me all the time. I wish I could get her to come out to Australia for a visit. I want you two to meet. Stewart is very fond of Fran. He likes cool, gentle women. I never could keep my emotions under control. Passion always drove me."

"Which is probably why you're such a marvellous actress," Rebecca soothed. "I don't want you to bother having to come with me, Fee. I'll slip over to the house by myself."

"All right, darling." Fee stood up, pressing her chiffon skirt against her trim thighs. "You might slip the necklace into one of the desk drawers in Stewart's study. Lock it, take the key. Explain to Stewart knowing its history you were uncomfortable wearing it."

Uncomfortable doesn't say it, Rebecca thought, glancing up to see Michael returning with her iced mineral water.

CHAPTER FOUR

AS REBECCA MOVED into the Front Hall she glanced at the French clock on the rosewood panelled wall. Twenty minutes after twelve. It had taken her all of that time to break away quietly from the guests. The gala evening was still going on in earnest. Another classic Outback gathering though Rebecca doubted many of them could be so lavish. Stewart had planned it all like a military manoeuvre, his organisation first-class. He had even decided on the flowers. Her mind blanked out *all for her.*

The revelries would go on until breakfast for those who were still standing. She would be really enjoying herself only for the fact Stewart had trapped her into wearing an important family heirloom, thus spoiling everything. What was his reason? To let people know he had his eyes on an attractive young woman he was considering as a potential wife?

It was a great pity he hadn't taken the trouble to ask *her!* He simply accepted he could have any woman he liked.

What arrogance!

The magnificent old homestead was very quiet though lights bloomed in all the major rooms and several of the bedrooms upstairs. Rebecca found her way to Stewart's study with its massive desk and cabinets, its hundreds of books, sporting trophies, marvellous paintings of horses being held by attendants and over the fireplace a large portrait of Stewart's late father, Brod's grandfather, Sir Andrew Kinross. It was placed exactly so the eyes followed the viewer around the room.

Rebecca paused for a moment to look up at him. Sir Andrew had been a very impressive looking man. Big, handsome, distinguished. Yes, the family face. But the eyes a clear green were so *kind,* Rebecca thought. Kind, calm and wise. Stewart's were filled with power, prestige, control. Those were the things that evidently mattered to him.

Broderick Kinross's brilliant blue eyes…burned with banked fires. She realised he was awakening in her feelings that could spiral out of control unless she clamped down hard. She had no desire to be caught into some furious dance with the cynical, judgemental, too damned seductive Broderick Kinross. She feared men who exuded such power and virility.

Rebecca moved around the massive desk, leaning against it briefly while she removed the diamond-set opal from her neck in one fluid movement. It had been wrong of her to wear it tonight. She should have risked going against Stewart's suggestion. She didn't feel proud of herself. In a sense she was a little overwhelmed by being catapulted into a world of so much obvious wealth. She had never experienced such wealth close up although she had interviewed many a celebrity with millions in her time. Sighing, Rebecca opened the top right hand drawer of Stewart's desk, placing the necklace gently inside. The light caught all the flashing lights of the large opal, sapphire, emerald, ruby, amethyst all embedded together, the dazzle of the surrounding diamonds.

It occurred to her now she really was a fool. At the far end of the drawing room, surveying the large room was a portrait of a dark-haired woman in a low-cut emerald green ball gown. Rebecca had admired it many times, knew it was Cecilia Kinross, Kimbara's first bride, painted in the early days of marriage to her kinsman, Ewan Kinross, who had taken up the great selection, the vast pastoral holding, after a big strike on the opal fields of New South Wales. Between the sumptuous gown, the beauty of the subject, the green eyes and wonderful hair, Rebecca's eyes had not dwelt on the pendant Cecilia was wearing around her neck. At first glance one could have thought the central stone was a sapphire.

She couldn't have made a bigger mistake if she tried. No wonder Liz Carol had been eyeing her so slyly every time she passed. Every guest without exception would have made the connection. There was no sense in lingering here. She would have to go back to the party.

Head bent, Rebecca turned the brass key in the lock, starting visibly when a voice addressed her from the half-open doorway.

"You know, Miss Hunt, you sure get around. So tell me what's so irresistible about my father's desk?"

Broderick Kinross pushed the heavy door open, walked into the study and stared at her.

"It was whatever was handy," she clipped. "I don't know the combination to the safe. Do *you?*"

He raised an eyebrow moving further into the room like she was a wild creature that would spring away at the first noise. "Well I might," he conceded. "Are you planning to tell how you know *exactly* where the safe is?"

She shrugged. "Your father showed it to me once. Not deliberately. I just happened to pass his study when he had the safe opened and he called me in."

He laughed, utterly amused. "You expect me to believe that?"

"Obviously not as you're looking at me like I was a first-rate con artist," Rebecca said as though she couldn't care less.

"So I ask again?" There was a gleam in his eyes. "What are you doing at my father's desk?"

"Doing what I should have done much earlier in the evening," she answered very coolly. "I'm putting the famous Necklace away."

His eyes flashed over her bare white throat. "You couldn't wait until after the party?"

She looked at him, the brilliant mocking eyes, the hard fine planes of his face, the raven shock of hair. "It's hard to imagine anyone more arrogant than you."

"Try my father," he suggested.

"*And* you don't listen when people explain. I had no idea of the significance of the Kinross Necklace. Now I know there's no way I'm going to leave it hanging around my neck." If she wanted to be safe it was time to run. Despite the fact he disliked her, a powerful attraction was running between them.

"But it's too late to undo the impact, Rebecca," he pointed out gently. "And I'm not buying your story."

"About what?" They might have been marooned together on an island.

"Women aren't the only ones to have intuition," he said. "My intuition tells me you're attracted to rich older men. I mean it could have something to do with your past life, about which we know amazingly little. You could be looking for a father figure. I studied a bit of psychology. It's textbook, Freudian stuff."

"You're talking nonsense." She broke his gaze.

"How can I be when I can see it all unfolding before my eyes."

"I'm going. I'm finding my way back." If she could get past him.

"Not for a moment." He moved like a panther to stand in front of her.

"I'll have the key if you don't mind."

She couldn't make herself touch him so he took it from her nerveless hand. "Thank you. I really ought to dare you to touch me." He inserted the key in the lock, turned it, opened the drawer, and saw the fabulous necklace within. "I wasn't accusing you of stealing it, Rebecca," he drawled.

"It hardly bothers me what you think," she answered with silky disdain.

"So why are you trembling?" He have her a faintly twisted smile, suddenly wanting to slide his hand around her creamy throat, down her neck to the delicate swell of her breast. She was small enough to pick up.

"I pride myself on behaving well," she told him. "What I'd really like to do is to take that smile off your face."

"That bad, is it?" His tone was frankly mocking. "So what are you waiting for?"

She was so affected by him she almost cried out, *Don't come near me,* instead she said with considerable control, "I think you owe me an apology."

"You're kidding me, Rebecca," he answered. "Why don't we put this in the safe? You'd better point out where it is."

She allowed herself a flash of malice. "Are you sure your father has given you the combination?"

He turned towards her, lean and powerful. "Tell me where the safe is then try me."

"Over there." She backed off, pointing. "It's behind the picture of The Hunt."

"God!" Momentarily he covered his eyes. "Dad must be losing his marbles. Come over here, Rebecca and stand by the window."

She did so borrowing some of his own mockery. "You want me to cover my eyes?"

"That's okay," he answered gently. "Just look out at the garden."

She gave a brittle little laugh. "You're really going too far, you know. Speaking to me like this."

"I don't think so," he said. "And with good reason. As a matter of fact I've been thinking about you all day."

That touched her like an electric shock. She swung about spontaneously just as he was closing the wall safe door. "I had assumed my father was well past falling in love," he said.

Her mouth curved in irony. "Did you? Then you've made an awful mistake. People fall in love at all ages. In the teens, forties, seventies, eighties. It's well documented. The great thing is *to love.*"

"Listen, I agree with you." He moved with his graceful stride towards her. "Who exactly do you love, Rebecca?"

"That's hardly your business," she said shortly, but her voice shook. It seemed to her reeling mind both of them were on the edge of the utmost folly. The heavy bronze and glass chandelier overhead sculptured his handsome face with light and shade. His eyes glowed an intense sapphire simmering with arousal. He was beautiful, powerful, in the end to be feared. He could only hurt her.

"Crazy isn't it?" He echoed her depth of feeling, close to her, lifting her face to him.

Then he began to kiss her, desire overcoming every other consideration. She was too much. Too much. The pearly skin, the slender body so made for a man's loving, the sight and the scent of her. He thought he could handle it. Hell, he had followed her, all suspicion, now he enfolded her, excited by her soft cry he swiftly cut off.

Her lips were so full and soft. Like velvet. They opened to him as if she, too, had been swept away like a leaf in a storm. No woman's body had ever felt so right to him. So small yet so finely fashioned, so *yielding*. He wasn't just kissing her—he became aware of that, covering her mouth and face with a hard, hungry yearning. She was melting into him, letting him take her slight weight. It gave him the most profound shock to realise he was falling in love with this woman. This near stranger. This woman he didn't trust.

Perhaps that was what she wanted. Father and son.

The thought gave him the strength to free her, though his body was on fire.

The power she possessed. The sweetness! The mystery! All of a sudden he bitterly resented it. He had always tried to do what was right, yet he could see if he didn't hold her she might fall. Why was she doing this? How could anything work out?

"Rebecca?" he warned, the anger inside him growing as he realised he had to fight to let her go.

"What do you want me to do? Tell me?" she pleaded in a soft, husky voice. She could have wept for her own surrender when she had spent years getting her defences in order.

He stared into her face, her eyes huge and shining with the shimmer of tears. "I shouldn't have done that," he said bleakly, thinking he should have known better. "I have to be half-mad."

There was even a possibility she was acting, witch that she was. Yet he put his hands squarely around her narrow waist and lifted her onto the desk, full of consternation that she was regarding him almost helplessly out of those beautiful eyes.

"In the bad old days, women with your powers would have run the risk of being burned at the stake," he said in a voice so mocking it splintered like wood.

"What pleasure would that have given *you?*" she retaliated, some colour coming back into her cheeks.

"Rebecca, I would have gone to your aid," he responded satirically. "No doubt about it. Probably got myself killed for my trouble."

Where was the rest of the world, he thought, wanting to kill sensation, but he couldn't. They might have been locked in some fantastic capsule.

Rebecca too was stricken. She pressed her two hands momentarily to her eyes. "I have to go back," she murmured twice like a mantra.

"I should think so." His voice had just a touch of cruelty. "Otherwise my father will be after you. Why if he found us together he could even think I'm trying to seduce you away from him."

"Except this is some nonsense you've made up. "She wrapped her arms around her.

"The tragedy is it *isn't.* You have real power in your hands, Rebecca." He reached out and lifted a handful of her long silky hair caressing it. "You even fascinate me. But there's no way I can accept your protestations of innocence. The way you've got my father eating out of your hand provides all the evidence

I need. Especially when I know him as well as I do. Here."
Abruptly, under intense pressure, he lifted her to the floor.
"We'd better go back but we'll take care with our exits. You go
first. I'll follow. It might come as a big surprise but Dad has a
damned expensive fireworks display organised for you."

"And he's done the whole thing on his own, without refer-
ence to me." All of a sudden she couldn't bear to be in the same
room with him. This man who had transformed her. She felt
utterly terrified of him in a sense. Of his seductive hands and
mouth, the dazzling eyes. She had never given herself up to a
man so freely. It was prudent to take flight.

With one hand Rebecca held back her dark tumbled hair,
gesturing with the other for him to stay in place. "I don't be-
long here," she said, seeing an end to Fee's book, her stay on
Kimbara. Everything.

"I can't make sense of it, either," he responded, his white
smile ironic. "But I can tell you this and this is the really scary
bit, I can't see any of us letting you go."

By noon of the following day all of the guests had begun the
return journey home. Rebecca who had slept very late after a
few broken hours, thought she wouldn't have to face Brod reminding herself he was flying out with the highly impressive
Cameron brothers who were obviously very close to him. She
didn't think she could deal with seeing Brod today but when
she finally made her way downstairs, moving quietly through
the house, she saw Stewart's study door was shut. Even from
the outside she could hear the terse sound of voices within. Father and son in a meeting. For a split second she wanted to race
back upstairs and barricade herself in. So he hadn't flown back
to Marlu as planned? Rebecca stood motionless for a moment
feeling vaguely distraught when Jean Matthews, Kimbara's
housekeeper, came up behind her.

"Good morning, Rebecca. Feel like some breakfast?"

Rebecca gave a little laugh detecting the humour in the way the housekeeper said it. "Tea and toast will do, but let me get it."

"Frankly that would save me, dear," Jean Matthews said. "I'm up to my ears in work. Come back into the kitchen. I'll join you in the cuppa."

"Fee not up yet?" Rebecca asked as they walked into the marvellous old kitchen huge by any standards and outfitted for the most demanding professional chef.

"Of course not!" Jean smiled. "I expect she's nursing a little hangover. Mr. Kinross and Broderick just keep going like nothing has happened."

"I thought Brod was flying back to Marlu today," she asked trying to sound casual.

"That was my understanding." Jean nodded, putting bread in the toaster while Rebecca made the tea. "He never stays long more's the pity but I understand there's to be a meeting with Ted Holland the overseer. Between the two of us, though, Broderick and his father don't see eye to eye—everybody knows it— Broderick is in on the decision-making. Sooner or later he'll get his due."

"They're not a happy family." Rebecca gave a sigh, pouring boiling water over the fragrant best quality tea leaves in the pot.

"It didn't take you long to find that out." Jean made a wry face. "The children could have loved their father mind. They wanted to love him but he rejected it. I go way back so I know. In the old days I was Nanny. Fee tell you that? Came here when I was barely sixteen as a domestic. Still can't believe Miss Lucille has gone. She was an angel. I loved her."

Something in her eyes conveyed she had given up trying to love her employer. "I stayed for the children. Turn a woman's heart in her breast. I worked in the house under Mrs. Harrington, my predecessor. A real old biddy I can tell you. She used to make me so nervous, but a wonderful housekeeper and a marvellous cook. Taught me everything I know. I still remember the lessons and her superior ways. When she left Mr. Kinross asked me to take over. It's so different these days. Broderick on Marlu. Ally gone away to Sydney. Lord she could have had Rafe Cameron," Jean wheezed, easing her plump frame into a kitchen chair, "but I fear it's too late. They were mad about each other but they'll never fit the pieces together again."

Jean's eyes misted so she took off her glasses and polished them. "Tried to talk her out of it. I know Broderick did. Rafe's his best friend. Even Mr. Kinross seemed upset."

"It's not possible they might get together again?" Rebecca asked, knowing that this issue had upset everyone.

"Take my word for it, luv," Jean sighed. "The Camerons are very proud men."

"No one else has got Rafe to the altar," Rebecca pointed out.

Jean's face brightened. "That's true."

Meanwhile in Stewart Kinross's study, the last thing on the agenda the decision to bid at a forthcoming auction of a well-known Central Queensland sheep and cattle station was taken. Brod went to stand up, gathering a whole sheath of papers and knocking them into shape. He'd been acutely aware his father had something on his mind he was keeping to discuss. Now it came out.

"Before you go, Brod." Stewart Kinross took off the glasses he used for reading and eased the marks on his nose, "I'd like to speak to you about what happened last night."

"I thought it was very successful," Brod said. "Everyone else did, too, going on the lavish praise."

"That wasn't the question I was about to ask." Stewart Kinross gave his son a cold stare. "Rebecca gave me to understand she asked you to put the necklace in the safe for her."

"Indeed she did. You were busy with guests at the time. She couldn't wait to take the darn thing off, though you'd never have known it. Cool as a cucumber, Rebecca."

"Can we be serious for a moment?" Stewart Kinross snapped.

"What do you want me to say, Dad?" Brod turned back. "Under the porcelain exterior she's one tough little cookie."

"Rebecca, tough? I hope you haven't been saying anything to offend her?"

"Would I do that, Dad?" Brod asked, trying to keep his temper.

"You take particular pleasure in stirring people up. What I want to know is did you find a way to make her feel uncomfortable in the necklace?"

"*I* find a way?" Brod slapped his handful of papers down on the massive desk again. "As it turned out, Dad, *you* did that. Given that the Necklace and its history is well-known, I would have thought any young woman would have found it awkward to wear. It is intended, as we all know, for my future wife."

Stewart Kinross shot back his huge swivelled leather chair. "Are you suggesting I'm way too old to consider remarrying?"

"God, Dad." Brod struck his fist into his hand. "I wouldn't have shed a tear if you'd married half a dozen of the women you've had in the past. Some of them were actually nice. But Rebecca Hunt is way off limits." The very thought burned him up.

Stewart Kinross smiled bleakly. "You've obviously led too isolated a life, Brod. Is it her age, twenty-seven you're getting at?"

Brod turned fully to face his father, his lean, powerful youngman frame crackling with energy. "Dad, she's too *young*. She's only a little bit older than Ally. She's younger than *I* am."

"So?" Stewart Kinross's face might have been carved out of rock. "I don't see that puts too much of a barrier in my way."

Brod sat down hard. "So you're really serious about this?"

Stewart Kinross's handsome face coloured. "She's exactly the sort of woman I've always looked for."

"You mean damned secretive?" Brod flared. "Even if she were in her forties you'd have to know more about her."

"I know enough," Stewart Kinross thundered. "I can understand your fears, Brod. Rebecca is young enough to want children."

"Well of course! Have you even *begun* to discuss this? It doesn't seem likely. Rebecca told me she had no idea of the significance of the Necklace. She wore it because she didn't wish to offend you. You were pretty insistent."

Stewart Kinross seemed to take a long time to answer. "You weren't there at the time, Brod."

God, *had* she lied to him? Brod thought bitterly.

"Of course I told Rebecca the whole story," his father answered emphatically. "Damned silly of me not to have. With people like you around someone was bound to tell her."

Brod wondered if he could take it in. "You told her it has only been worn by Kinross *wives?* That my mother was the last woman to wear it?"

Stewart Kinross shrugged. "Well I never mentioned your mother, Brod. I haven't spoken about your mother in many long years. She behaved very badly. She left me and you children. She broke her sacred vows and she was punished."

A look of furious distaste crossed Brod's face. "What a cold-blooded bastard you are," he said with profound resentment. "Punished, my God! My poor mother. If only I'd been older! She could have married just about anyone else. Some normal guy and she'd be alive to this day."

Stewart Kinross's eyes were as cold as ice. "Then you'd never have been what passes for my heir."

"I am your heir, Dad. Never forget it." Brod's face hardened to granite, his gaze so formidable his father was forced to look away.

"Well I think that's all," Stewart decided somewhat hastily. "You seem to think I'm not entitled to some life of my own, Brod. That being fifty-five I should scale down all my expectations."

Brod moved to the door, feeling shaken now. Rebecca had *lied* to him. "I've never known you to scale down on anything,

Dad. You think you're Royalty. Money isn't a consideration. If I weren't so damned efficient you'd have to be more careful about how you're getting rid of so much of it."

The fact it was true put Stewart Kinross on the defensive. "I can't imagine who you think you're talking to," he blustered. "I'm your father."

"Damned right you are," Brod answered grimly, "and a pretty miserable one at that."

"I think you'd better go now," his father warned. "I don't need any lectures on my sins as a parent. Truth is you're jealous of me, Brod. You always have been. Now there's Rebecca..." Stewart Kinross paused, staring at his son. "I've tried to stop thinking about you two last night. Some expression on your faces when you were dancing."

Brod gave an abrupt laugh and rubbed his chiselled chin. "Keeping an eye on us were you, Dad?"

"I made a bad decision last time," his father said. "One I don't intend to make again. I have to confess I was a little disappointed in Rebecca. You seem to disturb her. About what, I wonder? Did you threaten her?"

"To put it bluntly, Dad. I let her know it wouldn't be a good idea to get mixed up with you." It only struck him afterwards that hadn't been the smart thing to say. He should have let his father believe he and Rebecca were attracted. Hell weren't they? No matter what he thought of her. For now he had to get out of the house. He didn't think he could handle meeting up with Miss Rebecca Hunt without blowing his top. Grant wasn't due to pick him up until the following afternoon. He'd go join Ted, Kimbara's overseer. Take a good look around the station as they had already discussed. A good man, Ted. He had hand-picked him himself.

Fee didn't feel up to working, preferring to spend most of the day "resting" so Rebecca continued with her own research. When she called in on Fee she implored her to tell her all about

Cecilia's Necklace. Free, holding a hand to her throbbing temples, told her where to look.

"The library, darling. The bookcase to the left of the fireplace. Near the sofa. The middle section as I recall. It's all there."

"Sure I can't get you something, Fee?" Rebecca asked. The older woman was wearing a little make-up, she was never without it, but she looked decidedly under the weather.

"My youth back, darling," Fee called.

It was a very large library indeed. One of the finest private libraries in the country with thousands of leather-bound volumes and records going back to the earliest days of settlement. It was an important room in the house. Rebecca felt privileged to be there. She loved books with a passion. The look of them, the feel of them, the smell, all the wonder, the information, the excitement and wisdom they contained. Following Fee's directions she discovered the small leather-bound volume, with gold tooling published in the early 1870s giving an account of the Kinross-Cameron opal strike. Rebecca settled into the deep comfortable sofa, shifted a few piled-up cushions then began to turn the yellowing pages.

An hour later she was still reading. The adventurous young Ewan Kinross and his equally adventurous friend Charles Cameron, second and third sons respectively of good family had left Scotland in the mid-1800s to make their fortunes on the Australian gold fields. They hadn't succeeded in panning gold, not really knowing enough about it, but they persevered with their mining interests, all the time learning from the more experienced miners talk, until they were eventually rewarded by discovering a rich opal bearing seam southwest of the town on Rinka in New South Wales.

They took out a lease despite being told their find was probably worthless. The rest was history. The mine, Kinross-Cameron, gave up magnificent stones and made the men rich. Rich enough to do what they always wanted: take up adjoining great selections in far South West Queensland and raise the finest beef cattle in the land.

One particularly beautiful stone was kept to be made into a pendant for Ewan's kinswoman, Cecilia Drummond. Both young men were in love with her and the pendant was by way of showing their deep regard for her. The story was that both young men settled into trying to win her hand, adding a new dimension *rivalry* to their close friendship. It appeared at times Charles Cameron was the more favoured of the two. Indeed a family letter suggested Charles was her "knight in shining armour." But in the end Cecilia made her choice marrying Ewan Kinross and giving him four children.

Reading between the lines it appeared the marriage was not a happy one. Perhaps Cecilia would have done better to marry Charles. For a while it seemed the friendship between the two men was almost ruined then after the birth of Cecilia's first child things appeared to come right again. Charles Cameron in fact was one of the godparents.

Rebecca closed the book, leaning back into the sofa. Impossible to believe Stewart hadn't told her the full story. When she looked at the photograph of Lucille Kinross in full evening dress wearing the pendant Rebecca had almost felt the tears coming. She'd had no right wearing the necklace last night. Brod would never forgive her for it even if he could accept she had no knowledge of the pendant's significance.

She knew now Brod had gone out for the day with Ted Holland. He hadn't bothered with lunch at the homestead so she wouldn't see him again until dinner. Fee had already told her she was going to make an effort to get up.

"I see too little of my nephew," she said. "I could scarcely get near him last night for that Carol girl. I think she actually fears letting go of his arm."

Even so Liz Carol hadn't been able to keep Brod to herself. Rebecca, without appearing to notice, had seen him dancing with a number of pretty girls.

When she stood up to replace the volume on the shelf Stewart Kinross, impressive in his riding clothes, came to the door.

"How you do manage to lose yourself, Rebecca," he said, smiling rather fiercely. "I've been looking for you everywhere."

"It's a big house, Stewart," she pointed out mildly. "In fact the biggest private house I've ever been in outside of English stately homes."

"Now you're talking!" he said. "This would be a modest cottage compared to over there."

"This could never be a modest cottage anywhere," Rebecca said dryly. "There's something I wanted to talk to you about anyway, Stewart."

"Marvellous." He threw that off. "First get started on changing into your riding clothes. I feel like a good gallop. Get all that party feeling out of my system."

Rebecca resisted. "You don't think there might be an afternoon storm." She was a little scared of storms. "It's turned very hot."

"There could be I guess," he conceded, "but nothing to worry us. I've seen the most monumental storm clouds blow up. Great masses of purplish clouds rolling across the desert. But not one drop of rain. Before long a wind gets up and the clouds are blown asunder. If you get dressed I'll go down to the stables and organise the horses. If you're a particularly good girl I'll let you put Jeeba through her paces."

He turned and was gone, leaving Rebecca to climb the central staircase and find her way back to her room. Although it was so quiet, the day seemed to be thrumming with a strange kind of electricity. It was only when she was dressed in her riding gear, standing on the front verandah putting on her hat, that she took time to really examine the enamelled blue sky.

At the moment all seemed to be well, yet for some reason she had lightning on her mind. She and a friend had been caught once sailing in his yacht, one of the scariest experiences she had had. They were miles from anywhere with lightning flashing closer every time and the ninety-six-foot mast soaring to the lowering sky like a giant lightning rod. Her friend Simon had told her to get inside the cabin and disconnect the aerials and the power leads. If the worst came to the worst and the yacht was struck, at least the radio would still be working. She had never to this day forgotten the experience even though the storm passed over them without incident.

They rode southwards along a chain of tranquil billabongs where the River Red gums gave shade with their wonderful abundance of fresh green foliage. None of the pools was deep at this time though these same pools, Rebecca had been told, could flood miles beyond their banks. Stewart had pointed out flood debris caught high up in the branches of these riverside trees, indicating the height the floods had reached. A flat-topped mesa a few miles off looked remarkable in the brilliant afternoon light. It rose from the burnt umber plains to glow fiery red against the sky so blue it had turned violet.

The mirage, too, was abroad, creating such strange atmospheric tricks. It seemed to Rebecca's dazzled eyes a nomadic tribe was travelling across the landscape but the closer they rode the further off these wraithlike people appeared until they finally disappeared.

The desert birds most active early morning or getting on towards sunset were out in their countless thousands, their trilling and shrieking filling the air. Rebecca had often felt sorry for little budgerigars in a cage; now she rejoiced in the sight of them in the wild. They flew in great numbers across the increasingly incandescent sky, the dancing light throwing up vivid flashes of emerald-green from the wings and gold from the head and neck. Down in the lignum swamps nested the great colonies of Ibis. Kimbara was a major breeding ground for nomadic water birds, the spoonbills, the egrets and herons, the countless thousands of ducks and water hens. The pelicans stuck to the remoter swamps while the beautifully plumaged parrots, the pink and grey galahs and the white corellas tended to favour the mulga.

As they rode the trail back up to the grassy flats topped with tiny purple flowers in their millions Stewart, crouched low in the saddle, challenged her to a race. She took after him giving her spirited chestnut mare, Jeeba, all the encouragement she needed. It was hopeless; Stewart was by far the better rider and the big bay gelding he was riding much stronger and speedier than the mare. It should have, but it didn't seem to chase the cobwebs away. Rebecca was starting to feel quite alarmed by the sky. She stopped short near a clump of bauhinia trees and turned in the saddle, grey eyes anxious. "Stewart don't you think we should be heading back?"

He reined in beside her, reaching over to put a hand over hers. "Why so nervous, my dear?"

She withdrew her hand very gently pretending to adjust her cream Akubra. "I'm not normally nervous but the storm doesn't seem to be all that far away. Look at the sky."

"Goodness I've seen worse," he responded a little tersely, watching her start as a cockatoo nearby gave an agonised screech. "I know all about these things, my dear. I might look like a Wagnerian holocaust but we've been in drought."

"Well if that's what you think," she said doubtfully, still eyeing the lurid sky.

"So now's a good time to ask me what you wanted to earlier," Stewart suggested.

Rebecca decided to tackle the issue head-on not duck it. "I expect you know what it is, Stewart," she said. "I didn't have the slightest idea the Necklace you lent me was so important to the family. Why didn't you tell me?"

He gave her the look of a man who thinks himself insulted. "My dear I don't usually do things accompanied by an explanation."

"I think in this case you might have made an exception," she said very seriously. "I understand the Necklace was last worn by your wife."

His jaw tightened perceptibly. "Rebecca, that's no big secret. What is bothering you *exactly?* I saw you and Brod together last night. Did he take it upon himself to correct you for wearing it?"

"Not at all." Rebecca met his gaze. On no account was she going to create more discord between father and son.

"Please tell me," he urged, as though reading her thoughts. "Don't hold anything back."

She saw a flash of lightning appear on the horizon. "Stewart, it's a very beautiful necklace," Rebecca said, realising she was struggling with anxiety, "but it didn't make me happy to know it's promised to Brod's future wife."

Steward Kinross gave an icy chuckle. "My dear it belongs to *me* until such time. More to the point I could remarry. I've a damned lot to offer."

"I'm sure you have, Stewart." Rebecca felt she was floundering out of her depth. "It's just that it wasn't right to lend it to *me.*"

He hesitated, the grimness of his expression gentling. "You look like you're about to cry."

She set off deliberately. "I assure you I'm not. I think it has something to do with the colour of my eyes. You wouldn't believe the number of people who've told me that."

"They shimmer like diamonds." The look he flashed at her contained such a degree of feeling Rebecca, at that moment, felt she didn't have the strength to confront it. But she had to face the fact Stewart's infatuation with her had ruined things completely. If she didn't leave Kimbara, where would it all end?

"I really feel, Stewart, we have to get out of here," she urged, her face showing her strain. "The lightning seems to be getting closer."

He peered almost nonchalantly at the sort of sky he had seen countless times in his life. "My dear, it's many kilometres away. But if you're frightened…"

She felt no shame. "It's only reasonable to take precautions. I wouldn't like to be caught out in the open."

He continued to sit the big bay, silently staring at her. "You don't feel anything for me, do you?" he said eventually, his handsome face hard and flat.

She was almost too unnerved to speak. "Stewart, this is all a mistake," she cried. "I have to go."

"It's because of Broderick, isn't it?" He appeared to force out the words.

"Stewart, that's an insane idea," she protested, laying a calming hand on Jeeba's neck.

"Is it?"

The way he said it made her hair crawl on her scalp. "And you've no right to ask." She'd had enough bullying to last her a lifetime.

"There's no way I'll let him have you." He made a grab for her reins but Rebecca was waiting. She kicked a boot into Jeeba's side and the mare, already on the nervous side, responded by tearing off, its flying hooves crushing all the little wildflowers and scattering tufts of grass.

God was there no way out of this! Was she doomed to fire men's sexual obsession?

Rebecca let the mare gallop furiously across the valley, heading the startled animal towards the long broad hollow like a trench at the edge of a treeless slope. They had passed it on the ride out. There was a shorter time now between the lightning flash and the thunder. The lightning was coming closer. Why ever had Stewart chosen to take the horses out? They were so very exposed there seemed like no escape. He had put them at risk? She started to pray for the rain to come down so it could soak her to the skin. Much safer to have wet clothes when lightning was about. Any charge would conduct through the wet clothes rather than the body. She didn't even know if Stewart was far behind her.

* * *

Aware of the approaching storm, Brod headed back early to the homestead parking the Jeep in the drive. He worked his way through the house, saw nobody, then went to Fee's room, tapping on the door.

"Fee, it's me," he called. "Where's everyone?"

Fee, who had been lightly dozing, pulled herself off the bed and went to the door. "Hello there, darling. I've been catching up on my beauty sleep."

"Where's Dad and Rebecca?" he asked, sounding mighty taut.

"Are they missing?" Fee blinked.

"There's no one about."

Reluctantly Fee pulled herself wide-awake. "Ah yes, I know. Rebecca did come to the door to tell me they were going riding."

"When was this?" Brod frowned.

"Oh, darling, I'd say a couple of hours ago. What is it?" Fee, catching his mood, asked with a thread of apprehension.

"They're not home, unless they've arrived back at the stables. There's one hell of a storm about to break, Fee. It's been threatening all afternoon. Dad knows the risks of taking the horses out on a day like this."

Fee's mouth turned down. "You know your father, dear. He likes playing God."

"He's got Rebecca with him," Brad clipped off. "I'm really surprised he decided to take her out riding. For that matter couldn't *she* look up and see the sky?"

"For that matter I haven't seen it myself," Fee only half joked, darting away to the verandah. "Good Lord!" she breathed, reading the extraordinary sky. Her demeanour changed, becoming very serious. "That's pretty alarming even by our standards." She looked up at Brod who had joined her. "I'm sure they're safe, darling," she offered, recognising his deep concern. "My guess is they're taking shelter in the caves."

His lean face darkened. "Only a fool would head out that way today. They're more likely to have taken the Willowie trail. I'm going after them."

Fee put a detaining hand on his arm. "Be careful, darling, your father won't like that."

"A pity!" he rasped. "This is a disaster, Fee. The whole business. Dad's acting like a complete fool."

"He's only human, Brod," Fee said quietly, though sometimes in the past she had wondered if it were true.

"He told me this morning he explained all about the Necklace to Rebecca. Still she wore it."

He sounded so violently outraged, so betrayed, Fee had no hesitation speaking her mind. "I suppose you've considered your father could have been lying, Brod. I know that girl."

He turned away urgently. "Maybe she's making fools of us all. I don't know. For the first time in my life I don't *know*. But I'm going after her because I do know Dad. If anything goes wrong she won't be able to handle him."

He drove fast across the valley, cursing beneath his breath as the lightning flashes grew closer, followed in long seconds by the deafening crash of thunder. He estimated the lightning was only a couple of kilometres away. Whatever had possessed his father to ride out on such an afternoon? Was he full of hope if he had Rebecca alone he could convince her he cared for her? That he knew she could come to care about him? That he could cocoon her in a world of luxury? Had he even been heading towards the caves knowing at some point in the afternoon they would have to take shelter? Well he had no right to do it, Brod fumed. No right to harass her. Or was this what she wanted all along?

He didn't know the truth. He was only guessing.

Another brilliant flash of lightning forked from the clouds to the ground. Instinctively he winced. When he reopened his eyes it was to see a horse and rider galloping full tilt across the illuminated landscape with another rider hot in pursuit. He could see the first rider was a woman. She had lost her hat and her long hair was flying like a silk banner on the wind.

Rebecca! Whatever she was, saint or sinner, he felt relief pour into his body. He swung the Jeep in her direction. She appeared to be making for the deep depression that ran like a curving gully around the base of the nearest hillock. At least she had some sense. No one in their right mind would take shelter beneath a tree. The first big drops were falling now, striking the hard ground. This was the time of greatest risk.

Just as he thought it, suddenly, violently as though waiting for the exact moment to find its victim, a bolt of lightning was flung down from the leaden clouds casting a terrifying blaze before it forked into the second rider with a glow that burned the retina.

Almost blinded, caged in the Jeep, Brod felt such shock, such pain, it was almost as if his own heart had stopped. His father had been struck before his very eyes. Not only the man, horse and rider were down. Now came the inevitable clap of thunder, like the roar of some malevolent god, deeper, darker, devastating the ears. He could see Rebecca had become unseated, a small huddle on the ground, while Jeeba was struggling to her feet.

He felt compelled to go to Rebecca first. Drag her into the Jeep where she would be safer than anywhere else. Then he had to go to his father. He knew as well as anybody, lightning can and did strike more than once in the same place but he had to go all the same. His eyes stung behind his narrowed lids, as his whole life seemed to crowd in on him. He realised at that moment the whole day had blazed in an excess of strangeness and the threat of danger.

Rebecca was fully conscious, moaning a little. He ran his hands over her swiftly—he was certain no bones were broken then he lifted her high in his arms bundling her into the Jeep.

"Brod? My God, what happened?"

"Lightning, a lightning strike," he shouted. "Stay in the Jeep. Don't move." He slammed the door shut, enraged and saddened to see Jeeba tottering in pain. If she'd broken a leg she would have to be put down. Now inexplicably the ferocity of the storm abated, seeming to pass directly over them towards the eroded chain of hills with its network of caves.

He found his father on the now sodden ground, the big bay gelding dead beneath him. Desperately keeping his emotions in check he began massage and mouth-to-mouth resuscitation, stopping for a minute, starting again.

At some point Rebecca joined him, ghostly pale, her hair streaming water, looking so young she might have been home from boarding school.

"Brod," she said very gently, after a while, taking his arm, holding it, letting her head come to rest against his shoulder. "Your father is dead."

"What are you talking about?" he defied her. "He's living, breathing..."

"Brod, he's not."

Even so he had to make his last-ditch attempt, knowing beside him Rebecca was crying. "He can't be dead," he said, sounding so definite when he knew all life had fled.

"I'm so sorry...so sorry..." Rebecca crumpled as though all her energy had been burnt up. This had to be the worst day of her life. Such a dreadful thing for Brod. She wanted to comfort him, only exhaustion conquered her.

Now from everywhere men converged on the scene, pushing onwards until they reached the spot where Stewart Kinross lay dead on the ground, his son bowed over him holding his head in his hands. Rebecca was huddled in the grass, motionless though her lips were moving in prayer.

"What in the name of God has happened here?" Ted Holland demanded in the utmost confusion. "Brod, speak to me, man."

Slowly Brod turned up his head. "My father did something incredibly foolish, Ted. He rode out in an electrical storm. I saw the lightning hit him. I saw him go down, his horse under him. Both of them were struck."

"Lord God and the little lady?" Ted stared at Rebecca who appeared quite calm but disoriented.

"I'm afraid she's in shock," Brod said bleakly. "We'll have to get her back to the house. Get her warm. A shot of something. Fee is there, Ted. Take the Jeep then come back for me. I have to get my father home."

CHAPTER FIVE

ALISON KINROSS RECEIVED the news of her father's death when she was attending a party given for a visiting American film star.

"Take it in the study, Ally," her society hostess murmured, drawing her gently aside. "It's your brother."

There had to be a very good reason for Brod to go to these lengths to track her down, Ally thought, immediately panicked. She and Brod spoke often on the phone but if he didn't find her at home he always left a message on the machine. She hurried into the Sinclair study and shut the door after her. She was a strikingly beautiful young woman with a mane of dark curly hair and almond-shaped green eyes. Family eyes. Fiona Kinross had them, always using them to great effect.

"He's dead, Ally," Brod said very quietly when she picked up the receiver and identified herself. "Our father was killed in a lightning strike this afternoon."

She didn't cry though it was the last thing she had been expecting to hear. Her father had hurt her too badly over the years for tears but she felt a tremendous grief for what might have been. "Where, Brod? How?"

She listened while Brod told what had happened. Not *ex-*

actly what had happened. How his father had invited Rebecca to ride with him when he obviously knew a lot better. Unless as Brod suspected his father had some plan of his own in mind. That was a large part of the way his father had worked. Hidden agendas. Besides, he never had introduced the subject of his father's infatuation with Rebecca Hunt to Ally. He wasn't going to. Not *now*. Though Ally would hear of it. He was certain of that. He continued to talk, his tone grave and quiet

"I'll come," Ally said finally. "I'll fly out in the morning." She struggled with the thought of what it was all going to mean.

"Charter a flight," Brod advised her. "Just get here quickly."

"I love you, Brod," she said. Brod her powerful big brother. The brother who had always looked out for her and treated her with such affection.

"I love you, too, Ally." His vibrant voice was subdued. "I can't imagine how we're going to get through this, but we will."

When Ally put the phone down a moment later, she was conscious of the trembling right through her body. The party was over for her. She would make her excuses to her hosts then go home and pack.

The end of an era she thought. The beginning of Brod's reign.

As she walked to the tall double doors of the study, the light caught the lustrous gleam of her strapless emerald dress. There would be many difficulties ahead, she thought, not the least of them having to see Rafe again. Her father's funeral would be big. He'd been—dear Lord the past tense—an important man. Members of most Outback families would be there. Politicians, the legal fraternity, businesspeople. The Cameron brothers would be singled out as close family friends. The old gossip would circulate. Everybody knew of her love affair with Rafe. Hadn't she gloried in it? But in the end, overcome by the sheer tempestuousness of their feelings, she had run away. She had run like her mother and Rafe, her beloved Rafe, had wiped his hands of her. The very thought of him might still fill her with longing but she knew she had lost him forever.

* * *

When Fee rang her daughter, Francesca, in London she never expected Francesca to tell her, "I'm coming, Fee. I'll book a flight as soon as I get off the phone. I know you and Uncle Stewart had your differences. I know *why* but he was always very nice to me. It's the very least I can do. Besides, I'm longing to see you and the family, Brod and Ally." It seemed a far too inappropriate time to mention Grant Cameron even when his golden unashamedly macho image kept popping into her mind at the oddest times. Like someone you can't possibly forget.

"The funeral is on Friday," Fee was saying. "My poor brother in a cold room but it will give Brod the time to make all the arrangements. I can tell you everyone is shocked out of their minds. Not a lot of people have liked Stewart. A lot feared him. But he had such vigour. Surely he can't be dead."

"I can't really take it in, either," Francesca confessed distressed, sweeping her hair back off her forehead. "So now Brod is master of Kimbara. He's taken over the inheritance he was born for."

"Kimbara will be a different place," Fee vowed. "Though it grieves me to say it, Stewart served himself. Brod is like my darling, Sir Andy. He'll serve his heritage."

"It's so sad about Ally and Brod," Francesca said, depressed by her own intimate knowledge of family matters and the lack of love.

"Do you think I don't realise what *you* missed, Francesca," Fee asked with a pang. "I was a terrible mother."

Francesca couldn't help nodding. "I know!" She gave a kind little laugh, then sobered. "But I love you."

"I know and I don't deserve it." Fee cleared her throat." I couldn't feel more comfort knowing you're coming. Such a long flight! I want you to meet Rebecca. She was out riding with Stewart when he was struck so she's taking it very hard. In fact she wants to leave."

"Well I can understand it," Francesca breathed. "It must have been awful for her."

"Just like Stewart to go and do something dreadfully dramatic," Fee wailed. "Let me know your flight, dearest. We'll organise a connecting charter flight. Maybe that marvellous hunk Grant Cameron could pick you up. He's sure to want to meet you again."

I hope! Francesca thought, breaking the connection. She looked up from the bed where she'd been sitting to catch sight of her reflection in the pier mirror. She looked nothing like her beautiful mother. She took after her father's side of the family. She had a cousin, Alexandra, with the same red-gold hair and flower-blue eyes. People often mistook them for sisters.

The quintessential English Rose, Grant Cameron had called her with amused admiration, but with the suspicion her beauty and strength would be sapped in the harsh environment of the Outback.

Maybe just maybe, he didn't know enough about her.

Rebecca, who had sought refuge in a lovely cool seating area on the far reaches of the garden, lifted her head at the sound of footsteps on the gravel path. Hurriedly she tried to smooth the marks of tears from her face. Stewart's sudden violent death had hit her terribly hard, the shock compounded by feelings of guilt as though her rejection of him had somehow led to his death. It was irrational. She knew that, but it didn't help. It was Stewart who had made the dreadful mistake of not seeking protection for both of them yet her part in the tragedy weighed heavily on her.

Fee had given her the news Ally and Francesca were both coming for the funeral. Both intended to stay for a time. There was no place for her here with the family arriving, though Fee had been quick to beg her to stay. The footsteps grew louder. A man's footsteps.

Brod's. He was coming towards her, more formally dressed than usual as different people were flying in all the time to express their condolences and lend their support. Rebecca had never thought to see roses blooming so prolifically in the Outback yet now he passed under a double arch aglow with large yellow roses. Soon he would reach her.

Rebecca drew a deep, shaky breath, not fully understanding her own powerful reactions to the man. Both of them had made it their business to avoid each other. Now he had come to seek her out. For what reason? To ask her to leave? Innocent of all blame she regarded it as only natural. She threw aside a cushion, standing up as though readying herself for a verdict.

"Don't hurry away, Rebecca," he said, as good as blocking the narrow path with his tall, wide-shouldered frame. His tone was crisp but not unfriendly.

"What is it, Brod?" she asked without further hesitation, unhappily aware her voice was husky.

"I thought it was about time we had a little talk." He stored up the sight of her in his mind. "I haven't bothered you. I'm sympathetic to your shock but I want to know what happened yesterday."

It was so quiet only for the sound of the birds. She felt trapped.

"I can't talk about it, Brod," she said and turned away from him urgently, as he moved into the leafy garden sanctuary. She wanted comfort. She felt this man could have given it, except he had locked his mind and his heart against her.

"You *will* tell me, Rebecca," he warned quietly. "You owe it to me." He put out a hand not to restrain her but to turn her to face him. "Tears. Lots of tears. For my father?" She looked hurt like a child, her womanly powers of seduction not sending the usual messages from her beautiful drowned eyes.

"I can't help think I was somehow to blame."

Her voice was so deeply pained he found himself trying to ease it. "My father knew to seek shelter, Rebecca." He stared at her, trying to read her mind. "But I'm surprised you consented to go with him. Surely you could see a major storm was building up?"

She sat down again, with him towering over her, locking her hands tightly to calm herself. "I didn't want to go, Brod, but your father made it seem the tremendous build up of storm clouds was no more than some grand celestial display. He didn't expect a single drop of rain to fall."

Damn it! Dad and his tricks. "That *can* happen," he explained, "but my father could read the different skies as well as I can." He knew he would be too close to her to sit on the padded bench, her graceful body only inches from his, so he moved back a little to sit on the low stone wall surrounding a raised bed of flowers. "I want you to tell me where you were headed?" he asked.

She looked up briefly, grey eyes dominating her pale face. "Your father was going to show me the aboriginal rock paintings in the caves."

His suspicions confirmed. "He said that, did he?" he asked bleakly.

"I didn't really want to see them." Even then she vehemently shook her head. "I mean I do want to see them, but I'd been feeling so anxious all day. Now I know why."

"So you didn't manage to get that far?" he persisted with his line of thought.

"Put it this way—" she shrugged "—I kept heading in a different direction. Along the chain of billabongs. I love all the water lilies and the bird life."

"What are you hiding, Rebecca?" he asked all of a sudden, very blunt.

"What is it you think I should say," she pleaded. "I have to live with this."

God only knows what happened, he thought, sick to death of it all. "You sound distraught."

"I am." Her shadowed eyes flashed. "I want to go home."

He found he was violently opposed to that. "You're not a

child. You're a woman and you have professional commitments."
He said the first thing that came into his head.

"Your family is coming." She spread her elegant hands. "All
your friends. I have no place here."

His eyes blazed. "You've made quite a place for yourself,
though, haven't you, Rebecca. Did my father tell you he was
in love with you?" He wanted desperately to know what had
gone on.

"What does any of it matter, Brod?" She turned her face
away from him.

"That means he *did*."

"I don't know what he was saying," she evaded, when she
would never forget.

"Don't give me that. *Please*. He was so caught up with you."
The dappled sunshine fell over his taut face. "You knew it."

"I learned it the hard way." Now she almost gave herself
away.

"How?" he rasped.

"Your father never touched me," she whispered, a little
shocked by his expression.

"All right," he answered. "Calm down. But he said something to send you galloping madly away."

"And that's when it happened," she sighed deeply, "the tragedy. I don't want to talk about it any more."

"The thing is, Rebecca, there are consequences for our ac-
tions," he pointed out. "Look at me and tell me you didn't intend for my father to fall in love with you?" Hardness broke
through his quiet tone, cruelly cutting her.

"What difference would it make?" She flew up and turned
fully to face him, finding the very air was suffocating. "You
believe what you want to believe."

He caught her shoulders, smelling her fragrance. "That's a
cop-out really, isn't it?"

"I don't want to quarrel with you, Brod," she said, locked
into his magnetism.

Now the woman sprang to vibrant life. He saw it flare out of her eyes, wrapping them both in a desperate hunger. "Well tell me what you do want?" he asked harshly, his thumbs moulding her delicate collar-bones.

"I want to forget I ever met you," she heard herself saying. God knows he was out to hurt her. "I want to forget all of this."

"All of *what?*" he asked forcefully, feeling she was stealing something from him. His self-control. "I thought you were set on marrying a Kinross. You don't care which one?"

As antiviolent as it was possible for a woman to be, Rebecca, driven beyond her normal behaviour, threw back her hand intending to slap his beautiful, hateful face only he caught her wrist in mid-air, overwhelming her with his strength. His eyes flashed danger. "Tell me what you came here for, Rebecca? The biography was only the start. When did you decide there was a great deal more on offer?"

She could hear and see the tumult that was going on in him. Tumult that was heating her own blood. "Go on, lash out at me if it can help you through it," she cried, pushing against him with trembling hands. "I know I hate you."

"Ah, yes." He narrowed his eyes. "We've already discovered that." He brought her face up to him with insistent fingers, lowering his head to claim her mouth, while she in agony of mixed emotions tried to offer resistance.

Flames danced around them, locking them in a dangerous circle.

"You drive me mad," he muttered, as his lips finally left hers.

"I'm going home, Brod." Incredibly she leaned her head against his chest. She had to be crazy. Only he was so physically perfect to her she didn't know if she could possibly withstand him.

"Where's home?" Now he was absorbed in kissing her throat and she was letting him do it, allowing passion to convulse her.

"Away from you." Her voice broke with emotion.

"I don't believe that." He gave a little laugh, something like triumph in the sound. "God, I don't believe what I'm doing my-self. Is this a plan or are we just part of a pattern. Destiny if you will. You know my father brought you to this place?"

She grew very still within his arms, touched all over with alarm. "What are saying, Brod?"

"He never told you himself?" He lifted his head to stare into her eyes.

Now she had her free will back. "I weep for you, Brod," she said stormily. "For the sad life you've led. You can't trust any-one, can you?"

"I trust lots of people," he proclaimed. "But not a magnolia so white and pure. There's much too much mystery to you for that."

Some relationships are ruined before they start. "I'm going up to the house to pack," Rebecca said, disgust in her eyes.

"Won't do you much good." He gave a little shrug. "I'll take the pledge not to ask you too many tough questions but you're staying, Rebecca, make no mistake about that. No one will fly you out without my say-so and you owe it to my father to at-tend his funeral. You admitted as much yourself."

Alison arrived mid-afternoon, tired from the journey but thrilled to be home on Kimbara. It still exerted a powerful influence on her.

Her eyes filled with tears at the sight of her brother. Although they talked often, she hadn't seen that much of Brod in the past few years, now his striking maturity and the enhanced pres-ence of his inheritance was fully revealed to her. It occurred to her suddenly Brod had a decided look of Sir Andy about him. A quality their father by no means had had. She remembered that look of Sir Andy's well. Brod had it, too. The high met-tled pride. Not the arrogance but the pride of real achievement.

"Ally, it's wonderful to see you." Brod gathered his sister into a huge hug, fighting down the impulse to tell her she was much too thin. "I only wish it were happier times." Still holding her hand he led her to the Jeep. "Climb in. I'll take care of your luggage. I sure hope you're going to stay for a while like you promised."

"It's wonderful to know I can," she called back.

No more arguments with her father. No more stepping into the combat zone. No more scathing condemnation for not marrying Rafe.

"I don't suppose you were worthy of him anyway." The contemptuous words still rang in her ears. Years later.

It wasn't what one expected to hear from one's father.

Her few pieces of luggage loaded away, Brod got behind the wheel. "Fran is due in tomorrow. I've organised with Grant to pick her up at Longreach. I'd go for her myself, I guess I can call the Beech Baron my own, only so many people have been flying in and out paying their respects."

"I wonder if it's more wanting to offer you support than mourning Dad," Ally said bleakly, looking out the window at the vastness of the land. Kimbara was another world. "Dad had no idea how to make friends of people."

"That was his misfortune," Brod said gravely. "There was something I wanted to talk to you about before we got up to the house." He was worried Ally might hear it from someone else. "You know about Rebecca, of course."

Ally gave him a sharp look from her clear green eyes.

"What is that supposed to mean?" she asked in wonderment. "I thought Rebecca was here to write Fee's biography. Fee speaks highly of her. Obviously they've hit it off."

Brod's chiselled profile was serious. "They have but there's a little more to it than that. It will come as a shock to you but Dad was utterly infatuated with her." It had to be in the genes.

Ally blinked her astonishment. "What?" Her voice cracked. "Could Dad be infatuated with any woman? I hate to say this but I never thought he liked women at all. Not after our mother left."

"There were women in his life. You know that." Brod gave her a brief sidelong glance.

"True," Ally conceded, "but he never married one of them."

"I think he was beginning to see Rebecca in that light," Brod told her grimly. "She's very beautiful in just the way he liked. Cool, poised, patrician. Someone who could easily take over the role of his wife."

"For God's sake." Ally turned her head to study her brother's face. "I thought she was my age or thereabouts?"

"Ally, you'd be familiar with rich men marrying younger women," he countered.

"But Fee hasn't said a word about this," Ally protested, having difficulty taking it in. Her father thinking of remarrying. Now he was dead!

"Fee doesn't want to think about it." Brod said bluntly. "I wouldn't be mentioning it myself only chances are someone will tell you at the funeral, human nature being what it is. The real problem was Dad lent Rebecca Cecilia's Necklace to wear at the function the other night."

"Brod!" Ally looked her shock. "In that case, we could have a little gold digger right under our noses. She must have known."

His handsome mouth tightened. "I'm by no means certain of that. Rebecca says he didn't tell her. Fee believes her."

"And you? Why the doubt?"

Brod put a hand to his temple. "I can't rid myself of it. Maybe the fault lies in me. She certainly got rid of it before the night was over. I locked it away in the safe myself."

"Which seems to suggest Rebecca might have been another one of Dad's victims. He set her up? Maybe marked her in everyone's eyes?" Ally suggested shrewdly.

"Talk to her and find out," Brod said.

"You sound like the answer is important to you." Ally's mind was working overtime. She wondered about this Rebecca Hunt who had made such an impression not only on her father but on Brod as well.

"It's easy to see she'd get to a man, Ally," Brod confirmed

what she was thinking. "The thing is I can't reconcile all my images of her."

To his sister the look in Brod's eyes could only be described as tormented.

The four of them sat at one end of the long mahogany dinner table, eating without appetite, the conversation muted and desultory. Even Fee, a genuine extrovert, was subdued by the tragedy that had overtaken them. Given what she had heard, Ally didn't know what to expect when she finally met Rebecca Hunt. Rebecca had not intruded on her homecoming but had insisted on waiting until dinner to be introduced.

Now Ally watched the other younger woman as she sat quietly beside Fee. Just as Brod had said she was simply beautiful, Ally thought. Dressed in a deep violet shift dress that lightly skimmed her figure. The light from the chandelier glossed her smooth dark hair and illuminated the creamy white skin. She was small, inches shorter than Ally who was five-seven but she carried herself so elegantly she appeared taller. Her eyes, Ally considered, were her most striking feature apart from the piquancy of that full mouth. Every time she lifted her head, they glittered like diamonds with the light on them. She had a good hand shake, a lovely voice, and a decidedly refined air. She wasn't overly friendly, which Ally didn't expect at this time but when she did speak she said all the right things.

Ally couldn't fault her. In truth she didn't want to fault her at all. Rebecca Hunt didn't strike her as an opportunist or a social climber though Ally could well see how her father had become infatuated. Rather she struck Ally as a young professional woman like herself, who was very good at what she did, but hiding a multitude of hurts behind a carefully constructed facade. Ally's own dysfunctional childhood and adolescence gave her an insight into such things.

During the course of the evening Ally noticed, too, the tensions that were running back and forth between Rebecca and her brother, the intensity of the glances as though each was speaking to the other with their eyes. The tension peaked around half past nine when Rebecca rose gracefully to her feet.

"I must leave you all to speak privately," she said with the most exquisite sad smile. "I know you must want to." She addressed Ally directly. "I'm so glad to have finally met you, Ally. I've heard so many lovely things about you. Now I'll enjoy your show even more when I watch it. Night, Fee. You've been so kind asking me to stay on but I really feel I should return to Sydney after—" she faltered briefly "—the funeral. There will be lots of planes flying in and out. I'm sure I could arrange a lift to some point."

"How about the Never Never," Brod said discordially looking at her hard. "I thought we'd discussed this, Rebecca."

"Well we did." She looked flustered. "But Francesca will be arriving. Ally is staying on. You don't need me. We can leave the biography, Fee, until such time as you're ready to start again." The very tautness of her face showed her anguish.

"But, darling, I don't want that at all," Fee protested, casting aside her wondrously beautiful deeply fringed silk shawl. "I don't want you to live with this…sadness on your own. You've sustained a bad shock. Our lives have become entwined. Besides I'm looking on working on the biography as a sort of cure. A healing if you will. We haven't spoken one real word about my childhood yet. Stewart was alive and things were…" She threw up her hands theatrically.

"God, Fee, you're not going to make a full confession now he's gone?" Brod asked with a wry groan.

"What's wrong with the truth?" Fee demanded. "You don't know how miserable Stewart made me when we were children. He was a devil of a liar. Got me into terrible trouble all the time. Said I did everything."

"You probably did," Ally observed with the same wry affection Brod used when he spoke to his aunt. Ally transferred her gaze to Rebecca. "Please don't think of going on account of me, Rebecca. I can see we'll get on fine. Fran is a lovely person. Fee and I both want you to meet her. Anyway you heard Fee. She means to go on with the book."

Rebecca looked touched, but adamant. "You're being so nice but I really think…"

"Rebecca, why don't I walk you up to your room," Brod intervened, rising to his impressive height. "I can plead with you on the way."

"Do that, Brod," Fee said in heartfelt tones. "Rebecca really doesn't have anyone to go to. She told me. This isn't a kindness, Rebecca. We really want you." She sounded very definite as indeed she was.

"What's with Rebecca and Brod?" Ally asked her aunt in a fraught undertone as soon as the two had left the room. "You don't need an antennae to pick up the vibes."

"To be honest, darling, I think Brod's fighting his attraction to her. I think he's going through a bit of hell over your father, and Stewart's claim Rebecca knew all about Cecilia's Necklace before she wore it."

Ally continued to stare at her aunt. "You don't believe that?"

"Darling, I don't want to say it, but I know what a liar your dear father was."

"Well he's at rest now," Ally sighed.

"Wouldn't it be horrible if he weren't," said Fee.

Both of them waited until they were in the upper hallway before either of them spoke.

Even then in mounting furious undertones. "What a little coward you are waiting until you had Fee and Ally for cover," Brod accused her, when he really wanted to touch her. Soothe her.

"Am I going to go to hell for it?" Rebecca's pale face flushed with anger. "Why do you want me here, Brod? To mete out further punishment?"

His lean face tautened. "No such thing has occurred to me.

Besides it seems to me you're punishing yourself. How's it going to help you to run off?"

Rebecca let out a long mournful sigh. "Damn it, I'm not running off. I just don't want to intrude."

He couldn't help himself. He exploded. "Hell, that's good. You turn the whole household upside down, me included, now you're talking about hitching a ride on the first plane out of here. It doesn't fit the pattern."

"I thought it was what you wanted?" She stared up into his face, afraid of his power, his magnetism. She didn't need this upheaval in her ordered life.

He actually groaned. "I don't know what I want with your face distracting me. Maybe you ought to think of Fee. She employed you to do a job. You're a professional aren't you? It must have sunk in she wants you here." He gave a quiet, ironic laugh. "You've even talked Ally around."

Rebecca took a few rapid little steps away from him and went no further. "Honestly you take my breath away. I can't believe Ally's your sister."

"Good Lord, you haven't noticed we're very much alike?"

"Ally is a beautiful person." Rebecca ignored the mockery. "You're decidedly not. If I were you I'd be ashamed."

He tossed the idea around for a moment. "Tell me what I'm supposed to be ashamed of and I'll work on it," he said. Then suddenly in a voice that moved her powerfully he added, "I want you to stay, Rebecca."

Her heart quite literally rocked. "You want to keep an eye on me?" Despite herself her voice trembled.

"Like inches away." He moved closer, as graceful and soundless as a panther.

"I don't want trouble, Brod." She raised her chin.

"That doesn't seem to matter when it obviously comes after you. What are you afraid of, Rebecca?"

"I might ask the same question of you?"

He reached out and drew a shivery finger down her cheek.

"As it turns out I don't have the answer. What I particularly need to hear is more about you. You already know a lot about me. I think it's time you started talking. You don't speak of family. Of friends, lovers."

"I don't choose to," Rebecca said, the perverse pleasure in his company so keen she couldn't move.

"Fee said you had no one to go back to. What did she mean?"

She ought to try to move. *Now.* Yet her body turned more fully towards him like a flower to the sun. "My mother died when I was fourteen," she began quietly even now feeling the terrible pain of severance. "She survived a car accident but complications from her injuries killed her a few years later. My father remarried. I see him and his other family as much as I can but he lives in Hong Kong. He was an airline pilot. The best. He's retired now." She touched the tip of her tongue to her suddenly dry lips.

"Don't do that," he said in a slow deep voice.

"Brod, I can't stay here in this house. This beautiful sad house."

"Why do you think that is? Come on, tell me." He swooped to take hold of her wrists, drawing her close against him, bending his dark head to kiss her a little roughly but so sweetly, so passionately on her mouth.

He was becoming so precious to her she was really afraid. Don't stop. Don't ever stop. The feeling was stupendous. Her heart was burning inside her like a flame.

But he did, lifting his head like a man who was spellbound.

"This thing between us, I don't want to hurt you," he muttered, not even sure if he believed it himself.

"But it scares me." There she'd admitted it.

"You're the one with the powers." Now there was a shimmer of male hostility. "These past few days have been hell."

She recognised that herself. "I never thought for a moment your father—" She broke off, too upset to go on.

"Would fall in love with you. Want to marry you?" He held her away from him so he could stare down into her face.

"No." She averted her head so he could only see the curve of her cheek.

Something flickered in his brilliant eyes. How to control this power she had. "I don't see we're getting anywhere discussing this." He removed his hands quietly, watching her brush a long strand of her hair away from her face. "Don't embarrass us by calling on anyone to give you a lift, Rebecca," he said. "Don't hurt Fee's feelings. When you're ready to tell me what lies under that porcelain exterior, I'm here."

How can I tell him, Rebecca thought, her eyes trained on his tall figure until he reached the central staircase and without a backwards glance disappeared down the steps. Back to his family.

I had a family, too, Rebecca thought, walking desolately to her room, closing the door. A very happy family until her mother, a passenger in a friend's car, was badly injured when the car they were travelling in was struck by a speeding vehicle. Her mother's friend was killed. Her mother spent the rest of her life in a wheelchair devotedly nursed by her husband and daughter. A few years after her mother's premature death, her father remarried. A beautiful Eurasian women he met in Hong Kong. At this time she was at boarding school while her father shuttled between Hong Kong and Sydney. Even so they remained close and Vivienne, her stepmother, never let a birthday go past without sending some wonderful present. Vacations were spent in all sorts of exotic places. Bangkok, Phuket, Bali, twice to Marrekesch, but things settled down after Vivienne had her first child, an adorable little boy they called Jean Phillipe. A little girl, Christina, followed two years later.

It was at university she met Martyn. He was a few years older, studying law. She was doing an arts degree majoring in journalism. Although she was making lots of friends she and Martyn soon became a pair. He was exceptionally bright, good-looking, of excellent family, an only child. If Rebecca was soon to find his mother was very possessive she kept it to herself. Anyway Meredith actually approved of her if a little unhappy about the fact Rebecca's father had married a Eurasian who could have run rings around Meredith in any direction.

They were married when she was twenty and Martyn twenty-four. At first they'd been happy only Martyn didn't think she had any real need to finish her studies. His family were well-off. He was an up-and-coming young lawyer with a prestigious firm who had selected him because of his brilliant results. His mother had never worked. She had dedicated her life to becoming the perfect wife and mother. That was Meredith's primary responsibility in life. She fussed endlessly over her husband and son, kept a splendid house for them, arranged all the frequent entertaining. Rebecca's goal should be the same. It was supposed to be an all encompassing role. And some years on—Martyn was in no hurry to start a family—they would have children. Two only. A boy and a girl.

It took Rebecca a while to realise Martyn didn't want friends. Or her friends at least. He didn't want to invite them around to their very comfortable town house, a wedding present from his parents, he didn't want to go to any of their parties. Gradually people stopped asking altogether. As one of her girlfriends told her: "Martyn only wants you for himself, Becky. You're supposed to be so smart. Can't you see that?"

The marriage had lasted exactly three years. No time. An eternity. She refused point-blank to give up her studies. Her generation wanted a fulfilling job. She was supposed to be an outstanding student. At which point Martyn had always thrown back his head and laughed. "Journalism? What the heck's that? Stay at home and write a bestseller."

The arguments began. She felt he was caging her. Destroying her friendships. It wasn't a life, just the two of them all the time. It dawned on her that Martyn, for all his legal brain, wasn't interesting enough. What was important to him was he had her undivided attention.

The physical abuse started in the last year. First a hard slap across the face that sent her flying. Of course she had reacted in horror. Her father had been so gentle towards her and her mother. She left their town house that very night staying with Kim her most faithful friend. Martyn had come after her, in tears, begging her forgiveness.

"Don't go, Becky," Kim warned her. "It will only start again."

But he was her husband. She'd taken her marriage vows very seriously. The last time he hit her she ended in hospital with cracked ribs.

The marriage was over. She had her life back. Though it wasn't that simple. She had to endure a period of terrible harassment until she threatened to go to the head of his law firm, a fine man who liked her, to lodge a complaint. Soon after she moved away to London, determined nothing like that would ever happen to her again. It had been a long time before she had entered into another relationship. But somehow no one had ever touched her heart.

Until now.

CHAPTER SIX

AROUND THEM, everywhere they looked the ancient plains stretched to the horizon, the needle leaved clumps of spinifex that dotted them bleached bright gold against the fiery red of the sand they stabilised. Above them arched the limitless peacock-blue sky that at three o'clock in the afternoon was ruled by a scorching sun. People had come from all over the Outback to the vast station, this vast emptiness, to attend Stewart Kinross's funeral. Almost everybody except the infirm or the elderly had trudged to the low ridge where the Kinross family since the time of settlement had buried their dead.

The family cemetery in itself was impressive, surrounded by a stone wall with elaborate black wrought iron gates. Small and immense headstones were erected inside, some side by side. Kinross men and women. Children. Rebecca's eyes blurred as she tried to read some of the poignant legends on the marbles, unutterably saddened to see babies had died.

No tears from the family. Brod stood his six foot three, his hands clasped before him, his handsome blue-black head bowed. Ally dressed from head to toe in black stood with Fee, similarly attired as was Fee's lovely daughter, Francesca, the sheer perfection of her English skin and her marvellous titian hair a

striking foil to her black dress relieved only by an obviously
valuable string of pearls.

Other members of the extended family crowded around,
friends, VIP's, businessmen, partners in many of the Kinross
ventures. Prominent not only by virtue of their height and physical presence, were the Cameron brothers, Rafe and Grant, their
unprotected bare heads with the fabulous glint of gold.

Rebecca in a dark grey wide-brimmed straw hat Ally had
lent her, which matched the only suitable dress she had with
her, a discreet charcoal-grey, was glad of the sunglasses that
hid her eyes.

The clergyman, well-known to the family, continued with
the service while Rebecca gripped her fingers waiting for it all
to end. She half turned away at the final moments when the
heavy ornate casket was lowered into the ground, unable to witness it. Her own mother's funeral came back to her with dreadful clarity. She and her father had stood rigid, fighting to keep
back the floodgates but at that point they had both succumbed
to unrestrained weeping. At least her father had found happiness as her mother would have wanted.

That hadn't been her lot. Martyn had treated her so badly but
in the end she had been far from powerless. She had reclaimed
her life. Known success, won the respect of her peers. She'd
had no way of knowing when she accepted Fiona Kinross's
commission to write her biography such high drama would be
unleashed. What was she doing here on this day of all days?
How had she ever become so deeply involved with the Kinross
family, not knowing at that point Stewart Kinross had carefully
planned it all.

To Rebecca it didn't seem possible Stewart was dead. Only
she and Brod had seen him die. Nothing had prepared her for
such a shock.

Back at the homestead, people milled through the main reception rooms and out onto the surrounding verandahs, partaking

of the food and drink that had been prepared for them. Most stuck to tea and coffee with the selection of sandwiches but some of the men were knocking back whisky like it was mineral water. The conversation, though subdued, created such a persistent buzz it drove Ally, her nerves much on edge, to the far end of the side verandah. Worse yet to come. At some point she had to face Rafe. The very last thing she needed was hundreds of eyes on them.

Like most of the other women she had taken off her hat. Now damp tendrils of her curly hair that she had worn in a thick upturned roll at the back clung to her temples and nape. She turned away to look out over an avenue of palms. The home gardens were ablaze with colour. Soon the desert would burst into flower. Give it a month. The big storm that had robbed her father of his life would bring to Kimbara a marvellous profusion of wildflowers, millions and millions of everlastings, papery pink, bright yellow and white. When she was a little girl she had rejoiced in the way the everlastings didn't wilt. The Sturt Peas, named after the explorer, would trail their long stems of crimson flowers across the mulga plains, the fleshy leaved parakeelyas forming radiating patterns in the sand. The incredibly tough spinifex would turn from sun-scorched gold to deep green then later when it sent up its seed bearing stems great tracts of spinifex country were transformed from desert to a landscape that almost resembled vast fields of wheat.

How she missed it all! Though she had become successful at what she did—had indeed inherited some of her aunt Fee's great talent—she never felt truly at home in the city. This was her world, this incredible living desert; this sun-scorched land of fiery colours. The lush seaboard had its own unique beauty, marvellous Sydney Harbour, but nothing spoke to her like her own fascinating home, Kimbara. Brod's now. Lost in her thoughts, Ally started visibly when a man addressed her.

"Ally?"

She turned away from the white wrought-iron balustrade to

find Rafe studying her out of half-hooded gold-flecked hazel eyes. She willed on herself calmness but her head had gone spinning. A big man, even with her wearing her black high heeled shoes, she had to look up at him. His attitude was courteous. Rafe was always the gentleman, but a remoteness was there in his narrowed gaze. In the heat of the afternoon like most of the men he had taken off his jacket, his crisp white shirt showing the breadth of his shoulders, the top button of his collar undone so he could loosen his black tie. He looked as stunning as ever, the straight chiselled nose, the squarish chin with its distinctive cleft, the wide mouth, the clear gold skin that was so arresting with his thick shock of gold hair.

"Well am I looking better or worse?" he broke into her examination, his deep voice faintly wry.

"You look great, Rafe," she said. A masterly understatement. Like Brod he had found an impressive maturity.

"I haven't had a chance to tell you how shocked we were, Grant and I, by Stewart's death," he said with formal sincerity. "Please accept my condolences. Grant will catch up with you. He's still paying his respects to the rest of the family."

"Thank you, Rafe," she murmured, her emotions intensifying by the second.

"You're too thin," he said abruptly when he hadn't intended to say it at all.

"Have to be," she answered flippantly to cover her own agitation at seeing him. "The camera adds pounds."

Again he allowed his eyes to move over her. "You look like the breeze might blow you over," he said finally, dismayed by the stirring in his blood. "So, your career? Is it going as planned? You seem to have hit the jackpot with your show. Top of the ratings."

She leaned back against the railing. "It is a lot of hard work. I go straight home when the shooting is over. I have to learn my lines. I have to be up very early in the morning."

"That shouldn't leave you looking so stressed out," he said, disturbed despite himself at her look of strain.

"Is that how I seem?"

"Even given the shock of your father's death, you've altered." He wasn't going to tell her she looked beautiful, if too fragile for her height. The Ally he had held in his arms had more cover on those long classy bones. More curve to her warm, sweet breasts. How marvellous it had been then. Fantastic when they were alone together. Ally, his heart's desire. On the very day he intended to ask her to marry him, she provoked a blazing argument that left him dazed....

"I want it all to stop for a while, Rafe," she had cried, the tears smudging her cheeks, dust streaked from their ride, her long thick lashes stuck together spikily. "I want my own space!" When he finally calmed her down she claimed she loved him too much. That made him laugh. Not for long. Ally of the dark brown hair and slanting green eyes had made a fool of him with a capital *F*. She had run away to Sydney leaving him bereft. His heart broken until he picked himself up determined never to believe a woman again.

And what was he supposed to say to her now she was back? If only for her father's funeral. He knew, couldn't help knowing, he could have just about any woman he wanted. He'd had his casual affairs. He had to take it for granted Ally had had hers. She had it all. Beauty, freedom, style, wealth, a career that put her face on the cover of glossy magazines. God help him he had even bought a few. For what purpose? Another man might have thrown darts at her image. The great thing was he was over her. The Ally he had loved never really existed.

"You look so serious, Rafe," she was saying, lifting her emerald-green eyes to him. "Even grim. What could you possibly be thinking about?"

"I don't think you'd want to know," he said.

She couldn't bear the look in his eyes. "Not if it's about me. I know you despise me."

He heard his own deep-throated laugh. "Ally, beautiful as you are, it might be as well for you to know I'm now indifferent to your many charms. Fact is you're not the girl I knew all my life."

"You've written me off?" She stayed very still.

He nodded. "Had to." When he would have moved heaven and earth for her. "What about you? Anyone important in your life?"

She pushed tendrils of hair from her aching forehead. "People come and go, Rafe," she said, careful not to look at him. Not a one of them could measure up to you.

"How long are you staying?" He, too, sounded careful.

"A week. That's all I can spare. It's wonderful to be home. The comfort of it."

"Even if you were driven back by your father's death?"

She lifted her beautiful sad eyes. "You know all about our family, Rafe. You know why I'm not crying though I'm in mourning for what might have been. Like Brod. Dad never cared for me, Rafe. Think of that! He broke my heart."

He fought against saying it. Lost. "There's evidence you've got one?" One step. One error and he would pull her into his arms.

"I loved you. You were my world." With so many onlookers she managed to keep her face composed though her voice was unsteady.

"But you couldn't rest until you tried something else?"

"If only that were all of it!" she exclaimed. "I was too young, Rafe. I couldn't handle what we had. Our relationship was so powerful."

"Is that how you analyse it?" He spoke as though it were a clinical question.

"For what it's worth!" She managed to nod at people who were looking their way. Amanda Someone was staring. She seemed jealous.

"Well it doesn't matter now," said Rafe.

* * *

Grant followed Francesca's slender, black-clad figure out into the corridor. "How's the jet lag?" he asked, real concern on his open, strong-boned face.

"I made a fool of myself didn't I?"

He looked down at her and smiled. "I'd probably have fainted myself after such a long, gruelling trip."

She was amused by the very idea. He exuded such strength. "At least you were there to catch me." Within moments of walking into the bush terminal she, who prided herself on being a good traveller, had crumpled like a doll.

"I had the feeling I was catching a flower." He held her with his eyes gazing into what he considered the prettiest face he had ever seen. He knew Ally, the Kinross who had broken his brother's heart was beautiful in her vibrant challenging way. The young woman who had come to write Fee's biography, Rebecca, was beautiful as well, but so cool and controlled she might have been carved out of ice. This lovely creature had a warmth, a *sweetness,* a kind of innocence written all over her. It affected him powerfully.

"Don't write me off, Grant," she teased him gently. "There's a lot more to me than you can see."

"Was I doing that?" One tawny eyebrow shot up comically. "Writing you off?"

She nodded her head, all the while smiling at him. "I can see you don't think I'd fit in here."

Show me a rose growing in the desert, he thought. She was soft voiced. A lovely voice. Cut-glass accent but natural. She put him irresistibly in mind of a rose. Pink rose in a sterling-silver bud vase. "I do have that feeling, yes," he admitted. "For one thing you wouldn't be used to the heat." Yet he couldn't see the tiniest bead of perspiration on her flawless skin.

Francesca could have hooted. "You're not going to believe this but I think the heat's fantastic. I left some very miserable cold and wet weather at home. I want to thank you again,

Grant, for coming to my rescue. For flying me in. I know you're a busy man."

That he was. "There aren't enough hours in the day. I've got plans. Big plans. I want to—" He broke off and shot her a wry look. "I'm sorry. You didn't come all the way to hear Grant Cameron's visions."

"No, tell me." She took his arm. Beautiful, gentle, soft. "I know you run the helicopter service, of course. But you want to start your own airline to service the Inland. Is that right? Passengers and freight?"

He gave her a surprised, interrogating look. "Who told you that?" An elderly couple moved out into the corridor so Grant took Francesca's elbow moving her further down the parqueted passageway towards a side verandah.

"It was Brod." Francesca stopped walking to look up at him, struck again by his rare tawny colouring, the depth of copper in the thick burnt-gold hair swept off his wide forehead, the gleaming near-topaz eyes. "Brod is tremendously interested in your schemes. So am I."

He saw the sincerity. Was warmed by it. "That's wonderful." He grinned. "But are you sure you've got the time? I thought you were going home to your glamorous life in little more than a week?"

The topaz eyes were twinkling but Francesca knew what he was thinking. "I have to tell you, Grant Cameron, I'm finding it a lot more glamorous here."

Where else could you find a grand mansion in the frightening isolation and extraordinary savage beauty of the Australian desert? Where else could you find such a magnificent man? She might be setting herself up for a little heartache, a brief romance with no hope of resolution, but one thing was certain—Grant Cameron drew her like a flame.

Long after the household had retired, all of them diminished by the events of the day, Rebecca, more shocked than she knew, sought medication for a headache worse than anything she had experienced for a long time. Perhaps she was running a high fever. She seemed very hot. She stumbled into the adjoining bathroom to see if there were any aspirin left.

One. No good. She was going to need more pain-killer. It was downstairs in the large first-aid room stocked like a pharmacy. Her mind was whirling from her compulsive reviewing of the day. She couldn't forget Stewart Kinross's last words to her.

"There's no way I'll let him have you."

She couldn't possibly tell Brod that. It would drive him crazy.

She remembered the way she urged the mare Jeeba away. Poor Jeeba! It upset her terribly the mare had to be destroyed. Horses with their delicate legs. She didn't want to think about it but loving horses so much she couldn't push it away. Although the women of the family, Fee, Ally, and Francesca had supported her fully throughout the long afternoon, Brod hadn't come within ten feet of her. Of course people never stopped coming up to him, keeping him contained until it was all over but he had kept his distance from her as though she were poison she thought bleakly.

And there was still something he didn't know. He didn't know she had once been married. He didn't know that marriage had ended disastrously. Shattered beyond repair. He had invited her to talk to him but she had built up so many defences she doubted if she could speak of that awful time.

Dear God, she didn't want to be reminded. She didn't want to be reminded of the dreadful mistake she had made. The number of times she had cried. The shame of the things Martyn had done. She certainly didn't want to be reminded of Martyn's mother's visit.

Meredith had accused her—if Rebecca hadn't caused her injuries herself!—of driving him to hurting his wife with her demands for freedom, for a career. She had reneged on her sacred marriage vows. Back and forth they went, she losing the argument in the light of her mother-in-law's unswerving belief in her son, the fineness of his character.

Meredith had pleaded with her to go back to Martyn. He loved her. Didn't she know that? He would give her whatever she wanted if only she would go back.

Anything was better than going back. She was certain Meredith would face this problem again. Martyn liked making women suffer. Perhaps he was getting square with a suffocatingly possessive mother.

How could she tell Brod all about that? Though God knows it couldn't have been easy for him and Ally growing up in this house. Even Fee had spoken about her brother's destructive qualities. Now Rebecca began to see Lucille Kinross, like her, had been forced to flee a desperately unhappy marriage.

With a little shake of her pounding head, Rebecca caught up her robe, tying the sash tightly around her waist. There was no hope for her. She would live with her guilts forever. Real or imagined. She had never given Stewart Kinross the slightest encouragement. Indeed the thought had never entered her head but perhaps she had overresponded to his many kindnesses to her? She cursed some quality in her that drew certain men to her.

Downstairs she thought she heard a sound. She stood perfectly still for a moment trying to trace breathing, soft footsteps, anything. Both floors of the huge house were dimly lit with wall sconces, brighter at the head of the central staircase so no one could miss their footing if they descended during the night. She was conscious her heart was beating fast within her.

No one at all. Just all the little sounds of a darkened old house.

She had come downstairs for a purpose. Now she almost flew down the corridor that led to the kitchen taking a right turn to the large, well-stocked first-aid room. Lots of accidents, big and small went on at Outback stations. Kimbara was always prepared. When she snapped on the switch the light almost blinded her so brilliantly did it bounce off the white walls and fittings.

She saw her own startled face in a mirrored cabinet. She might have been a ghost her skin was so pale but her floating black hair was very real, the sleeplessness was in her shadowed gaze.

She needed something to work a miracle. She walked to one of the cabinets she knew housed a range of painkillers, letting her eyes run along the packages.

"I didn't think I dreamed it," a dark, eloquent voice said behind her.

"Brod!" She swung around, in her agitation dropping a packet to the black-and-white tiled floor. Now colour whipped into her skin as though a switch had been thrown.

"What's the matter?" He bent to retrieve the package, turning it over in his hand. "A headache?"

She lifted her hand to her temple. "I don't think I've had such a bad one in my life." Take that back, she thought dismally. In the last few years.

"Maybe these won't be strong enough." A frown drew his black brows together.

"I'll try them anyway."

"Why are you whispering?" He walked to another cupboard, took out a clean glass and filled it at the sink.

"Because it's very late. Because you frightened me." She gave a husky laugh. "What the heck else do I need?"

"Don't let's get into an argument." He turned to her, his eyes moving over her. "You look very pale. The fact is, Rebecca, I know how you feel. Only I've been drowning my pain with a few shots of whisky."

He pushed two tablets from their silvered sockets into the palm of his hand. "Here," he said quietly. "I hope they do some good."

She took them from him, feeling the rough calluses on his palms, wondering for a rocky moment how those same hands would feel on her body. She choked a little as the tablets seemed to stick in her upper chest, but swallowed more water at his urging.

"Come and talk to me," he said in a deep, low voice. "I'll let you lie quietly. I don't want to be alone."

Neither did she, still she hesitated. "Maybe…"

"Maybe what?" He looked down at her, so small in her slippered feet, her silky robe like the pale green sheaf of a flower.

"Maybe it's not a good idea, Brod."

"I can't think of one better." He took her hand, his handsome face taut and angular, his magnificent body in his everyday jeans, his soft blue shirt near undone to the waist in the sultry heat.

"Where are we going?" she asked, captured by his touch.

"Don't panic. I'm not taking you up to bed."

God, in her confusion she nearly cried out. Take me. Take me. *Hold me.* I want to be lost. Instead she walked with him very quietly. They paused at the study and he reached around with his hand to find the light switch. "You can lie down on the sofa," he told her, releasing her hand. "You don't have to talk if you don't want to I just need you to be there."

She went to the big burgundy chesterfield and curled into it, drawing up her feet. He picked up a cushion from an armchair and tucked it behind her head. "Relax, Rebecca. There's nothing to dread. I wouldn't hurt you for the world."

A soft cry of protest came out of her. "I never thought you would." The last thing she feared from him was sexual harassment. What she feared was her own passion, the tumultuous spill of emotion. She lay back and he ran his hand briefly through her hair.

"What a terrible day."

"I know. My heart aches for you, Brod."

He gave a short groan. "I'm finding it very difficult to mourn my father, Rebecca. Does that sound terrible? The hell is I'm not ashamed of it, either." He moved back across the room and sat in a big deep armchair with his grandfather's gaze on him. "Close your eyes," he advised. "Let the pain killers work.

"Parents shouldn't kill their children's love, Rebecca. Children have a right to love. Otherwise why bring them into the world?

"Dad chose an *heir*," Brod continued in a pained voice. "Kimbara needs heirs. He always acted as though I was one hell of a disappointment to him. Ally, too. Can you believe it? My beautiful, gifted sister. My mother was a hell of a disappointment to him, too. She couldn't live with that. She ran off."

Was it time to say something about her own marriage.

The time passed.

"Sometimes I think this house has a curse on it," Brod sighed. "The first Kinross bride, Cecilia, married the wrong man and was forced to live with it. She should have been a Cameron. My mother was another matter. After she was killed my father called me into this very study and told me all about it.

"No one gets away from me," he said.

Rebecca's eyes swept open. "He said that to his own child?"

Brod nodded. "He wasn't a man to pull punches. In our ignorance and pain Ally and I thought our mother had deserted us. The one parent who loved us. Later we knew what it was all about. You wouldn't have fared well with my father, Rebecca."

"Trust me," Rebecca pleaded, knowing full well it would take time.

"Well it doesn't matter any more." He released another sigh. "Has your headache eased?"

"A little."

"Let's see if this works." He came behind her and began to stroke her temples, his fingers moving with exquisite gentleness.

He had to be a magician. Almost at once she felt a warmth through her body, a warmth that spread to the smooth area under his healing hands.

"Oh, that's good. You have magic in your hands." She released a fluttery breath, loving what he was doing.

"Keep your eyes closed." His fingers began to move over her forehead and cheeks. They traced the curve of her eyebrows, the closed lids of her eyes, the whorls of her ears back to her satin temples as if he had all the time in the world. "Better?" he asked after a long while.

"Oh, yes!" she said softly, desiring his touch.

Then he picked her up. Cradling her before he lowered himself onto the chesterfield with her in his arms. "I just want to hold you. Okay?"

She let her head fall back against his shoulder. "I want to know all about you," she whispered. "Tell me."

For a moment he buried his face in her fragrant hair, then he began to speak, almost to himself at first. "It was really my grandfather who reared us. He was a wonderful man. Some people are kind enough to say I'm like him. He taught Ally and me to believe in ourselves…"

"Go on." She settled herself more comfortably and his arms closed around her. Her headache, miraculously, was gone. She was where she wanted to be.

When he finished speaking she knew more about his life than possibly anyone in the world, including his sister.

Somehow her position had changed. Her head was now pressed into his chest. One of her hands was clutching his shirt and she was breathing in his warm masculinity like incense.

"You're a good listener," he only half joked, wondering how so slight a body could seem so soft and voluptuous. God, if only…if only…

She lifted her head and stared into his eyes. "I didn't want you to stop."

"But I want to know who *you* are." He wound his hand through her long hair, moving very quietly into kissing her, wanting to do nothing against her will but moving perilously close to a man's driving hunger. "Rebecca?" he murmured against the side of her mouth.

She couldn't help herself. Her arm slid up around his neck arousing him still further. She clung to him, her body twisting in yearning.

His hands moved down over her breasts, caressing them

through the thin silky covering of her clothes, his thumbs gathering the tender nipples into tight electric buds. The sweet feverishness of it. He had fallen madly in love with her without realising it. This beautiful mysterious creature. All at once he needed to touch her naked flesh. He thrust his hand inside her gown as she turned her head into his throat.

"We're mad to do this," she whispered even as she let him touch her so intimately.

"When there's not the tiniest part of you I don't hunger for?"

"Someone might come." Yet she put her arms around him and held him to her breast.

"I don't know that they'll get through that locked door," he answered softly, his hands moving up and down the curve of her back, drawing her ever closer. This was the day of his father's funeral yet he was doing the strangest thing. Making love to Rebecca. Losing himself in her and her great fascination. Her mouth was her most revealing feature. It identified the deep well of passion that was in her. He looked down at her satiny dark hair tumbled over her eyes.

"Spend the night with me," he urged, his voice a little harsh with arousal.

She closed her eyes against his plea. "Then nothing will be the same again."

"Nothing has been the same since the moment I laid eyes on you," he mocked. The luminous eyes. The passionate mouth. Oh, yes, the mouth.

He kissed it again, so deeply she shuddered. "I want you beside me when I wake up."

"I can't do this." But her heart was racing, her whole body shot through with desire.

"You don't have a husband to betray?" he reminded her, exulting in her body's response to him. "Isn't that right?" He stared directly into her eyes, his own breathtakingly blue.

"No husband," she said at last.

"Then you need a man to tell you how beautiful you are?"

He lifted her, thinking he could use the small spiralling stair-case at the end of the hall. There was no turning back now. His need for her was too immense.

CHAPTER SEVEN

ONCE ALLY AND FRANCESCA went home after a stay that meant a great deal to all of them, Rebecca and Fee settled into a definite routine. They worked steadily on Fee's biography, averaging four or five hours each day but this time Rebecca began to delve more deeply into Fee's colourful life, looking for more information and treasures. This wasn't going to be a book that let *all* the family skeletons out of the closet but after that special night with Brod who had talked so eloquently and movingly about his life, Rebecca found she wanted to draw much more out of Fee than the glossed up and glossed over versions Fee had presented her thus far. Now thanks to Brod, Rebecca felt she had a far greater insight into the family; but there were difficulties.

"Darling, do you think we should say that?" Fee often asked doubtfully when in the course of their discussions Fee came up with some revelation.

Rebecca invariably replied; "Do we want an extraordinary memoir, Fee, a first-rate biography, or a give-away book for the coffee table?"

Fee being an extraordinary person wanted an extraordinary memoir so they restarted their journey going beyond Fee's childhood on Kimbara, the only daughter of the legendary cattle king, Sir Andrew Kinross and Constance McQuillan Kinross, a renowned horse-woman, herself the only daughter of a great pastoral family who had died a premature death at the age of forty-two after being tragically thrown from her horse in a cross-country race.

"I want it to be more than a biography of your life, Fee," Rebecca told her. "I'd like you to reflect upon *family*. A prominent landed family. A complex family as far as I can see. Marriages, starting with Ewan Kinross and Cecilia. Family influences. This business of inheritance, relationships."

"Lord, darling, you're looking at the best part of 150 years," Fee answered wryly. "That's a long time in this part of the world."

"It's more an overview of the family history I want, Fee. When you're speaking you paint such vivid word pictures. Brod has the same ability. Ally has it, too. I want to get it into print. Ally told me so much during her stay. It was wonderful to be able to speak together so freely. Brod even more. I'd like to use their recollections as well. I see this book as a marvellous kaleidoscope of Outback life as lived by a family who pioneered this vast area."

Fee smiled at Rebecca's youthful enthusiasm. "Heavens, darling, some of the stories would make anyone flinch."

"All your stories are safe with me, Fee," Rebecca told her seriously. "In the end we'll only reveal as much as you want to. I'm sure the reader will appreciate your candour, your generosity of spirit, not to mention your wicked sense of humour."

"If we're talking wicked I suppose I have to mention my sex life," Fee said in her rich, deep voice.

"Well it's not exactly a mystery, Fee," Rebecca teased. "We can change names of individuals to protect their privacy."

Fee looked saddened. "Darling, most of them are dead now, including my poor brother. I've found the most marvellous old photographs of him and me. We can use them. A lot of Lucille somebody has obviously hidden."

"That was Brod," Rebecca openly admitted, seeing Lucille's lovely face in her mind.

"Good God!" Fee gave a great sigh. "His father would have been furious had he known." The green eyes were searching. "For that matter, darling, how did you know? Brod has never mentioned hiding the photographs to me?"

Rebecca met Fee's gaze calmly. "We had a long conversation one night."

Fee lowered her head, knowing full well there was something going on between Rebecca and Brod. "Why not?" she replied. "I'm glad. You and Brod seem to be in harmony these days." She was far from oblivious to this new dimension in their relationship. "Both Brod and Ally have had to keep far too much to themselves," she added. "Now, let's have a cup of tea, then we'll get right down to it. This biography is taking on an entirely new character."

"Thank Brod," Rebecca suggested. No matter what happened she would always remember she'd had this very special time with him.

Brod came in around noon, telling them with wry humour about a staff dispute he had to settle. He snatched a few sandwiches and coffee, which he ate in Fee's sitting room, listening to Fee unearth another piece of family archaeology he had some doubts she ought to mention.

"Hell, Fee, you're going to reveal all our secrets," he ventured, tossing the last sandwich aside. "Within limits, darling," Fee corrected. "Silence won't sell the book. Besides Rebecca wants me to make the book more powerful."

"Then we might get Rebecca to write one of her own." His blue eyes flashed provocatively towards Rebecca's face. "From what you say, it's far from portraying some members of our family in a good light. Ewan who seemed to have tricked Ce-

cilia into marrying him. Alistair who ran off to Paris suppos-
edly to paint but ran through a fortune instead. Great Aunt
Eloise who married a thirty-five-year-old man when she was
sixty years old."

"But, darling, she was beautiful. She was famous," Fee offered by way of explanation, turning her head to preen in a
gilt-framed mirror. "She was also an heiress," Brod said, rising
to his feet and adjusting the red bandanna around his tanned
neck, "and her husband didn't have a razoo." He brought his
brilliant glance to rest on Rebecca. "If Fee can spare you for an
hour or so later on this afternoon, I'd like to take you out and
show you the wildflowers. I promised you they'd put on a tremendous display after all the heavy showers. Would you like
to come, too, Fee?"

"Not today, darling," Fee answered casually, not about to
play gooseberry. "I have a lot of mail to catch up on. That invitation to direct the Milton Theatre Company came right out of
the blue. I'd like to think about it. They have some wonderful
actors and some very good young ones coming up. I could be
of great influence there."

"So you're not set on going back to England, Fee?" Brod
asked, waiting on her answer.

She looked pensive for a moment. "You know I always said
I'd come home when my time in the limelight was over. I still
have a name but I think it's time to do something different. If
only I could persuade my dearest Fran to join me but she loves
her life in England. She loves her father and all their family con-
nections. She gets invited everywhere. She's madly popular."

"I thought she seemed a little disenchanted with her life as it
is," Brod mused. "Or maybe that was only the effect Grant was
having on her. If you ask me, Fran stole his heart when she was
sixteen years old and you brought her on a visit."

"That's right!" Fee said, her face lighting up with a smile.
"But Grant's got problems with Fran being who she is, if you
know what I mean. Lady Francesca de Lyle."

"Absolutely," Brod agreed. "He knows the sort of life Fran's been used to. She's beautiful, rich, titled, the darling of the society columns. An English rose that could never be transplanted in our wild horizons."

"But, darling," Fee protested, "aren't you forgetting, our own Cecilia was born to a privileged life and she became one of the most admired pioneering women of her time."

"Aw, shucks, Fee," Brod said breezily, "so she did." He walked to the door and sketched a little salute. "I'll be back to collect you around four, Rebecca. You know to wear a good sun-block. There'll be plenty of heat left in the sun."

"Will we be taking the horses?" she asked, lifting her chin a little as she spoke. Since that fateful day and the added shock of hearing the mare, Jeeba, had had to be put down, she found herself oddly reluctant to ride. In fact she had only ridden out three times since and that was because Ally had especially asked her.

Brod studied her squarely. "We'll be going a good distance so we'll take the Jeep. We might get around to discussing your little problem on the way. I don't want it to turn into a complex."

"Slight exaggeration, Brod," she said sweetly.

"Good." He nodded his approval. "I'd like to go riding with you now and then. You haven't lived until you've had a night out under the desert stars."

"Lordy, no!" Fee put both hands beneath her chin. "Marvellous fun! Of course you're going to need a chaperone."

Brod gave her a wicked grin. "I'll treat that as a joke, Fee."

It was a dream landscape. An endless shimmering ocean of wildflowers rolling over the plains so prolifically the bright red clay was all but hidden. It was a pageantry of flowers the likes of which Rebecca had never thought to see. White, gold, purple, pink, the papery ephemeral flora of this vast mulga region, which bridged the gap between the channel country and the true desert heart, with its glittering mosaic of gibber plains and rising pyramids of sand dunes.

"Enjoy it while you can," Brod said, holding her by the shoulders. "It's only going to last a few weeks then the earth will dry up again."

Rebecca felt her heart expand with delight. "It's a fantastic sight! Magnificent. I feel like I've landed in Paradise."

"All the more breathtaking because it only happens after heavy rains, which could mean once or twice in a year or two. Most of the time it's brilliant blue skies, searing sun and hot drying winds," Brod said.

"Wonderland!" Rebecca breathed. "I'd love to pick some to remind me."

"Why not." He smiled indulgently. "Stick to the everlastings—they retain their shape and colour for weeks after. They don't need water, either."

"How extraordinary!" Rebecca swung to face him, transformed from an ice maiden into the vivacious young woman she had once been. "How can anywhere that can produce a glorious show like this be called a desert?"

"You're wonderful," he said, suddenly bending to kiss her mouth. "You're like the seeds of the dormant wildflowers waiting to spring to life."

"That's because you've bedazzled me," she said, unable to hide her feelings.

"I think we've bedazzled each other." He drew her fully into his arms letting his mouth trace all over her face, savouring her scent and her skin, until it came to rest on the soft, silky cushion of her lips. His ardour conveyed powerfully his deep running desire. When he released her neither of them spoke, not wanting to allow a single errant word into their magic circle. It was joy. Incredible joy and a mind-spinning passion.

"Brod," she said, after a moment. "Broderick." She loved the sound of his name on her tongue.

"That's me." His eyes moved over her like blue fire. "What's your second name? You've never told me when I distinctly recall telling you and talking to you just about an entire night."

"It's very prim."

"When you're living such a fast life?" he gently mocked. "Amy? Emily? I just don't believe you're a Dorothy."

"Actually it's Ellen after an aunt."

"It should have been Eve." His eyes were full of lazy sensuality. He took her hand, leading her down from the vantage point into the shining sea of wildflowers. "We'll avoid that mob of emus to our left," he said. "They're having a great time now with so much herbage around but they can survive in the most arid areas."

Rebecca followed his gaze, feeling her small hand swallowed up in his. Though it was a common sight now to see the great flightless birds, Rebecca found them fascinating especially when running. She knew emus could reach great speeds over rough country. The kangaroos equally fascinating would appear in large mobs about dusk, bounding away on their long hind legs. In the heat of the day they sought the shelter of caves or dense shrub, avoiding unnecessary action and water loss. It was a pattern of behaviour developed over countless thousands of years. But the birds were out as usual in great flocks showing alternate clouds of brilliant colour from backs, wings and undersurfaces. Even as they moved near, vivid mulga parrots landed in a hollow of one of the curious stunted acacias that rose above the vast sea of everlastings showing no alarm at their presence.

Brod went first, gathering a bunch of white everlastings that he fashioned quite skilfully into a garland, placing it on her bare head. "Show me."

Rebecca straightened, eyes luminous, her dark hair escaping in a long, loose outcurving wave to fall across one cheek. She put up a hand to sweep it back but he said rather oddly. "No, leave it." Such an expression was in his eyes Rebecca felt her own vision blur and her limbs turn weak with longing.

"Imagine what you'd look like as a bride."

A bride. She could have cried aloud with the pity of it.

How that marvellous expression would fade if she told him the truth. She'd been a bride. She'd worn the pure shining dress, the long veil that had lent an unearthly radiance to her face. She had looked up at her handsome groom standing before the flower-decked altar with dreams in her eyes. She thought she had seen an answering dream in the intensity of the gaze he had bent on her. The same man who had caused her such misery and pain.

Almost in a twinkling her dazzling pleasure in the day was diminished. How could she ever tell Brod what had happened to her. She couldn't even tell him she had once been married, though he would have known she wasn't a virgin. Surely he might have expected that but she knew in her heart the fact that she had been married without ever revealing it would come as the final blow to his trust.

"No answer?" Now he spoke to her, tracking through the wealth of wildflowers, staring at her stricken face. "I thought every woman wanted to be a bride?" he asked quizzically.

"Well of course!" she realised the error of her reaction. Perhaps he would see what was there in her past.

"Well I'll be damned," he said gently. "Are you frightened of marriage, Rebecca?" He desperately wanted to overcome the huge shift in her mood.

"It's an enormous gamble, Brod. Everyone knows it," she said, tense as a wire.

"But when it works, marriage is so wonderfully rewarding. Most people try it. I thought your parents' marriage was happy despite the fact your mother never recovered from her accident?"

"They were devoted," Rebecca whispered.

"But you agonise about your mother's fate?"

"I'd give anything to have her back." Rebecca looked down at the colourful posy in her hand.

"That's exactly how Ally and I felt about our mother," he said. "I suppose our experiences are proof of our far from happy childhood. Ally apparently couldn't face marriage to Rafe despite the fact she was and I believe still is deeply in love with him."

"And you?" She raised her eyes a long way and stared into his marvellous face.

"I've had casual affairs, Rebecca—" he shrugged "—but I've tried to be scrupulously honest with the women in my life. Marriage is a very different thing from a romance. When I choose a wife I'm going to take darn good care I find the right woman. I've had my life torn apart once. It's not going to happen again."

She felt exactly the same way.

They were quiet on the return trip; Brod stunned to discover the passionate young woman he now knew Rebecca to be could genuinely be disturbed by the thought of marriage. Hadn't he seen something like horror expressed in her face back there? Perhaps someone had hurt her badly? Someone about whom she refused to speak. Feeling as he did, he would have to give her time. He understood now the "coolness" of the facade she had cultivated. It was all about throwing up defences. Defences he now realised he badly wanted to break down.

"Where are we going?" Rebecca asked some time later into the quietness. They had been driving for miles yet the flowers went on, the everlastings turning to carpets of snow, native poppies and hibiscus, undulating seas of green pussy tails, lilac fan flowers, the flaming fire bush, the salt bush and the cotton bush and the spreading Opomoea. This wasn't the legendary Dead Heart that had claimed so many victims, it was the biggest garden on earth. The Jeep left the flower smothered plains heading towards a dense line of green, which could only mean a lagoon or rock pool was feeding it.

"I want you to see my favourite swimming pool," Brod said. "That's when the time is right. We'll have to stop soon and walk the rest of the way. It's a glorious place. It even has a little waterfall."

"I think I can hear it," Rebecca said, aware of rushing

sounds. As they drove closer she was certain. Tumbling water. It sounded marvellous in the glittering heat. Brod stopped the Jeep in the shade of the trees and switched off the engine.

"It's a bit of a way down. Are you up to it?" His eyes gleamed.

"Of course I am!" A growing excitement was reigniting her spirits.

"You won't be sorry... I promise you."

He held her hand all the way, holding back branches in case they whipped at her face or body; stopping when she became a little puffed. Finally, when they had almost reached the bottom of the slope crowded with white spider lilies in their thousands, he picked her up and carried her the rest of the way. When she exclaimed at the beauty of this secret spot he lowered her gently to her feet.

"But this is...ravishing." Rebecca was thrilled by the tranquil beauty of the pool and the much cooler atmosphere. From high up among the trees a small silvery waterfall tumbled over rocks and into the pool, which was shaded at the edges a pale jade, emerald in the depths. A place for lovers, she thought. Paradise before the Fall. A beautiful quiet secret place with the scent of a million wildflowers held in suspension in the golden green air.

"I knew you'd like it," Brod said, delighted by her expression.

"I love it. Does anyone come here?"

"Only me. Ally, too, when we were kids. There are dozens of lagoons to swim in on Kimbara. This is my private place. No one comes here. Not even the cattle. Probably no one even knows about it and I'm not about to tell them."

"*I* know," she boasted.

"So you can see, you're honoured."

Rebecca turned away, overcome by her feelings. As a kind of respite she bent to an exquisite little flower that grew in an isolated clump beside a rock.

"What's this?" She fingered a delicate mauve petal.

He glanced down. "I've no idea. There are so many beautiful nameless flowers tucked away."

"Name it after me." She looked up and let her eyes linger.

"I know what." His voice was deep and indulgent. "Rebecca Lily. You have the same delicate air."

"Okay. You stick to that. Rebecca Lily. Is that a promise?"

"It's Rebecca Lily forever as far as I'm concerned."

She stayed where she was and undid the laces of her shoes. "I'm going to paddle."

He let her go, watching her slender figure clad in pink cotton jeans and a matching shirt move across the sandy bank to the crystal clear water. Now she was standing in ankle deep, tugging at the hem of her jeans. "Crazy!" she called. "We should have brought our swimsuits."

Desire swept through him like a fire through dry grass. He had wanted her long before he had actually known her beautiful body. Now that he had it was an everyday battle just to keep his hands off her. His need for her was immense, the strength of it gaining with every passing day.

"Brod?" she ran back to him laughing, the water she had splashed so lavishly all over her face glistening on her magnolia skin, running down her neck into her pink shirt, wetting it so it clung to her breasts. His eyes tracked the water's progress. She wasn't wearing a bra. He could see the naked sensitised nipples peaking against the sodden material. It was too much. Too much. He was a desiring man and he couldn't stand it.

"We could always take off our clothes," he suggested very softly, drawing her to him by the collar of her shirt, letting his hands move to the top button.

"I'm too modest." Yet she leaned into him, tingling cascades of sensation running down her spine.

"When I've kissed every inch of your beautiful body?" That memory would stay with him forever.

"At least I had the cover of moonlight," she whispered, beginning to tremble.

"You didn't in the dawn." When he had taken her without speaking.

"When I had to leave you."

"I've never let a beautiful woman visit me in my bedroom before," he told her, looking deeply into her eyes.

"I'm the only one?"

"I mean what I tell you." His vibrant voice was deep. He began to undo the little pearly pink buttons one by one giving her all the time in the world to draw back, watching her intoxicated, the stars in her eyes. Finally he peeled it off her like the petals of a flower. At her little affirming cry he swooped like a falcon out of a clear cobalt sky pulling her unstoppably into his arms and planting his deeply desiring kiss on her mouth.

She might have been a violin in the hands of a master, her whole body one sweet seamless vibrato. She craved his embrace, revelled in it. It was almost as if this place was watching over them. The encircling trees, the broad sweep of spider lilies, the ancient rocks, the emerald pool, sparkling waterfall, the swarm of iridescent insects that hovered over a blossoming shrub with a waxy flower that resembled a native frangipani.

The spirit of the bush. She had to glory in every moment.

On a rippling tide of emotion, Rebecca broke away from him, her eyes like liquid diamonds. She tilted her head back, laughing aloud with pure joy, the action lifting her small breasts and tautening her creamy torso so her ribs showed. "I want to swim in the pool," she announced blissfully.

"I want to dive off the ledge and touch the sand at the bottom. I want to swim several lengths then for a finale I'm going to jump up on that flat rock out there and sun-bake until I'm dry." Without hesitation or the slightest show of self-consciousness she slid off the rest of her clothes, jeans and briefs then took long springing steps, gazellelike, into the clear sheet of water.

"Listen I'm ready to join you," Brod called, the lightness of his tone belying the mounting intensity that was in him. His hands swiftly stripped off his denim shirt and moved to the silver buckle of his leather belt. This woman, this incredibly beautiful naked nymph kept transforming herself. One mo-

ment one thing, something different the next. Every image fresh
and new. She was creating something approaching a delicious
frenzy in his blood.

Soon he was stripped of his clothes, his lean powerful body
deeply tanned all over, the dappled sunlight playing over gleaming skin and long, taut muscles. He could hear her calling to
him, as alluring as a siren who lived in the emerald depths, lifting her arm to beckon.

"It's wonderful, wonderful," she cried. "So cold I can't stand
it."

She'd warm up, he vowed, moving into a smooth, powerful
dive. My God she would! He'd make love to her until she was
on fire. Utterly his.

Stock mustering and drafting went on at a back-breaking pace.
One of Kimbara's top stockmen, Curly Jenkins, miraculously
escaped serious injury when during the course of the drafting at Leura Creek a mob of bullocks broke free and crashed
through an iron gate leaving the unfortunate Curly crushed
behind it. Brod, who was at the homestead when the accident occurred, had the news from Curly's offsider who rode
at break-neck speed to the homestead to give the alarm. Brod
immediately contacted the Flying Doctor who flew Curly out
to hospital suffering, as was confirmed, from badly bruised
ribs, and severe bruising to the trunk. Less than a week later
Grant Cameron called on Brod to join in a ground search for
one of his helicopter pilots who had begun mustering cattle on
one of the Cameron outstations but had not called in at the end
of the day. Grant had been unable to reach him by the company radio and the pilot had not cancelled his SAR, his search
and rescue time.

At first no one was all that worried; Grant himself said radio
problems weren't that unusual. The pilot, an experienced man,
could simply have landed somewhere and set up camp for the
night. He had his swag aboard.

* * *

The men searched all day with no luck. First light the following morning the search was stepped up to full scale with planes and helicopters retracing the pilot's course. Brod flew the Beech Baron and Rebecca, caught up in the now general anxiety, begged to go along as a spotter. It was her first time flying with Brod but this wasn't the exciting joy trip it might have been. It was she who first saw the wreckage, distressing her terribly, scant moments before Brod who began circling the area pinpointed the fatal spot. A short time later the rescue helicopter arrived to land on the difficult terrain.

The fatality affected everyone. The pilot was well-known and liked reminding them of the dangers that were a normal part of station life. Rebecca began to find it very difficult not to dwell on Brod's safety. There was hardly a day he and his staff weren't challenged. Rebecca had watched him on a motorbike mustering a herd of bullocks with her heart in her mouth. Then there was all the flying he began to do to the outstations and other Kinross stations in the chain. Over vast distances the only way to go was by air. Rebecca found herself fighting anxiety until he was safely back.

"Darling, Brod is a wonderful pilot," Fee reassured her. "A natural. He's had his licence for years. It's essential in his job."

Still Rebecca prayed.

CHAPTER EIGHT

IT WAS AN idyll that had to end. Rebecca was to learn the past is never past. It keeps coming back at you.

Up in the pre-dawn Brod left Fee a reminder their financial people, accountants and tax solicitors would be flying in for a meeting that afternoon. In all likelihood it could spin out to the next day. Four in all. Barry Mattheson and his associate and Dermot Shields was bringing someone, too. He had given instructions to Jean to make up the guest rooms just in case.

"I can't bear talking money," Fee moaned, "but I'm involved in it all. Sir Andy left me with a lot of clout. He wasn't going to give it all to Stewart. His affairs will take *ages* to finalise."

"Well I've got plenty to keep me busy," Rebecca said, folding her napkin and rising from the breakfast table. "In fact, we're moving along very nicely, Fee. This is going to be a winner. A marvellous read."

"I won't be glad when it's over." Fee, who was still seated finishing off a cup of tea, caught Rebecca's hand. "I've loved having you here, darling, and Brod is happier than I've ever seen him in his life. Close as we are I'm giving you *all* the credit for that. Would you come around here, girl, so I can see you?" Fee teased.

Colouring Rebecca moved back giving Fee a little bob. "Yes

m'lady." She tried to speak gaily, but emotion throbbed in her voice.

"You're in love with him aren't you?" Fee asked very gently, retaining Rebecca's hand and staring up into her transparent face.

"I thought I knew what love was," Rebecca said dreamily. "I didn't. This time I do. Every time I see him my heart sings, Beloved! I can't describe what I feel for him as anything other than sublime." Her beautiful eyes suddenly glittered with unshed tears.

"Have you told him any of this?" Fee was enthralled.

"Not in so many words," Rebecca confessed. "I couldn't bear to tell him about my life."

Fee looked alarmed. "Darling girl, you're making it sound horrifying."

Rebecca's luminous grey eyes darkened to pewter. "I'd give anything for a lot of it not to have happened, Fee," she said, gravely.

"Do you want to tell me?" the older woman urged, quite concerned. "Goodness I really do feel like your aunt."

"I mean to tell you, Fee," Rebecca decided. "But I must tell Brod first."

"Of course," Fee murmured. "My every instinct was you've had a bad experience in life even if you do look exquisite."

"I've been hiding myself away," Rebecca said. "I don't mean literally. I've seen a lot, done a lot. Had my success. It hasn't been easy but I thought that was what I had to do."

"But you've talked about your family. Of your love for your mother and father and your family in Hong Kong." Fee continued to look up at her with concern.

"It's something else, Fee. Someone I met when I was very young. And on my own."

"Well I know all about that," Fee confided in her wonderfully expressive voice. Forty years later still with faint bitterness. "All I can tell you, dear, is it will be much better to get whatever it is out in the open. Tell Brod. It will only get harder as more time passes."

"I know." Rebecca gave a little shudder.

Fee shook her head. "Don't be too nervous, Rebecca," she warned. "Maybe I should tell you Ally said Brod was madly in love with you before she left. Take into account that upsetting little experience with my poor brother. Brod felt it badly. My advice is, darling, and I've got a lot of insider knowledge, don't keep any secrets from Brod."

"I won't!"

If it kills me, Rebecca thought.

Brod dashed in for a quick shower and a change of clothes before Barry Mattheson and party were due in at Kimbara's airstrip.

"I'll make myself scarce," Rebecca said, standing on the staircase, looking over her shoulder to speak to him as he was making for the door.

"Stay and meet them," he invited with a smile.

"No, I'll let you all get on with it. I have plenty to do."

"Well you'll meet them all at dinner." Brod shrugged. "We've got one hell of a lot to sort out. I doubt we can get through it all this afternoon."

"Take care." She blew him a kiss.

"I mean to," he said.

For you. He wasn't pushing Rebecca even when he was crazy about her but he intended to take their relationship a whole lot further. Like an engagement. Pretty soon after that she was going to become his beautiful bride. Despite herself. He was going to do everything in his power to make his wife happy.

Rebecca!

He started down the steps filled with incredible life and vigour.

Rebecca heard the visitors arrive but she made no effort to go to the window and look out. She kept working, realising she was almost at the point of making a first draft of Fee's biography. Fee, in her private conversations, was always very honest; now that same honesty had been extended to the book. In Rebecca's opinion, it was turning into a rather extraordinary chronicle, not only Fee's life but the Kinross family life down through the generations. She knew it would be every bit as good as Dame Judith's memoirs, which had received excellent reviews. It was nice to get praise. One reviewer had referred to her "elegant, even lyrical prose." She hoped it was matched by realism. Fee had entrusted her with quite a commission. This would be a bigger and better book than Dame Judith's because there was so much more to say about a long line of extraordinary characters.

Fee tapped on her door around six, her beautiful face touched with exhaustion.

"How's it going?" Rebecca asked, sounding concerned. "It's been a long session."

"That it has!" Fee put a hand to her temple. "Sir Andy used to have a small army of lawyers. At least we've cut it down a bit. All I can say is it's damned fortunate Brod is so clever. He's right up with them. Doesn't miss a single solitary thing. I get bogged down a bit. We used to have an enormous fortune you know. It's mind-boggling how much Stewart got through. Lived like a prince while Brod handled everything from the minute he was able to."

"Are you going to come in and sit down?" Rebecca asked. "You look a little tired."

"I am, darling," Fee confessed, "but I'll keep you company at dinner."

"Good. I didn't want to be the only woman there. What are they like?"

Fee glanced at her watch. "Well I've known dear old Barry since forever. I knew his father before him. Dermot is a new one on me but sounds like a good man. The other two are much younger but very bright. Early thirties. I'll go off now and soak in a long, luxurious bath.

"Do you good." Rebecca gave her an affectionate smile and turned back to the word processor. She'd work for another half hour or so then draw her own bath.

She took her time when she was usually eager to go downstairs, selecting a two-piece jersey outfit in her favourite colour, violet, probably because it looked good on her. It had a simple high-necked sleeveless top and a long fluid skirt, which she wore well. Some of her girl-friends thought you had to be tall to wear long skirts. She found just the opposite. They actually made her look taller and she liked the sensual feel of soft fabrics against her legs.

Her hair was getting very long. She hadn't had it cut for months. She parted it in the centre and brushed it to a high glow, pushing it behind her ears and letting it flow down her back. Next diamond stud earrings she had bought herself to mark her New Journalist of the Year award. A few swishes of O de Lancôme—she was never without it—and she was ready.

All through the afternoon, even when she was working on the book, her conversation with Fee stayed at the back of her mind. No doubt getting it all out into the open was good advice but her extreme reluctance was proof how badly she had been traumatised.

Rebecca sank into a gold brocade armchair burying her head in her hands for a moment.

"Brod," she rehearsed in her mind, "there's something about me I haven't told you...."

"Brod, I've wanted to tell you this for so long but..."

"Brod, I've been married. Years ago. To a violent man. Well he wasn't violent at the beginning. He used to be so nice... Nice, God!"

"Brod, I married a charming, unpredictable man."

It was going to be a terrible shock his finding out. Their relationship, never casual, had escalated so rapidly into a grand love affair all the more extraordinary because neither of them had put their deepest feelings into words. In a way both of them had a problem saying, "I love you," though Brod told her the most beautiful things about herself unable to hide his desire and need.

What a ghastly mess she'd made of it all. It was now imperative she speak out. If she left it any longer she would lose him. This man who had given her back her dreams. This man who put so much store in trusting. In a way she had been leading a double life. Now she would have to face reality.

Rebecca stood up and went to the mirror, looking deeply into her reflected eyes. "Go on, do it. I dare you. Tell Brod about this man he has never heard of. Your husband. Your ex-husband who liked to hurt you. Tell him about your husband's mother, the real head of the family, who would never hear a word against her perfect son. Go on. Tell him. And tell him very soon."

Rebecca smiled ruefully at herself, feeling better. There was no crime in having been married. Her only sin was not telling the man she loved.

Moments later while she was waiting for half past seven when she would go downstairs, Brod came to collect her wearing a soft open-necked blue shirt with grey trousers and a summer weight navy blazer trimmed with gold buttons. She had always thought him as stunning, burning with life, but with whatever had happened between them his looks were positively hypnotic, this man with the wonderful blue eyes.

"Hi!" she said, her heart thudding beneath the thin violet jersey.

"That's nice," he said in a low voice his gaze moving very slowly over her. "Purple is definitely your colour."

"How was your day?" she asked.

"Not completely satisfactory." He rubbed the back of his neck as if to ease it. "But we're working on it." He took another glance at her mouth. "I'd love to kiss you. I mean I want to kiss you all the time really, but we'd better go downstairs." He put out a hand, unable to resist sliding it down her satiny waterfall of hair. "I like your hair longer. It's perfect parted in the centre."

"I aim to please you," she said, feeling a bit intoxicated.

"You *do?*"

"What do you think, Brod?" She lifted her dark head to him. "I've gone to pieces over you."

He laughed; a flash of beautiful white teeth. "Gone to pieces of course. But are you in love with me?"

"You don't believe me?"

"Yes, but I'm not exactly sure what yes means. I'd really like to know what you want of me, Rebecca?"

"Nothing. Everything," she said.

He moved her back against the wall, bent his head, just barely grazing her mouth, but the effect was sizzling, robbing her of breath. "You're a magnet for me."

She stared into his eyes. "I know so much about you. So much about your family. You know so little about me."

"I thought you were going to tell me everything one day," he challenged.

She frowned, very serious. "I want to tell you *tonight.*"

If it were possible the colour in his sapphire eyes deepened. "Rebecca, you little Sphinx, I'll be waiting for you."

As they walked to the head of the staircase, Fee, who had been playing hostess, came out into the Front Hall, looking amazingly rich and famous. "Ah, there you are, my darlings. Jean has dinner ready for eight. "You'll want a pre-dinner drink."

The four men who had been seated in the drawing room, a pleasant relaxed group, now came to their feet, wondering who the beautiful young woman was on Brod's arm.

Three were wondering.

One had no reason to. He already knew Rebecca Hunt. He knew she had been commissioned to write Fiona Kinross's biography. He'd seen it in the papers. Rebecca had become more successful than he ever would have given her credit for. Now she was happily at home with these megarich people. These top people. This great landed family. Who could beat that?

Rebecca totally unprepared thought she might faint from the shock. It was amazing she *didn't* faint, her vision had become so blurred. But she would have known him anywhere. Martyn Osborne. Her ex-husband.

Dear God she pleaded inwardly. Don't punish me any more.

Brod, about to make the introductions, became aware of the tiniest little flutters in Rebecca's body, the quickening of her breath. Something was perturbing her. He looked down at her face swiftly and saw it confident, exquisitely poised. She wore the smooth mask he had almost forgotten. The shields were down. But he knew something was very wrong.

Speak to him as though you've never seen him before in your life, was Rebecca's first frantic thought. Play a role. Be as brilliant as Fee. She had nothing to be ashamed of. It was Martyn who ought to be deeply ashamed. There was no way she was going to fear him any more.

She got a vague impression of the older men. One silver haired, distinguished, the other portly, the younger man almost a matched pair with Martyn. Fair, well-bred, good looks and near identical smart casual clothing. Martyn had obviously left his old legal firm to join Mattheson & Mattheson. Another good career move. It was an incredibly bizarre situation but one she had to get through. The decision taken, she moved smoothly into speech, countering her turmoil with courage. Just too ridiculous to pretend she didn't know him at all.

"But, Martyn, what a surprise!" she exclaimed, with mild pleasure. "Martyn and I were at university together." She looked to Brod and Fee in explanation. "I swear it's a small world." At least *that* was true.

"How nice!" Fee stared at her, not in the least fooled, even if she applauded the acting.

He'd thought she'd be struck dumb with shock, possibly make an utter fool of herself, yet here she was extending her hand, withdrawing it very promptly before he had a chance to tighten his grasp. "How are you, Martyn?" she asked, feeling his eyes eating into her.

"Fine, Becky. Never better. Someone was only talking about you the other day. It was my mother actually. Why don't you call her?"

Because she disgusts me. Like you. "Lord, I'm terrible keeping up with all my phone calls," she answered lightly, allowing Brod to move her on to the leader of the group. Barry Mattheson responded with genuine pleasure, remarking on Rebecca's professional success. "I've had the pleasure of reading your biography of Dame Judith Thomas," he said. "My wife read it first and gave it to me. Both of us thoroughly enjoyed it."

"You won't have to buy a copy of mine, Barry," Fee told him, patting his arm. "I'll be sending you and Dolly an autographed copy."

"I'll hold you to that, Fee."

The portly Dermot Shields came next, his good-natured face intelligent and alert. Jonathan Reynolds, Dermot Shields' aide stood to attention, impeccably groomed and a little overawed by the grandeur of his surroundings. This was the first time Jonathan had ever visited one of the country's great historic homesteads and he was mightily impressed.

By the time they went into dinner it was apparent to Rebecca Martyn was going to play along with her. At least for the time being. She knew he was quite capable of denouncing her the moment he saw fit. Perhaps he was hording the pleasure. Or quick-witted at all times he had divined Brod's interest in her and as a consequence was trying to work out how best to proceed.

Destroy her or maybe make a big career error, Martyn Osborne thought, taking his place at the big gleaming dinner table with its swanky appointments. The Kinross family were at the top of his firm's long list of wealthy clients. He had even thought with secret contempt old

Mattheson positively worshipped them. It would be incredibly stupid to upset this lot. Or be seen to be upsetting them deliberately.

He had noticed Kinross's swift reactions on his oh so superior face. Handsome as the devil with that shock of blue-black hair, too damned long—who did he think he was... Mel Gibson?—and those startling blue eyes. What an arrogant bastard he was. Of course he was in love with Becky. Imagine she was more beautiful than ever with a cool poise that was entirely new to him. He'd given her so much and it meant nothing to her. He'd loved her too much and she had twisted that love. Turned him into someone else. It was all her fault. Everything. He had never forgiven her. He had never got over it.

Carrying a deep grudge all these years. He'd worked hard to manoeuvre himself into the position to accompany old Mattheson on this trip, never for a moment volunteering the knowledge he knew his ex-wife was on Kimbara helping that over-the-hill actress, Fiona Kinross, to write her silly memoirs.

Mattheson knew he had been married of course. Knew the marriage had ended in divorce but he had no idea his ex-wife was Rebecca Hunt. Needless to say Beck would revert to her maiden name just to spite him. He wanted to give her a bad time, but wanted to be able to think of the best way to go about it. He'd like to shake that acting cool and banish the gleam in Kinross's blue eyes every time he looked at her. The worst bitterness was he still wanted his ex-wife. Wasn't that the reason for pursuing her out to this godforsaken wilderness?

Rebecca went through dinner in a trance of some sort, somehow holding to her end of the conversation, a little slow to answer Martyn's trick questions. He's crazy, she thought. Nothing to indicate it. He's handsome; very correct in his behaviour. Charming to Fee. Just the right amount of deference when speaking to Brod and his senior colleagues, a touch patronising with Jonathan Reynolds who was totally lacking in Martyn's overweening self-confidence. Nicely friendly with her. Old chums from way back exchanging light conversation.

Except for his eyes. She could see the malice in them. The venom. She tried to understand how she had ever come to marry him. But then she had known nothing about the dark side of men.

Brod for his part, decided to say nothing. He allowed Rebecca to carry on with this charade. He was so close to her now, so at *one* with her he knew under the polished facade disturbance ran deep. Without appearing to in the least he kept Osborne under close scrutiny. Osborne, too, was doing his best to cover the feelings that were rife in him but Brod knew his instincts were right. Even during the flow of conversation he kept turning things over in his mind. He was beginning to believe this smooth-faced lawyer with his faintly pompous demeanour and his small mannerisms, the little twitch of the eyebrows, the restless hands, the fake laugh, was the man who had brought much unhappiness into Rebecca's life.

Becky, he called her. Not surrounding the sharpness of the word with cushioning grace. It sat oddly with Rebecca's delicate appearance. Brod understood there was a story there. He intended to find out about it. He hadn't liked Osborne from the moment he had met him. Somehow Osborne had struck him as a malicious schoolboy. Just a fancy but long experience had taught him he had little need to question his judgement.

A malicious schoolboy. One who liked to pick the wings off butterflies.

They lingered over coffee, taking it out onto the verandah at Fee's suggestion so they could enjoy the welcome coolness of the night and the glorious vault of the heavens filled with a billion glittering stars. Nowhere did they sparkle so brilliantly or in such infinite numbers as over the rarefied air of the desert.

It was Barry Mattheson who suggested to his colleagues they should turn in. Martyn turned to Rebecca. "Once around the garden, Becky, for old times' sake. I haven't gotten around to telling you about some of our old friends. Remember Sally Griffiths and her sister? Dinah Marshall? They've set up their

own school for gifted kids. Doing well to. Gordon Clark? He
was mad about you. Weren't they all!"

You included, Brod thought, wanting to pull Rebecca into
his protective arms,

But she wanted to go with Osborne. "I've got a little time to
catch up." She stood to join Martyn, knowing she had little alternative. Because of the conversation at the dinner table, Martyn knew for certain now both Brod and Fee believed her to
be a single woman. Fee had even commented Rebecca would
make some man the perfect wife one day. "We'll be ten minutes no more," she told Brod. "I know you like to lock up." In
fact Brod never locked up. Who was there to raid him? This
was his own kingdom.

Fee, her antennae working overtime, felt driven to whisper
to Brod, "Keep an eye on her, darling. There's something about
that young man I don't like."

"I'm going to," Brod confirmed grimly. "I can recognise
menace when I see it."

"Poor little Rebecca!" Fee said, her heart sinking. "She's
hiding something, Brod."

"Don't I know!" Brod's expression was taut. "I can't tell you
what exactly but she's very disturbed."

When their guests retired, Brod kept Rebecca and Martyn
under silent surveillance, moving soundlessly along the length
of the side verandah, then moving out into the darkened garden all the while listening to the murmur of their voices. This
was something he had never done in his life—eavesdrop—but
he had no compunction about doing it now. He knew something was badly wrong. He knew the two of them had been
playing along.

Until *now* when they thought themselves alone.

As they moved further away from the house, Martyn clamped
his hand around Rebecca's arm but she freed herself by jerk-

ing away forcefully. "It wouldn't be good for you if I started to scream," she warned in a soft, furious voice. "Brod would pound the life out of you."

"He'd have a go," he scoffed, secretly hating to have to put it to the test.

"The hell he would!" Rebecca said with disgust. "He's head and shoulders over you. And I mean in every way."

"In love with him, are you?" he sneered, all the old memories flooding back. His jealous rages.

"You don't need to know," Rebecca replied quietly.

"Oh, yes, I *do!*"

"You need help, Martyn. You always did."

He wasn't about to listen to that. Women with the way they twisted things. "Nothing would ever have gone wrong between us except for you," he hissed.

Their voices were pitched deliberately low but Brod caught it. His suspicions confirmed. No surprise. This was the man in Rebecca's life.

"What is it exactly you *want,* Martyn?" Rebecca asked.

"Can't you see. I want you back. Everything that happened was your fault."

"You need to believe that," Rebecca observed wearily. "Like I said you need help."

"I engineered this trip out here," he told her, a kind of triumph in his voice. "Saw in the paper some time ago you were working on a new biography. Fiona Kinross. Fate with just a little jump start from me let you fall into my hands. I knew all about our Kinross clients. Big. *Very big.* Next thing there's a trip scheduled for Kimbara. Another associate was lined up to go but I'm good at manoeuvring."

Are you indeed, Brod thought, moving ever closer.

Again Rebecca's voice sounded inexpressibly tired of it all. "What could you hope to possibly gain? If you were the last man on earth I'd never come back to you."

I'd never let you.

"That's put another knife through my heart," Osborne burst out.

"You haven't got a heart, Martyn. You've just got a big inflated ego."

"So what's the plan?" Osborne demanded. "Kinross? Are you after him? You always were a high flier."

Listening Brod clenched his fist.

"You mean when I settled for you." Rebecca's voice was icy with contempt.

"My family aren't any ordinary family," Osborne bragged. "We're very well connected. That was a big inducement for you. Do you think I don't know that?"

She tried to swallow. "Martyn, I'm going back. You still talk more rubbish than I've ever heard in my life."

He caught her shoulder. "I'll make you pay. I swear it."

"Do your worst." This from Rebecca, as she flung away.

"Whatever *that* could possibly be," Brod suddenly appeared on the path before them. In the faint light from the verandah he looked very tall, powerfully built, very angry. "You're a visitor here in my house, Osborne," he grated. "It appears to me you're harassing Rebecca. I'm here to help her."

Osborne seemed to gasp for breath. "Harassing?" He sounded shocked, wounded. "Believe me, Mr. Kinross, that's the last thing I would do. You've got it all wrong."

"Have I? Rebecca, come over here." Brod indicated with his arm where Rebecca should stand. Beside him. "Then I think you ought to explain. You've been goading Rebecca all night. I'm not a fool."

"A fool. That's the last thing I'd say you were." Osborne's confident voice wobbled. "I was shocked out of my mind when I saw Becky here. How would I ever know?"

"You'd better tell me," Brod invited pretending he didn't already know.

"He read I was here in the newspaper," Rebecca supplied,

not daring to look up at Brod's steely profile. "He managed to convince Mr. Mattheson he was the best person to bring."

"Why exactly," Brod asked.

"If you only knew." Osborne suddenly clutched his head with his hands giving every impression of a man driven by grief to speak out. "Is it a crime to try to get your wife back?"

"Dear God!" Rebecca burst out imploringly to an indifferent heavens. Brod, totally off guard, reeled back as if taking a king hit. The bliss of these past weeks was smashed into the ground. Trust destroyed. The madness was she had brought it all on her own head. She understood it all. One terrible mistake could change a life forever.

"I only want her back." Osborne's low, impassioned voice came again, an assault to Brod's ringing ears. "I love her. I never ceased loving her."

It rang true. Nevertheless, or perhaps because of it, Brod moved suddenly, jerking Osborne forward by the lapels of his jacket. "Wait a minute. You're trying to tell me Rebecca is your wife? You came here to my home to this station to try to effect a reconciliation?"

"I swear I didn't know what else to do." Osborne's voice broke almost in despair. "She refused to see me, answer my letters, my mother's pleas all these years."

"Years? What are we talking about here? She hasn't been with you for years?" Brod sounded very, very, angry.

Rebecca knew Brod probably wouldn't want to hear from her again still she spoke. "Martyn and I were divorced years ago. It was a very unhappy marriage. I never wanted to lay eyes on him again."

Even with the roaring in his ears Brod heard the word divorced, the only word that pulled him back. "I can understand that," he rasped.

"What is a man supposed to do if his wife won't honour her sacred vows?" Osborne's voice throbbed with raw emotion as he held up a hand as if to shield his face.

Yes, I'd like to punch you, Brod thought. I'd like to lay you out cold but I shouldn't because I'm supposed to be a civilised man.

"Damn you for thinking you could start here." Disgustedly Brod let his hands fall. "Let me understand something—" finally, his face grave, he turned on Rebecca "—is there some remote possibility you could go back to this guy?"

She shook her head, wrapping her arms around her. "No." It would be like being driven back into hell.

"Did you hear that?" Brod swung back to Osborne, terse and powerful.

"I just wanted to hear it from her own lips." In the midst of his humiliation Martyn knew a moment of pure triumph. Vengeance was sweet. If there was anything going on between Kinross and Becky—and he was sure that there was—dear little Becky had well and truly blotted her copy book. What was the old saying? Second hand goods. A man like Kinross wouldn't want a woman with the merest hint of scandal in her background. He could beat this up for all it was worth, only chances were it could all rebound on him. Better to play the poor fool. "Can you blame me for loving her?" he asked in a quiet, defeated voice. "I'd apologise to you abjectly if it would do me any good."

"It won't," Brod returned, very bluntly. "If I were you I'd go inside and reconsider your position. You came here under false pretences. Do you think I couldn't get you sacked?"

"I'm sure you could." Martyn hung his head. Remorse was the way to go.

"I'm half-way sure I *should*." Brod cut him off, looking at him with cold suspicion. "I may even get around to it if you feel you should spread your story. It wouldn't do anyone any good now. Rebecca has told you there's no chance of any reconciliation. None whatsoever. You'd better accept that. For all time."

"I know when I'm beaten," Martyn answered. Glad, yes glad to see Becky so stricken. He wanted her to understand he could still reach out and hurt her. "But surely you can find it in your heart to forgive my coming here? For acting the way I have? Rebecca promised to marry me till death do us part. That meant everything to me. In the end it meant nothing to her."

They stood seemingly like statues listening to Martyn's footsteps trudge back to the house.

Brod was the first to break the highly charged silence.

"He can stick to his room tomorrow," he said, his voice still deeply angry. "Tell Barry he's ill. I don't want him privy to any more of my family's affairs. God I can't take it all in even now. I'll tell Barry I want someone else on the job. Someone with more seniority. Barry can think what he likes."

"I'm sorry, Brod. So sorry."

He caught her chin, looking down into her shocked face. "Are you? You had no intention of telling me, did you?"

There was a little shift in her shoulders. "You don't really understand. My marriage was a time of great unhappiness. I have great difficulty thinking about it let alone talking about it."

"To *me?*" He felt cut to the heart. "To the man you've lain with in such intimacy for all these weeks. The man you claimed made you so happy?"

She turned her tear-blinded, shamed face away. "I was afraid to tell you."

"*Why* exactly?" he demanded, filled with disbelief. "Am I some kind of an ogre?"

"You don't trust me, Brod," she said simply. "Underneath it all you've *never* trusted me. You're not completely in love with me as I am with you."

He could scarcely hear her over the thud of his heart. "Ah, don't give me that!" he said in a contemptuous rush. "I've been waiting for you to speak to me. I've been so patient. I've given you plenty of time. I'm not a patient man."

"I love you." She stared up at him as if committing his face to memory.

He laughed, even now feeling a deep well of desire. "You're

saying this *now*. How long was it going to take you? Or were you waiting for me to ask you to marry me?"

"I never believed you would," she said, profoundly fatalistic.

He grasped her by the shoulders as if to shake the life out of her, the brief surge of violence conquered by his natural gallantry towards women.

"You thought you were destined to be my mistress?" He let his hands shape her delicate bones, their strength quietened.

"I've come to believe bad karma might be the pattern of my life. All the agony with my mother, growing up. Praying for her to get better and she never did. My marriage to Martyn. When I look back on it I was just a kid looking for a safe home. I had no one. I visited my father maybe a couple of times a year."

His eyes showed their bewilderment. "Is all of this so terrible you couldn't tell me?"

She knew his effort to control his anger with her wouldn't extend to Martyn. And Martyn was still in the house. Brod wouldn't take her story of physical and mental abuse without confronting Martyn with it. A terrible argument would take place. Perhaps Martyn would get what he thoroughly deserved. But at what price? Fee would be terribly upset at such ugliness. Barry Mattheson and his colleagues would be made aware of it, without question.

She didn't know how long she stood there without answering. "I can only say I'm sorry, Brod." Maybe she could redeem herself. But it would have to be another time.

His hands finally came down in rejection. "Well, sorry, Rebecca, it's not good enough. All this time in your own way you've been lying to me. To Fee. Have you really grown so close to her or is it all an act? I don't understand you at all."

"I don't understand myself," she admitted openly. "Perhaps I should have counselling."

"Have you always concealed things, Rebecca?" He searched her face, pale as a pearl in the brilliant starlight.

"You have to believe I was going to tell you everything to-night."

He gave a brief torn laugh. "The truth at last, only your ex-husband, Martyn, beat you to it. I can't say I took to the pompous son of a bitch but I'm damned if I can condemn him. He said he still loves you, Rebecca, I believe him."

"That's because you don't know the kind of man Martyn really is. He doesn't know what true love means. All he knows is right of possession. As if you can ever own a human being."

"You don't want to be owned?" he asked quietly.

Now *she* was angry. "I *won't* be owned."

"You fear entering into another marriage? You think all men are mean and possessive?"

"No, not you." Never you. There was nothing in her beautiful Brod to dread.

"Yet you thought I was totally devoid of human sympathy," he said, in a deep, wondering voice. "Loving you and God help me, Rebecca, I do. You thought I couldn't listen to your story. Help you fight all your perceived dark places. You talk about this Martyn, your ex-husband. Well I've got news for you, Rebecca, you don't know what love means, either."

CHAPTER NINE

BACK IN SYDNEY, Rebecca wrote with obsessive nervous energy, virtually unreachable to her friends. She was on her third draft of Fee's biography. The final copy. The phone rang many times. She never answered it. Who did she have anyway? She kept in touch with her father, Vivienne and the children. Vivienne had been going on about a visit. They hadn't seen her for such a while and they longed to. What about Christmas in Hong Kong?

"I won't give up until I've persuaded you," Vivienne said.

It seemed to Rebecca an ocean separated her from the ones she loved. An ocean of sea. An ocean of desert sand. In the month since she had left Kimbara she and Fee kept in touch but her sense of isolation had deepened terribly. Even Fee hadn't been able to persuade her not to leave. Rebecca frowned to herself, remembering...

"I despise that young man coming out here trying to make trouble." Fee's voice was sharp with denunciation. "Let the dust settle, Rebecca, Brod will come around. Though there's no denying you made a big mistake not telling us, darling. It didn't do anyone any good. You do see that?"

"Of course I do, Fee," Rebecca answered her. "I promised you I'd tell Brod that awful night and I meant to but it was doomed never to work out."

Fee had gazed at her for a long while. "You poor girl! If only you'd come to me for help. Heavens, darling, it's not as though you did something dreadfully wrong. I've been divorced twice myself. I never kept it a secret."

"You're famous, Fee."

"I wouldn't have kept it a secret anyway. What was this Osborne? A beast? I'm sure there must be something."

"He has problems, Fee." What was the use of going into it now. God knows she had put it off for so long. Her secret, silent, other life. Although Brod was scrupulously polite she knew he had locked himself away from her.

How had she reacted?

She'd left with the freight plane while Brod, finding his own refuge, was staying out a full week at stock camp.

Rebecca shut off the word processor, sitting immobilised, lost in her thoughts. The book was good. It had taken on a real identity. At least she had given Fee that. The Kinross family, too. She had worked at a punishing pace. An act of atonement.

Brod!

Every time she thought of him she tried for her own survival to push his image away but her whole body remained pierced with longing and regret. She had fallen fathoms in love now the loneliness of it all. The febrile feeling in a body deprived of glorious sexual pleasure. No wonder she was so tightly strung up. But it hadn't hurt her work. In fact it gave a little credence to the old adage an artist had to suffer before inspiration flowed. If only Brod hadn't turned away from her. Not that she had given him much time, awash with her own bitter regrets.

For an instant Rebecca felt a sense of self-pity but she thrust it away. It was all her own fault. She had become entrapped in playing a certain role, adamant after Martyn her defences would never crumble. As a consequence she had paid the price.

Rebecca stood up determinedly. Enough writing for today. She needed a distraction. She really ought to go out and do a little shopping. It was Friday, the stores would be open until

9:00 p.m. She felt stiff from sitting too long in her chair. She placed her hands near the base of her spine, bending back gently, straightening up. She didn't have to look in a mirror to see how much weight she had lost. She could feel it. Very soon someone was going to mention the word anorexia but that wasn't her condition. She took care to eat the right things only sadness had shrunk her. She had always had chicken bones.

She decided to walk to the shopping village and get herself some smoked salmon, fresh fruit and vegetables. Some of those wonderful little rolls from the bakery, some dark rye bread for breakfast. Maybe a bottle of a good Riesling. It would keep for a couple of nights. She had to make a big effort to get back to normal. She had to be strong. It wasn't beyond her. She'd made a comeback after Martyn.

An image of Brod flashed before her eyes. Before grief flooded her.

Ally put her foot down and her small BMW accelerated smoothly, obedient to her touch. She'd been on location in tropical North Queensland for almost a month so many, many messages were waiting for her when she got home. One was from Fee to ring her, which she had immediately, listening as Fee told her all about the dramas that had been enacted at home.

"You're joking, Rebecca was once married?" Ally felt shocked, even a little outraged. "Why on earth didn't she tell us? I mean what was the big deal?"

"Obviously it was to Rebecca," Fee answered wryly. "Brod is terribly affected. He really loves her, darling. I'm sure of it."

"Well she mustn't love *him* if she can't confide in him," Ally countered sharply, then relented. "Heck who am I to judge? I've made a mess of my own life?"

"Do you think you can go and see Rebecca, darling?" Fee asked hopefully. "I can give you her address."

"Actually I've got it." Absently Ally turned up a page in her little black book. "That wouldn't be a problem, Fee. I suppose Brod's got very withdrawn?"

"I think he feels like murdering someone." Fee was driven to exaggeration. "You know Brod, darling. You know men."

"Not droves of them like you, dearest Fee."

"How naughty!" Fee wasn't offended. "I can't help thinking Rebecca is still hiding something."

"About her husband. Lord preserve us!"

"*Ex-husband* please, darling. He couldn't have been in jail. He works for James. Wait he's not with James any more. I suppose Brod had something to do with that."

"Did you ever think Rebecca might have experienced physical abuse in her marriage?" Ally wondered aloud.

"That little thing!" Fee's voice soared in shock. "Who would ever want to hurt such a beautiful little creature?"

"That's what I plan to find out."

When Ally reached Rebecca's block of flats she went to the floodlit entrance, let her gaze slide over the names and numbers. Hunt. R. Third floor, Unit 20. She found the buzzer, pushed it. No answer. She tried again. Damn, Rebecca wasn't at home. She should have rung first but she wanted the element of surprise. She had truly liked Rebecca from the moment she met her, a liking heightened by the knowledge her beloved brother had fallen deeply in love at last. Now Ally wanted to get to the bottom of what was keeping them apart. Was Rebecca a true enigma? A woman dangerous to love? Anything was possible.

Ally glanced at her watch, was about to move back to her car when she saw Rebecca walking down the road, a shopping bag in each hand. She looked as elegant as ever but Ally saw with concern she looked positively breakable.

"Rebecca!" Ally called brightly, waving a hand. She hurried forward to help with the parcels.

Rebecca came to a complete standstill, unexpected pleasure pouring into her. Ally was so emotionally strong. So vivid. "I thought you were away on your TV series?"

"All over." Ally flashed the radiant smile so well-known to her public. "Here, let me take one of those."

"Is everything okay?" Rebecca began, her face in the lamp-light suddenly very pale.

"Lord, I've gone and frightened you," Ally said with quick understanding. "Everything's fine or as fine as it will be until you and I have a little talk. Tell you what, why don't you and I unload these and have a bite to eat somewhere. There must be dozens of restaurants around here."

"Why don't you let me make dinner," Rebecca offered. "I have a chicken, smoked salmon, all the ingredients for a salad. Fresh rolls. Even a good bottle of wine."

"Lovely!" Ally said cheerfully. "I haven't had time for a bite to eat since breakfast. And I make a mean salad dressing. Paul Newman eat your heart out."

It was amazingly companionable. The best time Rebecca had had after the worst of times. Ally encouraged her to eat. "We're in no rush. I've nothing on." Her glance moved over Rebecca's petite frame. "You've turned positively fragile."

"Take a look at yourself then." Rebecca smiled.

"I eat all right—" Ally confirmed it by reheaping her plate "—but I'm on the run all the time. I haven't asked how the book is going?"

"I'm proud of it, Ally." Rebecca raised her eyes to Brod's sister's stunning face. So much like him. Except for the eyes, so perfectly like Fee's. "I know Fee is going to be very pleased with how it's turned out."

"We *all* will be," Ally corrected with a smile.

They cleared away first before they had coffee, taking it to the comfortable seating area in the combined living-dining room.

"You're a puzzle aren't you, Rebecca?" Ally said. "A puzzle I'm determined to solve. I adore my brother. When I came home for Dad's funeral I saw he was in love with you. I saw you returned his deep feelings."

"I love him," Rebecca admitted freely, "but there are so many things..."

"What things?" Ally set down her coffee cup. "Go on, explain. You can't close yourself in like a tomb. I'm here to help you, Rebecca. I'm not only Brod's sister, I'm your *friend*."

"I need one, Ally." Rebecca was very close to tears.

"Talk to me, girl." Ally leaned closer, her green gaze compelling. "Tell me about that ex-husband you were forced to leave."

After about an hour the flood tide of words simply ran out.

"My God!" Ally breathed, rising to her feet and going to the balcony as if to get some fresh air. "What a monster!"

Rebecca caught her long hair and dragged it to the back of her head. "I thought I could never get over it until I met Brod."

"Brod!" Ally threw up her arms. "Brod could never behave like that to a woman. Never in a million light years." She shuddered at the very thought. "Why the man needs denouncing. And he had the hide to come after you. To set foot on Kimbara. I think Brod would kill him if he knew. No wonder you've found it so terribly difficult to speak. It must have been dreadful for you, Rebecca."

"Yes." Rebecca simply nodded, feeling strangely at peace and unburdened. "But I got away." She looked across the coffee table as Ally resumed her seat. "I think the image I wanted to present to the world was borne out of pain. Shame, too, I suppose."

Ally's vivid face looked saddened again. "And you didn't tell Brod because you thought he would think less of you. As though your husband's brutality had somehow infected you."

"That's it, exactly, Ally. Once I actually liked it when a male colleague told me I was like a white camellia. *Untouchable.* That was the image I wanted to project. Not a woman who had once crumpled under a man's hitting hands."

Ally's expression was very serious, even sombre. "But you've won through, Rebecca. You've earned respect on all sides. It's that brute you were married to who was the coward. What you've told me makes my skin crawl."

"*You* wouldn't have put up with it, Ally."

Ally took a deep breath. "I had a family to call on, Rebecca. A very powerful family. Whatever my father's sins of omission he would never had stood by had I become involved in a disastrous marriage like that. Brod, well Brod, I wouldn't have liked to be the fella."

Rebecca nodded. "That's why I didn't tell him that night. I just couldn't start a terrible fight even if I did want Martyn thrown off the property."

"But you have to tell him now, Rebecca. You know that."

"I can't say to him what I've said to you, Ally. We're women. From what Fee told me Brod has already taken some action. Martyn's no longer with Matthesons."

"Great!" Ally applauded with a clap of her hands. "I think he might try another state. Western Australia wouldn't be far enough! Clear across the continent. Look, you've been working too hard. That's very clear to me. You need time off. A friend of mine has a gem of a beach house at Coff's Harbour. We could drive down tomorrow night. Spend a few days. What do you say?"

"To friendship." Rebecca raised her empty coffee cup, her eyes lighting up. "But what about you. You must have lots of things lined up?"

"I have, too, but I'd much rather go with you. You're going to come through this, Rebecca, or my name isn't Ally Kinross."

The weather was perfect. Glorious blue skies, marvellous surf. Ally's friend's little gem of a beach house was big and fantastically beautiful, consisting of a series of pavilions, some open air filled with wonderful Thai furniture from Bangkok. Perched on the hillside overlooking the Pacific Ocean, it had breathtakingly beautiful views and a long flight of steps that led down to the white sandy beach. Even the sheltered front garden was filled with beautiful things: palms, ferns, orchids, water lilies and giant pots that lent a wonderfully exotic touch.

In such an environment with Ally's company and the healing powers of the blue sea and golden sun, Rebecca began to relax. Ally was such a good and generous person Rebecca felt a deep gratitude for all her help. Serious conversations punctuated the relaxation. Ally's own love story came tumbling out. It was a warm, close time. A time of getting to know each other properly. By day they went for long walks along the beach, swam, did a little sun-baking, explored the beautiful coastline by car, visited all the little galleries and craft shops, had al fresco lunches that turned into hours. They stayed home at night making a meal, watching television, listening to music, before turning in, calm and quiet.

It was on the Tuesday afternoon as Rebecca was relaxing in the open-air pavilion covered with its dark timbered roof, Ally, looking marvellous in white shorts that showed off her beautiful long legs and a little yellow top that left her golden midriff bare, came up the stairs from the garden.

"Rebecca, love, we have a visitor," she called, a decided lilt in her lovely voice.

"Really?" Rebecca swung her feet to the ground, expecting to see the owner of this marvellous place. Like Ally she was wearing beach clothes only her outfit was a beautiful sari she had bought at one of the local boutiques, its silky black background covered in brilliantly coloured tropical birds and flowers.

She waited a few seconds, receptive to whatever came, hearing the sound of footsteps coming up the stairs.

"My big surprise!" Ally announced as their visitor appeared, lifting herself up onto her toes to kiss her brother's lean, handsome cheek.

"Brod!" Rebecca drew in a sharp breath, the book she had been reading falling to the floor.

"Now I'm going to leave you two alone," Ally laughed. "I know you've got lots to talk about. I'm going down to the vil-

lage. If Brod's going to stay we'll need more of everything."
She turned jauntily, gave them a little wave. "Back in a hour
or so you two."

While Rebecca stood rooted like some exotic flower, Brod
walked towards her, taking his time, a quiet approach but his
eyes were blazing over her.

"Hi!"

"Hi, yourself." It came out like a whisper and all because
she was ecstatic to see him again. "Tell me how you got here?"

He put out his two hands and cupped her face. "Ally and I
have the same friends."

"Oh!"

"By the way, you look beautiful."

"So do you."

"That's hard to believe."

They stood for a moment silent while Ally's BMW tore off
accompanied by a loud honk of the horn.

"The only question is did you miss me?" He brought her
close to him and kissed her mouth. Tenderness and passion,
the sweetest of wild honey.

Sensation swallowed her so she took a while to answer.
"Never!" She shook her head at the same time, flashing him a
luminous glance.

"The same for me," he teased. "I never thought of you once."

"You say the nicest things." There was an explosive excitement beneath the banter. He touched a little fold of material at
her breast, indulging his senses in the satiny feel of her skin.
"Well hardly at all," he amended, "except for the hours between
one dawn and another. Night was the worst."

A feeling of intense joy rose in her. "For me, too. It's been
a torture."

"When I think of what you had to suffer!" His voice was
low and impassioned.

"Hush, it's all over." She raised herself on tiptoe, putting
gentle fingers against his mouth, delighting in his little nipping
kisses. "Ally told you?"

"Isn't that what sisters are for?" he asked gratefully. "Ally is amazingly intelligent and perceptive."

"You don't blame me?" She gazed intently into his eyes.

"Rebecca!" He held her questing glance for a long highly charged moment, the great surge of protectiveness he had experienced at the first sight of her, her femininity, her vulnerability, alchemising into pure passion. This was the woman he wanted with all his heart and soul. Nothing would have stopped him coming after her. With or without Ally. Abruptly he lowered his head covering her upturned face with kisses, then as her head fell back, the length of her neck. "You were right not to tell me about Osborne that night at the house. I think I might have gone crazy had I known what he did to you. I can easily see now how you built up your defences and why. What we have to do now is burn them down."

"When I'm already engulfed in fire." An answering moan of desire rose in her chest. "I love you, Brod. I adore you."

He felt an enormous surge of elation. "Are you absolutely sure of it?" He stared down into a pair of liquid diamond eyes.

"I'm going to die if you leave me," she said.

"My precious Rebecca!" He gathered her closely to him. "You deserve so much. I want to give it to you. Marry me."

Totally at peace, he began to kiss her again, moving his tongue against hers, exploring her mouth deeply, while sensation after sensation shot through Rebecca like little jolts of electricity. Down the length of her body, her limbs, her spine, between her legs.

"When is it Ally gets home?" he groaned against her mouth.

She whispered fluttery little endearments back. "An hour. Make it two. You know Ally."

"I do." He thought for a moment, then swept her up into his arms, causing another wave of sexual pleasure.

"Then we'll take it very...very...slowly," he said.

* * * * *

The Bridesmaid's Wedding

CHAPTER ONE

BRISBANE IN JUNE. Sky meets the bay in an all-consuming blue, glorious in the sunshine. Brilliant flights of lorikeets dart in and out of the blossoming bottlebrushes, drunk on an excess of honey. Chattering parties of grey and pink galahs pick over the abundant grass seeds on the footpaths, not even bothering to fly off as someone approaches. The twenty-seven larkspur hills that surround the river city glow with wattles, the national emblem, a zillion puffballs of golden yellow flowers drenching the city in irresistible fragrance.

In the parks and gardens, the ubiquitous eucalyptus turn on an astonishing colour display as do the bauhinias, every branch quivering with masses of flowers—bridal white, pink, purple and cerise—like butterflies in motion, a foil for the pomp of the great tulip trees with their scarlet cups. All over suburbia, poinsettias dazzle the eye while the bougainvillea, never to be outdone, cover walls, fences, pergolas and balconies with sweeping arches of pink, crimson, purple, gold and bronze, but none more beautiful than the exquisite bridal white. A surpassing sight.

It was on just such a June afternoon, beloved by brides, Broderick Kinross, master of the historic cattle station Kimbara, in the giant state of Queensland's far southwest, was married to his beautiful Rebecca in the garden of the graceful Queensland colonial Rebecca's father, a retired airline captain, had bought when he and his second family returned home from his long-time base in Hong Kong. The wedding ceremony and reception were deliberately low key in accordance with the bride's and groom's wishes, with family and close friends, but a huge Outback reception was planned on Kimbara when the couple returned from their honeymoon in Venice.

Now in the rear garden bordered by the deep, wide river, some seventy guests were assembled, revelling in the sparkling sunshine and the stirring uplift of emotions. Even the breeze gave off soft tender sighs, showering blossom out of the trees like so much confetti. All faces wore smiles. Some like the bridegroom's aunt, the internationally known stage actress, Fiona Kinross, superbly dressed in yellow silk with a marvellously becoming confection on her head, registered transports of rapture. This was a wonderful day; the family wedding, the culmination of a great romance.

As the hour approached, everyone looked expectantly towards the house when quite suddenly the bride's four attendants, three bridesmaids and one little flower girl, the bride's enchanting little stepsister Christina, appeared, moving down the soaring palm-dotted lush sweep of lawn to some wondrous floating music by Handel.

Each bridesmaid was a natural beauty. Each had fabulous long hair, sable, titian and blonde, left flowing over bare shoulders, with tiny braids at the sides and back woven with seed peals, miniature silk roses in the same shade as their gowns with flashes of gold leaves. Their ankle-length sheath gowns of delustred satin showed off their willowy figures to perfection, the strapless bodices decorated with delicate pearl and crystal beading that glittered in the sunlight, the precise shades of the gowns chosen to be wonderfully complementary, rose pink, jacaranda blue, a delicate lime green.

In their hands they carried small trailing bouquets of perfect white butterfly orchids on a bed of ferns. The little flower girl dressed in lilac silk organdie with a wide satin sash, was smiling angelically, scattering rose petals from her beautifully decorated flower basket. All four of them shimmering in the radiant light, irresistible in their youth and beauty.

"Oh, the magic of being young!" Fee whispered with a catch of emotion to the tall, distinguished man standing next to her. "They might have stepped out of a painting!"

A sentiment apparently shared by the other guests who broke into cries of delight and a great wave of "Aahs."

Only one person felt strangely alone, almost isolated, but no one would have ever guessed it. Rafe Cameron, best man, with his golden leonine mane, fine features and air of authority and pride. Rafe had his own thoughts, far-ranging yet fiercely close. Thoughts that stirred an unwelcome rush of bitterness that had no part in this wonderful day. But Rafe was human. A strong man of correspondingly strong emotions who had known rejection and heartache and never got used to it.

Now he stood rooted, staring up at the ravishing tableau, his eyes drawn hypnotically towards the chief bridesmaid in her beautiful rose gown. Ally Kinross. Brod's much loved younger sister. The girl who had stolen his heart and left him with a bitter dark void in exchange. It was an agony to him how beautiful she looked, a smile of utter luminosity on her face, her magnificent curly dark hair—cosmic hair he had once labelled it in fun—hair with a life of its own, tracking down her back, the sun striking all the sparkling little gems woven into the long strands. Her perfect olive skin was pale but high colour burned in her cheeks, a sure sign of her inner excitement.

Oh, Ally, he mourned deep inside of him. Have you any idea what you did to me? But then, they never had used the same measure. Ally's protestations of undying love were like tears that quickly dried up.

Brod and Rebecca. It should have been Ally and me. He could scarcely credit it now, but this joyous occasion could have been for them. Hadn't they planned on getting married, even when they were kids? It was almost something they took for granted. The two great pioneering families, Kinross and Cameron, were surely destined one day to be united? Even Stewart Kinross, Brod's and Ally's difficult, autocratic, late father had wished it. Except it didn't happen. Ally had turned her back on him, running off to Sydney to make a name for herself as an actress just like her extraordinary aunt Fee, who now stood smiling brilliantly, looking fantastically nowhere near her age. Ally would look just like that when she was older. Both had the same marvellous bone structure to fight the years. Both had that laughing, vibrant and I-can-do-anything nature. Both knew how to take men's hearts and break them. It was in the blood.

Determinedly Rafe pushed the thought from his mind. This wasn't the day for self-pity, God knows. He rejoiced in his great friend's good fortune but he was beginning to feel his practised smile stretch on his mouth. It was this first sight of Ally that had thrown his hard-won detachment into uproar. He only hoped no one would notice, not realising how very successful he had become at masking his emotions. But hell, he was supposed to be tough. A Cameron which counted for a lot in this part of the world A Cameron respected by his peers. A Cameron brought unstuck by a Kinross woman.

And it wasn't the first time. But they were old stories. Everyone at the wedding would know them.

Rafe wrestled down the old anguish, rewarded by a moment's powerful diversion as right on cue the bride, on the arm of her proud father, appeared on the upper terrace moving from the shade of the wide verandah into the sunburst of light. She was wearing a lovely smile, posing for a time as though exquisitely conscious of her impact.

Rafe for all his hurt felt his own mood lifting, hearing Fee exclaim, "Magic!" above the great wave of spontaneous applause.

The bride remained on the terrace a short time longer so everyone could look at her, her great sparkling eyes dominating her face, her hands clasped loosely on her beautiful trailing bouquet of white roses, tulips and orchids. Like her bridesmaids she wore a slim-fitting gown, an overlay of gossamer-thin silver lace, over an ice blue satin sheath that reached to her delicate ankles and showed off her exquisite handmade shoes. She didn't wear the traditional veil. Her thick glossy hair was drawn back into the very fashionable "Asian" style, a little reminiscent of Madame Butterfly, decorated high on the crown with tiny white orchids and little cascades of seed pearls and crystals. She wore no jewellery except for the dazzling diamond studs in her earlobes, a wedding present from her adoring groom.

For the shortest time, something she couldn't possibly indulge on such a day, a kind of broken-hearted sadness swept over Fee. Memories she had learned to suppress. Her two failed marriages, all wrong really, right from the start, but she had her child, her beautiful Francesca, more precious to her with every passing day. In retrospect it seemed she had failed though she had been judged highly successful in the eyes of the world as an acclaimed actress; a countess for almost twelve years until the terrible divorce when she had been out of her mind with a short-lived passion for her then lover, an American film star more famous than she. The lunatic years, she thought of them now. Lust never becomes love. And she had had to say goodbye to her lovely little daughter who remained in the custody of her father.

"Fee, darling, you're looking very sad." Her companion bent his pewter-coloured head. "Is anything the matter?"

"Memories, Davey, that's all." Fee turned slightly to squeeze his arm. "My mind was wandering like a bird in the breeze. I'm an emotional creature at the best of times."

Lord wasn't that the truth! David Westbury, first cousin to Fee's ex-husband, Lord de Lyle, the Earl of Moray, smiled down on her wryly. The bold and bewitchingly beautiful Fee. He couldn't remember a time when he hadn't found her captivating, for all the family had never wanted de Lyle to marry her. They feared what his own ultra-conservative mother, sister to de Lyle's mother, had called her "gaudiness," her palpable sex appeal, the richness and "loudness" of her voice, which was really her training, the resonance that could reach to the back seat of a theatre, the terribly foreseeable conflict of interests. The family turned out to be right but David knew for a fact Fee had given his cousin his only glimpse of heaven for all it came with a heavy price.

"Here comes the bride," Fee began to hum, doing her best to forget her own deep regrets. "Be happy, my darlings!" she breathed.

"Amen!" David seconded beneath his breath, feeling enormously proud of his own young relative, Francesca, the titian-haired bridesmaid in the lovely blue gown. He was so glad Fee had kept up the family ties, inviting him out to Australia for the wedding and the promise of a long luxurious holiday in the sun. Four years now since he had lost his dearest Sybilla, the *nicest* woman he had ever known. Four sad rather empty years.

Even from as far away as Australia Fee had shown her concern. "You want a bit of mothering, Davey," she had announced over the phone in that still wildly flirtatious voice. Even steeped in depression that had made him laugh. Fee had never known how to "mother" anyone, least of all her own daughter Francesca.

The focus of all eyes, Rebecca and her father began to move down the short flight of stone steps flanked by golden cymbidium orchids in great urns, smiling at the guests in front of her. It was all dreamlike in its perfection, Fee thought, her eyes stealing to the Gothic arch-way specially erected for the wedding ceremony. It was decorated with masses and masses of fresh flowers and beneath the arch stood her adored nephew, Brod, looking wonderfully handsome, his traditional male attendants by his side; the splendid Cameron brothers, Rafe, the best man, then Grant, the sun flaring off their golden heads. Next to Grant, a six-footer-plus like the rest of them, Brod's long-time friend and fellow polo player, Mark Farrell, all four, lean, rangy bodies resplendent in long-jacketed slate blue suits with white, pleated, front-wing collared shirts.

The bridegroom wore a royal blue Italian-style cravat, his attendants, silver. It was all dreamlike in its perfection, Fee thought. As one's wedding day should be.

Now the ceremony was due to begin. The celebrant was waiting, moved by the atmosphere of reverence that settled over the assembly like a veil....

Throughout the marriage ritual, Rafe stood fair and square beside his friend, smoothly handing Brod the bridal ring at just the right moment, his heart deeply touched by the obvious happiness of the bride and groom. Rebecca had changed greatly from the ice-cool young woman he had first met. Secure in Brod's love she had blossomed like a closely furled bud into radiant flower, the warmth that had always been in her, quenched by a disastrous first marriage, bubbling to the surface. Nowadays Rebecca was brimming with life, a wonderful transformation with Brod beside her.

As bride and groom were pronounced man and wife, he couldn't control the pressing desire to look towards the young woman who had beguiled then betrayed him, though it showed him danger. Those *laughing* green eyes, witch's eyes, forever promising and cajoling, were glittering with tears.

Tears?

His jaw was sore from clenching it. Where was his strength? He wasn't going to share any tears with her though her glance locked with his at precisely the same moment, as though reminding him openly. It perturbed him there was so much anger left inside him, so much misery he had shoved into a dark corner. She had hurt him that badly. But she wasn't going to know about it. The tenderness towards her that had been so much a part of him at least had vanished. Ally might be a superb actress but he wasn't too bad at acting a part himself. God knows he'd had plenty of practice.

His tanned, golden face wearing a masterpiece of a smile,

Rafe congratulated his friend, clamped him affectionately around the shoulders, and kissed Rebecca's satin cheek, wishing her all the happiness in the world. He told the bridesmaids, Francesca, Fee's beautiful daughter, and Caroline, Rebecca's long-time friend, they looked absolutely perfect before turning to Ally, who was unashamedly wiping the few spilt tears from her cheeks.

"It must be fantastic to marry the woman you love," he remarked as though there wasn't a single dark corner left in him. "I've never seen Brod so happy or so utterly at peace."

His voice was deep and relaxed, yet Ally winced as if from a sharp sting. Knowing him so well, she was aware of the fires that burned deep inside him, the feelings of betrayal so smoothly hidden but a hundred times worse since the last time she had seen him at her father's funeral. The message behind his words told her very clearly he would never take her back again. She wanted to go into his arms. Hug him. Beg his forgiveness, his understanding. But she knew she couldn't.

Instead she answered gently, "It was a beautiful ceremony. Perfect. I'm going to miss my big brother." Her expression turned nostalgic. "Motherless, and with the way Dad was, Brod and I were so close."

Rafe tried to deal with a stab of pity. He wanted to stretch out a hand to her. Stroke her sumptuous wild hair. Wind it around his hand like he used to. Just the slightest breeze and it ruffled into a million curls.

"You haven't lost him, Ally," he managed.

"I know." Ally felt the same old powerful tug towards him. "But Rebecca is the number one woman in his life now."

"And rightly so." Rafe's tone was crisp. "You want it that way, don't you?" He looked across the throng of guests to the radiant bride and groom happily receiving kisses and congratulations and a little bit of warm teasing.

"Of course I do!" She lifted her face to him in her spirited way. "I'm thrilled. I love Rebecca already. It's just that…"

Of course he knew. He was just trying to stir her up a little. "The family has regrouped," he relented. As a Cameron, Brod's best friend, and Ally's once-taken-for-granted future husband, he knew just how dysfunctional the Kinross family had been. The late Stewart Kinross had been a hard, complex man, barely hiding his resentment of his charismatic son, subtly making Ally suffer. Brod and Ally had had to look to one another for understanding and support all their young lives. "Brod is married now," he continued, "life goes on. But you haven't lost your brother, Ally. Just gained a sister."

"Of course." She gave her beautiful smile. "It's just that weddings are serious times, aren't they? Full of happiness, but a little sadness, too. Days when none of us seem to be able to tuck our emotions safely out of sight." She allowed herself to look into his eyes. They were so beautiful. Gold-flecked, neither grey nor green but an iridescent mix of both.

"Is that a shot at me?" he challenged.

At least they were talking, she thought gratefully. "Will we ever be friends again, Rafe?" she asked, avoiding an answer.

He chose to ignore the traitorous twist of his heart. Friends? he thought grimly. Was that what we were? He wasn't going to permit this blatant appeal to his senses, either. "Why, Ally, darling," he drawled, "I can't remember a time when we weren't."

She didn't have to touch her cheeks to know they were on fire. She supposed she deserved this. His distinctive strong-boned face with the Cameron cleft chin, looked forged in gilt. He was a splendid creature full of power and energy, beautiful really with that mane of gold hair, another Cameron hallmark. There was an enormous guardedness in his expression, yet a glimmer of something even he couldn't control, the powerful physical attraction that had once dictated their lives.

Oh, God. I need you, Ally thought. I want you. I love you. I bitterly regret running away from you and bringing about my own destruction. She realised with hidden grief the strength of her feelings far from abating over time had become more desperate. Only Rafe was a proud man like all the Camerons. A man who placed an immense value on loyalty and she had betrayed him. One of those false steps in life when she had placed self-fulfilment or how she had thought of it then, above a love so strong and deep it had all but taken possession of her. Love isn't always safe. At twenty years old the force of it had panicked her. Against everyone's wishes, she had fled. Now this. Lifelong estrangement from Rafe. It made her want to weep.

"Why look so heartbroken?" He cocked a golden brown eyebrow.

"You forget how well I know you." Though she smiled, Ally kept her telltale eyes veiled. "You're even more remote since the last time I saw you. I'm fearful you've *totally* shut me out."

"For good, darling," he assured her without apparent regret. A dark wing of her hair with its decorated little braid fell forward onto her cheek and despite himself he found he was tucking it back.

Fool! Only Ally always had been too much to handle. When he spoke it seemed imperative he make his position perfectly clear. Now his eyes were trapped by the wide beautiful shape of her mouth. The eager, ardent mouth he had kissed a thousand times. And never enough. "I've got my life together," he said by way of explanation. "I'd like to keep it that way. But don't think I'm not grateful for what we had. The bond between us will last. It's just I'm not your willing captive any more."

She gave a low sceptical laugh. "Captive? I could as easily capture an eagle. In my memory it was the other way round."

"You were always one-eyed," he said in his deep seductive voice. "Who was the girl who at age fourteen told me she adored me. That she wanted to live with me all her life. You were going to marry me the day you turned eighteen. Remember, Ally? You the born seductress. Remember how you told me you belonged to me? Remember how you drove me crazy with desire when I'd made a sacred vow I wouldn't touch you until you were old enough to handle our relationship. Poor me," he mocked, "it was my duty to protect your vulnerable innocence."

Her eyes flickered, moved away. "You were always very gallant, Rafe. A gentleman in the grand manner."

She gave a passing guest that incandescent smile that somehow flooded him with anger. "But you changed all that, didn't you?" He looked down into her face. "And maybe that was the big mistake. When it came right down to it, the fire you *thought* consumed you couldn't match the fire in me. You were the candle to the inferno, or something like that. A reckless child to the man. Is that what frightened you away?"

Because there was a hard kernel of truth in it, Ally tossed back her head, causing her long hair to bounce along her back. "You didn't find fault with me when I was in your arms," she retaliated, her heart swelling with emotion. She had a vivid flash of the way it was, an experience so momentous, like nothing else that had ever happened to her, their bodies bonding passionately in the great front bedroom at Opal. A bedroom not slept in since Sarah and Douglas Cameron, Rafe's and Grant's parents, had been killed in a light aircraft crash returning home to the station. But Rafe had wanted it that way. Wanted their first mating in the immense ancestral bed. A night without sleep. Delirious making love.

Rafe. Her first love. Only love. There had been other relationships since, a very few; the ones she had settled for a second best, none with that tremendous *significance*. None who could make her soar. Mind, body, spirit. No one. Rafe was her past, her present. Life without him in the future was unimaginable. He was the missing piece of the jigsaw of her life without which the whole design could never be resolved.

She should have married Rafe years ago when she'd had the chance, instead of fleeing his powerful aura. Rafe, like her brother Brod, had inherited wealth, power, responsibility. A life of service to the land. She understood it, bred to the same heritage, but she couldn't pretend she had the same dedication.

Now years later she would give that dedication gladly. Her career had brought her public admiration, the respect of her peers, but it hadn't brought her either happiness or fulfilment. It had brought her a good deal of hard work, terrible hours, and increasingly a level of anxiety she had never remotely anticipated. There was a high price to pay for fame.

"Ah, well, it's all in the past," Rafe was saying gently without sounding remotely friendly. "I propose we leave it there instead of raking over the dying embers. You know that. So do I. Although it seems a pity your great career isn't as fulfilling as you thought?"

With an abrupt movement she took a little step back from him, raising her chin. "Who told you that?"

He wagged a finger at her. "Ally, Ally, because I can match you step for step, beat for beat, word for word. I know you as well as you know me. You're not happy in your make-believe world. You used to say you couldn't breathe in the city. *And* because I liked you the way you were," his gaze moved down over her, deceptively silky, "I have to tell you you're way too thin."

"Great! I look awful?" she mocked. She knew without vanity how good she looked even if stress was taking its toll.

He considered the question briefly, golden head, metallic in the sunlight, to one side. "Well, put it this way. You're not quite as much woman as you used to be. There's not an awful lot on top." He glanced meaningfully at her fitted strapless bodice. "But you look beautiful. The sort of woman one can't take one's eyes off. Totally desirable. Which makes me wonder why there's never any affair of yours splashed over the cover of the women's magazines?"

"Somehow I still believe my private life is my own. Anyway, since when have women's magazines appealed to you?" She spoke sweetly, aware as Rafe must be, they were the focus of many eyes. A splendid affair gone wrong like Scarlett and Rhett.

"Ever heard of women friends?" His dry tone glittered. "I was over at Victoria Springs only the other day, submerging myself in old issues with Lainie. The two of us went through them together. Lainie has always been one of your greatest admirers. Four pages of Ally Kinross wears seductive separates, that was in *Vogue*. Mercifully you put them *together*. I figured you could have worn a bra with the see-through number, Lainie predictably thought you looked fabulous. There was Ally Kinross acting up a storm; Ally Kinross tells us about her working life. No wonder you've lost weight, but no mention of your love life, though. I say that's odd. Neither of us is getting any younger."

Which was true. "Perhaps you'll show me the way," she retorted with a spark of anger. "You and Lainie share the same tastes. Very establishment, very conventional and so forth." Was she so jealous? Of Lainie, their friend?

He made a soft, jeering sound. "To hell with that! You're talking nonsense."

"Am I? It seemed to me the relationship has flourished," she commented, believing it to be true, "so don't look down your ridiculously straight nose at me. Though at five-seven, allow a couple more inches for heels, not a lot of people do. But *you* can." Rafe, like her brother Brod, stood an impressive six foot three.

"I expect being a tall woman has its problems?" he said, a lazy smile to his so sexy mouth.

"You found your way around them." Despite herself she sparked again. "You've changed, Rafe. You never used to be sarcastic."

"Forgive me. I'm so sorry." He seemed to find that amusing. "Anyway, that's the least of your problems." He saluted a passing guest who didn't make the mistake of butting in. Rafe's and Ally's unique relationship was known to all of them.

"I didn't say I had any problems," Ally began to realise she and Rafe had stood a little too long talking. Everyone was moving off to the huge white marquee erected in the grounds, among the guests an attractive young woman in an exceptionally pretty flower-printed chiffon dress with a sparkling ornament securing her cascade of long, thick, fair hair. Lainie Rhodes from Victoria Springs Station. Lainie, although a couple of years younger than Ally, had been part of everything from childhood. "So you're not admitting you've turned up the heat on your friendship with Lainie?" Lainie wished it was otherwise but she couldn't control her need to know. Her eyes followed Lainie's high-spirited progress, arm in arm with Mark Farrell, the groomsman.

"It sounds like you don't care for that?" Rafe countered very dryly, trying to blanket out his own warring emotions. Lainie was a nice girl. He was fond of her, but he hadn't gotten around to seeing her as more than "the girl next door."

Yet. The hard fact was he had a responsibility to get married. Produce an heir for Opal. It was imperative he find a solution to Ally. A good woman to combat her.

Knowing him so intimately Ally picked up on his wavelength. "Lainie is one of us," she said almost in quiet resignation. "We used to compete in the show ring. She's fun and very loyal."

"Totally different from you." It was cruel. A bitter accusation he couldn't prevent from rushing out.

Cut to the heart, Ally, the accomplished actress, turned her response into provocative banter. "You mean, I don't remind you of a friendly puppy?"

But Rafe, too, had recovered his equilibrium. "I meant that in the nicest way possibly." He wasn't at all fazed by Ally's reminding him of a chance remark he had once made about Lainie. There was a time she had practically leapt into his lap every time she saw him, which was the way her teenage crush seemed to take her.

"Obviously." Ally nodded in agreement. "May we expect an announcement?" Though she continued to speak breezily it was taking all her training. She felt she couldn't bear an answer that suggested a growing involvement.

"Ally, darling, let me set you straight." Rafe reverted to a sardonic drawl. "My private life no longer has a great deal to do with you. No offence. Just a simple statement of fact. What we had I'll remember all my life, but it's *over.* Something that happened at another time. To different people. Ah, here's Grant and Francesca coming our way," he exclaimed like a man granted a reprieve. "I'm sure you've noticed they get on amazingly well, though don't read anything into that. The Lady Francesca has her own brilliant life in London."

"She might like to change it." Ally, too, watched her cousin Francesca and Rafe's brother Grant walking arm in arm towards them. Francesca of the glorious titian hair looked ravishingly pretty in her jacaranda blue bridesmaid's dress, not even reaching to Grant's broad shoulder. Grant, like Rafe, was outrageously handsome. He and Fran looked wonderful together, their laughter spinning out to reach them. Happy, carefree laughter. The sort of laughter one wants to hear at a wedding. Ally was enormously fond of her cousin, Lady Francesca de Lyle. The idea of having Francesca around all the time had immense appeal.

Not apparently to Rafe.

"Don't say that!" he murmured, half amused, half alarmed. "I don't want to see my brother's heart broken, as well."

Her breath seemed to leave her. *As well?* "Are you admitting you still have some feeling left for me?" She held his eyes, eyes that had once been infinitely loving. Eyes that still had such power over her.

"I'm saying I *did,* until you got bored and ran away." His marvellous body relaxed. "Sometimes it seems a pity your spell lost its potency, Ally. I might never feel that kind of heat again. Ah, the feverishness of youth!" His voice was light with nostalgia. "Such a dangerous time."

"At least it gave you a good excuse to hate me."

"Hate you?" He stared at her in mock shock. "I can't get stuck with that one, Ally. I'd never dream of hating you. What do they say about one's first love? Never mind." He extended a courteous arm to her. "Why don't we join up with brother Grant and your Francesca? Most people have made their way to the marquee. I want to see all the delectable things to eat. I let lunch go so I'd have plenty of space. I just love weddings. Don't you?"

CHAPTER TWO

THE RECEPTION HAD been arranged as a buffet with long tables, covered in white linen cloths that had been given a deep lace edging, laden with delicious food: glazed ham and turkeys, great platters of bay oysters on beds of crushed ice, luscious seafood of all kinds—crab, prawns, lobsters, crayfish, scallops, silver trays of whole smoked salmon and capers ringed by the old favourite, quartered boiled eggs. There were fish dishes done in mouth-watering pastry, succulent slices of roast beef and lamb, pasta dishes, chicken dishes, mountains of piping hot rice and a variety of garden salads to refresh the palate. But the greatest fanfare was the dessert table. Guests stood looking at it transfixed. Some of the younger ones even started to applaud.

There were cheesecakes, shortcakes, splendid gateaux, tortes, mousses, trifles, the much loved meringues, their snowy peaks running passion fruit, or for the more sophisticated the meringues were filled with hazelnut cream and drizzled with chocolate, the delectable whole dominated by a four-foot-high fruit and chocolate brandy wedding cake, like some wondrous sculpture. The Corinthian pillars were perfect in every detail as were the garlands of handmade flowers and lace work. As the guests continued to exclaim at the ravishing effect of decor and food, waiters in black trousers and short white jackets began to circulate, offering the finest champagne.

The moving ceremony over, the festivities began.

The idea was for the guests, all known to one another, to mingle freely, moving from table to table as the mood took them, the whole atmosphere wonderfully relaxed. Only the bridal party had defined seating at the top table.

Stage one was the feasting that everyone enjoyed tremendously, then came the speeches. The next stage was the dancing, balloon and glitter-throwing. Someone even threw two or three plates before they were reminded it wasn't actually a Greek wedding.

Later on, after the bride and groom had left for their flight to Sydney where they would spend a night in a luxurious hotel before embarking on the first leg of their trip to Europe, the rest of the bridal party and some of the younger guests were going on to the theatre with supper after if anyone possibly had room for it, and there was talk of continuing on to Infinity, the "in" nightclub. No one wanted such a glorious day to end.

When it was time for the bride to change into her going-away clothes, Ally went up to her room to help her.

"This has been the most wonderful day of my life!" Rebecca announced, smiling emotionally through her tears. "Brod to share my life. I adore him. You've been wonderful to me, too, Ally. I'm so grateful for your friendship and support. You played a big part in bringing us back together. You're such a generous spirit."

"As I should be." Ally took charge of Rebecca's beautiful wedding gown. "I've taken over the role of sister."

"That's true!" Rebecca laughed shakily, stepping into the skirt of her fuchsia bouclé wool going-away suit. "I know you're going to be the best sister I could have."

It sounded so heartfelt, so full of gratitude, Ally stopped smiling. She went forward to kiss Rebecca's cheek. "Thank you for that, Rebecca," she said gravely. "Thank you for becoming part of my family. You're going to change Brod's life in the most wonderful way. Give him such love. Family. That's what he needs."

"And you, Ally?" Rebecca looked at her new sister-in-law with her great shining eyes. "You must be happy, as well."

"I'm going to try, love." Ally was amazed her voice was so steady. "But I don't think Rafe is ever going to change his mind about me."

"You still love him." It wasn't a question but a sad statement of fact. There were no secrets between the two young women. They'd shared many a heart-to-heart discussion.

"I'll always love him." Ally went to the wardrobe to hang up Rebecca's dress. "That's just the way it is. I'll continue to love him even if he marries someone else." She closed her eyes in involuntary pain.

"You don't think your friend, Elaine...?" Rebecca asked tentatively. She couldn't help noticing Rafe had danced with Lainie Rhodes a number of times, Lainie staring adoringly into his eyes.

"Anything's possible, Becky," Ally was forced to admit. "Lainie's really nice. Warm and kind. Not a major brain perhaps but competent. She'll develop beautifully, too. She's a country woman above anything else. She knows how to continue a tradition."

"And you don't?" Rebecca turned to scrutinise her new sister-in-law, loyalty in her eyes.

"I think Rafe has convinced himself I'm another Fee," Ally explained sadly. "God knows I love Fee. We all do. It's hard not to. But Fee always took care of herself and her career above every other concern. Fran must have been a very sad and lonely little girl, for all her father tried to make it up to her. I suspect her life now isn't as glamorous as it's supposed to be, any more than mine. To love and be loved is a woman's greatest joy. Children her greatest achievement. And my biological clock is ticking away."

"And mine." Rebecca sounded as though she had just the right plan to stop it in its tracks. "I had to avoid falling pregnant with my previous husband Martyn, our life being what it was, but Brod is my dream come true." She picked up a silk cushion and hugged it. "I feel today my life begins with him. My *real* life with me functioning the way I am, not keeping everything locked up inside. My love for Brod has invaded every aspect of my life. Loving has taken away the pain."

"I can understand that." Ally nodded. "You've been wonderful for him, too. Brod and I have also had our bad times. Now," Ally paused, seeking to lighten the conversation, "what are you going to do with your hair?" Rebecca had removed all the ornaments.

"I'd thought I'd leave it long," Rebecca picked up a brush, whisking it vigorously through her waterfall of hair. "Brod likes it this way." Finally she turned. "What do you think?"

"Beautiful," Ally smiled, handing Rebecca her fuchsia jacket.

'I mustn't forget my bouquet." Rebecca looked back at the exquisite arrangement lying on top of a small circular table. "I want my chief bridesmaid to catch it."

And so Ally did, though Lainie was powerfully disappointed. She, who had manipulated herself into a good catching position, saw the bouquet sailing right for her, but somehow at the very last minute, never mind how, misjudged her timing. The bouquet cleared her outstretched hands though she was sure she stood on someone's toe to get it and landed against Ally's flawless, infinitely sexy, breast.

The irrepressible Aunt Fee, who was too much, Lainie and her mother had always thought, burst out clapping in a kind of triumph. "Isn't that great?" she demanded of the tall silver-haired man, exuding Englishness, who had certainly never left her side the entire afternoon. "You know what that means, Ally, don't you? You're next."

"Don't forget me, Mamma," Francesca laughed, holding up

a single white orchid that had separated itself from all the rest. She felt wonderfully happy and alive anticipating the long evening with Grant beside her. He was so completely different from anyone she knew at home. So strong, so straightforward, so self-reliant, full of his hopes and plans. She couldn't seem to get enough of his company.

"Congratulations, darling," Rafe murmured in Ally's right ear. He was smiling sardonically, showing his perfect white teeth. "Possibly it's to someone you haven't yet met."

"Oh, that makes me so cross!" Lainie interrupted, turning round to them. "It's not as though you even tried, Ally, when I pray for a good husband every day of my life. No joke, Rafe," she cautioned him, "so stop laughing."

"Sorry, pet," he answered lazily. "Catching things was never your strong point but Ally here, was raised as a tomboy. She has an excellent eye."

"She's so amazingly beautiful she doesn't need to catch any bridal bouquet," Lainie half grumbled, looking up at him with intense helpless delight. Rafe was always charming and agreeable to her but she could scarcely believe someone like Rafe Cameron, so eligible in every way, could ever find her sexually attractive. Not after Ally who was like a bright flame, but—well everyone in the Outback knew their story. The reason for the split up. Ally, like her fabulous, over-the-top aunt, had wanted to become an actress. Simply dumping one of the most gorgeous men who had ever lived.

"How could she do such a thing?" Lainie's mother had often asked, shocked. "I don't suppose I should say it, but bolting seems to run in the family."

Now Ally was a star who won gold Logies for best actress. Lainie loved her show and tried never to miss an episode. Ally was the sort of person, who could easily make the big-time like Cate Blanchett and take on the world. She was lost to Rafe and he had to accept that. Besides, Rafe had started to spend much more time over at Victoria Springs.

"Don't be modest, Lainie," her mother had encouraged her. "You'll make any man a wonderful wife."

Possibly, but she only wanted Rafe.

So Lainie hoped and prayed and didn't enter into any other relationship. The worst part, she truly loved both of them. Ally and Rafe. She would have to have a talk with Ally as soon as she possibly could. Find out the lay of the land.

Tumultuous cheering broke out as Rebecca and Brod climbed into the limousine that was to take them to the airport. Everybody began to wave. Ally, hair flying, holding the little flower girl's hand, ran once more to the car and leant in to land yet another kiss on bride and groom. "Take care, you two. Have a wonderful time! I'll be expecting to hear from you," Ally said.

Rebecca smiled at her and her small stepsister. "Darling little Christina! I'll miss you. I'll miss you both so much."

"With me by your side?" Brod, looking unbelievably handsome in a well cut grey suit, laughed at his bride.

"You know what I mean, darling." She leaned to kiss him, a kiss that tasted of champagne and strawberries.

"It's a good thing I do." Brod's eyes left his bride's beautiful face for a moment. "Take care, Ally. You'll be hearing from us often. I've asked Rafe to keep an eye on Kimbara. *When* he can find the time. Ted's a good man but it makes me happy knowing Rafe is on hand. I'm grateful to him for so many things."

"So you should be!" Rafe, overhearing, called with affection. "Have the best time in the world, you two. Now take it away." He signalled to the chauffeur as the bridal party threw more confetti. Fee wiped it laughingly from her own and David Westbury's clothes then grasped the little flower girl's hand while Rafe got an arm around Ally's narrow waist drawing her backwards so he could shut the limousine door.

Heat like an electric charge, rushed up his arm as it came in contact with her body. Heat to his heart, to his head, to his loins. For a moment he almost despised himself with his reaction. This was like a haunting. There had to be some way to exorcise Ally. He let go of her before his whole body dissolved.

They all watched until the limousine was lost to sight then everyone began to walk back to the house, those that weren't going on to the theatre starting to say their goodbyes although Rebecca's father assured them they were welcome to stay as long as they liked, an offer a lot took up.

Lainie waited until the powder room cleared before she decided to conduct her own little investigation. She had to find out for sure if Ally still carried a torch for Rafe. She knew in her heart she would find it hard to come between them if they still cared for one another. Though one didn't hear too much about grand passions any more, thank the Lord. She could talk to Ally. Woman to woman. They went back a long way. Big TV star or not, a member of one of the great pastoral families. Well, a patrician in this part of the world, Ally was very down-to-earth and friendly.

"You look wonderful, Ally. Superb," Lainie said for starters, her large, soft, brown eyes admiring as she watched Ally make a few minor repairs to her make-up. Gosh, how did she get her eyeshadow like that? It made her slanting green eyes look like emeralds.

"Thanks, Lainie." Ally gave her lovely smile. "It's been such a beautiful day. A day I'll remember with great joy. A little sadness, too." She began to remove the decorations from a braid. They'd be too much for the theatre. Fran had removed hers, twisting her beautiful hair into a very elegant knot. Maybe she could do the same even if she couldn't get the same result. Fran's hair was wonderfully manageable, hers was downright difficult. Ally experimented for a moment until she became aware of Lainie's expression. "For heaven's sake, Lainie, why are you staring at me like that?" she asked wryly. "Has my mascara run?"

When it actually came to it, Lainie's mouth went dry. "Sorry, pal. I apologise. I was staring, I know. You must be used to it, anyway. You're gorgeous."

"You're not too bad, either," Ally reminded her. "That dress looks wonderful on you."

"I haven't been able to eat to get into it," Lainie freely admitted. "Ally, I just wanted to ask you something personal—I'd never ask if I didn't think… I mean I'd never…"

"You want to know if Rafe and I still mean something to each other?" Ally had a shot at it.

"Right on," Lainie sighed in relief. "Please don't tell me if you don't want to. I'm not a person who is ever going to be called confrontational."

"Fairly forthright nevertheless, my girl." Ally felt she no longer had the energy to fool around with her hair. She would have to leave it as it was. "Lainie, love," she explained patiently, "you know as well as anyone Rafe and I are an old story."

"But you were wonderful together." Perversely Lainie mourned. "Mum thought you had to be nuts."

"Unfortunately I was." Ally looked her regret. "But that was years ago. I was younger than you are now. I thought I needed more time before I could face so much responsibility. Rafe was master of all he surveyed. We all know what the Camerons are like. I wanted to find myself, show the world what *I* could do."

"Oh, I know, Ally." Lainie was understanding. "You wanted to be like your aunty. She was *very* famous though you don't hear much of her these days. But those challenges lost you Rafe."

"You don't have to sound pleased about it," Ally said reproachfully.

"Oh, I'm not pleased." Lainie's reply was genuine and hasty. "I feel sad. Like everyone else did. We thought we were guaranteed a huge wedding on Kimbara. You might even have chosen me for a bridesmaid."

That really shook Ally. It could have been a possibility. Now she was looking on Lainie as a possible successor.

"Are you still in love with him?" Lainie wanted everything made clear to her.

"What do you want me to say?" Ally held out a hand for Lainie to get up. It was time to go. "Rafe will always have a place in my heart. The Camerons and the Kinrosses are almost kin. We grew up together. But things happen. Rafe and I have changed. We're different people now. I have my career. It's no secret I've had movie offers."

Ally stayed a hand as Lainie's pretty mouth framed "What?" "Rafe is wedded to Opal Downs. Like Brod, his inheritance is his life. We've moved on as people."

Lainie's cheeks flushed as wild relief swept her. She clasped Ally's hand tightly. "So you don't mind if...?"

"You have my blessing, Lainie." Ally freed herself gently from Lainie's surprisingly strong grip. "But I should add some sisterly advice. I don't want to see you hurt, either. Rafe has any number of women clamouring for his attention. At least four of them are probably waiting patiently for us outside the door."

"But he was having a ball with *me*," Lainie argued.

"That's what one does at a wedding, Lainie," Ally warned her. "Have a ball."

Lainie considered that for a time. "*You're* the only one who worried me," she said finally. "Mum woke me up to the fact Rafe might consider me for a girlfriend."

"So good luck, then," Ally answered feeling she had done her best. Having a ball at a wedding didn't add up to a romance. Or did it?

The theatre show was as brilliantly entertaining as the reviews had promised. Everyone came out of the theatre feeling a flood of warmth, smiling, humming snatches of the catchy tunes.

"You're coming on with us to the nightclub, aren't you, Ally?" Francesca asked as they stood amid the swirling crowd in the foyer.

Ally was long used to all the glances of recognition that

came her way. In another minute someone would come up and ask for an autograph. Meanwhile she smiled at her cousin, anxious now to be off. She certainly didn't want to see any more of Rafe with Lainie in tow. "I have to fly back to Sydney in the morning, Fran," she explained. "I have a pretty hectic schedule next week."

"What a pity. I'd have loved you to come." Francesca couldn't hide her disappointment even as she understood.

"So how are you getting home?" Grant, who was holding Francesca's slender arm, turned his tawny head to see if he could catch sight of his brother. "Rafe is somewhere back there. Maybe he could give you a lift?"

"No, that's okay." Ally smiled back. She realised Grant, like her own brother, Brod, had never given up hope she and Rafe would some day be reunited. "I can catch a cab."

"You can share ours." Francesca didn't like the idea of Ally's going home on her own.

"You're going the other way, love," Ally reminded her.

"That doesn't matter." Francesca looked up to Grant for confirmation.

"Of course not." He was more than happy to oblige. "We can drop Ally off then come back into town. Where is it, Ally? Some friend lent you their unit, didn't they?"

Ally nodded. "Pam is holidaying on the Barrier Reef for a week. It seemed nicer than staying at a hotel. I like to be a bit anonymous." Keep my whereabouts a secret, she thought a little grimly.

"Ah, there's Rafe now. Rafe?" Grant called to his brother who was clearly enjoying something Lainie was saying to him.

"Be with you." Rafe lifted a long arm, turning to shake the hand of a male guest who was moving off.

"I'm sorry, but I don't think it's a good idea if Lainie falls in love with Rafe," Grant announced out of the blue.

"You think she might?" Fran looked like she'd never considered it for a minute.

"I'm sure she already has," Ally confirmed, turning to a youngster who came up with a program to be autographed.

"Gee, thanks, Ally, that's cool!" The boy, who had to be all of fourteen, whistled behind his braces.

"Does he know you?" Grant looked after the departing fan.

"No. He just thinks he does." Ally smiled. "I've had complete strangers come up and start talking as though they'd known me all my life."

"I don't think I could get used to it," Grant said with a slight frown. "Anyway, to get back to Lainie. Rafe isn't flirting with her, he's only being nice."

"Well he's got her up in the sky somewhere. Floating on cloud nine," Ally offered wryly. "Mind you, Lainie is sweet. She's entitled to her dreams."

Grant wrinkled his broad forehead. "Just between you and me. Rafe needs a great deal more than Lainie can offer." He laughed shortly, the tiniest spark of anger in his hazel eyes. "Do you honestly think she's woman enough for him?" He held Ally's gaze in his direct manner.

"Don't ask me—it's too close to home."

Francesca stared from one to the other, looking thoroughly intrigued. "Are you suggesting someone should tell poor Lainie to back off, Grant, dear?"

"It might save her a lot of heartache." Grant looked serious. "No one wants Lainie to get hurt."

Lainie, smiling brilliantly, was starting towards them and Ally began to brace herself for what was to come.

"I'm trying to talk Rafe into joining us at the nightclub," Lainie announced. "You have to help me." She appealed to Ally and Fran.

"Rafe's really not one for nightclubs, Lainie," Grant tried to warn her.

"But on such a *night*." Lainie clutched at Francesca's arm in her enthusiastic fashion. "Quite a few of us are going on. There's absolutely no need for him to rush off."

"Well, *I* have to," Ally told her lightly. "We start shooting very early Monday morning."

"I'd love to get a bit part in one of your shows," Lainie confessed. "But I suppose I'm too short."

That struck Grant as utterly irrelevant and he said so.

"It was just a thought." A little warily Lainie eyed Rafe's younger brother, knowing Grant Cameron wasn't as sweetly tolerant as Rafe was. Grant was one of those men who didn't suffer fools gladly.

Into the group came the rangy, elegant Rafe, looking super relaxed. The overhead lighting gilded his fine features and played around the smile on his sexy curving mouth. "So is everyone off?"

"You're coming, then?" Lainie rejoiced, all but rubbing her cheek against his slate blue jacket. "It's wonderful to know I could persuade you."

"Well..." Rafe looked down a moment at her fair head. "Lainie, I find it hard to disappoint you, but I'm flying off home in the morning. Grant is staying on to line up some more business, but I have to get back to the station. As well, I promised Brod I'd keep an eye on Kimbara. You've got a dozen people to keep you company," he consoled her. "Fran and Grant are going on. So is Mark Farrell. I thought you two got on rather well." He referred to the groomsman. "And Ally must do this sort of thing all the time."

"You obviously haven't heard about my killing schedule," Ally said in a wry voice. "I have to get lots of beauty sleep so I can get up the next morning without telltale bags under my eyes."

"Bags? Not you," Lainie retorted.

"So can I drop you off at your hotel?" Rafe looked on sardonically. "You're staying with Fee and Francesca?"

"Not this time." Ally shook her head. "Fee has commandeered the best suite. Davey has another."

"I have to settle for deluxe," Francesca smiled.

"And a friend has lent me her place while she's away," Ally added.

"Rafe are you *sure* you won't come?" Lainie persisted, desperately wanting it to happen.

"Sorry, pet." He gave her his maddening nonchalant smile.

"Well, that takes care of that then," Grant said with satisfaction. "We were going to drop Ally off, Rafe, but I'm sure she's happy for you to take over."

"I don't *have* to go," Lainie looked about vaguely, wishing secretly Rafe would simply take her off to bed.

"Sure you do!" Grant took hold of her arm purposefully, with Francesca, blue eyes twinkling, taking the other. "Let the good times roll."

Grant looked back at his brother and Ally and tilted a tawny eyebrow.

CHAPTER THREE

THEY WERE QUIET in the taxi, each sitting as far away from each other as possible, but feeling the effects of their enforced intimacy coming at them in electric waves.

"Are you coming in for a moment?" Ally asked when they arrived. "You can have a nightcap. You don't need to drive."

He wanted to tell her no. He had already begun to shake his head, but Ally threw open the door, peering up at the apartment block. She didn't want him to see her nervousness. She didn't want him to know the cause of it. She moved towards the well-lit entrance, assuming Rafe was paying off the driver.

"Nice place," the driver said to Rafe. "Beautiful woman. I'm sure I know her from someplace. Your wife?"

"She shied away from accepting me," Rafe found himself admitting.

"Fancy that!" The driver, of Italian descent, looked amazed. This guy looked like he had it all. "I haven't seen such a glamorous couple in a long time."

The lift was empty, the hallway a blaze of illumination. They were quiet again until they reached the door of the unit.

"You know, Ally, you're nervous," Rafe observed calmly, taking the key off her and fitting it in the lock. "Not of me, surely?"

The fact was she was excited but edgy, as well. These last

months had taken their toll on her. She was starting to act like someone with a real problem, which, in fact, she had. But who could hurt her with Rafe around. He was very much the man in control.

"I could do with a cup of coffee," she admitted, giving a husky laugh.

He unlocked the door and held it open so she could precede him into the apartment. She'd left a few lamps burning as she always seemed to do these days. Now in the low rosy light she glanced automatically towards the sliding doors that led out onto the terrace with its spectacular views of the cityscape.

Something moved. She stood perfectly still, muscles tensing, adrenalin pumping into her blood.

"What is it? What's the matter?" Rafe registered her alarm instantly, grasping her arm and staring into her stricken face. "Ally?" She looked primed for panic as though her emerald eyes saw some great wrath. "What the hell's going on here?"

At the sound of his voice relief flooded into Ally's face. She could diagnose her own delusion born of months of harassment. She turned to him, her heart still racing, grateful beyond words for how he filled the room with his commanding presence.

"Rafe!" It was little more than a gasp as she waited for the adrenalin in her blood to dissipate.

"For God's sake! What did you think you saw?" he burst out, letting go of her, moving with a lithe, purposeful tread to the sliding-glass doors. Obviously she thought someone or something was out here. He saw only the night-time dazzle of the city lights and glittering towers, the graceful sweep of the Expressway spanning the broad deep river that meandered through the centre of the city in grand curves.

He turned back to her, shaking his head. "There's nothing here. Nothing to be afraid of."

"Good." She gave a small delicate sigh.

Perturbed himself now, Rafe unlocked the doors, slid them open and walked out onto the terrace. Nothing disturbed the peace. There was a collection of potted plants, a white wrought-iron table with two chairs. Quietly alert he walked to the balcony. Looked over. Directly below him five floors down a young couple was entering the building. They were laughing, hand in hand, eyes only for one another.

Ally watched him come inside, feeling slightly ashamed now of her instinctive reaction. The moment of panic. "Just a trick of the lighting," she offered by way of explanation. "I thought I saw something move."

"Something or someone?" His arresting face framed by that burning gold hair was etched with hard concern. Obviously she wasn't telling him the whole story but he intended to get it out of her. He could see she still looked scared when the Ally he knew was the least nervous of women. She had never jumped at shadows. It made him angry suddenly that life in the city should have made her so. He recognised what he felt was possessiveness. Possessiveness permeated with a sense of powerlessness. She wasn't his Ally any more.

"It was nothing, Rafe." Ally tried to shrug the moment off. "Stop looking like you want to pummel someone. I have an overactive imagination." She turned quickly towards the galley kitchen. "I'm having coffee, would you prefer Scotch?"

"Coffee will be fine." He began to roam around the open-plan entrance, living/dining room, furnished quietly but comfortably with one stunning piece of art dominating. "This must be like living in a birdcage," he muttered, a big man in a small, confined space.

"Not everyone can afford grand houses," Ally pointed out, "and vast open spaces. Actually this is quite an expensive piece of real estate."

"I imagine it would be with that view." He glanced back at the sparkling multicoloured lights reflected in the indigo river, then walked nearer the kitchen looking over the counter to where Ally was measuring coffee into a plunger. "Your hand is shaking." How beautiful her fingers were, long and elegant, the nails gleaming with a polish that matched her gown. Ringless. He still had the engagement ring he had planned to give her.

"So it is," she agreed wryly. She wanted to tell him everything. How awful it had been for her. But he might see it as a deliberate play for his sympathy.

"Why, exactly," he persisted, his lean powerful body tensing as it might against a threat.

"It's been that sort of a day."

"Something is really bothering you." He watched her closely, all his old protective feelings coming into play.

"Lord, Rafe, I'm just a little tired. And overexcited. Sit down and I'll bring the coffee over."

"It might make sense to tell me," he remarked, his face reflecting his concern. "Do you mind if I have a quick look through the place?"

"Be my guest," she answered a little weakly. Her heart was still quaking. "Two bedrooms, one used as a study, two bathrooms, a laundry."

"My God!" He sounded amazed anyone could live like that. The cattle baron with his million wild acres.

Rafe walked down the narrow corridor checking each room in turn. He even looked inside the built-in wardrobes, accepting now some terror large or small was preying on her mind.

"Well?" She arched a brow. So hard to believe he was here. So wondrous. So real.

"Everything in order." He crossed to one of the couches upholstered in some light green fabric and removed a few of the overabundant cushions. "I bet this is nothing like where you live in Sydney?" Ally had tremendous flair. They had spent a lot of time walking round the homestead on Opal planning what they would do to refurbish it after they were married. Opal Downs boasted a marvellous old homestead like Kimbara, but whereas Kimbara homestead had been constantly refurbished and updated, Opal had been caught in a time warp. Nothing much had been changed since his grandfather's time. His mother had been contemplating a lot of changes in the months before she and his father along with six other passengers, had been killed when the light aircraft they had been travelling in crashed into a hillside in the New Guinea highlands.

He couldn't bear to remember that terrible time. The shock and the grief. The last time he and Grant had seen their parents alive they had been laughing and full of life, waving from the charter plane that had taken them away from Opal. Forever.

"I've decorated my apartment. We all do our own things. You've gone very quiet." Ally, as sensitive to him as he was to her, set the tray down on the coffee table.

"Memories. They come on you without warning."

"Yes, they're the very devil!" Ally agreed, remembering all the times she had to push her own back. "I'm glad we can have this quiet time together, Rafe."

She was a siren seducing him into her arms. He could smell the perfume that clung to her, stirring his blood. He had lived almost like a monk for years. The odd go-nowhere affair. But there was a huge difference between having sex and making love to the woman who aroused his every longing. Ally belonged to the category of women one would have to call unforgettable. He was mad to touch her. But he didn't move, instead saying quietly, "Your hand isn't shaking any more."

"You're here," she said, her eyes alive with emerald light. "Stay for a while." Rafe always had been an intensely strong and reassuring presence.

"You feel the need to be protected?"

"Believe it." She gave a brittle laugh.

Rafe took a quick gulp of the fragrant black coffee, hot and strong the way he liked it, then set the cup down. "I'm picking up a lot of bad vibes here, Ally. You're not going to tell me you're being harassed by some crank? I know it happens to people in the public eye."

She was struck by his perception. She knew she flushed.

"You mean that sort of thing is happening?" he asked, almost incredulously.

"On and off." She tried to appear unfazed.

"Keep talking," he ordered, his strong handsome face turning grim.

She sank back into the sofa opposite him, the light glancing off her beautiful satin dress, making all the little crystals on the strapless bodice twinkle like stars. "I've had letters, phone calls. The calls must be made from public phones. The police can't get a trace on them."

"Someone speaks? A man?" He gave a dark, forbidding frown.

"I'm afraid so, though he seems to use a device to disguise his voice. It's really rather scary."

He stared at her, decidedly the object of any man's desire. "Scary? I'd like to get my hands on him." His voice rasped. "Does Brod know?"

Vigorously she shook her sable head. "You think I'd spoil his wedding? His honeymoon? No way! It's not like this creep is actually doing anything. I've never been stalked. At least I don't think I have." She realised her characteristic blithe self-confidence was breaking down.

For a split second Rafe felt even he couldn't cope with it. "When did it start?" he asked very quietly, his eyes pinned to her expressive face.

Of course she knew exactly. "Four months ago. The channel is very good to me. They've arranged security for me. I have someone to see me to my car."

He let out a hard, tight breath. "No wonder you nearly jump out of your skin when you imagine you see a man's reflection."

"Maybe I'm not quite sober." She tried to make light of it. "I had rather a lot of champagne at the reception. I'm not afraid."

"I think you've proved you are. And why not? This modern world is turning into a jungle. Have you told Fee?"

She rubbed her arms. "I've told no one in the family. Only you. It's an occupational hazard, Rafe. I have to live with it."

His expression was formidable. "This is really bad, Ally. I don't like it at all."

Her mouth trembled. So he still cared something for her. "I have hundreds, maybe thousands of fans who only wish me well, but this guy is something else."

A gust of wind came up and moved the plants on the terrace, causing Ally to lift her hands to her temples. "I thought I'd prefer to stay here rather than a hotel where I'd be recognised." She leapt to her feet. "Now I'm not so sure. I expect I'm feeling a bit more vulnerable after such an emotional day."

"Sit down again," Rafe said. "Let's face it, Ally, there's a decision to be made. You don't have to spend a single night feeling threatened. Not while I'm around. You mightn't be my Ally anymore but the Kinrosses and the Camerons go back a whole lot of years." Brod looked to him to oversee the running of Kimbara in his absence, the idea that his only sister was in any danger would upset him greatly.

"What I'm offering, Ally, is friendship allied to the age-old tradition of man as a protector. It's the way of the Outback." He tossed off the rest of his coffee, watching her slide back on the couch. "I think what I should do, what Brod would want me to do, is stay overnight. I can sleep on this sofa. Maybe shove the two of them together."

She didn't know what to say, a thousand sensations crystallising into a feeling of great warmth. She also remembered Rafe's tenderness. "Rafe, I don't want you to do that."

"The lady protesteth," he raised an eyebrow, "but I can see relief in those beautiful almond eyes. I don't want to hear any more about it. I'm staying. I won't tell anyone if you don't."

"I imagine it would upset Lainie for days on end." Her gaze flickered to his. Found it sardonic.

"I'm not sure what you're on about as regards Lainie, and I don't actually care. You're nervous about staying here and I don't blame you. I'd just like to run into this guy who's been giving you such a bad time. Are you sure it's not someone you know?"

The police had said the same thing. "You mean, someone I work with? One of the actors, one of the crew?"

"Take it easy," he soothed, watching her reaction. "Tell me the sort of things he writes. What he says on the phone."

"Rafe, you wouldn't want to hear it." She slid her heavy hair back from her face.

"So it's a sexual thing?"

"Of course." She glanced away, her high cheekbones stained with colour. "He claims he's in love with me. He can give me everything I need. He likes to say how he's going to do it. I crash the phone down. I've had three different ex-directory numbers but he always finds out. That's not easy to do."

"And the letters? There aren't any fingerprints?"

She shook her head. "The police have checked all that out."

"They're taking it seriously?"

"Yes, they are. One of the anchor women from another channel resigned because she was being harassed. I don't like the idea of some nut dictating my life."

"That figures. You've still got the letters?"

"The police have. They think it's someone who knows me, as well. He certainly knows what I'm wearing on any given day."

"And you've kept all this to yourself." He had a tight control over his voice.

"I'm trying to be brave, Rafe."

"Sounds more like you're being foolish. Brod and I could have solved this. You should have told him. You should have told at least one of us."

"I have," she reminded him. "With Brod there never seemed to be time. I didn't want to spoil anything for him or Rebecca. God knows Rebecca had her bad times with that first husband of hers. I didn't want to stir up any bad memories. I'm glad you're here," she finished on a gentle sigh.

"So am I," he answered, but his expression was grim. "But I have to tell you in Brod's absence I intend to take over his role. I think we should get some competent woman to come and stay with you until this thing is straightened out. I'm thinking of Janet Massie here." He referred to a long-time friend. "You've always liked her and Janet knows how to handle herself. She's been a lost soul since Mick died. Looking out for you will give her something positive to do. And the money would come in handy."

She kept her eyes down. "Rafe, Janet wouldn't want to come to Sydney. She's never left the bush."

"Try her. If you want her, Janet will come. Better yet, I'd like to see the guy to confront her. Janet has developed as much muscle as I have."

"I don't know." Yet she felt like going with his instincts. "My apartment isn't much bigger than this one. I'm used to living alone. So is Janet since she lost her husband."

"Let's talk this through," Rafe suggested. "Janet is a good bloke. She's got a great sense of humour. She won't get in your way. It's not forever. As soon as I can settle a few of my own affairs I'd like to conduct a little investigation of my own. The police have enough on their hands. They don't have the manpower."

"Let me think about it, Rafe," Ally pleaded, though she honestly couldn't think of anyone better than Janet to man the fort. Janet was a real character with the proverbial heart of gold. The sort of woman you could pour out your heart to. It would be comforting, too, not to have to come home to a dark empty apartment. At least while this was going on.

She had thought of confiding in Fee but decided against it. Fee being Fee couldn't help turning everything into a great drama. Fee would have told Brod. Francesca. Anyone who had ears. Fee sometimes could be positively unnerving. Francesca, on the other hand, who could always be relied upon to keep her head, lived on the other side of the world. She was just going to have to go along with Rafe's plan.

CHAPTER FOUR

IT WAS LUDICROUS to think Rafe at six foot three could pass a comfortable night on the couch.

"Why don't you take the bed?" Ally implored. "I don't mind in the least where I sleep."

"Why don't I simply move in with you," he said, his voice laced with heavy sarcasm. "Then you wouldn't be on your own in the dark."

"I don't think you're serious." Her heart rocked at the very thought. She couldn't suppress flashes of how it had been between the two of them. Turbulent bliss. Surely feeling like that could never be lost?

"No, I'm not," he told her bluntly, brushing her with his iridescent gaze. "You're not the woman in my life any more, Alison, my darling." Yet what woman could fascinate him so.

"So, then, who is?" Ally began to shake out the boronia-scented sheets with unnecessary vigour.

"Hey, lady, that's private." Masterfully he took the sheets off her, draping one over the sofa and leaving the other on a chair close by. "What I really ought to do is roll up like a hedgehog."

"I know." She stood there worrying. "You're much too big."

"I've slept in a whole lot worse places. I've actually perfected the art of falling asleep in the saddle. Now, push off," he said, his tone remarkably casual, considering her proximity was like some kind of purgatory to him. Ally was so good at this.

She had already taken off her beautiful rose pink bridesmaid gown, replacing it with a tightly sashed brocade robe with satin lapels that matched her eyes. Her polished olive skin glowed in the light. Her curly mane rained down her back and shoulders. Her beauty stunned him. No matter what she had done to him he would never tire of looking at her. He'd created this situation, now he was stuck with it.

"You have to fly home tomorrow," she added, as though it were an outrage to ask him to sleep on the couch.

"Ally, darling, be a good girl and go to bed," he told her, praying for patience. "You can leave the blanket."

"But what about pyjamas?" She continued to hover, wishing she could come up with something that might serve. But there was nothing in this feminine abode.

"Hell, girl, I don't sleep in pyjamas," he drawled. "If it's really cold I might get into a tracksuit. But it's not cold. It's balmy."

"So, what then?" she persisted, radiating concern. "It isn't all that warm at night. This is June. Officially Winter." He had taken off his slate blue jacket, the silver cravat, and unbuttoned a few buttons of his finely pleated white shirt. He looked so wonderful, so vigorous and full of life she was terrified she was going to make a fool of herself.

"Go, Ally." He pointed firmly to her bedroom door. "You've seen me naked. I've seen you naked. There's nowhere else for us to go. Anyway that was a long time ago. But don't panic. I intend to stick to my briefs."

"Right." She drew her robe closer around her, knowing she was outstaying her welcome, but longing for closer contact, the touch of his hands, his mouth, his skin. "Good night, Rafe, dear." She thought she might try to kiss him like a sister but she realised that would be impossible.

"Damn it, Ally, stop it!" he exploded. "And you can forget the dear. I don't think I can cope with it."

"So I've used up all my credit?" She looked at him with sadness in her gaze.

He straightened, staring across the small distance that separated them. The overhead light glanced off his taut, arresting face, accented his strong cheekbones, put a deeper groove in the cleft in his chin. "Can I be honest with you, Ally?"

"Of course." She held the satin lapels of her robe to her throat, starting to look apprehensive.

"You'll always be part of me. Part of my heart. But what I feel for you, what I felt for you, is like a great weight that's dragging me down. I have to get on with my life. I've virtually had no life since you took off and left me. A few affairs that never came off. I know sweet little Lainie imagines herself in love with me but I don't intend to break her girlish heart. I don't like hurting people."

She winced as though he'd hit the rawest nerve. "Are you saying *I* do?"

He looked as her with cool condemnation in his glittering eyes. "Yes, Ally, I am, but I forgive you. Forgive but not forget is my motto. I'm well on the way to being healed so don't just stand there flaunting your warm, sweet body in that gorgeous robe. Go to bed and sleep well. I'll be right outside your door like ghillie Brown with Queen Victoria."

She took a deep breath, trying not to feel deeply wounded. "All right, Rafe." She had some pride, after all. "I do appreciate your staying. I'll be up early in the morning. I'll make breakfast."

He shook his head. "Don't worry about me. Cup of tea and a bit of toast."

"Good night, then," she bid him quietly, turning to walk away.

Good night, Raphael. My golden angel.

Good night, Ally, my torment.

Hours passed. Hours Rafe dozed fitfully, unable to find a comfortable position, unable to fall off to sleep however much he willed it, unable to quiet the tumult in his body, the images of Ally that bloomed in his brain. Finally he pulled the blanket around him and sat in the armchair propping his feet on the footstool Ally had found in the study. God! he thought desperately, wishing his blood was as cool as the breeze that was coming in from the half open sliding-glass doors.

He never could sleep without lots of fresh air. He hated the times he had to stay in hotels. The confinement and that damned air-conditioning. Down the hallway Ally was sleeping the sleep of the innocent, he thought ironically. He could actually hear the quiet rhythm of her breathing. So she hadn't shut the bedroom door. An invitation? He wouldn't put it past her. He fancied he could hear her very heartbeat, causing him to jam his head between his hands to block it out.

Face the horrifying truth, mate. You're still in love with her and there's nothing you're going to be able to do about it. Except not show it. He hadn't survived all the pain to lay his heart wide open again. He would suffer a lifetime denial rather than let Ally treat him like a fool again. Not that she wouldn't like to try it. Tugging on his heartstrings was a part of her. Probably she'd never been totally happy unless she knew what they had would never be over. She had been truly glorious to make love to. His perfect woman. The goddess with feet of clay.

Lainie had given him the news Ally was considering a movie offer. Why not? She was a born actress. A natural. She'd look brilliant on the big screen. She had such a luminescent quality. What was to stop Ally if Hollywood beckoned? He knew she could slip into an authentic American accent. Sound as English as Francesca. Another part of her training. Accents.

He only wished to God this guy who was harassing her would appear on the terrace right now. After he finished with him it was unlikely he'd ever harass Ally again. From down the hallway came a little catch of a moan. She was having a bad dream.

He wondered if he should check. Decided not to as her breathing became quiet again. You have to overcome this, sport, he thought wryly, bring your mind to bear on getting to sleep. Mind control is what it's all about. But desire for Ally continued to saturate his blood.

It was late at night. She was in the underground car park, moving urgently towards her car. Arnold the security guard wasn't with her. The lights were too dim. She always thought that. There seemed to be a haze, as well. She thought she smelt cigarette smoke. Cigarette smoke made her ill. She turned her head, casting her eyes around swiftly with false bravado. She was nervous. As nervous as a cat with a Rottweiler in sight. One of the cast, an older woman, told her to always carry a small can of hair spray in her bag. If you couldn't get hold of the illegal mace, hair spray would have to do. Anything to give you a minute to get away.

She was conscious she hated all this. The fear. Why should women walk in fear? It wasn't fair. She could hear her breath whirring in her chest. Her car wasn't far away but she couldn't seem to close the distance. It was almost as though she was walking through water. She tried to increase her pace, approaching a pillar with a big black H on it. She almost passed it only to be confronted by a figure. A nightmare figure. It was wearing a balaclava, a black mask like a storm trooper. She could clearly see the eyes.

She tried to cry out but nothing passed her throat. She was struck dumb by fear. The man in the mask spoke. The voice was muffled by the balaclava over his head. Yet she knew it. It was the same voice that whispered obscenities to her on the phone. She made a move towards him. Hit out. A reflex action that turned into a furious swipe. If only she could claw the mask from his face. So near to him she thought she knew the odour of his sweat. She wasn't going down without a fight. He tried to backhand her but he couldn't seem to connect. She found her voice screaming for help. If she could only hold on someone would come to rescue her.

"You miserable swine! You bully! You coward!"

Now he held his hand over her mouth and she tried to bite it hard. Something was holding her like a winding rope. She kicked and fought, blind with fear and frustration. I have to live through this, she thought. I'm young. I have to find a way to make Rafe love me again. I have so much to live for. She could use her nails. They were long and sharp. Only the hands that were holding her were strong. Too strong for her. She could feel her wild thrashing slowing, slowing, like a woman undergoing sedation.

The nightmare face above her seemed to have disappeared....

She stopped fighting altogether. Sagged.

"Ally, Ally."

The terrible muffled whisper was gone, as well. The voice was deep, bracing, full of command. And, so blessedly familiar. Rafe.

The certain knowledge jolted her right out of it. She snapped open her eyes.

She was lying in a bed, trussed up like a mummy. Bedclothes. Rafe was staring down at her, his gold hair tousled, holding her firmly by the arms.

"For God's sake, Ally, snap out of it!" he urged. "You're making my blood run cold."

Full consciousness took hold of her clouded brain. She sat up, groaning. "I'm sorry. I'm sorry." She tried to push her own wild mop of hair away from her face. "I was having a nightmare."

"You can say that again!" His voice cracked with irony. "Hell, you were trying to bite me. I had to stop that screaming before the whole building cried rape."

"I'm sorry," she moaned again, kicking out in frustration at the bedclothes that had somehow tied her in a knot.

"Here, let me do that." Roughly he freed her, letting her tumble on her side. The room was white with moonlight. He could see her clearly. She was wearing a nightgown that had long clingy sleeves but the low oval neckline revealed the exquisite slopes of her breasts.

"Do you suppose someone is going to knock at the door?" She wasn't fooling, either.

"Hell, I'm surprised someone hasn't called for the police."

"As bad as that?" She made a supreme effort to pull herself together.

"It would have been if I hadn't muffled most of it. My God, Ally, what were you dreaming about?"

"My phantom stalker," she said bleakly, suddenly punching the pillow. "I was putting up a fight."

"Your bites are specially good. It's a wonder you didn't try to scratch my eyes out."

"I didn't hurt you, did I?" She rolled towards him, tried to grasp his hand. "Heck, you're cold."

Abruptly he withdrew his hand from her warm clasp. "I didn't have time to put on my nightie," he said with heavy sarcasm, his brain telling him to get out of here as quick as he could.

"You don't need to," she said huskily. There was something about a man's bare torso she thought, staring up at him. Broad in the shoulders, tapering to a narrow waist, his chest hazed with golden brown hair that ran in an arrow and disappeared into his dark briefs. Not an ounce of superfluous flesh on him. She was about to reach out and stroke him, but caught herself in the nick of time. "I suppose it was triggered by talking about him, the stalker," she explained.

"I guess so." Why the hell did she have to turn into the beam of moonlight, her body curved invitingly. An erotic vision.

"There was something about the figure in the dream," she confided with a tiny edge of hysteria, "but I've lost it." Her breath fluttered and the neckline of her nightgown moved down further, exposing her breasts as creamy as roses.

"Don't you dare try anything on," he warned her, a dark frown drawing his brows together.

She swung up in mock outrage. She wanted him so badly she was prepared to try anything. "I have no idea what you're talking about," she lied. "You know perfectly well…"

"What? What is it I know perfectly well?" he challenged her.

She surrendered all of a sudden, propelled by her mounting urgency. "I want you, Rafe," she said, her whole body quivering with nerves and desire. "Sometimes I wish I didn't, but I do. I want you to hold me close. I want you to come in beside me."

This nightmare of hers could be no more than trickery, he thought with sudden anger. She was a marvellous actress. "I see." His voice was harsh. "We make love until dawn, then you fly off to Sydney and your brilliant career. Lainie only told me tonight you've been offered some big part in a movie. You didn't tell me."

"I don't know how much I want it." She caught at his hand, held it, despite the fact his fingers had gone rigid as he steeled himself against her touch. "How can you be so cold to me," she implored, carrying his hand to her breast, holding it there so he could feel the chaos inside her. "I know I did something dreadful but can't you try to understand?"

He took his hand back deliberately, his voice heavy with scorn. "Ally, please, no more. I've spent years killing off my feeling for you. Roll over and go back to sleep, I'm not even tempted."

That, when desire was shafting through his body, so hot, so powerful it was agony. In truth he felt electric, out of control.

"I'd say you are a dreadful liar." She confounded him, shaking her head. "You're in as much pain as I am." Again she grasped his arm, arresting him.

She had beautiful hands. How he remembered the way she used them. Delicate long fingers, tantalising nails, hands that could stroke a man's body so sensuously, the yearning became unbearable.

Her magnificent mane of hair burst around her face, her emerald eyes glittered. Her silken rose-tipped breasts were revealed as she leaned towards him. There was even a teardrop shaped like a pearl clinging to her lashes.

So it remained. The wild love of their youth. How could he not be aware of the passion that had always been between them.

"I want you, Rafe." Her lips parted on a shaky breath.

"So what?" he asked with deep cynicism. "The pleasures of the flesh aren't lasting, Ally. You've always done what you want. Now you offer yourself to me because it just happens to suit."

She was beyond pride. The room was filled with his aura, his energy, his scent. "Rafe, stay with me."

"You're mad!" he said bitterly, while his heartbeat hammered right up to his throat. "Mad to ask this of me."

"I need you." It came out as a quick sob. She needed to tell him how much she loved him. How she had always loved him. Always would. She needed...

He was desperate to stop her entreaties. A grown man filled with furious frustrated desire for a woman. He pushed her almost roughly back onto the bed, for the moment forgetting his own strength so her head came into sharp contact with the mahogany bedhead.

"God, what am I doing?" He groaned, his voice full of self-disgust.

Ally, too, was a little shocked, but full of a jagged excitement. She started to rub the back of her head, though in truth the crack had been cushioned by her abundant hair.

"I never knew you were violent." She forced herself to breathe deeply, trying to quiet the flames that were leaping between them like a bonfire about to go out of control. "Rafe?" she whispered as he shoved the bedclothes aside.

"What part are you playing now?" he taunted her. "The innocent virgin? It doesn't suit you. I think you'd better stick with seductress. You know all about that."

She couldn't bear his contempt. "Listen to my heart," she begged him. "It beats for you."

"Ally, you're a bitch. You really are!" he breathed, his mind carried back to the number of times she had whispered those very same words to him...listen to my heart. It beats for you....

He moved then with breathtaking speed, going down on the bed, all six feet plus of him, radiating male energy and power and a dangerous frustration. While her heart did a crazy cart-wheel he took possession of her, pulling her into his arms, shaping her body so masterfully he had it perfectly moulded to his.

"Rafe!" Her face flushed as if from a raging fever even as she had an overwhelming sense of coming home.

"Ally. Damn you."

His mouth came down on hers with bruising strength. A punishment. Only to find her lips open and waiting as though she intended to steal the very soul out of him.

Ally. Unchanged. Ally, his obsession.

He flung his arm over her, imprisoning her as he lowered her back against the bed, realising as he was losing himself neither of them were breaking the long feverish kiss. It went on and on. Ally writhing beneath him, while his free hand, the hand that wasn't clutching her riotous hair, moving with power and urgency over her body.

I've thought about this one million times. Thought about it. Fought it.

Rafe moved his mouth blindly across her eyes, her nose, her cheeks. Her skin had the texture of satin. Now his hand closed over her delicate breast inciting the nipple. She moaned, the same little mewing sounds he remembered from before.

He had tried to despise her. A futile exercise.

"Don't hate me, don't hate me," she implored, still effortlessly reading his mind. Still making it so easy for him to caress her beautiful body. Women like her knew how to turn the tables. She was the victim now. He was the man with a heart of stone.

His body tensed, bringing hard muscles into play. Immediately she locked him with her long slender legs. Threw her arms around his neck. "Don't leave me, Rafe."

His heart thudding so loudly it might have been trying to break out from behind his ribs. "You're a witch," he accused her harshly. "A witch and worse."

"But you can't do without me." She stared into his eyes.

He wanted to hurt her as much as she had hurt him. "When it comes to sex, I guess we're perfectly matched." He bent his golden head, burying his face in the curve of her neck while she began to whisper strangely. Little incantations she once told him, Lala Guli, a powerful old aboriginal woman on Kimbara had taught her. The same incantations she had used years ago. Magic. Woman magic. In reality, potent.

The blood roared in his veins like a great tumult of water over a canyon. He lifted her in his strong arms. Hoisted her over him, held her while her hair, that incredible hair, fell, covering them both like a curtain. Then slowly, tortuously he lowered her against his intemperate body.

He was mad for her. Quite simply mad. One word said it.

Now, witch that she was, was kissing him all over his face. Little fluttery kisses like a butterfly dancing. Kisses that got right under his skin. Tiny traitorous kisses that he had to put a stop to.

He took hold of her head between his two hands, holding her, kissing her until he almost put a stop to her breath. In defiance of everything, his will and his pride. She was Ally. His one and only woman. His desire for her had grown ever more insatiable over time.

So long. So long.

The heat between them was sparking, running like a flame towards dynamite. Rafe drew a deep shuddering breath pushing her nightgown to her waist, lowering his head so he could kiss her swelling breasts, take the fragrant, tightly bunched berries right into his mouth. Too late now to curse himself for his human frailty. Yet he had never felt more powerful, more virile.

"My love, my love!"

Her frenzied little cry sent him totally off balance. She *knew* this had been inevitable. A kind of angry laugh broke from him even as he readied her body to receive him, realising as he entered her, her beautiful face was wet with tears.

Ally woke with a start and leapt to her feet, reaching for her discarded nightgown to cover her nakedness. Her body still bore the imprint of Rafe's, the male scent of him clung to her skin. She thought she remembered exactly how it was, the feeling that poured over them like a king tide, but nothing could match what happened between them last night. Her skin drenched with colour and her eyes blazed in her face. She would remember it all her life.

Afterwards she thought she could never sleep, her body still throbbed and pulsed, but Rafe had lain beside her so quiet, so profoundly thoughtful, she had turned her head into the pillow and, exhausted, had fallen into a deep dreamless sleep. Now she tied her mass of hair into a rough ponytail and hurried down the hallway. The apartment was very still, like there was no one there.

"Rafe?" she cried in earnest. Her normally melodious voice high-pitched with a residue of powerful emotion.

"I hear you."

He was out on the balcony, looking at the streams of traffic that moved over the Expressway spanning the river. Now as he walked back into the apartment looking not the least bit dishevelled but terribly dashing, his eyes moved over her, taking in the stained cheekbones, the brilliant eyes, the way the sunlight rayed through her nightgown, outlining her figure.

"Good morning, darling," he drawled, mockery in his eyes, his attitude, in the very twist of his mouth.

"You shouldn't have let me sleep in." All of a sudden she felt profoundly unbalanced.

"I was about to call you." He glanced casually at his watch. "You have plenty of time."

"I wanted to make your breakfast." Uncertainly she turned towards the galley.

"How charming!" His iridescent eyes glinted. "Actually I attended to myself. A quick shower. Tea and toast."

She'd heard nothing so deeply had she slept. "About last night..." she said in a faraway voice.

"Should be the title of a book, don't you think? A screenplay. A film starring the glorious, sexy, Ally Kinross. No wonder men worship you."

By this point she knew exactly where she stood. "Can't we talk about this, Rafe?" she begged.

"Darling, no. I must dash off. But I had fun."

"Fun? Is that what we had?" She looked at him questioningly, pain in her eyes.

"What do you want me to say, Ally? I'm about to shoot myself. Unrequited love?"

"I meant everything I said."

"How astonishing!" He lifted one golden brown eyebrow. "We didn't *talk* at all, though you had a particularly good time with all Lala's jargon."

"It's not jargon and you know it. It's ritualistic love magic."

He laughed, a discordant sound, but attractive. "Whatever the hell it is, it works. For a time." He checked his watch again, stretched with a graceful movement that put her in mind of some lithe big cat. "Ally, I adore you. Thank you for having me over. Now I intend to stay until it's time for you to leave for the airport. I'll ring the cab and put you in it myself. Then I have to beat it back to my own hotel, pick up my things and settle my account. The Piper is at Archerfield. I'll only be a little late for takeoff."

She turned her head away to hide her distress. "You don't *have* to wait for me." It was almost as though she had dreamed last night or had their lovemaking existed in another dimension?

"But I intend to." He had turned up his sleeves in an attempt to appear more casually dressed when he returned to his hotel. The finely pleated white shirt was obviously a dress shirt but open-necked, long sleeves tucked up, with the beautifully cut slate blue trousers, his gold hair perfectly groomed, he looked more like a movie star than a cattle baron. "You see, Ally," he trod softly past her and pinched her cheek, "I briefly considered treachery but discarded it. I'm taking this harassment problem of yours very seriously. I'm going to get on to Janet this very day and ask her to help us out. Something tells me she'll jump at the chance. I'll arrange for her to fly to Sydney, give her your address and ex-directory number. It might be an idea to write it all down and you can take it from there."

"You'll do this for me?" Her voice was grateful.

"I certainly will. I can hardly forget I once loved you dearly. Anyway you're a Kinross. My best friend's sister. Brod and Rebecca would be deeply disturbed if they knew what's been going on."

"You won't tell them?" she pressed him. "You won't let them know. Not while they're on their honeymoon."

He agreed with a faint niggle of worry. "You must let me act in Brod's stead. But I insist you go to Fee while you have the locks to your apartment changed. I think you should tell her. I expect her to be terribly concerned, but please tell her to leave it to me. Make her understand we don't want Brod and Rebecca caught up in it yet."

"I hate all this," she said. "The terrible unease. I can't get accustomed to it at all."

"It will soon be over," he promised, his expression turning grim. "I have some urgent business that will keep me on Opal for the best part of this week but I'd like to come to Sydney after that and look around for myself. Have a chat to the particular police officer in charge of your investigation. Maybe your bosses, your producer. Why don't you go off and have your shower while I make some coffee. I know you don't like tea."

She nodded. "I hate to drag you into this thing, Rafe. I know better than anybody how hard you work. All your responsibilities."

"Don't worry about it, Ally," he said. "I have the will and the energy and I'll feel a lot better when the whole matter is cleared up. In the meantime I want you to be very, very careful."

"Tell me about it!" A shadow of her luminous smile. "Did you know Fee will have Francesca and David staying with her?"

"Fee told me. So what? I haven't seen it but Brod said your aunt bought herself a great house right on the harbour."

This time Ally gave a genuine laugh. "It's really something. Much too big for one person but you know what Fee's like. She's used to splendour. The ex-countess and all. She has live-in help, a husband and wife, and she intends to entertain a lot. She's been approached by important people in the Arts to give of her enormous experience."

Rafe nodded. "I'm sure she'll enjoy it. A woman like Fee should never retire. I happen to know she adores you and she worships Brod, so take advantage of the situation. Your aunt will always be there for you. She's returning home today, isn't she?" he questioned with a slight frown. Maybe she wasn't.

"Afternoon flight," Ally confirmed. "Fee never can get up in the morning. I expect Fran will want to spend every moment with Grant."

His shapely mouth tightened. "Fran is a beautiful girl and she has all the charm in the world but I hope you're not promoting any romance. I know Fran's your cousin and you're very fond of one another, but an English rose won't transplant easily to the desert. Francesca is a titled young woman. An aristocrat from the other side of the world. Lady Francesca de Lyle. It suits her beautifully."

"Of course it does," Ally said with a return to her usual spirit, "but she has a Kinross for a mother. Her father doesn't have as much money as you might think. It's been Kinross money that's been allowing Fran to move easily through her privileged world and incidentally helping out the earl."

Rafe's brows shot up. "Well then, that's a surprise."

"It would be a surprise to a lot of people, I guess," Ally said simply, "including Fran."

"You mean, she doesn't know?" Rafe gave an incredulous laugh.

"I'm certain she doesn't," Ally said. "Fee didn't intend her to know. Perhaps Fee felt guilty about all the lost years and thought money wouldn't serve. Who knows. All I'm saying is, it's my family who have the money, Rafe. Not the earl. He has the stately pile but it has nearly sent him broke."

Rafe drew a whistling breath. "That's a pretty big secret. You think you can trust me with it?" He challenged her with his iridescent eyes.

"I'd trust you with my life," she said. It had the ring of perfect truth.

CHAPTER FIVE

FEE WAS IN wonderful form, enjoying herself enormously. Her mother was one of those women who could go on for hours and hours without ever losing her audience, Francesca thought, torn between love and a lifetime of regrets.

Lady Francesca de Lyle, the poor little rich girl, sent to live with her father after her parents divorced. "A marriage that had started to disintegrate from day one," her father always said. She had suffered and her father had suffered. Victims of Fee's relentless pursuit towards fame. With her many long years in the public eye, the luxurious lifestyle she had led, her fame as an actress, her two prominent marriages, one to a reserved English aristocrat, her father, the other to a handsome, flamboyant vagabond of an American film star who had cast his spell over millions of women around the world, it was only to be expected Fee had many a riveting story to tell. Not only that, she kept changing voices for all the various people she portrayed.

"Such a marvellous raconteur," David murmured, his elegant face full of admiration. "The most beguiling woman I've ever met."

Francesca gave a little wry smile. "Some piece of work," was the way her father phrased it. She tried to push to the back of her mind the sad lonely years when there had been far too many things going on in her mother's brilliant career for her to pay attention to a small daughter. Still I love her dearly, Francesca thought, seeing, as a woman, how her mother and father had been almost totally incompatible.

"Living with your father was like living without conversation," Fee once told her. "The most exciting communication was how the home farms were doing, or how much it was going to cost to fix a section of the blessed roof. Some part of it was always caving in. Decent man that he is, one could scarcely call your father profound." But for a long while he had been kept captive.

Dinner over, Fee got them all moving to the living room for coffee and liqueurs. Fee loved people. Obviously what she couldn't suffer was silence. How very different we are! Francesca realised it more and more with every day. An only child, she had been thrown back on herself for entertainment, relying heavily on her love of reading and roaming her father's beautiful estate.

Like all the de Lyles she was a born country woman. And her love for the land didn't stop at England's green fields. She found her mother's ancestral home, Kimbara, the most thrilling place on earth. The sheer immensity of it, the frightening isolation, the savage beauty and most of all the colourations of the extraordinary landscape, the hot pinks and yellows, the fiery brick reds and the white and black ochres that contrasted sharply with the blazing blue sky. She loved the burnt umber of the great plains, the mile after mile of parallel sand hills breaking to the horizon in a blue sea of mirage.

She'd been ten years old when her mother had first brought her to Australia. "Home" to the great homestead where Fee had been born. A homestead which, far from appearing insignificant in comparison with her father's magnificent Ormond Hall, had a quite extraordinary impact of its own. When she really thought about it, Kimbara stood alone as another fascinating planet might stand alone. All she knew was she loved it. She could even settle there.

An English rose in the desert? She heard Grant Cameron's deep drawling tones.

Hadn't he forgotten this great country of theirs was opened up by settlers from the British Isles? There had been plenty of English roses, Scottish roses, Irish roses, you name them, all mentioned in their history books. Strong, fearless women who had imposed their own kind of civilisation on the Timeless Land. The Kinrosses and the Camerons had their origins in Scotland. There had been powerful women figures in the family. She must remind Grant of that, whenever she saw him again. God, she had really complicated her life allowing herself to fall in love with a man from the Outback.

"Come on, my darlings!" Fee came up, arms outflung. She swept them from the entrance hall into the luxuriously appointed living room, dominated by a wonderful portrait of her at the height of her beauty and fame. It hung in splendour above the Italianate fireplace, a focus for all eyes.

"*Absolutely dazzling,* David thought. The artist had caught her very essence. Passionate, histrionic, wilful, possessed of a boundless inner energy that had driven her brilliant acting career. She was dressed in an exquisite haute couture ball gown of emerald silk, posing on a small gilt and embroidered silk settee that was part of a suite in his brother's Gold Drawing Room. The pose was pure Singer Sargent, Fee leaning forward slightly to display the beautiful curves of her shoulders and bosom. Not a man to take a great deal of notice of women's fashions, David remembered that gown well.

Francesca had not inherited her features or Fee's flamboyant nature. She was a de Lyle. The one who most resembled Fiona Kinross, the star, was her niece, Alison. Both of them had that flamelike quality, a combination of strength and a strange, touching, vulnerability. Alison, too, was making her mark, Fee had told them at dinner, while her niece tried to stop her. Alison had been offered the female lead in an exciting new film. A thriller. David supposed if the film took off Alison would go to America and perhaps never come back. The Kinross women seemed to choose a career before marriage.

Suddenly he felt enormously grateful Fee had retired, although people were always offering her jobs. At the end of the year her biography written by Brod's clever wife, Rebecca, would come out. How far would it go? Whatever her faults Fee wasn't the woman to want to deliberately hurt anyone. He thought of de Lyle, now quietly but contentedly married. How had Fee and his cousin ever got together? They couldn't have been more different. It wasn't as though Fee had been looking for a step up the social ladder. She was a princess in her own country and, let's face it, Fee had brought to her marriage a magnificent dowry. Fee the golden girl with the Midas touch. David suddenly realised he couldn't bear to let her go out of his life. In his mind she was like a ray of glorious sunshine and he so loved the Australian sun.

Ally waited until long after their guests had departed and Francesca and David had said their good-nights. Fee, the habitual night owl, was still as bright as a button, sitting on a sofa, talking over the events of the evening.

"I had mixed feelings about asking Miles and Sophie but it turned out rather well, don't you think?" she asked rather slyly.

"Yes," Ally agreed with a degree of amazement. "Not everyone asks along a ménage à trois, present husband, ex-husband."

Fee laughed. "Honestly why Miles and Sophie broke up, I'll never know. They were a team!"

"Fee, I have something to tell you," Ally interrupted before Fee had a chance to summon up an anecdote about her theatrical friends.

"Darling," Fee patted the sofa beside her, "come here. Of course you can tell me anything you like. There's something on your mind. I've been trying to get it out of you since you arrived."

"It's not about Rafe," Ally answered wryly. She sat down beside her aunt, taking Fee's elegant beringed hand with its knockout brilliant cut seven carat solitaire diamond, a love token from her second husband. "Is this darn thing insured?" Ally rearranged the ring a bit.

Fee shook her head. "I can't keep up with the premium."

"Fee, you're a very rich woman." Ally looked her in the eyes.

"That's because I don't give my money away."

"That's news to me." Ally pecked her affectionately on the cheek.

"Darling, I know what you're getting at, but that's a family secret. De Lyle hated taking my money but I insisted. Francesca had to have the best of everything."

"She only wanted her mum."

"I know." Fee nestled closer to her niece for comfort. "Don't remind me of the egocentric woman I was. Tell me your little problem. Not Rafe, of course. He's a big problem."

"I'm being harassed, Fee," Ally said bluntly.

Fee looked around so nervously an armed intruder might have found their way through the open French door. "My darling girl. This is terrible." Her voice rang with concern. "One can get a maximum of fifteen years for stalking. Have you spoken to the police? You absolutely must."

"If you promise to sit quietly, I'll tell you," Ally said. Fee had a tendency to turn everything into a play starring herself. Ally had seen it before. It didn't take that long to tell her everything with Fee turned to face her full-on, obviously wanting the dialogue to be two-way but holding off valiantly until Ally had finished.

"My darling, don't think I don't know what you're going through!" Fee exclaimed, pushing a silk cushion out of the way. "There was a time, I'd rather not think of it now, it was pretty scary, that wretched person…" Fee broke off, managing to steer herself back on track. "But we can't *not* let Brod know!"

"Hang on, Fee. I have your promise," Ally reminded her.

Fee shuffled her pretty feet in her beautiful Italian evening sandals. "I never realised what you were about to tell me. This is a terrible thing for a young woman to have to endure. Any woman. No wonder you nipped around to my place. You must stay here. Never leave the house. I can arrange everything. Bodyguards, security people."

Ally placed her hand over her aunt's. "Fee, dearest, I'm going back to the apartment after work tomorrow. I know you want to entertain Fran and David. I've heard about all the outings you've lined up. Fran only has a couple more days before she goes home. I don't want you to worry her with this business."

Fee sat back and gave a deep sigh. "Darling, she loves you. She would want to know."

"She can't *do* anything, Fee and I don't want to spoil her stay with anything unpleasant. David, either. He's looking so much better than the last time I saw him."

"I married the wrong cousin." Fee made a wry face.

"That's okay. David was married himself at the time."

Fee thought hard for a moment. "I suppose he was. He's so fond of me. That's the final irony. His mother, God rest her soul, always treated me like a stampeding rhino let loose in the castle. So you're going to leave this all up to Rafe?"

Ally nodded. "Janet Massie will be with me tomorrow night."

"What help would another woman be, darling?" Fee asked doubtfully.

"You haven't seen Janet." Ally smiled. "She's a great character, she's built like a barrel. She ran a cattle station single-handedly after her husband died. You'd have to stomp over Janet to get to me and by then you'd probably be bleeding to death."

Fee was impressed. "So this Janet is going to be your shadow until Rafe arrives?"

"Something like that." Ally nodded.

"If you ask me, the man is still madly in love with you." Fee the expert in such matters sounded utterly convinced.

"Even if that were true, I've convinced him totally I'm not marriage material. He needs someone he's certain is always going to be there."

"Not the little Mary Poppins character, Lainie Rhodes?" Fee gasped. "Why, darling, she fades into insignificance beside you. Though I have to say she's very much more attractive than she used to be but she still puts me in mind of an exctitable…"

"Puppy." Ally uttered a low groan. "Rafe used to say exactly the same thing."

"Darling, I think I need a drink to soothe my nerves." Fee went into a sort of foetal crouch.

"Not if you don't want to wake up with a hangover?" Ally was unmoved. "You know you're off to the Blue Mountains in the morning."

"Forget the Blue Mountains!" Fee swung upright, her rich resonant voice booming with outrage. "I can't possibly go away and leave you."

"Well, good for you," Ally responded, patting her aunt's hand. "But, Fee, it isn't as though this person has ever shown his face. He gets his kicks out of sick letters and obscene phone calls. I'd be really worried if he decided to send around six dozen pizzas. No, you go, Fee. Rafe thought you should know."

"Of course I should know!" Fee flared. "With your father dead, I'm head of the family. Nothing wrong with a bit of tradition."

"Rafe also thought we should keep this strictly between us," Ally added meaningfully.

"All right." Fee gave in with reluctance. "But I'll have Berty," she referred to the husband in her Dynamic Duo team, "drive you right to the door of the studio. I could never ever forgive myself if something happened to you."

It came out with such incredible drama, Ally leaned over to kiss her aunt resoundingly.

"Nothing is going to happen to me, old girl."

Fee laughed. "My darling, you'll be an old girl in time."

"I very much hope so." Ally felt a little prickle of fear run down her spine. "Janet will be there to keep an eye on me and the apartment and Rafe wants to do a little investigation of his own. He'll be here in a few days."

"Thank God for the Camerons!" Fee breathed. "Crossing either of them would be like crossing Crocodile Dundee. You do know our ancestor, Cecilia Kinross, loved Charlie Cameron not Ewan Kinross the man she married."

"Perhaps they were all under the weather," Ally suggested. "The Scots love a wee drop of Highland malt."

"That they do," Fee agreed fervently. "You're a really good actress, my darling. For what it's worth, fractionally better than I was at your age, but I can't help thinking you missed a glorious opportunity when you let Rafe Cameron slip through your fingers. My best advice to you, based on wide experience, is, go to bed with him. Nothing like bed to cement a relationship. I have my darling daughter to prove it."

When she slept it was to dream. Fragmentary dreams tumbling one on the other born of the late-night conversation with Fee about the stalker. She was always in some dark place waiting for him to come for her, helpless, at the end of her resources, waking herself up moaning only to fall back into the same dream. She would have emerged wild-eyed, only towards dawn her dream turned to the remembered rapture of earlier years when she and Rafe were inseparable. When Rafe's mother and father had been alive, welcoming her to Opal like her second home. Home really. She had never tasted happiness at Kimbara since her mother had left vowing to gain custody of her and Brod in time but facing an enormous uphill battle against their father's power and influence. They had never seen their mother again, heartbroken children with a father who was a commanding near stranger.

For all of her childhood and adolescence Brod and Rafe had been her heroes. Every time she hugged one, kissed one, she hugged and kissed the other. She adored both of them from infancy. Her brother and her brother's best friend, Rafe Cameron. Five years separated her from her heroes, consequently she had happily taken over the role of little sister. Until, as such things happen, she and Rafe had fallen in love. Then the whole landscape changed and the sweetness of affection, the unshakeable childhood bond became a love so overwhelming it became too much for a young girl's heart to hold. Not that Rafe had ever made her miserable demanding more than she could give him. Even as a boy Rafe could have written the book on self-control. Rafe was very honourable indeed and she had the powerful security of knowing she mattered deeply to him. Rafe, her perfect knight. But they were passionately in love.

Behind her closed lids, half-waking dream sequences stole into her mind...the summerhouse her grandfather had built on the banks of the creek that meandered through Kimbara's home gardens. It was there Rafe had kissed her for the first time as a woman, not a little girl....

There was a party on at the homestead. Past midnight it was in full spate. Her father was entertaining some visiting Asian prince who had taken a fancy to playing polo and bought several of Kimbara's excellent polo ponies. She could see all the lights blazing through the house flowing out onto the gardens. She could hear the music and the laughter, drown in the heady sweetness of jasmine that smothered the white lattice walls of the summerhouse. The night was marvellous with a huge copper moon that spread its radiance all over the desert landscape.

She was sixteen and the tiniest little bit tipsy. Rafe had gone off to get her a cold drink but she had sneaked a glass of fine champagne from one of the waiter's trays, quaffing it quickly, loving the taste and the bubbles, the way they filled her mouth, then the sensation of stars exploding inside her.

"Hey, Ally!" Rafe came back and saw her with the champagne flute, his expression very much big brother.

"Don't be a spoilsport!" she laughed, loving the sparkle that had settled on her. Loving him. She was moving onto the terrace intent on the night, running across the lawn, full of her first intoxication, with responsible Rafe in pursuit. She was breathless by the time she reached the summerhouse, feeling pure joy she had managed to beat him. Him with his long legs and superb male athleticism. Still laughing she held on to a white pillar for support, fragrance in her nose, jasmine flowers catching in the long cloud of her hair. She was wearing a green silk taffeta dress to match her eyes, a new dress, a beautiful grown-up dress, a present from Aunt Fee who lived halfway across the world but never forgot her.

Rafe laughed, too. A lovely indulgent laugh that would be forever in her ears.

"Just look at you," he teased.

"What do you see?" In an instant she was sober, taken over by some unstoppable emotion, an intensity of awareness, suddenly years older. Different.

"I see a sixteen-year-old with the giggles," he said in the same teasing ways but something didn't fit. An edge.

"I only had one glass!" She made an effort to defend herself.

"I know, but you're not having another," he clipped off, already twenty-one and a man. "Time to go back now, Ally. We can't leave the party."

"Why not?" She was full of mischief, a sense of a woman's power. "Who's going to miss us?"

"I'd hate to see you get into trouble," Rafe, long used to Stewart Kinross's severe ways, retorted. "You know what your father is like."

"Perfectly." Suddenly tears pricked behind her eyes. "Loving me and showing me off are two different things. I'm just a possession in my father's world, Rafe. You know that. God help me if I were plain or stupid."

Rafe sighed in tacit agreement, holding out his hand. "Let's go back, Ally." He sounded kind and tender but her blood was fired.

"I absolutely refuse to. And you can't make me." She lifted her face to him with the old childhood dare.

A curl of a smile touched his mouth. "Oh, yes, I can, Ally Kinross. I can pick you up and carry you anywhere. Anytime."

"Dear, darling, Rafe, why don't you do it?" she challenged, seeing the sudden glitter in his eyes, overjoyed he was responding despite himself.

"I'm joking, Ally," he said sternly just to prove it. "Don't make it hard for me."

"Come on Rafe, it's Ally," she said. "Nobody looks after me better than you do." Something sweeter than the jasmine, more powerful than the moonlight surged through her veins. She moved towards him in total silence. Walked right into his arms.

"I love you, Rafe," she said with exquisite pleasure. Words of endearment she had used all her life but never with the unmistakable depths of a woman.

"Ally!" He turned away his splendid head with its thatch of golden hair, but not before she saw torment hone his features.

"I love you," she repeated, never quite completing the word as he acted like lightning sweeping her into his arms in the most wonderful way imaginable, masterful, romantic, all she had ever dreamed of, his beautiful mouth swooping down to cover hers, warmly, deeply, searchingly, raging with desire. It was simply...a revelation. Heaven.

Afterwards neither of them spoke as though each recognised nothing would be the same between them again. She wasn't his "little chick" any longer. His responsibility. The chick had found wings....

Ally came completely awake, still savouring Rafe's phantom kiss on her mouth. She fancied she even had the scent of him on her skin, the marvellous maleness. She was as needy of him now as she had been then, but in seeking to distance herself from him to gain some perspective on what was happening in their unique relationship she had only succeeded in distancing herself from him completely. If only she'd had a mother to advise her, to sort her out, to help her get a handle on her tumultuous emotions. She realised now Rafe had kept a tight control on his own desire, but then Rafe was five years older, heir to a great historic station and well used to handling responsibility from boyhood. On that score alone they'd been helplessly mismatched.

It was after Rafe's parents had been killed so tragically they had consummated their love. Rafe trying to bury his grief in the rapture her body gave him. She had been awesomely good at offering him forgetfulness, aching for him, aching for lost relationships, the fine man and woman who had fostered her and shown her so much affection. Maybe if Sarah Cameron had lived Ally would have been Rafe's wife today but she'd had no mother figure to call on then and she, too, was missing Rafe's parents terribly.

Is it any wonder she made so many youthful mistakes.

Ally was up early to see the family off. She knew they planned to spend the day in the beautiful Blue Mountains less than an hour's drive from Sydney. The whole area covering some five hundred square miles was famous for its tourist attractions, taking its name from the early settlers because of the marvellous bluish haze that hung over the mountains. Though it looked magical the haze was caused by fine drops of eucalyptus oil in the atmosphere, the heavily wooded slopes being covered with eucalypt trees. Fee had a great friend who lived in the beautiful township of Leura with a very grand garden, so that was an additional attraction.

Ally had just started breakfast prepared by Polly, the female half of the Dynamic Duo—Ally suspected quite correctly Berty and Polly weren't their real names at all, but some invention of

Fee's—when Francesca entered the morning room, her lovely serene face lit up with a smile.

"You know Mamma had this room decorated to look almost exactly like our trellised orangerie at Ormond."

"Sweetheart, I know that," Ally said, tipping back her head to look at the fabric-tented ceiling. "What a pity you're not going to inherit the stately pile."

"It's a pile, all right." Francesca bent down to kiss her cousin's cheek, then took a wheelback chair opposite her. "I don't know how it hasn't sent poor Papa broke. It passes to my cousin, Edward, you know, unless I produce a male heir. I don't mind, really. I don't need that kind of inheritance. The upkeep is killing and it's dreadfully cold. I'll settle for Mamma's view of Sydney Harbour." She looked out the open French doors to the balustraded terrace and beyond that the dazzling blue waters of arguably the most beautiful harbour in the world. "Oh, I wish I could stay!"

"So do I!" Ally looked back. "We'd make a wonderful team, we could go everywhere together. It would be such a pleasure to have you."

"I can see it, too, but I have my P.R. job waiting for me back in London."

"Surely you don't have to go back to resign?" Ally poured her cousin a cup of coffee. "You could easily find something here. That patrician face. That patrician voice. Lady Francesca de Lyle ain't bad, either," Ally joked. "Besides, I know you want to stay."

"*That* obvious, is it?"

"It's a woman thing, love. We always know. Actually, I've been working on a plan."

Francesca gave her cousin a speaking glance. "Trouble is, I don't think Grant would ever buy it."

"Why do you say that?" Ally pretended to be shocked. "You don't know the plan yet."

Francesca put out a hand to cover Ally's. "I love it the way you're always thinking of me, but Grant knows how his brother suffered after you left. He's vowed never to make the same mistake."

Ally glanced away, nibbling at her lip. "I was the one who made the mistake, Fran."

"So why don't you tell Rafe that?" Francesca urged.

Ally shook her dark head. "I made a fool of him so he can't and won't forgive me. You don't know those Camerons. They're far too proud."

"Maybe that's just a front?" Francesca asked hopefully. "I know I could get Grant to fall in love with me."

"Sweetheart, as it happens, any man could fall in love with you," Ally said laconically. "I'm certain Grant recognises you for the lovely young woman you are but as a realist he sees you were born into a world infinitely different from an isolated Outback cattle station. Maybe he thinks you couldn't survive in such an environment. Come to think of it, it is a big ask."

"But, Ally, I'm an outdoorsy girl," Francesca said firmly, but not loudly. Polly was due with her breakfast.

Ally rolled her eyes. "Darling, roaming your father's green fields and rolling hills, is a far cry from losing yourself in a killer wilderness. And it is a killer, Fran. Make no mistake. There have been plenty of fatalities to prove it from the early explorers to overseas adventurers who think they can conquer the Wild Heart."

"*You* love it," Francesca maintained. "You grew up on Kimbara. I fell in love with it at age ten. I'm a Kinross, too. On my mother's side."

"Sure you are!" Ally saluted her with her coffee cup. "So what you have to do is change Grant's perception you're not a terribly suitable candidate for Outback wife. It's up to you to make it all happen."

"Ditto!" Francesca smiled.

CHAPTER SIX

JANET MASSIE ARRIVED that same day and immediately slotted in. Though there were thirty years and more between them she and Ally fell into an easy rapport. Both were Outback women, after all.

"You leave it to me, love," Janet told Ally firmly, "no one will go bothering you with me around. What's the world comin' to? It's not manly to harass a young woman. It's a coward's role. Rafe is worried about you. Remember how he solved who was heading up that cattle duffing gang in '96? With a bit o' luck he'll be catching this fella who's been bothering you. Right bastard he is, love, pardon my French. Just let him try and hide from Rafe."

The thing was he'd been doing a very successful job of it, Ally thought.

The next morning when Janet went to collect Ally's mail her attention was directed to a long yellow office-style envelope on which someone had printed Ally's name and address. It wasn't neat. It stuck out jaggedly like a threat. Janet badly wanted to open it and read what it said herself. She couldn't stand the idea of Miss Alison of Kimbara Station, a real lady, being in this kind of trouble. It must be a dreadful strain, but it wasn't her place to rifle through Ally's mail no matter what it was.

Mercifully, Rafe was flying in midafternoon. He would know what to do. Rafe for all his gentlemanly ways was as tough as tempered steel.

'How many more takes before we finish?" Ally asked the show's director, Bart Morcombe, testily and she wasn't testy often. "Why can't Matt ever get his lines off?"

"Because his tiny brain keeps getting in the way?" Zoe Bates who played the affable wife of the local pub owner in the series, suggested.

Morcombe, looking decidedly frazzled around the edges, tried to soothe his star. It was most unusual for Ally to get this uptight, but then she had a lot on her mind lately. They all had with Ally being harassed. It affected every single one of them. Except Matt Harper who had grown up in a very tough neighbourhood and was very nearly punk. "The thing is he's not as professional as you, Ally, and he doesn't have your photographic memory."

"He's an imbecile, that's why," Zoe, who had a pounding headache, cut in. "It's all that coffee."

Morcombe looked at her thoughtfully, scratching his head. "I thought coffee was good for you? Isn't that what they're telling us these days. Anyway it doesn't help much griping, Zoe. We have to keep telling ourselves Matt has gone over big with the viewing public. Our ratings are sky-high. Ally and Matt generate sparks on the small screen."

"'Struth, I thought he was gay!" Zoe snorted beneath her breath, though there was no evidence to support her supposition. Most people in the business tossed the idea around because Matt Harper, an extremely good-looking young man rarely had a girlfriend in tow. His dangerous wrong-side-of-the-tracks looks had won him a lead role in Ally's series. He'd had no training whatsoever, nevertheless he had a definite brooding presence on screen that translated into fireworks.

Without really liking him Ally had tried to help him in all

sorts of ways for which he always appeared grateful in his highly defensive fashion, but sometimes, like today, she felt like jamming the script down his throat. Bart was too soft on Matt when he was known to be pretty scathing with lesser lights when it came to getting things right.

It was nearly five o'clock in the afternoon and they'd been hard at it since their 6:00 a.m. call.

Matt eventually sauntered back from his dressing room and gave them all a what-the-hell-are-you-looking-at-me-for look.

"What's taken you so long?" Bart surprised them all by barking.

"I've been teasing my hair." Matt had insolence down to an art form.

Ally exhaled sharply. "Do you think we can wind up this scene, Matt? I'm really tired."

"Sure, princess." He gave her a smile that displayed perfect teeth courtesy of the studio. "Don't have a nervous breakdown. If you all just relax I might be able to remember my lines."

"*Please* do, Matt," Ally pleaded.

He looked down at her, not tall but looking very strong. "I love it when you beg."

The scene called for Matt, the town's angry young man, to come into Ally's surgery, aggressive and slightly drunk.

Matt did it in a single take.

They were just wrapping the episode up when Bart's senior assistant, Sue Rogers, came rushing in like a small tornado. "God, the most exciting man I've ever seen in my life is outside talking to the boss. I tell you he's better than Redford in his prime."

"Oh, I don't think so." Zoe gave a languid wave. "I see you're not wearing your glasses. No one but no one looks like Redford."

"Just see how you react!" Sue sounded faintly hysterical. "He's big and tall and lean and he's got hair a woman would spend a fortune on. I tell ya it's pure gold!"

"Could be a hallucination," Zoe suggested, getting her gear together. "It's been a rough day."

Ally was the only one who knew exactly who it was. It had to be, from that description. Rafe. He'd finally arrived but she never thought he would come to the studio to collect her. Now he was here and her heart rose in her breast like a bird taking flight. She was desperate to see him.

"It'll be a friend of mine," she told them, smiling in Sue's direction. "Rafe Cameron."

"Lordy, lordy, I think I'm going to faint." Sue pretended to stagger. "This is *the* Cameron, the cattle baron?"

"One and the same."

"There!" Sue rounded on Zoe. "What did I tell you? I knew he was someone special. The walk! Boy, oh, boy, stand tall. The scent of the great outdoors! The cattle baron comes over loud and clear."

"I'd like to meet him." Bart sounded fascinated.

"Thank you very much but I'm on my way." Matt spoke rudely, staring hard at Ally. "From the look on your face you really fancy him?"

"Rafe is a sort of a big brother." Ally deftly hid her annoyance. It was none of Matt's business. "With my own brother away on his honeymoon, Rafe wants to look into this harassment business."

"You don't think the cops are doing enough?" Matt couldn't keep the snarl out of his voice. "They gave me a bad enough time."

"A good thing you can't *write*." Zoe's voice was flat and unkind. Matt Harper brought out the worst in her but even she didn't see Matt as Ally's tormentor.

"What is that supposed to mean?" Matt marched right up to her, his black eyes on fire.

"Nothing, Matt, just a silly comment." Ally checked him by putting her hand on his arm and clutching it hard. "It's OK, OK."

"I take it back," said Zoe with a little shudder.

Matt seemed to quieten, looking down at Ally's elegant, long-fingered hand on his arm. "You're a real lady, Ally, you know that. The *only* one I ever met in my life."

"Didn't you say you were going, Matt?" Bart asked, not wanting any trouble. He tried to take it easy with Matt, damned near raised as a street kid, but he was an arrogant little bastard and he had a mean temper.

That wasn't about to happen. Before Matt could make a move, Rafe walked onto the set accompanied by the boss of the station, Guy Reynolds, a top executive with the national channel.

"Now I know what you mean about the golden boy aura?" Immediately Zoe turned to whisper to Sue. She was highly impressed but Matt's face took on an extra hard edge.

"God, the cattle baron born with a sterling silver spoon in his mouth," he said with amused contempt. "I bet he's got a handshake that could crack coconuts."

Ally shrugged lightly. "Why don't you stick around and find out?"

They all focused on Rafe Cameron as he approached. A full head taller than Reynolds, he was dressed casually in beige trousers, an open-necked shirt and a classic blazer, but his height, his walk, the perfectly coordinated body, the tanned golden skin and the mane of shimmering gold hair, lent him a powerful drawing power. All of a sudden the familiar set seemed to teem with light.

Up close they saw the authority, the *real* authority, the high intelligence in the iridescent eyes, the way little sun crinkles radiated out from their corners, etched in white. A cattle baron if ever there was one.

They could all see how he would look astride a horse, a bandanna around his neck, a rakish akubra pulled down over his eyes. It took all of them a few moments more to realise they were staring. Even Ally who had loved him all her life couldn't take her eyes off him.

Matt didn't get a chance to leave. Introductions were made

all round. Rafe was as charming as ever, so charming the cast and crew appeared to be exulting in his presence and his easy, friendly ways. Even Matt smothered his aggressions opening up unexpectedly to the sheer manliness of their visitor, the commanding aura that made for respect.

All frustration with the long day seemed to fall away. Though it was easy to see Rafe Cameron could, if the occasion demanded it, be extremely formidable, a man to be reckoned with, if he liked and approved of you, if you did nothing to harm Alison Kinross, he couldn't be nicer. Even when he put out his hand to shake Matt's, Matt hadn't shied away from it, rather he look flattered.

Twenty minutes later Rafe and Ally were out on the road joining the peak traffic, Ally driving her small BMW.

"So what did you really make of my work mates?" She flashed him a glance, the golden carved profile.

"Pleasant people for the most part," he observed. "But you never can tell."

Ally surrendered to a deep sigh. "The police questioned everyone, as you know. They spent most of their time questioning poor Matt. I believe there's a little file on him downtown. Nothing terribly serious. Years ago when he was a kid, but it all sticks."

"I'd say the guy's had a hard life." Rafe knew all about hardships. "He's like a wound-up coil."

"A terrible life!" Ally confirmed. "In and out of homes. I don't know that I like him. I try, but he makes it difficult for all of us. I have to make allowances."

"What he wants is to start caring about himself before he can start caring about anyone else," Rafe said. "He probably has a poor self-image. I damned near felt like offering him a job. That usually straightens these troubled young guys up. I've seen really bitter kids nobody cared about turn into different individuals when they're given a bit of responsibility."

Ally knew Opal Downs worked in with a welfare program

for troubled youth. Rafe had taken it on board after he was approached. Her father had refused point blank.

"The land works its magic," Rafe said. "Being around horses. I don't think Harper's at home with the acting business."

"Just a way to make money," Ally said. Matt had told her that a thousand times. "The strange thing is, he has a decided screen presence. The talk is, believe it or not, people love to talk, Matt's gay."

Rafe gave her a very straight look. "No, he's not, Ally. No matter the rumours, or how they got started. I'm quite sure he fancies himself in love with you."

The traffic was too heavy for Ally to take time off to stare at him. "Wha-a-t?" she cried. "Matt hasn't looked sideways at me, Rafe. Not ever. We play a part. It's called acting."

"Obviously the camera sees what *you* don't," he said crisply.

"I don't believe this." Ally shook her head. "Matt has no girlfriend…"

"Maybe he's focused on *you*." Rafe, who had gone to the studio deliberately to size up the people Ally worked with, began to speak his thoughts aloud. "Let's think about this. Maybe he's allowing the rumours to circulate. Maybe it suits him. Protective cover. Maybe he doesn't know what to do with his passion. You're Ally Kinross. You have a *name*. A privileged background. You're a heroine to him in a way, but he's afraid of you. And how does he overcome his fear? His shame in his own background? He harasses you."

Ally's hand gripped the wheel in rejection of Rafe's theory. "It's not true, Rafe. We've worked together for quite a while. Heck, he's right under my nose. He had to endure being spoken to by the police for nearly half a day."

"Do you think the police don't know what they're about?" he countered. "The last person you suspect might be all right for the late night movie, but most crimes against women are committed by men close to them. Ex-husbands, ex-lovers, jealous boyfriends, men they come into contact with in the workplace.

Men who become obsessed with them. Unfortunately for him Harper does have a police file. We all regret the fact he had to grow up in a violent environment but Harper could have a demon in him and don't you forget it."

He timed his departure, waiting until they pulled out of the car park. The woman was driving. That struck him as funny. The big cattle baron actually allowing a woman to *drive!* Something he never did. Women had no feel for machinery, no road sense. They were rotten drivers. Men were the masters of the world.

Except, for a woman, Ally Kinross was special. Rich, well-born, sexy and very beautiful. He'd give anything if only she would look his way, but that wasn't going to happen. Not with guys like the millionaire boyfriend around. How did these people get to have so much money, anyway? So much power. He had none and his breeding was questionable, as well. Hadn't his slatternly mother taken the trouble to tell him early. "You're not Danny's kid." He hadn't understood then but he did by the time he was seven and already into petty crime. Anyway, Danny's real brood wasn't handsome. Being handsome had earned him good money. Some silly bitch had stopped him in a shopping centre one day and asked him if he'd like to get into model-ling, maybe even a TV show. It was unbelievable the way she made it all sound.

"Sign up and leave it to me!"

He had. His looks had even been improved especially since they got his teeth fixed. The perfect white flashing smile. What he hadn't expected was for the silly bitch to fall in love with him. She had to be damned near forty and he hated the colour of her brittle blonde hair. But Ally Kinross! Thunderbolts on sight! Ally the untouchable. That was when he decided to punish her.

Send her letters. Phone calls. It was extraordinary the thrill they gave him. The feeling of power over her. Clever him. He was clean as far as the cops were concerned.

He knew where Ally lived. He had her latest ex-directory

number though it wouldn't be so easy to get the next if she changed it. He knew all about the brother's wedding though he hadn't followed her to Brisbane. He knew about the aunt in the great big mansion on the harbour. Now he knew about the boyfriend. The Greek god cum cattle baron.

He had to know what was going on between Ally and her old buddy. Somehow he knew in his bones Cameron was a dangerous new element. But then, all his life he'd enjoyed playing wild games.

When they arrived at Ally's apartment block she ran her car down towards the underground car park, pausing for a moment to activate the huge security door. With Rafe beside her she was spared all sense of nervousness. She knew he was wrong about Matt Harper. It came as a bit of a surprise. Rafe was an excellent judge of men. Obviously he wasn't letting anyone off his list.

On the way home she learned he had already spoken to the detective assigned to her case. The sad fact was the police had no evidence on anyone. They were waiting for whoever was harassing Ally to make a mistake. No one wanted an actual confrontation but the possibility had to be addressed.

Janet was waiting with the yellow envelope. Rafe took it from her, opening it up carefully with the paper knife she passed him.

"Is your name Ally Kinross?" Ally asked him wryly.

"Yes, is it," he replied, his eye glued to a single sheet of ordinary white typing paper, the contents not ordinary at all. Written in misshapen block letters it was ugly, melodramatic, scary.

"What does it say?" Ally sat down hard, her whole body vibrating with upset.

Rafe waited a moment before he answered. "There's something here that might be checked out by an expert." He ran a finger along his clean-cut jaw line. "An odd kind of speech pattern common to all the communications. It could be feigned, again the obvious misspelling could be, too."

"Matt can spell," Ally said with relief, knowing Rafe's doubts about Matt. "The police checked that out."

"You mean you have someone already. What a blessing!" Janet visibly brightened.

"Rafe suspects everyone," Ally said.

"So would you if you had any sense." His golden brown brows were drawn together in a heavy frown.

"So what does it say?" Ally repeated. "Am I going to get to know?"

He laughed shortly, no amusement in it. "It's not that interesting." Rafe went to refold the letter to put it back in the envelope when he checked abruptly, a decided glint coming into his eyes. "Well, well, well." He focused on the yellow envelope. The back flap had been reinforced with a strip of transparent tape as the glue wasn't all that effective. "Maybe our friend has left a calling card, after all?"

"Tell me, Rafe," she begged. "I feel ill."

He passed her the envelope. "Notice anything under the tape?"

Immediately the sick feeling dropped away. She looked back at him, her whole expression sharpening. "If I'm not mistaken that's a tiny hair. Maybe the sort of hair off a man's wrist."

"Exactly." Rafe took the envelope back from her. "I'll hand this over to the police first thing in the morning. I might even give Detective Mead a ring."

"We're talking DNA?" Ally's expression returned to brooding.

"Hasn't it revolutionised crime fighting?" Rafe nodded. "I'm certain we might get something from this."

"That's wonderful!" Janet beamed. "Now both of you have to eat. Are you staying to dinner, Rafe?"

"As long as you don't try feeding me peanut butter sandwiches." He smiled at her, harking back to a time Janet had done just that. "Unless you'd like to go out?" He glanced across to Ally, seeing her deepening expression. "No one needs to cook."

"You know that's a great idea," Janet said with enthusiasm, "but I won't come along. There's an old movie with Robert Mitchum in it I want to see. Fancy restaurants are for the young and well-dressed."

"Maybe I'd better change." Rafe gave his open-necked shirt an amused glance.

Ally shook her head. "You look fine." He looked wonderful. She would never tire of looking at him.

"Tell you what." Rafe stood up. "I'll go back to my hotel and then I'll pick you up around seven-thirty. It will give you time to relax a bit. Run a bubble bath." As he said it he had an instant vision of her beautiful body barely concealed by glistening foam. "I have one or two calls to make." One to Mead, he thought but didn't say. "Victoria's suit you?" He named a top restaurant.

"You'll be lucky if you get a table," Ally warned. "It's usually booked well ahead."

"I'll get one," he said almost idly.

Janet laughed, her faded blue eyes crinkling with wry amusement. "I bet he will."

With Rafe back in her life, even if he was only looking after her welfare, Ally came alive. She had her scented bubble bath with foam spilling everywhere, relaxing her body in the fragrant, blue-tinged water. Her blood was running like quicksilver as excitement surged through her veins.

The memory of the night they had spent together, that extraordinary night of Brod's and Rebecca's wedding, had stayed with her with absolute clarity. The pounding force of their passion, the desperate hunger that had plagued them both endlessly totally assuaged. Afterwards she had felt peace but Rafe had lain so quietly, arms raised, his hands locked behind his golden head. It couldn't have been plainer. Their passion was mutual. What went on in Rafe's mind kept them apart.

Why, oh, why, had Lainie decided to tell him all about the

film role she'd been offered, Ally agonised. It was her own fault mentioning it. Telling Lainie Rhodes anything was like hiring a loudspeaker. She hadn't even read the script yet but Lainie had obviously made it appear she was on the verge of accepting. Fame came before love. Alison Kinross's career was everything. Even Fee was convinced she was going to take the role. Everyone in the business said it was inevitable she would move to the big screen.

"A face made for the movies," Bart always said. What he didn't know was her so-called career had brought her no great joy. The excitement, the satisfaction levels had declined early. The underlying reason was she didn't live for acting. It was Fee who fell in love with her roles. Fee who had found her career on the stage utterly fulfilling. Even to the exclusion of her family. It wasn't Fee who had raised her beautiful little daughter. Fee had been locked into her Art.

Ally had met Francesca's father, Lord de Lyle only twice in her life, found him wholly different from her aunt, even different from his own cousin, David, but no one had disputed he hadn't tried very hard to be a good caring parent.

No one could make up for the absence of a mother. She and Brod had lived with that loss. Fee was born lucky. She's been given the blessed opportunity to get to know her beautiful daughter all over again. It was the strong resemblance between herself and Fee that was always remarked on. Was it any wonder, then, Rafe had come to believe any relationship between them was unworkable. Ally Kinross was set to follow in her famous aunt's footsteps.

When Rafe returned with a box of Belgian chocolates for Janet, Ally met him at the door, the two of them calling a good-night to Janet who had made herself comfortable in an armchair, turned on the television and gleefully opened the delicious assortment. Janet just loved chocolates and these were the very best.

For dinner Rafe had changed into a beautifully cut dark grey suit with a white-collared blue and white striped shirt and a ruby silk tie. For a man who spent most of his life in riding gear he had great taste. Not only that, he had the tall lean body to show clothes off. Ally was pleased now she had worn a new outfit in textured silk. She looked good in black. It was chic, it was elegant, it was sexy. And tonight she was relying heavily on her sex appeal. Sex was a woman's not so secret weapon and she had to come armed if she wanted to convince Rafe she was still necessary in his life.

The maître d' led them to their table, which Ally realised was one of the best in the room. Other diners looked on, absorbing the fact that was Ally Kinross, the TV star, but who was the amazing man beside her? He was clearly someone. He had the looks of a film star but a quite different aura. Absolutely extraordinary. He filled the room like some great beautiful golden thoroughbred.

"Like a martini?" he asked with easy charm.

"I'd enjoy that very much. It's been an awful day, an awful tiring day."

"You don't look the least bit tired," he told her. He could have said you look dazzling, but didn't. Ally made a black dress look the ultimate in sex appeal.

"Aah, that comes with clever make-up," she responded lightly.

"I've seen you without it."

His eyes were so distinctly sensuous, so sexually disturbing, she burst out, "You've seen me…"

"Leave it there, Ally." He seemed to shake himself out of it, picking up the wine list.

"Very well, Rafe," she answered with mock obedience. "But we did have our good times."

"Looking back, yes." His expression unmistakably tightened.

"I seem to do a lot of it these days." She gave a genuine sigh. "Looking back."

He glanced at her over the top of the wine list. "That might get you into trouble, Ally. I'm following the sign post. Straight ahead."

"I just can't see you and Lainie," she offered dryly.

"As it happens, neither can I." He shrugged lightly. "But I'm still out there looking for the right woman."

"Not me?"

"Certainly not you, Ally." He smiled. "The way I hear it, you're moving on to bigger and better things. Hollywood calls."

"I think I'll pass on Hollywood," she said.

He appeared to ignore that as just so much talk. "Can they afford to lose you?" he asked suavely, breaking off as the waiter approached.

Ally sat back while Rafe ordered, nodding her head when he suggested a particular wine. "I've had another card from Brod and Rebecca," she told him more neutrally after the waiter had gone. "That's four up to date. A phone call from their hotel in Venice."

"I can claim a letter." Rafe's handsome mouth relaxed into a smile. "Brod could very easily miss me if he rang. He made it sound as though married life is very well worth the risk."

Her green eyes glittered. "Do you have to sound so cynical?"

"*I* don't have any choice, Ally, darling, but I'm glad Brod has married the woman of his dreams. He deserves his happiness."

Ally nodded her dark head, centre-parted, a mass of curls and waves. "Marrying Rebecca was the best thing he could have done. She loves him with all her heart and of course she's very clever. Kimbara will be the perfect place to write. She told me she'd love to make a start on a novel. I'm sure she's got something in mind with an Outback setting."

He seemed amused. "Surely she got enough inspiration delving into the Kinross past. Sex and family secrets."

"All right, all right." Ally waved an acknowledging hand. "The Kinrosses never were as free of scandal as the Camerons. Anyway it's going to be a mystery thriller."

"Great! I hope it's brilliant. I can even think up a title. 'The Disappearing Bride.'"

"The things we do to each other," Ally mourned. "I used to be a part of your life."

"Darling, you were part of *me,*" he corrected, a sudden flare in his eyes. "You had it all. I know it was a long time ago, but let's get that straight." He was damned if he was going to tell her she had taken the life from him and left him a terrible emptiness in exchange. Obsession was a raging monster he had to conquer.

A great sadness came over Ally, a sense of having spoilt both their lives. "Now I'm your sparring partner."

He shrugged a wide shoulder. "It's better than being abandoned, believe me. Your kind of hold is tyrannical. There must be quite a lot of women with the underlying wish to own a man."

She stared at him out of her black-lashed green eyes. "I thought I could come back."

"You thought you could have an arrangement." His brows knit together. "Sorry, darling. I'm an all or nothing man. Obviously you can still affect me. I couldn't resist you the night of the wedding. I suppose I was off my head."

"Don't say that." She reached out urgently for his hand, wrapping her fingers around his.

She didn't see his knuckles whiten. "You use sex like a tool, Ally," he said, trying to harden his heart against the appeal in her beautiful eyes. "You're as near to being a dangerous woman as there is."

She sat back shocked, but not surprised. She wasn't wrong about Rafe Cameron. He had the pride of the devil. "I'm as needy as the next woman."

"Except the next woman doesn't have a fraction of your allure. Add to that, you're an actress." Mockery lit his sparkling eyes. "You've just gotta have that great response."

"Are you saying you've never slept with anyone who offered better?" Blood rose to her cheeks. She felt hot in her silk dress.

"Not in my experience. *So far.*" He smiled at her, brittle, a little taunting. "Even though something profoundly significant has been lost, we still share a powerful bond."

"God, yes!" Neither of them could deny it. Ally bowed her head, toying with her wineglass. "That's very important to me, Rafe."

"I know." He was consumed by the desire to take hold of her, crush her mouth under his. "It's proof of the goddess syndrome. You let a man go on the condition he always returns."

Midnight was breaking by the time they returned to Ally's apartment. Riding together in the back of the taxi had been an emotion-fraught experience made all the more tantalising knowing neither could have what their bodies so desperately craved.

There wasn't even a chance he would kiss her, Ally thought, deeply conscious of the languorous heat in her body, the flower of desire that was trembling for release.

Rafe paid the taxi off, joining her on the footpath and looking around.

"You shouldn't have let the taxi go. You mightn't get another."

"Why are you whispering?" he asked, taking her by the arm.

"I'm damned if I know." She could actually feel herself swaying uncertain of what was to happen next. She even felt guilty because she wanted him so badly, her whole body stirring in seduction.

Rafe kept her walking, taking time to check the dense foliage around the landscaped entrance. "They really oughtn't let this get too high," he said, looking at a hedge. "I might have a word with the caretaker in the morning. Don't worry about me, Ally, I'll see you to your door. I'll be sure to pick up a roving cab. I could walk back to the hotel for that matter."

Why not? He had abundant energy. He was a big, strong man. He knew how to defend himself against a charging bull. Lord he had taken on a half a dozen cattle duffers on his own, then went back to the muster.

The lift doors opened and they walked in, the small mirrored panels on the walls reflecting their images. She felt strung up. Ragged.

"Why do you look like that?" he said under his breath.

She gave a little delicate shrug and put her hands to her flushed cheeks. "All I want is for you to love me."

"*Make* love to you, don't you mean?" All night he had been resisting the violent urge to touch her, now she was inches from him, staring at him with those emerald eyes. Her olive skin was flawless beneath the overhead lighting. Her short silk dress showed off her beautiful legs. The style left her arms bare but was cut high at the neck, covering her breasts. He knew exactly what they looked like beneath the black silk, the delicate curves, the points of her nipples. Did women know men regarded breasts as miracles?

"Rafe?" she whispered low in her throat. A consummate actress playing a part? All he knew was he answered her with a soft growl, pulling her to him with one arm around her narrow waist.

Such an exquisite forbidden mouth!

"Rafe!"

"Don't bother talking," he muttered, given over to consuming her mystery, though it was the source of his pain.

Her mouth opened fully to his exploration. He could feel the silk of her tongue, smaller, more pointed than his. She had closed her eyes, her head thrown back against his shoulder. He wanted to tear her clothes off, lay her beautiful body on a bed. His own body was filled with passion and agony, a great hurt having her in his arms couldn't block out.

He was dimly aware the lift had arrived at her floor. The door was opening. She was pressed against him, her arms going around his neck clinging as though without his support she would slip to the floor.

He drew them both out, walked a few steps along the corridor, before allowing his mouth to sink on hers once again. What she was offering might have been the elixir of life. Wall brackets were burning. No one was around though there were four units to each floor. He could feel her shuddering against him and his hand swept down over her breast uncaring. He remembered how it was those years ago. The first time in the big bedroom at Opal. She was frantic for him then. His little virgin.

She was frantic now.

Time to do something, Rafe thought, chiding himself bitterly but unable to think straight with Ally in his arms. He knew if Janet Massie weren't inside Ally's apartment he would have Ally on her own bed. Such passion for a woman was astonishing, bewildering. His mind said one thing while his body did a total turnabout. What he had often thought despairingly, was *exactly* right. Ally was in his blood. But he had to remember he had come here because she deeply needed his support and attention. There was something about that Harper character, though he tried hard to be affable, something quickly covered over like a blanket. To hide what? Psychological damage? It could well be severe.

Rafe's feelings of protectiveness released him. "You have to go inside now, Ally," he said, his voice changing from emotion-charged tones to the voice of authority.

"I don't want to go." She stared up at him, seeing the glow in his eyes, the passion that had emanated from him dissolving into a hard decision. "A pride of lions" is how people used to speak of the Camerons. Douglas Cameron and two sons. Rafe's hair was glinting beneath the lights as bright as an angel's.

Rafe saw the shadowy figure moving towards the stairwell before Ally. The figure seemed to be draped in some sort of dark cloak, still Rafe had the definite sense it was a man.

"Hey, you," he yelled on impulse. "Come back." His strong hands closed on Ally's shoulders, pushing her towards the door. "Get inside and stay there, Ally. And while you're at it, ring the police."

"No, Rafe!" Immediately she knew his suspicions. The figure had given off an unmistakably sinister aura. "He could have a weapon."

"If it's who I think it is I'll fight him with my bare hands." Rafe had learned many hard valuable lessons in life. One was how to defend himself no matter how rough the going.

He took off with no thought of his own safety, hearing the hard pad of footsteps on the internal stairway. With little more to go on than instinct he was convinced he wasn't far away from the man who'd been harassing Ally. The whole building was slumbering. There was no one on the stairs, no lifts opened and shut.

Just him and me, Rafe thought, hard in pursuit. Even if he found he had the wrong quarry, the figure in the cloak had no business being inside the building. Whoever it was, it was no woman. This was a fit man equal to the chase. He tried to put a face on the fleeing figure. Came up with Matt Harper. It had to be him. He fitted the profile too well. Mead had confided as much glumly, unhappy they couldn't catch him out.

"He's probably writing up one of those letters now!"

This time, however, Harper had made a mistake.

The cloak, the surprise bit of apparel was thrown down early. Rafe leapt over it to the landing, with his long legs and his athleticism gaining on the quarry.

Three floors down it all came together. Rafe sprang in a rage, his anger made all the more formidable because it was deeply personal. He grasped the back of the man's neck and shook him like a rabbit, expecting violence, all that hate to detonate into an explosion of fists. Instead to his huge surprise, his quarry turned victim, shouting out a frantic, "Help!" He even ducked his head in his hands as though expecting to be beaten. Only Rafe had no killer instinct. He swung the man to face him, his whole demeanour incredibly tough and daunting.

"What the hell are you up to?" he demanded.

Matt Harper laughed shakily, rubbing his neck. "Jesus, are

you cattle barons totally mad?" He laughed again, a choking sound.

"Pretty much so when someone tries to stalk our women," Rafe told him with contempt.

"*Your* woman, is she?" Harper gave Rafe a twisted smile. "You coulda hurt me, Mr. Cameron."

"I still can," Rafe warned. "What are you doing in Ally's apartment building and why did you run?"

"I did something stupid," Harper admitted. "But hell, man, I've got nuthin' to feel ashamed of. Since all this bad stuff has been goin' on I've been keeping an eye on Ally."

"Yeah…sure…. Don't make me throw up."

"Hey, mister, it's the truth!" Harper straightened his hand-some head, his expression proud. "It just so happens I care about Ally. She's the only one who has ever acted like a friend to me."

Rafe nodded grimly. "Then it's a terrible way to repay her. You're as guilty as sin, Harper. I can see it in your face. I can smell the guilty sweat off your body. Anyway, for your infor-mation, I'm making a citizen's arrest. Ally has called the police. You can give your cock-and-bull story to them."

Harper's black eyes flickered. "You won't come out of it too well, either, *Mr.* Cameron. There are laws against assault."

"What's the betting you won't find anyone to look into it? I wanted to nail you, Harper, and I did. So now we walk. We're going back up the stairwell and you're going to wait quietly until the police arrive."

"Oooh, you are a big strong man!" Harper said, sliding into a simpering camp voice.

"Forget that!" Rafe muttered in disgust. "That was just a smokescreen." He got hold of Matt Harper's arm and held it tightly behind his back. "Now start walking. I haven't hurt you but I'd like to. Remember that."

They were almost at the first landing when Ally appeared at the top of the stairs. Her first reaction when she saw Harper was to cower against the wall. "Oh, God, Rafe," she moaned. "You were right, after all."

At that Matt Harper's chiselled features contorted. "Right about what, Ally?" he shouted, sobbing a little in perverse shame when he saw her beautiful stricken face. "I've done nuthin', I swear. Your big muscled boyfriend here has been belting into me. For what? For lookin' out for you. I've been doin' that since all that harassment stuff started."

"Go back upstairs, Ally," Rafe ordered, unimpressed with Harper's explanation, but Ally, being Ally, pressed forward unexpectedly, no longer fearful but violently outraged. Matt was lying. Of course he was lying, the miserable little rat. Why hadn't she recognised it? This was the person who had given her months of hell. Him with his black jeans, his black sweatshirt and that silly damned cloak.

"You bastard!" There were tears in her almond eyes. "And to think I stuck up for you. What a fool!"

"Go back, Ally," Rafe warned, knowing how impetuous Ally could be.

But she was focused on Harper. "You're going to pay for all you've done, Matt. I've rung the police."

"This is a set-up," Harper yelled, trying to stare her down, but Ally was flying down the stairs, badly shaken inside, but wanting to confront her tormentor. Those letters, those phone calls! She felt they had violated her. This repulsive creature needed a little time in jail.

"Ally!" Rafe yelled, rapid-fire as though she was about to step out into a mine field.

The tone of his voice checked her at the very moment her high heel caught in that damnable black cloak. She had a moment of pure panic, the realisation this was going to turn out badly, then she was pitching forward, throwing out her arms in desperation to break her certain fall.

This *can't* be happening! It was her last conscious thought.

Both men moved. Both cried out her name. Rafe felt he could

have reached her, cushioned her fall with his body, only Harper, remorseful now, got in his way. Ally came down hard, her slender body at a sickening angle.

It chilled him to the bone. He literally had to heave Harper, who was howling like a pained animal, out of the way. "Move, you fool!"

"God, God, I'm sorry!" Useless words that made Rafe furious. He flung out a hand, crashed it down on Harper's shoulder, forcing him down on the step. Immediately his handsome features distorted. Harper began, of all things, whispering to himself, his head buried in his hands.

As Rafe bent over Ally, his mind slotting through all he knew about first aid, the door opening onto the stairwell burst open. Two men appeared, Mead and a uniformed police officer.

Rafe lifted his head, something dangerous in his face. "Get an ambulance quick. We have to get her to the hospital. She's had a fall."

The police officer acted on the instant, pulling out his mobile and punching in the emergency numbers.

"You got him?" Mead cried, his eyes on Harper who was screaming, to Mead's amazement, he hadn't done anything. They were trying to fix him with something he hadn't done.

"I got him," Rafe responded bleakly, working not to turn around and shut Harper up. Forcibly. Maybe for good. He kept hold of Ally's slender hand, his eyes glued to her white unconscious face. If anything bad happened to Ally, life as he knew it was over.

CHAPTER SEVEN

FEE ENTERED THE ward with great urgency, her face white and tense. She was followed closely by David Westbury, concern lines etched deeply into his forehead.

"Rafe, my dear!"

Rafe stood up as Ally's aunt went tearfully into his arms. "I've never been so shocked in my life. This is terrible, terrible. My beautiful Ally! Where is she? Where have they taken her?"

"They're running tests, Fee." Rafe tried to speak reassuringly, nodding over Fee's head to David who responded with his eyes. "She's broken her wrist. I don't know exactly *how* bad the break is. It's the crack on the head that's the greatest worry."

"My God, not head injuries." Fee's voice was frightened. "This could be very serious."

"I pray God not, Fee," Rafe responded, his hazel eyes grave. "Ally came to fairly quickly. She responded to my voice. She *knew* me though she was having a problem remembering what had happened. The paramedics were there almost immediately. She's having the best of care."

"We'll have to let Brod know." Fee looked terribly dejected. "On their honeymoon but they have to know."

"Yes, Fee," Rafe agreed. "I feel responsible for this somehow. My turning up seemed to have triggered Harper off."

"It certainly brought him out into the open," David said supportively. The young man had nothing to reproach himself for. Rather the reverse.

"Rafe, dear, you can't blame yourself for anything." Fee shook her head. "We both know Ally. She wouldn't stand by idly if she thought you were in any danger. It's that psycho Harper we have to blame. Is he still denying he's had anything to do with it?"

Rafe nodded grimly. "His claim is he's been looking out for Ally, but the police aren't having that. He's been taken into custody and he'll be charged with being on private premises unlawfully, sending offensive material through the post, stalking, and there's the little matter of his violating privacy laws, ex-directory numbers and so forth. I expect he'll be released on bail with an order to appear in court a month or so on."

"Will Ally have to appear? She'll hate that." Fee shuddered.

"Not if he pleads guilty. If he doesn't she'll have to appear as a witness and be cross-examined by defence counsel. I don't think it will come to that, Fee. He'll be convicted and put on a good behaviour bond with a hefty fine. He'll also be ordered to stay away from Ally. I think it's something like a kilometre, so there goes his TV role."

"Who could care about that?" Fee's eyes shone with anger.

"Please," Rafe extended his arm, "why don't we all sit down. The doctors won't be back for some time."

A nurse with a kind capable face approached to ask them if they wanted tea or coffee, but all three declined.

Finally the doctor Rafe had spoken to earlier, a consultant neurologist, came down the corridor, his clever face expressionless in the manner of doctors, yet it turned the blood in Rafe's veins icy. He stood up to take the news while Fee, equally strained, clutched at David's arm. "Oh, Davey, I'm so afraid. I keep remembering Ally when she was a little thing and her mother had gone away."

David forced a smile, fighting down his own anxieties. "Ally's a strong girl, Fee. A fighter. She'll come through."

Rafe introduced Fee and David, and the doctor began to fill them in. The scaphoid bone in Ally's left wrist had been broken but he didn't foresee a problem with that. She was young, she was healthy. No reason to believe she wouldn't knit well. The head trauma? Well.... The doctor went on to explain Ally had a good strong bony skull which protected the tissues of the brain. Also she was fortunate in her abundant hair which unquestionably had cushioned her fall. Nevertheless, she had a split to the scalp that had required urgent attention.

He was awaiting the results of the MRI, the magnetic resonance imaging, which would provide him with all the information he wanted. He needed to know what was going on inside the cerebrum though he told them pools of cerebrospinal fluid acted as an internal shock absorber. The patient was badly concussed, but there was no significant impairment of physical function apart from the broken wrist. She had a very bad headache, as could be expected, but so far, and this was crucial, no visual deficits.

Her short-term memory however was at this stage poor. She would have to be held for observation. Perhaps for several days. The implications of any head injury had to be regarded seriously. He was at this stage reasonably predicting a quick recovery. There was no coma. The paramedics had reported the patient had recovered consciousness by the time they arrived, a matter of minutes.

"Can we see her?" Fee asked, standing up suddenly as though she wouldn't brook any other answer.

The doctor hesitated a moment, taking in her distress. "For a very short time."

"I only want to kiss her." Fee stared back into the doctor's eyes.

Immediately he turned, beckoning to a nursing sister who was standing at a station nearby. "Sister Richards will take you."

"Thank you so much, Doctor." Fee looked at David, who had no thoughts of intruding.

Feeling a shade dizzy with relief, the two men sat down as Fee and the nurse moved off. The doctor looked down at Rafe with a sympathetic eye. "Of course you may see your friend for a moment, Mr. Cameron." Obviously they were romantically involved. The young man was deeply troubled.

"Actually I'd like to stay through the rest of the night," Rafe said, hoping the doctor wouldn't argue.

"You don't have to." He was assured. "The hospital will call if there's anything worrying to report."

"I'll stay all the same."

The doctor nodded. "Very well. I'll have my pictures then. If you're still around I can give you a first-hand report." He began to excuse himself. "Now I have another patient I must see to. When your aunt comes back, Sister will escort you to Miss Kinross's room."

"Rather better than we thought?" David said after the doctor had gone, looking at Rafe with kindly eyes.

"I can't relax until she's been given the all clear," Rafe answered, unconsciously twisting his strong hands. "This has been a nightmare."

"But a major breakthrough, Rafe. Ally is very fortunate you were around. They should really lock Harper up and throw away the key. One tries to make allowances for his deprived background, but he sounds a piece of goods."

Rafe nodded. "He's got a lot of psychological baggage. I'm putting my hopes on the DNA. Mead tells me he's got himself a good lawyer already. That doesn't make any of us particularly happy. The police or me."

"Ah, here comes Fee," David murmured, looking down the silent corridor. "Is it my imagination of does she look twice as fragile."

"Shock," Rafe said. "She and Ally are very close."

Closer in a way than Fee and Francesca, David thought, but didn't have the heart to mention.

Fee was deeply upset by it all, so both men encouraged her to return home.

"I'm staying for the rest of the night, Fee," Rafe told her. "With any luck they might allow me to sit quietly in her room."

"This has been a horrible shock," Fee said. "She knew me but she couldn't really talk to me." Fee went to Rafe, hugged him. "Thank you, Rafe, dear. The break is in the same arm she broke as a child, you know."

"When she was ten." Rafe easily cast his mind back to the day. Ally the tomboy had followed them, him and Brod, out to their new secret swimming hole about three miles northwest of Kimbara homestead. It was a wonderful spot, a fair-sized lagoon with sparkling volumes of water pouring over giant boulders and swirling down a narrow gorge of multicoloured rocks with stripes of desert red, pink, yellow and black.

They were having a wonderful time in the water, surprisingly deep and cold, but both of them were fine divers and swimmers when suddenly the ten-year-old Ally appeared out of nowhere. Even as a kid she'd been a great tracker. She'd waved to them from the top of the rocks, tall for her age, in her T-shirt and jeans, her wildly unruly dark hair decorated with a garland of white daisies.

"Hey, you two! As soon as I get my clothes off, I'm coming in."

Both he and Brod had reacted with alacrity. That was all right when they were small and she was hardly more than a baby but not now. He and Brod were fifteen years old, nearly men, and both of them held Ally very dear to their hearts.

Immediately Brod had turned for the bank, starting to protest when Ally took off like a bird, her small feet flying among the stones. She probably would have made it to the creek only a sulphur-crested cockatoo chose that very moment to fly shrieking into the branches of a white-boled limewood that flanked the stream. He fancied he could still hear her sweet piercing cry, a cry resembling the cry she had made tonight.

They'd fixed her up with a stout stick along her arm, tied with his bandanna, carrying her all the way home on a make-shift stretcher they'd rigged up, leaving the horses, including Ally's, to find their own way home. Nearly fainting with the pain, Ally had been very brave. Even when all three of them had had to face Stewart Kinross.

No mother like his own to fly out onto the verandah filled with loving concern for her child, Kinross had given them all a tongue-lashing. Ally included. Rafe always thought Kinross would have liked to give his son a hiding but at fifteen both he and Brod had stood a boyish but extremely fit six feet. Brod and Ally had found little comfort in their father whereas he and Grant had had immense love and respect for theirs.

Now, when he was shown into Ally's hospital room, his heart literally sank in his breast. She was lying back in the bed, her left forearm in a cast, her normally vivid face robbed of every vestige of colour, her beautiful green eyes dull and heavily lidded. She didn't look remotely like a young woman in her mid-twenties. She looked little more than the child he had known and loved. A felled child after one of her famous escapades. Her wild silky hair was scraped back from her face and she had a surgical dressing over the left side to the back of her head.

Yet she tried to smile at him, her voice barely above a whisper. "Could have been worse!"

A standard joke between them when things had gone wrong.

"Ally." He approached the bed, bending to touch his lips to her temple. "My poor little Ally."

"You used to love me, didn't you?" she said, glancing down at her injured wrist. "Would you believe it, it's the same arm I broke all those years ago when you and Brod had to carry me home on a stretcher."

"I remember." He turned a tender, twisted smile on her.

She stared back at him almost dreamily. "I remember how

you stood up to Dad when he started to yell at us. He really wanted to knock Brod flat, you know."

"He was under a strain," Rafe said it for the Sister's benefit.

"No he wasn't," Ally protested.

"Don't let's worry about it now, Ally." He tried to soothe her agitation.

"I've got a lovely big gash on my head," she told him hoarsely. "They had to put a dozen stitches in. And they cut out a patch of my hair."

"No one's going to notice, Ally. You've got lots of it." The old sweetness hovered around his sculptured mouth.

"Rafe." She tried to swallow down her panic. "I've no real idea what's happened. You've got to tell me. Fee didn't get an opportunity. They hurried her out so quickly."

"She was told she could only stay a minute, Ally."

She looked very haughty, eyes flashing. "Lovely to see you, too."

"Here, now." He took hold of her free hand. "We can talk all about it in the morning. By then you'll remember for yourself."

"That's right, dear," Sister intervened. "You've had an unpleasant experience. Doctor wants you to rest quietly."

Ally lifted her head, winced. "Rafe, here, will take full responsibility," she said. "He's used to lots of responsibility. He's Cameron from Opal. The Chosen One."

"Now there's a vital piece of information." Rafe bit back a laugh. "Do you remember we had dinner?" he asked. He drew up a chair to the bedside.

Ally frowned, concentrating hard. A movement of the brows that appeared to give her pain. "I remember we had dinner. I remember the two of us in the lift, then it starts to get hairy."

"The very reason why I think we should wait to talk about it in the morning. I'll stick around. The doctor said I could."

"Stay here." Ally began to grumble as he started to get up. "They couldn't give me much in the way of pain-killers. Not with concussion. I want you *here*."

"I think not, dear." Sister sailed in, an authority figure.

"I'm the patient," Ally pointed out, for all the world like Fee in one of her imperious moods. "And I say I want him here." She appeared to grow angry.

"Right you are," Sister agreed cheerfully, nodding her head at Rafe. "If you can sit down a little way from the bed, sir."

"I want him *right* here." Ally waved Rafe back. "I'm a must-go-where-he-goes sort of person."

Rafe had no idea why she said it. This was Ally, who had left him.

It was Rafe's first experience of a night in hospital. How the patients were supposed to sleep with all the light and noise he couldn't imagine. Nurses made regular checks on Ally, lifting her eyelids, checking her pupils, noting things on her chart, smiled kindly on him. In the dawn light before she was even stirring he was told to leave. Someone, he found out later a woman doctor, gave him coffee and a couple of muffins she'd been actually saving for herself. He went to the washroom, saw his own face in the mirror, weariness and worry apparent in his eyes and as he ran an explorative hand over his face felt his jaw with its golden stubble. He powerfully needed a bit of good news.

He got it as he was coming back from putting a call through to Fee. David had answered the phone. David who was fast becoming a fixture in Fee's life. Fee had been unable to sleep for hours, David told him. Finally she had dropped off in an armchair about six o'clock. As for himself, like Rafe, he had spent a long sleepless night. Stress was affecting them all.

When the neurologist told Rafe there was nothing in Ally's tests to cause worry, he fully understood what gratitude was. A tremendous sense of relief spread through him, as though a great burden had been lifted from his shoulders. He marched right back to the phone and put through another call to Fee's home. This time Fee answered in an uncharacteristically tiny voice that totally changed when Rafe gave her the good news.

"Oh, thank you, God," she cried, her resonant tones vibrating down the wires. "I've been so afraid. As a family we've been rocked by tragedy. You, too, Rafe, darling. I know Ally loves you."

Rafe put down the phone, shaking his head. Yes, Ally loved him in her fashion. Neither of them would ever forget their shared childhood, or their beautiful, romantic bonding, but inevitably after Ally got her strength and confidence back she would return to her career and the proposed movie despite her claim she wouldn't take up the opportunity. At least this time there wouldn't be a Matt Harper on the scene. Even if that tiny curl of hair didn't come from Harper's body, he'd have a hard time keeping to his trumped-up story.

"I want to go home," Ally told him the minute he saw her. "I'm perfectly all right. I remember everything." She did look a little better, eyes brighter, but nervy, obviously still traumatised.

"That's wonderful," he said with relief, "but you'll have to be patient, Ally, you're here for a few days."

"I'm leaving this afternoon." She was enunciating too clearly, moving her uninjured hand up and down on the coverlet. "I hope you can help me, Rafe. You're my pal, my protector."

"That I am," he agreed quietly, saddened and angry this had to happen to her. "But think about it, girl. Your doctors want to keep an eye on you. They're the experts. Not you or me. It makes good sense to do what you're told."

"I suppose," she said. "I'm just being stupid. Remember how I was always getting into trouble when I was a child?" The expression in her eyes softened. "Ally the daredevil, always trying to be one of the boys."

"Yes, darling, I do." Her sheer vulnerability and her physical weakness were bringing back all the old powerful urges to shield and protect her.

"Thank you for still calling me darling." She rested a trembly hand over his.

"That's quite all right, kiddo." He yielded to the impulse to lift her hand and kiss it.

"You know I idolised you and Brod," she said with sweet recall. "You were both big brothers to me then. The two of you so famous for your bushcraft, the wonderful way you had with a horse. Fee used to call you The Twins though your colouring is like day and night. You the golden boy, Brod with his raven hair."

"You always trying to tag along." He smiled as memories began tumbling over one another.

"You mustn't have wanted me all the time but neither of you ever got annoyed. I used to love your visits. I used to love going over to Opal." Her eyes started to sparkle. "Your parents were so kind to us, the motherless Kinross kids. Your mother always made a point of kissing me good-night on our stay-overs, sending me home with some beautiful little gift. She was a lovely, lovely person. I think of her so often."

Rafe could feel a harsh throbbing in his own chest. "She certainly loved you," he told her, his tone suddenly clipped. "The little girl she never had."

Both of them were quiet for a time, then Ally said, "She really believed we were going to get married one day."

She hadn't lived to see the break-up.

"Ah, well, Ally, we blew it," he said steadily, his gold-flecked eyes cool as a rock pool. "But I'm still in your corner when anything goes wrong."

She felt his withdrawal. Saw it in his eyes. "I recognise that, Rafe, and I thank you for it." Ally looked down thoughtfully at the cast on her forearm. "I was lucky, wasn't I?"

"Lord, yes." He raised a hand to his temple. "It makes me ill just thinking what could have happened. You're so damned impetuous. Even as a child, you seemed to have no regard for life or limb."

"Excuse me," she said with some affront. "It was *you* I was worried about. I thought he might have a weapon."

"No weapon," Rafe responded tersely. "That will work in his favour. God knows what he came for. I didn't think he meant to confront you. I think he wanted to discover what you and I are to each other."

Her badly bruised body still reacted, filled with glittering spirals of heat. "Well, he got a damned good idea. All that frantic kissing!"

Though his heart twisted at the memory, he managed to speak lazily. "It's not as though we plan to do it again."

"At least until I'm out of plaster." Ally slumped back against the pillow. "Oh, that black sweatshirt." She shuddered as it all swam back to her. "The look in his eyes. Like a dog apologising for giving you a good bite. What I wanted to do was give him a piece of my mind."

He couldn't help smiling, his iridescent eyes crinkling at the corners. "I told you, Ally Kinross, you're a dangerous woman. By the way, I sent a fax to the Cipriani in Venice. Brod and Rebecca weren't there when I rang so I faxed the message to ring me or Fee. I explained a bit. Not much. I didn't want to alarm them at that stage. Now, the Lord be praised, we'll have better news when they ring in."

"I don't want them to come home." Ally spoke emphatically.

"They might have other ideas." Rafe knew how much Brod loved his sister, and Rebecca was pretty fond of her, too.

"Not on their honeymoon," Ally maintained. "I'm not going to ruin their lovely time together. I'll convince them I'm quite all right."

"Don't get uptight." Rafe soothed her. "I happen to agree, but you'll need help when you go home. Janet, I'm sure, will stay on."

"You've spoken to her, of course."

He nodded. "She sends her love. Like the rest of us, she was terribly upset."

"Poor old Janet, she's had too many upsets. It's not the apartment I want to go back to, Rafe. I want to go *home*."

"To Kimbara?"

She lifted her face to him and looked straight into his soul. "The place where I was born. The place I love with all my heart. The place my father kept me from."

Rafe winced with the memory of so much heartbreak. "He wasn't much of a father, was he?"

Ally sighed deeply. "He simply didn't have the qualities that went with the job." Of a sudden, her lovely voice became muffled. "Oh, Rafe," she murmured. "I'm so afraid."

"Of what?" He leaned towards her. "It's not your nature to be afraid."

Weak tears welled in her eyes, tears dashed impatiently away. "I'm afraid Matt will talk himself out of this. He can be very convincing. God, he even convinced me he was my friend. I just couldn't stand it if he was around. I'd rather quit the show."

His heart sank at the thought of her resuming her career, but of course she would. "So go home for a while, Ally," he advised. "We'll take care of you. It's only natural for you to feel this anxiety, but hang in there. Even if the hair that was caught on the Sellotape is something else, a fibre of some kind, I know the police will break his story. Innocent people don't run. They don't act unlawfully. They don't dress up in ridiculous cloaks. Of everything, that's what gets to me. It's so damned bizarre."

"Maybe he fancied himself as Batman." Ally tried to joke. "But he's ruined it all for me. I can understand now how that TV presenter, Gillian Craig, got out of the business."

"Being harassed would make anyone extremely nervous. One crucial thing, though, he didn't lay a hand on you. This is in the hands of the police now, Ally. Concentrate on your future." He spoke gently, trying to calm her, though his heart was heavy. "A very bright future if all the critics are to be believed. I'm sure you'll get to make your movie yet."

CHAPTER EIGHT

A FAMILIAR LANDMARK was coming up. Manarulla, a vast naked rock of ever-changing colours that dominated the approach to Opal Downs' southwestern border. Ally felt excitement beat inside her like wings. Like all the rocks of the inland, Manarulla put on a daily pageant of changing colours. From a distance it rose from the vast red plains in a blue sea of mirage that turned an astonishing violet before the atmospheric haze disappeared as they flew through it. Looking down she could see all the horizontal bandings of raw earth colours that signified Manarulla's tremendous age.

At the start of the good season the endless plains were thickly vegetated with soaring river gums and ghost gums along the countless watercourses, the spreading billabongs and the chain of lagoons that dominated the Channel Country landscape. Even the arid mulga scrub showed off varying greens, the stunted branches, sculptural in their stark, outflung arms. While the pungent spinifex with its tall seed-bearing spears was so thick across the fiery earth from the air it resembled scorched fields of grain. These same mulga plains that ran on to the horizon within a few weeks of good rains turned into the greatest garden on earth, with an astonishing palette of colours. No one who had seen them could ever forget Nature's fantasy.

Beyond Opal lay Kimbara. Home. The Kinross desert fortress lay further towards the great living desert, with its rolling red dunes, salt lakes and shimmering gibber plains of polished quartz. She was thrilled to be back. Thrilled! So intense was her love for the land. As a child she had gloried in the daring deeds of her ancestors, the Outback's legendary heroes. The Kinrosses and the Camerons had covered themselves with distinction, their families interconnected down through the generations.

More important she was coming home to *peace*. Much as she grieved for what might have been, the fact her father no longer reigned over Kimbara gave her release. No more being hurt. No more baffling black moods to contend with. No deep regrets, no frustration for lack of understanding and communication. No futile craving for affection. Her father had been such a complicated man.

Her brother, Brod, was a man of a very different character, like their grandfather, Sir Andrew, Fee's beloved Sir Andy. Brod loved her and wanted her. Her sister-in-law, Rebecca, was blessed with a tender nature.

Now they were in clear sight of Opal's runway with its huge silver hangars emblazoned with the station's name on the roof. Three Cessnas were on the ground. A distance away was part of the helimuster fleet. Ally counted four in number, maybe the yellow tip of one positioned in one of the hangars.

"How many helicopters has Grant got now?" she asked, full of admiration.

"Six," Rafe said with satisfaction. "My kid brother is a very shrewd businessman and he's a great pilot. He has eight on the payroll now. Three other pilots, all experienced older men, a couple of top bush mechanics, maintenance men, office people. He's doing very well. Better than we both anticipated."

"That's the Cameron name. That counts for a lot."

"Sure, but Grant is *young* to have such big ideas. Young to run a company that's getting bigger every day."

"He's full of confidence. Like you." Ally smiled. "I'm certain he's going to be a big achiever."

Rafe nodded, a smile around his handsome mouth. "He has visions of starting up his own airline."

"Qantas eat your heart out!" Ally laughed. "What's he going to do when he gets married?" She meant, where was he going to live? Was he going to continue to operate from Opal? Was he going to build his own home on the station? He was bound to find a suitable spot in five million acres.

Rafe shook his head. "I'd like him to stay single for a while longer."

"Drat it, you can't live his life for him, big brother."

"I'd like to give him a fighting chance at any rate." Rafe turned his head to give her a quelling glance. "He needs time to work up the business."

"The right wife could help him." Ally was enjoying teasing him.

"The right wife, of course, is the lovely Francesca, your cousin."

"Might I remind you, Francesca is a country woman."

"Take another look down there, Ally," he urged. "It's beautiful, it's savage, it's immense. It's unique. It's *empty* except for a handful of people, the great herds and the native fauna. It has absolutely nothing in common with the tranquil green beauty of England with its constant rainfall. This is the sun-scorched land where it mightn't rain for years. You love it. I love it. We were born to it. We're part of the desert scene. Francesca is a beautiful young woman. Warm, friendly, intelligent, but an exclusive creature. I'd be very careful if you're trying to promote a romance."

"Promote a romance indeed!" Ally chuffed. "Grant has always been greatly taken with Francesca. The same goes for her."

"It's not *her* kind of life, Ally," Rafe warned.

"Might I remind you our ancestors hailed from the misty Isles. Now their bones have become part of the desert sand."

"God, Ally, you're a matchmaker," he groaned.

"Maybe I am."

"Except you're not set on marriage yourself." A sardonic glance.

"I could be."

"Is hubby going to stay at home while you're off making movies?" he asked suavely.

"I haven't committed myself to anything, Rafe," she frowned, realizing it was an uphill battle convincing him she spoke the truth.

"You will." He said it casually, like he didn't care any more.

"Are you sure you don't want to land on Opal?" she asked a moment later.

He shook his head. "No, I'll get you home. You'll want to rest. You won't want to start up again. You can come over to Opal anytime you like."

"Don't think I won't take you up on that," she said.

It was a magnificent clear and cloudless day. Rafe turned downwind in preparation for the descent. There was Kimbara homestead, a jewel of colonial architecture set down in the ruggedly majestic wilderness, the main compound surrounded by its outbuildings like a small town. Kimbara was a self-sufficient community with its overseer, stockmen, ringers, jackeroos, fencers, mechanics, cooks and gardeners. There was even a small schoolhouse with a resident school teacher for the children of employees. Even during the hard times, Kimbara hadn't suffered much in the way of cutbacks, thanks to the excellent management of the cattle chain and the family fortune.

The sparkle off Barella Creek that meandered through the home gardens was almost blinding as was the glinting corrugated iron roof of the hangar with Kimbara Station painted in huge black letters picked out with cobalt blue.

She felt ecstatic! Safer in the vast empty bush than she had ever felt in the nation's largest city. Of course her experience with Matt Harper had coloured her perceptions and robbed her of some of her natural resilience. So, too, her injuries which might curtail her normal station activities. Ally was a fearless rider. She had grown up adoring the companionship of horses. Now she wondered how best to go about station life with her forearm in a cast. Driving, too. How well would she handle the jeep? She had no intention of sitting around twiddling her thumbs. The wild bush called with its solitude and wonder.

Rafe turned sharply over the homestead, dipping his wing to signal to Ted Holland, Kimbara's overseer, they had arrived, then they were coming in to land, making a perfect touchdown despite the brisk cross-winds.

Ted was waiting, with his wife, Cheryl, who had opened up the homestead and stocked the refrigerator in preparation for Ally's arrival. In Brod's absence Kimbara's housekeeper was off visiting her sister in New Zealand, so Ally would have the homestead to herself. Something she wanted. Fee and David planned on arriving the following week. Fee had wanted to come at once but Ally had persuaded her she needed a little time on her own. She wanted to *think* in this other world of her childhood, in the freedom and immensity of the ancient land, without the city's jarring discords. She needed to compose herself in mind and body.

While Rafe stood in discussion with Kimbara's overseer, Cheryl accompanied Ally into the house which smelt of flowers and furniture polish. Cheryl had placed a huge bowl of brilliantly coloured zinnias on the library table in the front hall and Ally stopped to stroke a scarlet petal. All the time she half expected her father to stride out; tall, muscular, strong, in his riding clothes, always slapping at his side with his riding whip, extraordinarily impressive. *Alive.* Ready to pick an argument on the slightest provocation.

"Thank you, Cheryl. The flowers are a lovely touch," she said, genuinely appreciative.

"I'd do anything to make things nice for you, Ally. You know that. Brod took time off to send us a card." Cheryl smiled, obviously happy about it. "Venice looks wonderful. Another world. We were so pleased to get it. They're having a lovely time."

Ally nodded. "I had a hard job convincing them not to come home," Ally told her wryly. "They were really shocked by what happened to me."

"You and Brod are so close. It must be really scary being in the public eye." Cheryl, who rarely left Kimbara station said in a kind of awestruck tone. "Rafe told Ted the young fellow who's been harassing you has changed his tune."

Rafe came up behind them, his tall figure silhouetted by brilliant sunshine. "Guilty," he said with satisfaction. "Once he knew he'd left a little calling card, he folded. The police will let us know when the case comes before the court but Ally doesn't have to go."

"Well, it was a dreadful thing to happen." Cheryl looked dismayed at the cast on Ally's forearm. "Not that you haven't done damage to that arm before. Now..." She started to bustle towards the rear of the house with them following her up, a small wry woman with a cap of salt and pepper curls, snapping dark eyes and a network of fine lines etched into her face. "I made a lovely cake first thing this morning. You'll love it, Rafe, men have such a sweet tooth, and a batch of biscuits. You can have them with your cup of tea. I'm happy to make it for you," she offered.

"That's all right, Cheryl." They moved into the huge, shining kitchen and Ally patted Cheryl's shoulder. "I'm not an invalid and I don't want to put you out. It's a comfort to know you're around if I get into any trouble, but mercifully it's my left hand."

"Don't try to be too independent, dear," Cheryl warned her. "Don't forget I've known you all your life."

"Are you saying I misbehaved?"

"You're telling me." Cheryl clicked her tongue. "Wasn't it Rafe here who christened you the naughtiest little girl in the world."

Ally smiled sadly. "Most of the time I was trying to get my father's attention."

In the end Rafe made coffee for them both, slicing a couple of thick slices of Cheryl's delicious cherry and ginger cake.

"Let's have it on the verandah," Ally suggested. "I want to breathe in our wonderful air."

"You're not a bit daunted at the prospect of staying here on your own?" Rafe asked when they were comfortably settled. He wasn't too happy about it himself but Ally was very stubborn.

Ally shook her head, her mass of curls piled untidily but very fetchingly on top of her head. "This is my home, Rafe, it might be full of ghosts. I'm sure I've seen little Mary Louise Kinross playing in the garden even if she did die at age six over a century ago. Kimbara's ghosts and I understand one another."

Rafe sighed in agreement. God knows his own heart jumped around Opal. "I know what you mean. But it so happens, I'm talking about your managing with that hand out of action."

"Give me a little credit, darling." She spoke briskly. "I'm Ally, remember?"

He gave her a very attractive lopsided grin. "You have to be feeling a little emotional to call me darling."

"You're kidding me." Ally shrugged, setting her cup down. "I've called you darling a million times."

His expression was frankly mocking. "Strange, I haven't heard it since you were a teenager."

"When I thought you had an excellent memory, Rafe?"

"You mean the night of Brod's wedding," he retorted smartly, "it was never too clear what you were saying."

"You're not curious?" she asked, trying to sound casual, leaning back in the white peacock chair.

"Too damned scared to be curious," he drawled. "I remember the last spell you laid on me."

"Now you're too proud." A stray ray of sunlight was making a glory of his thick golden hair, gilding the fine modelling of his face with its distinctive cleft chin. She took great pleasure in the shaping of his wide shoulders, the hard muscles of his arms and chest. He was a wonderful-looking man. The same tough Outback stock as herself. She began to feel her emotions churning and it showed in her eyes.

"Don't try to pick a fight with me, Ally," he warned lazily, watching the breeze further tousle her hair. She was wearing a pink cotton shirt and a matching full skirt. Clothes she must have found easy to get into. He couldn't help noticing through the unbuttoned neckline she wasn't wearing a bra. A problem with the cast on her wrist. Again it was there. The quick rush of desire, the waves of urgency that made him want to sweep her into his arms. They had been so companionable these last few days, but he knew how easy it was to get swept into the rapids. "Let's have a pleasant time," he now murmured. "We might take a walk later if you're up to it. I'd like to have a look around."

"That would be nice." *Nice?* When being here with Rafe was some way to a miracle. Ally turned her head, looking towards Kimbara's historic home gardens. Five acres in all. She could see three cowboy-gardeners going about the never-ending job of maintenance. It was a wonderful view from the wide verandah; great stands of native gums, tea-trees and palms, sweeping lawns kept green with bore water, a million blue and white summer-flowering agapanthus, the same huge semicircle of hydrangeas given welcome protection from the big heat by the trees. There were hundreds of flowerbeds, providing brilliant splashes of colour, a formal rose garden to the rear of the house with pergola bush roses everywhere, the sparkle and sound of running water, meandering Barella Creek with its flotilla of black swans and a small colony of ducks, its clumps of bullrushes, arum lilies and other water plants like the wonderful tropical blue lotus.

With all the nectar-yielding shrubs in the grounds it was a garden of birds. They filled the dry aromatic air with their songs and whistles, the flash of their brilliant plumage. As a child she had run around the garden imitating the bird calls, delighting in confusing them so they actually answered back. She had been a wonderful mimic. Still was for that matter.

Rafe was following her gaze, soaking up the garden's beauty and tranquillity. "Every time I come here I mourn what's happened to Opal's garden," he said. "It sorely misses my mother's presence. I detail some of the men but they're no gardeners. They just know how to clean up."

"You need a woman, Rafe," she said gently. "You need a wife."

I want you back, he thought with a harsh throb of pain. Instead he nodded. "I'll have to give it serious thought. I've let things drift so long. Ours was one hell of an emotional entanglement, Ally. I can understand sometimes how you had to flee from it."

"Can you?" She turned her head to stare at him with her green eyes.

Underneath he was still a touch hostile. "It frightened you as much as it gave you excitement. We always had easy communication. Sex just turned our world topsy-turvy."

Her glance wavered. "I never wanted to leave you, Rafe. I never wanted to make you unhappy. Making people unhappy isn't part of my nature. You had such strength, such maturity beside you I guess I felt like a wild kid out of school. I was the chosen one. I had the greatest joy and pride of being your choice for a bride."

He carefully suppressed the old anger. "Ally, darling, you weren't a shy awkward kid," he drawled, "you weren't any quiet little virgin blushing when a man sought you out. You weren't a young woman just beginning to explore your sexuality. You were born knowing the lot! I didn't seduce little ole you. You were dead set on getting us *both* into bed."

She laughed mirthlessly, unable to deny it. "You can say that again. You were everything in the world I wanted. I couldn't wait to know your body. God knows I'd admired it often enough. I thought I had it all figured out."

"Then you got swept up by something else. The big career. You were always full of wild enthusiasms. Marrying Rafe and settling down on the farm didn't seem like such a good idea, after all."

"You hurt me as much as I hurt you." She turned her face to him.

"Lovers usually do. Anyway we're older and wiser now, Ally. Unloved. Unattached." He was simply teasing but she reacted sharply.

"Don't make it sound like it's all too late!"

"No, there's always Lainie," he said in deliberate provocation. "Now there's a girl with a lot of colour in her cheeks. A healthy girl with a good womanly body."

"A good breeder?" she asked ironically.

"A man needs children, Ally." Abruptly he sobered. "They provide us with an excellent reason for living, for striving. I like to think my genes are immortal."

"Well, you'd better get a move on, then," she answered tartly, unable to catch herself.

"All I need is your blessing, Ally. Now," he sidetracked. "Don't be surprised if Lainie decides to call on you. All that business with Harper hit the papers. She's bound to want to call. She's a very sweet girl."

An hour or more later when Rafe was leaving she made him take Cheryl's cake and her homemade biscuits. No cake-makers on Opal. No live-in girlfriend. No wives.

"Wouldn't you rather keep it?" he asked as she went about putting the biscuits in tins, crisp cookies in one, raspberry coconut slices in the other.

"No, these will be a treat for you and Grant. I love cake but I don't eat a lot of it. I have to watch my figure."

"What figure?"

It was just a little joke but some deep ache quickened. She turned abruptly away.

"Ally?" He couldn't imagine that he had hurt her. His beautiful Ally.

She shook her head but he could see her face screwed up fiercely just like when she was a kid and fighting the desire to cry.

"Ally, I didn't mean anything at all." His hand gently cupped her shoulder, turned her to him. "You've got a beautiful figure. It's just that you're really too thin."

"Oh, to hell with my figure!" she burst out, knowing she sounded foolish. "Do I have to beg you to kiss me goodbye, Rafe Cameron?"

"Ah, Ally, what can I say." Violent longing shook him but he bent his head intending to peck hr cheek then fly off home, only she moved. He couldn't endure not kissing her any longer. Her injuries had quickly gutted his sense of self-preservation. She was always in his heart. Day and night.

He moved his mouth gently but strongly over hers, finding it waiting, open, as sweet as the fruit from the tree of knowledge. He tried to keep the high level of sensuality down to a manageable level, but it swirled around them like licks of flame. She was standing very quietly, not moving at all, allowing him to kiss her, to slide his hand through the open neckline of her shirt, another button coming loose as his hand claimed the warm ivory silk of her breast. He could feel that wonderful sexual energy crackling between them, wrapping them in coils of gold. Ally, intensely aroused as ever by his ministrations, the highly sensitive nipples of her breasts drawing into dusky peaks as sweet as berries. She was so perfectly shaped for loving. His loving. He took profound pleasure in her.

She was moaning a little, delighting in sensation, he the expert on her body, the sound rising, circling like a singing bird freed from its cage. It extended his desire, making it terribly hard to retreat. He could feel the tremble in his arms starting, a sure sign passion was eating him up.

Rafe threw back his head, full of sudden, explosive frustration. "If I don't get out of this damned kitchen..." Ally was the only woman in the world capable of doing this to him. It was enraging, humbling. And yet...

"Maybe we should undergo counselling," Ally suggested wryly, her voice reflecting her own struggle. She was so hungry for him. In so much need. Being apart had been terrible.

"Maybe we oughtn't be alone together," he grated.

She gasped at the implications. "Don't say that! It's horrible. I want to come over to Opal. I haven't seen it for so long."

"Did you really expect to?" He cast a stern eye over her beautiful, flushed face. Deep as his voice was, it rang. "I wanted marriage. You rejected the whole idea."

"But, Rafe," she pleaded, laying her head against his chest, grateful beyond words when his arms automatically enfolded her. "I want to come."

"Then how can I possibly deny you." His smile was grim. Ally, the consummate temptress. Every part of her he knew intimately, her satiny flesh. The scent of her skin. Her flavour. Would it ever work out or would they always be coming at each other through barriers. "One thing, my on and off lover," he warned. "You're not *sleeping* over."

She knew just what he meant, her body sparkling with relief. "Would I with Grant in the house?" she joked.

It was his turn to laugh. He had to. "Ally, you'd dream up a way," he said dryly. "You'd even risk breaking your bones."

For two days Ally roamed the station in the jeep. From cool early morning when the sky was tinged with indigo and yellow to the glorious sunsets that set the sky on fire. There was simply no other place on earth that filled her with such a sense of peace, of belonging, of ancestry. Remote it might be, frighteningly lonely to some, she saw beauty everywhere. Desert, dunes and plain, the ancient eroded hills and the hidden valleys, that magic of the caves with their extraordinary rock paintings, the endless chains of billabongs that were a major breeding ground for nomadic waterbirds.

Her favourite birds were the ones that didn't migrate, the sulphur-crested cockatoos, and white corellas, the galahs and the brilliant parrots; the zillions of small birds: the crimson chats and the wrens, the finch and the quail, the great flights of budgerigar flying in formation over the plains, literally turning the sky overhead to emerald with flashes of gold.

It troubled her to see scores of pretty little zebra finch feeding on the ground only to have a hawk leisurely swoop on the group. The falcons and the great wedge-tailed eagles liked to take their prey on the wing. That was nature. She had never become so thick-skinned that she didn't hate the kill.

At first, Ted, feeling responsible, was dead against her taking the jeep out, although she promised she would drive slowly to allay his fears.

"What if you go over a damned pothole?" Ted said. "What if you run into a bloody camel? They're ill-tempered beasts at the best of times. There are two big males on heat out in the hills. We came on them only the other day, fighting each other and roaring with rage."

"You didn't shoot them?" Ally well knew the wild camels, descendants of animals imported into the desert in the early days of settlement did a great deal of damage, particularly to fences.

Ted shook his head. "We try to tolerate them. But they're a worse nuisance than the donkeys."

"I'll keep to all the recognised tracks," she promised, full of zeal to oblige.

"You'll have to, Ally." Ted twisted his battered akubra round and round in his hands. "Rafe would tear strips off me if you had an accident."

"So who's going to tell him, then?" Ally asked with insouciance. "Anyway, I haven't done anything stupid for years. I've been driving around the station since I was twelve. I'll have no difficulty controlling the jeep. Besides, when has a broken arm or a broken leg for that matter stopped you?"

Ted scratched his balding head. "That's all very well, Ally. I'm a tough old bird."

"So am I." She laughed. "Don't feel bad, pardner. Your concern is charming."

And she was true to her promise. She took care, keeping to the main tracks and limiting her speed. Once a kangaroo leapt out from behind a boulder to stop dead on the track right in front of her, staring at her in the familiar dopey, endearing, fashion as if she could possibly do anything to harm him. Ally obliged by going around the big marsupial. She visited the mustering camps, watched a couple of fine-looking brumbies being broken in by Barney Crow, their part aboriginal stockman who had a wonderful way with horses.

The men at first were a little shy of her, even the ones who had known her all her life. She wasn't one of them any more. She was Miss Kinross who had gone away to become famous. It didn't take Ally long to make the awkwardness disappear as she enjoyed a cuppa and a slice of damper baked over the hot coals with them during a break.

Ally had always found it easy to make friends. Her father would have been coldly disapproving. He was one of the old school who kept himself many, many steps removed from the station staff. Ted Holland was the only one who had ever been allowed into the homestead. And then only to give an accounting.

Her nights were unsettled, the old fears clawing at her dreams. It would take her a while to recover from her trauma, but by day she was always on the move, causing Cheryl to remark on her energy.

"I would have thought your nasty experience would have made you want to relax, Ally," she called from the verandah of the Holland's comfortable white timber-framed bungalow.

"I am relaxing, Cheryl," Ally answered her. "I adore being

home. My biggest fear here is having an emu or a kangaroo jump at me."

The house was enormous after her apartment. In the evenings she turned cupboards out. Had a look inside. She found lots of photographs of herself when she was very small. Many of them when she was a baby. She never realised she was so cute. Even then she had a mop of curls. She couldn't imagine her father had taken them. It had to be her mother or Grandpa Andy.

Her mother! Even the word was an elegy. *Mother.* Was it possible her own relationship with Rafe had been influenced by her parents' disastrous marriage? When it got right down to it, at that point, she was so *young,* she had feared marriage. There had been such an overload of emotion. All her childhood and early adolescence there had been a near mystical bond between herself and Rafe. The relationship that had been definitely non-sexual, more like family, overnight culminated in Rafe's becoming her fantasy lover.

All those hormonal upsurges! She blushed to think of them, the powerful needs and the crazy wishes. In its way growing up had been a traumatic experience for her. She had fallen wildly in love too early when love meant: *pain. Her mother going away.* Her mother had been passionately in love with her father at the time of their marriage, but in the end she'd been forced into leaving him. Maybe in fleeing Rafe she had been trying to protect herself against such a bleak eventuality.

Except Rafe was an entirely different being from her father. As a woman who had been intent on mastering a career, she recognised that fully. Even if Rafe had slammed a door on her. Rafe wasn't into control and dominance that masked a fragile ego. Rafe wanted a wife as his life's partner, with the full security of his support and love. She thought establishing herself as an actress was a worthwhile goal. Now she found she didn't want that at all. The Dream was still the same. The Dream was Rafe.

CHAPTER NINE

ON THE THIRD morning she heard the most welcome sound in the world. The sound of Rafe's Piper circling the house. Now at long last she would get to see over Opal, the historic homestead she had once expected to go to as a bride. The homestead where she had fully expected to live out her days as Alison Kinross Cameron. Both sides had fully supported that once. Even her father who had related far better to Rafe than he ever had to his own son. Why that was, she had ceased to wonder. Perhaps it was because Rafe was a Cameron, a different dynasty. Brod was the Kinross heir who for years had performed the real tasks of running the chain. It was Brod, like Rafe, who had the true dedication.

She was waiting for him at the airstrip when he landed, leaving the jeep parked in the shade of the trees. Within minutes they were airborne, Ally filled with anticipation for what the day might bring.

"Should I bring my nightie and a toothbrush?" She tried a joke when he rang to invite her over, wanting to behave perfectly but finding herself too darned nervous to manage it.

"Whyever would you need to do that?" he'd answered suavely. "I'll have you home before sunset."

"You used to invite me for the night," she'd reminded him

with some nostalgia, trying desperately to get back on the old easy footing.

"Sorry, Ally, darling, you're banned for life."

So that was that! Nevertheless she'd tucked a toothbrush into her tote bag in the wry hope he might relent. She realised she was all but flinging herself at him, but her pride seemed to have flown out the door.

Her first sight of Opal's homestead brought a flood of memories surging back. Rafe's mother had always been up there on the verandah awaiting their arrival. A warm friendly woman but always maintaining her dignity. They had been great friends. She so needy for motherly attention, the older woman with a household of men, touchingly appreciative of young female company.

"What are you thinking about?" Rafe asked, almost reading her mind.

"How your mother was always waiting for you on the verandah."

The dull pain never went away. "How you and she used to talk. Chatter, chatter, chatter. Even Dad had to ask you to put it on hold." Delighted to see them both laughing and happy.

"We women had tons of important things to discuss. Fashion and gossip. Novels we had read. Who was getting married. Who was breaking up. Families who were in trouble and what could be done to help. What was going on in the rest of the world. We talked about everything. Your mother loved to hear what Fee was up to. I think she got a lot of vicarious pleasure out of Fee's glamorous life without ever wanting to lead it."

Rafe smiled. "I know. We used to tease her. Obviously two husbands aren't enough for Fee?" He gave Ally an amused sidelong glance. "David has settled in very nicely."

She could only nod in agreement. "I think he's always had a crush on Fee. Not that he didn't love his wife."

"Not trying to pair them off?"

"Fee means a lot to me," Ally said. "I think she and David could be very happy together. David is a very cultured man

of wide interests. Fee's at a time of life when she's ready to
settle down."

"I'm strangely moved by that."

Rafe's mouth curved in the way she loved.

"But it wouldn't go down too well with Francesca's father,
would it?" he asked.

"Mmmmm." Ally took time to consider. "He could hardly
object. He and Fee were divorced years and years ago. The earl
has happily remarried."

"But why pick his *cousin*?" Rafe raised a questioning brow.

"David is the best man, that's why. Don't be a spoilsport,
Rafe Cameron."

"I'm sorry," he apologised, a decided glint in his gold-flecked
green eyes. "I adore your fabulous aunt. She provided us all
with a lot of colour."

The 4WD swept around the circular drive, gravel crunching
under its heavy tyres, Rafe bringing it to a halt at the base of
the short flight of stone steps that led to the verandah.

Opal Downs homestead, a single-story structure, lacked the
conscious splendour of the two-storied Kimbara built in the
style of a grand English country mansion, and its home gardens,
as Rafe had warned her, had suffered badly, but Ally loved it
probably because the homestead had soaked up all the love and
devotion that had gone on within its walls. It had a palpable aura
of serenity and comfort.

The house was a fine example of English Regency adapted to
suit the harsh Outback conditions. Wide verandahs surrounded
the house on three sides, protecting the central core. The timber
balustrades, the fretwork and the classic pillars were all painted
a pristine white, the series of timber shutters at the French doors
a dark glossy green, lending a charming airiness and sense of
coolness to the house.

The main structure was composed of a particularly fine rose-
coloured brick that had mellowed to a graceful desert pink. The
slate roof added another touch of elegance, the green toning

harmonising with the all-over colour scheme. Like Kimbara, constructed at the same time, a wealth of skills in the way of tradesmen had been borrowed from around the colony, builders, woodworkers, plasterers, stonemasons. Charles Cameron and Ewan Kinross had been in competition to see who could complete their homestead first.

Charles Cameron, less concerned with grandeur had finished many months before. Ewan Kinross marked the completion of his splendid gentleman's residence by taking to it a bride, Cecilia, his kinswoman, whom both men loved. Rebecca, as Brod's bride, would get to wear Cecilia's famous opal and diamond necklace now. Indeed Rebecca had already worn it to a ball, drawing a great deal of attention to herself as her father had intended. Just to think of the old story, Ally found upsetting, so she pushed it away. Brod and Rebecca were married now with a long happy life in front of them.

"Let's make a ceremony of it, shall we?" Rafe asked as he helped her alight from the Toyota.

She tipped her face to him, her eyes challenging. "You're not going to carry me over the threshold?"

"I doubt I could stand the weight."

"I thought you were the one who kept telling me I was stick thin." She let go of his hand, breathing in deeply to cover a whole range of emotions. "It's such a beautiful day I suppose Grant is up and away?"

He nodded. "Pretty close, as it happens. Victoria Springs."

"What?" she stared at him hard. "I really hope he doesn't tell Lainie I'm here."

"Should that put a dampener on anything?" he enquired very suavely.

"Don't be nasty, Rafe. So what form is this celebration going to take? I'm always open to suggestions." She shook her curly head tied at the nape with a silk scarf.

"Now isn't that a fact! Actually I put out a brand-new doormat in your honour. It says Welcome."

"But *am* I?"

"I don't know. You wouldn't have been up until recently." The remark came out a lot more crisply than he intended but it was intensely unsettling having her back on his home ground. Having her back where they had first made love together. He could still feel the enormous wound to his pride, to his psyche, when she had gone off and left him. Sure the wound had healed over, but the place still plagued him like a phantom limb.

Going to bed with Ally was as inevitable as taking his last breath. That hadn't changed, but he wanted no more deep confusion in his life. She would return to her career and her large network of friends within the business. He would have to accept what couldn't be changed and find himself a satisfactory wife. There were any number of beautiful, desirable, intelligent women out there. Let's face it, he figured on the Most Eligible list. He'd find a good wife if it killed him.

"So are you deciding this was a bad idea?" Ally confronted him in her spirited fashion, in her own way extremely proud.

He shook his gleaming golden head, a certain measure of wry resignation in his voice. "Opal welcomes you back, Alison Kinross. I guess your spirit will never leave."

"No, it won't!" Her green eyes glittered like emeralds. She turned to him so quickly, her sable-sheened hair whipped around her face. "I laid a claim to you, Rafe Cameron, when I was a child. I love you better than anybody. Better than anyone else will. You just remember that." She swallowed convulsively on the emotion that rose to her throat.

He studied her with a taut smile on his mouth. "Make sure to remind me at my wedding. Much as I love you, Ally, I can't go through life with your hooks in me."

"Hooks?" Ally winced involuntarily. "You really don't want me back?"

His heart lunged, though he spoke satirically. "Are you ready to toss your career aside?" he countered, taking hold of her hand

and leading her to the steps. "I don't think so, Ally. It makes me awfully sad, but that's life."

She spoke what was uppermost on her mind. "You know it scares me sometimes the way everyone believes I'm going to follow in Fee's footsteps."

He froze. "Hell, Ally, isn't that what you've been working for all this time?"

"I have no pretensions to stardom," she said as emphatically as she could.

"You could have fooled me." He was mocking now, holding her hand on the verandah.

"I guess I have," she agreed quietly. "I thought I wanted to prove I could act. Or prove I could be somebody out there in another world. I suppose I wanted a *choice*."

His mouth twisted ironically. "Yes, you did, and you made one. You've put in a lot of hard work and it has paid off. I'm not into watching much television, as miraculous as it's been for the bush, but I've watched your show and I have to say you're something special. You're beautiful, you're spirited, you radiate warmth and intelligence. You're delightful. The camera loves you, the way you walk and talk, the radiant flash of your smile, the bubbly laugh. You have an individuality about you, a glow. I'm not in the least surprised the movie offers are starting to come in."

She went to the balustrade and slid her uninjured arm around a white pillar. "Everyone is very disappointed I'm leaving the show. They're planning on killing me off while I'm out on some errand of mercy. Needless to say, Matt has buried his career."

"I'm not surprised." Rafe's voice was a rasp. "He's barely civilised. Do you have to go back to finish some scenes?"

"No." She paused to watch an eagle in flight. "They're working on it. I'm still having nightmares. I'm even hesitating before I pick up the phone."

He joined her at the rail and placed his hands lightly on her shoulders. "It'll pass. Give yourself a little time to regain the harmony in your life, Ally. You're strong. You'll find yourself again."

His attitude plainly warned her he gave no serious credence to any talk of her abandoning her career.

He let her wander around the main rooms of the homestead at her leisure.

To the left and right of the spacious hallway graced by arches, flowed the old drawing room and the formal dining room with their matching richly carved fireplaces and mirrored overmantels. The beautiful ceilings with their detailed plaster work had unquestionably been done by the same team of craftsmen who had worked on Kimbara, with very fine crystal chandeliers adding their own elegance and splendour. The formal dining room led to the library through wide folding doors with pedimented overdoors that almost reached the sixteen-foot-high ceiling, beyond that the huge study Rafe had taken over from his father, and a smaller one on the other side of the passageway used by Grant.

The mainly Victorian furnishings with a selection of rather splendid Oriental artefacts were still in an excellent state of preservation, but Ally itched to replace a lot of the soft furnishing as Rafe's mother had planned to do.

Virtually nothing was changed since the last time she had been in the homestead. It was fairly obvious, too, the brothers, Rafe and Grant, kept almost exclusively to the less formal rooms of the house, using the morning room, which adjoined the huge old kitchen, for meals and the large informal sitting room facing the rear garden and a loop of the creek, to relax.

While she was exploring Rafe stood quietly watching her circle each room in turn. If she hadn't been an actress she could have been a dancer, he thought. Her movements were so graceful, so fluid, so springy. He remembered all the dances and balls they had attended together. Outback people revelled in such occasions.

The balls on Kimbara had been marvellous. Stewart Kinross

had been very much the lord of the manor with his wonderful good looks and his dark glinting sardonic manner. Ally had a high look of her father, as did Brod, except for his startling blue eyes, but when you saw Ally you automatically thought of the brilliant Fee. It must have broken Sir Andrew's heart when his adored daughter left her Outback home to set sail for England, Rafe thought.

Fee's father, Ally's grandfather, had loved his only daughter deeply. Fee's spreading her wings had stopped all his plans. Of course, Sir Andrew wanted her to marry someone like his own father and settle down to life on the land. Sir Andy had wanted grandchildren. Lots of them. He had three, it was true. Two he'd adored so openly, and little Francesca, born last, almost inaccessible to him, shielded by her father's English family.

It was very quiet in the old ballroom, which hadn't been used in many years. The Kinrosses had built their great hall to accommodate cattlemen's conferences and their gala functions; the Cameron dances had always been held here with homage paid to their Scottish ancestry, an ancestry the Kinrosses shared as did many Outback families.

Ally stopped in front of a magnificent portrait of Charles Cameron in full Scottish regalia that hung in the ballroom above little gilded settees and chairs that were pushed back against the walls. A few feet away was a companion portrait of his wife, with the Cameron tartan arranged with great panache around her bare shoulders and her billowing white silk ballgown. Another Scot. She was smiling, a lovely-looking woman with a generous figure, reddish gold hair, large hazel eyes and high colour in her cheeks. Smiling radiantly no matter she had been married on the rebound after Ewan Kinross had wedded the legendary Cecilia.

"I wonder what went wrong between our ancestors," Ally paused to ask. There were any number of theories, but no one ever knew and the main characters had never said. "I can't imagine marrying one man when I was in love with another."

He looked at her, masking a flash of pain. "People make accommodations all the time, Ally. The girl I marry mightn't be *you* but I'm damned sure I can learn to love her."

"You can transfer your affections that easily?" She swung her head, fixing him with her eyes.

He nodded calmly. "I'm not going to doom myself to the bachelor life. I want family. Children. I love children. You should see me with my godchildren."

Whatever had she done walking away from this fabulous man. "I know you'll make a wonderful father." Ally moved further along to stare up at the portrait of Charles Cameron's wife. "This is where that wonderful flamboyant hair comes from. And the gold-flecked hazel eyes. Grant's colouring is tawnier. You're pure gold." Ally sighed, looking up at the painted familiar eyes. "She looks a lovely, open, good-humoured woman. I really like her."

"Not Cecilia the temptress," he pointed out, very dryly.

"Cecilia was doomed to be very unhappy, but this woman wasn't."

He gave a faint grimace. "I expect, like me, my ancestor reasoned the best way to go was get on with life. The marriage turned out to be long, happy and fruitful."

"I'm glad." Ally turned about, giving him her incandescent smile. "You Camerons are such nice people. My grandfather had hopes Fee and your father would fall in love."

"Yes, I know. I don't feel bad it turned out differently. Dad admitted once he had a crush on her. I might even go so far as to say everyone did, but he knew Fee wasn't going to settle down like a good Outback wife. Fee was going to fly the coop and never come back." Even as he was speaking, Rafe felt the old traitorous twist of his heart. Like aunt, like niece.

"Dance with me?" Ally suddenly asked. "Let's pretend it's the old days. Didn't we have the mot wonderful times? I remember as a child staring into this room, watching all the grownups dancing." She closed her eyes and began to sway around the room. She was sick to death of the cast on her arm. She couldn't wait to get rid of it. "Isn't it romantic, da da da da da." She couldn't really think of the words, on a night like this.... "Isn't it romantic."

Around and around she went in a loose summer dress, sleeveless, low in the neck, the fine, white cotton printed with one huge yellow hibiscus across the skirt. A little girl's dress, except Ally wasn't a little girl. She was all woman. With the cast she was forced to keep one arm to her side but the other lifted as if to go around a partner's neck.

Everyone had wanted to dance with Ally. All the boys. Ally as light and drawing as a flame. She had a lovely clear singing voice to match her voice. Absolutely true, but she was making a mess of the lyrics. He had to stop himself from joining in. He wanted *her* to stop. He wanted to prevent her from reclaiming his heart. But he wanted the taste of her lips on his tongue. He wanted to pick her up and carry her through to the silent master bedroom with its great four-poster bed. Memory of the first time he had taken her slid into his mind, an experience so profound he knew if he lived to be a very old man it would be one of his everlasting recollections.

"Dance with me, Rafe." She called to him. "Come on, please. Some memories never go away. I remember the way you looked at me when you saw me dressed for Corrie Gordon's twenty-first birthday ball."

And Ally was sixteen. Overnight turned from a tall, graceful, skinny, tomboy who used to pop up out of nowhere into the most alluring woman. How had it happened so fast? One day she was still caught up in the craze to go fishing for barramundi, the next she was wearing a dark green velvet dress with long tight sleeves, a low oval neckline that showed the sweet curve of her delicate breasts and a swaying bell of a skirt. Instead of riding boots, evening shoes with the glitter of diamanté adorned her feet, her customary untidy plait as thick as a rope transformed into a gleaming dark cloud of curls that framed her beautiful vivid face.

"My God, would you look at her!" Brod, at his shoulder, had cried, the brotherly pride vibrant in his voice. "If she isn't Aunt Fee all over again!"

Even then Brod's remark had struck at him forcibly like a cold fist, though he had buried the remark deep. Fiona Kinross had gone away when she was only a few years older than Ally.

Now Ally slowed up to face him. "You're not a bit of fun any more," she accused.

"I'm not into *dancing* any more."

"It's a bit early to give it up," she lightly mocked. "You were a wonderful dancer. Everyone used to stop to watch us. It's funny how big men can be so light on their feet. I expect in your middle years you'll stomp around like John Wayne." She lifted her curly head. "This one for me? Please, my Raphael. My angel."

"No man in his right mind should get so close to you, Ally," he said, feeling skeins of desire unravelling.

"Remember how I used to call you that? My angel. You with the golden hair and the golden skin and the dazzle of your eyes."

"Lay off, Ally," he said, his iridescent eyes flickering with deep buried hostility.

She arched her swan's neck and gave a great big sigh. "Hell, Rafe, you're not going to turn into a *frog*?"

His reaction was immediate. Fierce, a little savage. He threw out one arm and jerked her to him, holding her body very closely against him, his breath coming deep and harsh. "What *is* it you want?"

She strained back a little so she could stare into his taut, handsome face. "I want you to marry me." Now that she had said it, it almost stopped her breath.

"What?" His deep voice was a thunder. She could feel the force of his anger like it was *live*.

"I said, I want you to marry me." A sudden rush of tears glittered in her eyes.

He knew he was a heartbeat from losing it. Maybe less. "Do you actually *mean* it or is this some cruel joke?"

"Never." She shook her head. "I want you. I need. I love you."

"You mean you want to ruin me." He gave her a terrible look of contempt.

"How could I ever do that?" She tried to put everything she felt for him into her eyes.

"I couldn't stand your going away, Ally," he grated. "I couldn't stand it then. I couldn't stand it now. My wife has to be with me. I have to know she's there. I have to know she's someone who's going to want our children. Who's going to be *there* for them. Look how Fee wrecked lives. Your cousin Francesca had a miserable childhood. I suppose to this day her husband doesn't feel free of her."

All of which was true, but Ally fought back. "Don't transfer Fee's curse to me, Rafe. I am not Fiona Kinross, I'm Ally."

"And you want me to take you back?" he asked with hard incredulity.

"You're going to take me back," she flared with her own powerful temper.

Incredibly he laughed. "You're right, Ally. I'm going to take you. You want me to make love to you, don't you? Like wild sex is going to heal everything?"

"Not *wild*," she said very gently, touching the tips of her fingers to his sculptured mouth. "You have to be careful with me. I've got fading bruises all over my body. I have this forearm. I have a big scar buried in my hair."

"You know all about seduction, don't you?" He took her face between his hands, outlining her wide beautiful mouth with the tip of his tongue, deliberately teasing her when he could feel that rising, head-spinning, extravagant passion.

"I'm not ashamed of it," she said, her dreamily beautiful emerald eyes closed. It wasn't said in arrogance, or triumph, but a simple statement of fact. Yet it gave him the lash he needed.

"Well, it's not on, Ally." Very slowly he released her, gratified his voice sounded cool and ironic though it cost him a huge effort. "You're as spellbinding as ever you were, but I'm older and wiser now. I still retain a handful of my marbles. I don't know what's the matter with you today. I suppose the ordeal that Harper put you through has made you a little afraid. Your injuries have slowed you down, but in another few weeks you'll be out of that cast. Your head will be properly healed and you'll be thinking about resuming life. Your real life, that is."

All her blossoming hopes plummeted. Sure she hadn't thought it was going to be easy. "So what do I have to do to prove I'm on the level?"

He looked down his straight nose at her. "I don't know if you can, Ally," he said, trying to sound philosophic. "Maybe you are. Maybe you aren't. Who knows with a woman? Let alone your kind of woman. I tell you what..." He took her arm with great courtesy. "Why don't we leave the whole thing alone until you're feeling more like yourself? I was thinking we could have an early lunch then take the horses out. I've heard all about your exploits in the jeep, now I can find you a quiet hack, not the usual temperamental firecracker you go for, and ride to Pink Lady creek. It's literally covered with the most dazzling waterlilies. You'll like that."

"Thanks, Rafe," she said quietly, knowing she was outmanoeuvred.

But not outmatched!

It was midafternoon. They were returning to the house after a ride of real companionship based on their mutual love of the land when they heard the sound of a chopper splitting the quiet air. It was apparent the chopper wasn't putting down at the airstrip, the sound was coming even closer.

"That'll be Grant," Rafe said, screening his eyes with his hand and looking skyward. "He's early, I didn't expect him until sundown."

"It will be nice to see him," Ally said with genuine affection. It would have been marvellous to spend the rest of the time alone together, but Ally had always been fond of Grant. "He's been mad about aircraft since he was a kid. Now he's made a thriving business out of it. I suppose you worry?" She knew he would. None of them after the Cameron fatalities had ever felt *really* safe.

"I try not to," Rafe sighed. "But it's not easy. Grant's all I've got."

"And me. And Brod." She glanced at him.

"And Lainie," he added slyly. "I expect you'll see her one of these days."

They saw her a lot sooner than expected. Grant set the helicopter down as lightly as a bird on the lawn while they watched from the verandah.

"He's got someone with him." Ally crinkled up her eyes against the brilliant sunlight. All hopes of having Rafe to herself were vanishing.

"I'm afraid so. Party's over."

The rotors slowed, then stopped. Grant was out on the grass helping his passenger to alight.

Lainie.

"Speak of the devil," Ally moaned.

"How can you say that of such a sweet girl? Smile, Ally, they're on their way."

"Howdy, you two!" Lainie yelled, and began to wave. "I cadged a ride with Grant."

"That's just awful!" Ally glanced wryly at Rafe. "Did Grant really have to tell her I was here?"

"Surely you want to have a word with one of your biggest fans?" he countered, amusement in his hazel eyes.

"I suppose I must," Ally sighed. "I don't know why I'm speaking like this. I like Lainie. There was a time we used to laugh ourselves silly."

"I take it you've sobered up?"

"Especially since she's taken a great interest in you," Ally told him tartly. "I expect you're the one she's really come to see."

"Let's find out." His face under the black akubra he still wore had a casual power.

Lainie and Grant made their way across the lawn to the front steps, Grant looking very much the action man in his khakis. Lainie dressed attractively in a rather fetching drawstring peasant blouse of many colours teamed up unexpectedly with tight designer jeans. Her thick fair hair, one of her greatest assets, flapped in the breeze as beautifully groomed as a show pony's mane.

"Ally, great to see you!" Lainie gave her infectious laugh. "As soon as Grant told me you were visiting I insisted he let me join in the fun." Her sparkling eyes moved to Rafe. "Why didn't you let me know, Rafe Cameron? Ally is one of my dearest friends."

"I would have, Lainie," he drawled, "only it took me ages to clean up the house."

Lainie leapt up onto the verandah, about to give Ally a big hug, stopping when she saw the cast on her forearm. "Oh, you poor thing! That's awful. We were all absolutely dismayed when we read what had happened to you in the papers. Mum said you made one big mistake when you left the bush."

Before Ally could react, Grant went to her and kissed her cheek. "Hi, Ally. It's true, we've all been anxious about you."

"And you've got so thin." Lainie's tone suggested Ally was visibly losing weight by the second. "That dress is hanging on you."

"That's what it's supposed to do, Lainie," Ally said. "I need things that are easy to put on."

"And end up with something very easy on the eye." Rafe's mouth curved in an appreciative smile.

"Thanks for that." She turned her head to him.

"Not really. I just loved looking at your bare legs when we were out riding."

Lainie wheezed abruptly, then started to cough. "You rode in that?"

"I've got nothing to hide. I tried but there's no way I can manoeuvre myself into jeans," Ally said. "I'll have to wait until the cast comes off."

"Yes, but…"

"Shut up, Lainie," Grant said calmly.

"I've had some news from Fran that might interest you, Grant." Ally briskly changed the subject. "She's quit her job."

"Blimey. I thought girls like her didn't need a job," Lainie interrupted. "Lady Francesca de Lyle. I thought Fran was just filling in time until she married a jolly old lord."

"So what is she going to do now?" Grant locked onto Ally's gaze, ignoring Lainie entirely.

"I think she wants to spend more time with her mother." Ally had the air of a woman who thought it a very good idea. "She can always get a job here."

Lainie fought to contain herself, failed. "It's all *your* fault, Grant. You were making goo-goo eyes at her at Brod's wedding. Leading her on," she teased.

"I was not!" he clipped off, bristling just a little. "Don't get my goat, Lainie, or I won't drop you back home."

"Only joking. Can't you take a joke?" Lainie punched him playfully on the arm. "I think Francesca is absolutely lovely and she *sounds* such a princess. I quite see why you were smitten."

"What about a coffee or a long cold drink?" Rafe smoothly intervened. "Are you going back right away, Grant?" He turned to his brother.

"I'll wait for Lainie," he said in an all-suffering voice. "Relax for a while. What else did Fran have to say?" he asked Ally as they all walked indoors. "More to the point, when is she thinking of coming?"

"I expect she's after him," Lainie confided to Rafe in a whispered aside. "Some of those old aristocratic families haven't got a razoo any more."

In the kitchen Lainie took over the making of the coffee with brisk efficiency, the men wandering off as soon as they saw she was handling it. "Aren't you a bit nervous over at Kimbara all on your own?" she asked Ally, going to *exactly* the right cupboard for coffee cups and saucers.

"I'm not on my own, Lainie." Ally stood over by the window, looking out. "There's Ted and Cheryl. All our people. Any one of them would come to my aid if necessary."

"I know. I meant on your own at the homestead." Lainie ground fresh coffee beans, continuing to talk over the noise. "Heavens, I could never manage to find my way around. It's so big."

"Not for me. So what have you been up to?" Ally asked, trying to divert Lainie without real hope of success.

"We've got a new dog, Kaiser," Lainie announced, looking pleased and proud. "He's magnificent."

"Don't tell me, a German shepherd."

Lainie laughed, selecting the largest plunger. "We love the breed. I know cattle dogs are more to your taste."

"Kimbara *is* a working station."

"So, when are you off again?" Lainie asked brightly, making heroic efforts to hide her jealousy.

"Give me time, Lainie," Ally pleaded wryly. "What's all this about?"

Lainie bit her lip. "You and Rafe are just friends. So you *said*?"

"So?"

"Gee, I don't appreciate having to ask you this, but have you any plans for staying over?" Lainie's fair, attractive face grew hot and ruddy.

"The things people ask you," Ally sighed. "Actually I packed my toothbrush."

"You didn't!" Lainie stared back at her horrified, glancing swiftly in the direction of the hallway as Rafe came back into the kitchen.

"Can I carry something out?" He couldn't fail to notice Lainie's open-mouthed expression. "What's up?"

Lainie felt so close to crying she couldn't hold back. "You've never asked *me* to stay over." She couldn't control her sudden hostility towards Ally.

"What do you mean?" Rafe looked from one young woman to the other.

"If Ally's staying, I'd like to stay, too," Lainie told him firmly. "We could make up a foursome and play cards."

"Are you crazy!"

"Now there's a mood booster," Rafe drawled. "The only snag is, Ally isn't staying over, Lainie. Neither are you. I've learned how to protect my reputation."

All anxiety left Lainie's face. "You tease, Ally," she said. "You and the toothbrush! You always like to kid around. I was just asking Ally how long she's going to stay with us, Rafe. When *are* you going back to Sydney, Ally?"

"When it's safe," Ally offered laconically.

"I can never work out if you're fooling or not," Lainie complained. "That wretched Harper. You'll have to make sure he stays away. Anyway, now you're going to be a famous movie star you'll be surrounded by security people. It's so exciting when you come to visit us. We envy you all your glamour."

She was jealous. Of course she was jealous, Ally thought, but she's making her point and, being Lainie, hammering it home.

"Where's that coffee?" Grant's voice called nearby. "I feel like I've been waiting for hours."

Lainie smiled brilliantly in Rafe's direction. A woman who could be relied on to be there. "Be right out!"

CHAPTER TEN

ALLY HAD CHERYL up to the house to help her prepare for Fee's and David's visit. They were arriving at the weekend, taking a domestic flight to the nearest Outback terminal where they would be picked up by Grant.

Bedrooms were opened up and aired, fresh linen fragrant with the scent of the native boronia, placed on the beds. Little welcoming touches were brought in, books, ornaments, the bathroom stocked with fresh fluffy towels, bath mats, washers, soaps, bath gels, toothpaste, hand creams, little luxury items. Cheryl went down the list, marking everything off. Fresh flowers would be placed in the rooms on the morning of arrival.

It was exciting to have members of the family at home, Cheryl thought, happily going about helping Ally. Brod and Rebecca, the new Mr. and Mrs. Kinross, would return home at the end of the month. Kimbara would blossom. Stewart Kinross hadn't used friendliness as a means of communication. His children did.

With a couple of hours of daylight left Ally decided to take the jeep out for a short run. She needed to think and the desert fringe was the place to do it. She'd received a long, newsy letter from Bart Morcombe, the director, with an accompanying script for a film the brilliant young New Zealand director, Ngaire Bell, was seeking to make. It was an adaptation of a fairly recent prize-winning Australian novel set in colonial times and offering a very challenging role for the female lead.

"This will take you right up the ladder of success," Bart had written. "Haven't I told you all along you've got the right stuff for a major actress?"

She wasn't the only actress Ngaire saw in the role but apparently the brilliant director had been very impressed when she spotted Ally in an episode of her country doctor series. "She loved your appearance and personality, Ally," Morcombe wrote. "The kind of passion you're able to generate. I really think you should forget the other project and concentrate on getting into Ngaire's film. I tell you it's a showcase role. And you being a Kinross from a landed family would have the background off to a T."

Ally read the script through in one sitting. She couldn't put it down. But strictly speaking, wasn't her interest professional, much in the way she would devour the performance of an acting icon like Dame Judy Dench or Katharine Hepburn. Where was her own drive to success? The absolute conviction she wanted to play this part, allowing Ngaire Bell would even settle on her for the lead. Surely she would snap up established stars. It was a risky business starring a relative unknown. But then it happened. Bart hadn't talked about budget, big or small. The film would be shot on location in and around Sydney before moving inland for the Outback scenes. No exact location as yet.

Ideas were buzzing in Ally's head as she headed out to the sand gravel flats. She had seen them so often smothered in wild flowers, "the white and golden glory of the daisy patterned plains," as some bush poet had put it. She only intended to run out a few miles to Moorak Hill, another monolithic red rock to the northwest. It was a spot that gave her great pleasure. A small stream, more a tranquil shallow billabong lay at its feet, a haven for waders and small birds who made their nests out of the large hollowed-out branches of fallen trees. Desert rivers and streams were marvellous places, their cool refreshing beauty providing such a contrast to the heat and red dust of the spinifex plains, such a huge part of the desert landscape.

Near the rust red eroded summit of Moorak with its small caves and series of small cliffs like a pyramid grew a beautiful ghost gum, its stark white trunk and bright green feathery crown standing out boldly against the glowing, opal blue sky. It had been growing proudly out of the sheer rock of the ancient bastion for as long as Ally could remember. A sight to fire the imagination.

When she reached her destination, Ally parked the jeep in the only protection she could find, a grove of gnarled little trees with precious few leaves to hide their extraordinary skeletons. It wouldn't be long before they succumbed to the arid conditions. Gnarled mulgas were a symbol of drought but good winter rains had fallen and better yet the far tropical north was expecting a rainy Christmas. When the monsoonal rains filled the great rivers of the north, life-giving water flooded down through an inland system to the Channel Country a thousand and more miles away. If the rains were really flooding they could reach to the very centre of the continent and into the vast basin of Lake Eyre, the largest salt lake on the continent, which filled maybe twice every century.

Ally reached out a hand to a leaf but it crumbled at her touch, releasing a strangely attractive scent, like dried herbs. Overhead coasted falcons and hawks forever on the lookout for prey. Ally reached back into the jeep and poured herself an iced coffee from the thermos. The big heat of midday was over, shadows were lengthening but the sun never lost its power. It was important never to become dehydrated. She drank slowly, revelling in her surroundings. The peace and quiet was extraordinary, like being inside an Outback cathedral.

How different it was being home. Home where she looked into the eyes of her beloved. This was where she grew up. This was what held her in place. She had seen enough of the outside world to know this was where she belonged. To know what was important to her. She had faced herself, confronted her needs. It came down to two choices. She could work hard and perhaps become famous in the career she had embarked upon or she could find her way back to being the only woman in Rafe's life. That might prove harder than winning a leading role in a Ngaire Bell film, she thought wryly. They'd had such a wonderful relationship. Beyond the physical. The spiritual, the emotional. She wanted that again. She wanted Rafe's full trust. She was ready in her mid-twenties to make a full commitment. To life. To family. She'd seen quite a few of her friends, fellow actors, women lawyers, busy P.R. consultants, career-oriented women becoming very reflective once they reached their thirties. There was a certain fear they might be going to miss out on their role as *women*. As wives and mothers. They knew they probably couldn't have it all like a man.

Nothing meant anything without Rafe. Ally's vision of herself as a highly successful career woman had burned out. She saw it very clearly now. Rebuilding her once marvellous relationship with him was her major priority. She was happy to forgo a career. It wasn't a very real sacrifice, either. It was her choice. Her way of settling the biggest issue of her life.

Feeling happier and more at peace, Ally returned to the jeep, turning it in a half circle before driving off through the tangle of cane grass. With the approaching sunset the smouldering blue of the sky was being invaded with billowing clouds of colour, rose, pink, amethyst and gold. Hundreds of birds flashed across the sky, going into the long smooth glides that landed them in the lignum swamps. Dawn and sunset in the Outback were magical times. Ally was watching a large squadron of brolgas flying in V formation just ahead of her when she became aware the jeep was overheating. Wisps of smoke were issuing from the bonnet. Her eyes flew to the temperature gauge. The needle was moving steadily into the danger zone. How could that be? She always checked the radiator for water. Number One rule. The jeep like all other station vehicles underwent routine checks.

"Oh, hell!" she muttered to herself, distracted enough to hit a fairly large half-hidden bough that flicked over and up into the air. A little awkwardly she climbed out, cursing her injured wrist, she managed to lift the bonnet without too much trouble then she began to make her inspection inside.

Damn! The radiator hose was coming away. She would have to tighten the clips holding it. Not much of a problem. A few minutes later she was on her way, realising she wouldn't reach home in daylight. Cheryl was bound to tell Ted when he came in. Both would be worried. Ted would most likely drive out to check if everything was all right. At least Cheryl knew where she was heading. She never left the homestead without leaving general directions. With her arm in a cast she had to be more careful than usual, more considerate of other people.

Ten minutes on with the burning red sun sinking towards the grape blue horizon she was forced to stop again. Not only had the hose come away again it was obvious the clips simply weren't going to hold it. The whole thing would have to be re-newed.

"What now?" she asked the darkening bush. She wasn't frightened. There was nothing in the bush to hurt her. No wild animals, only innocent wild creatures. It grew cold at night, but she had a rug. She could throw it around her. There was a small bar of chocolate, a large red apple, the rest of the iced coffee. She could get a fire going. News she hadn't returned would travel fast. If they couldn't find her in the pitch black, blackness so acute it couldn't be imagined, someone would come for her at first light.

Ted saw the helicopter coming in, bright yellow with the Cameron logo an interlocking GC within a dark blue circle. He figured it had to be Grant calling in on his way home, probably to finalise dates for a Kimbara muster, but it turned out to be Rafe. He had the chopper set down before Ted reached the airstrip.

"Now this is a real surprise." Ted beamed, swinging out of his sturdy Nissan. "I thought it was Grant fixin' up for the muster."

The two men shook hands. "Grant's got his hands full right at the moment Ted, but he'll be contacting you soon. I was over at the McGrath place helping out with a problem when a new pile of mail came in. Quite a bit for Brod. Some of it I expect you can take care of. I collected ours and yours in advance. I'll say hello to Ally if you'll run me up to the house, then I'm off home. I prefer not to fly the chopper in the dark."

They found Cheryl waiting in an attitude of anxiety on the verandah of the homestead. "I expect it's nothing to worry about but Ally's not back yet," she called to them the minute they stepped out into the drive.

"So where did she go?" Rafe felt like swearing, his gaze checking the sky. Ally sure needed watching.

"She always tells me her plans." Immediately, Cheryl was on the defensive. "A few jobs needed doing this morning, Rafe, what with Miss Fiona arriving with her friend. Making up beds and such like. Ally likes to get out every day. She loves the sunset."

"So where did she say she was goin', luv?" Ted interrupted patiently.

"Northwest. Out Moorak way, I'd say. I'm just sitting here waiting for her to get home."

"Best go fetch her," said Ted, proceeding to turn back to the Nissan. "Why the hell Ally wants to rattle around in that jeep I don't know." He let out a great sigh. "I would definitely class Ally as a mighty independent woman."

Rafe made a quick decision, based on his intense involvement. "If you lend me the Nissan, Ted, I'll go check if she's on the way back. She wouldn't need to leave it too much longer or she'll be driving home in the dark."

"With one good arm," Ted said, clearly unhappy about that.

"The keys, Ted." Rafe held out his hand, not pushing his authority but it was instantly clear.

None of them dared think. Ally might have had an accident.

"Let me get some food in case you get stuck, Rafe," Cheryl called. "I won't be a minute."

"Fine." Rafe turned to Ted who obviously shared his concern. "I'll either see her coming in or she's had a breakdown of some kind. That's always on the cards. Either way I'll find her. If we don't make it back by nightfall you might give Grant a call. Explain what's happened. It won't be the first time we've spent a night in the bush. You might meet up with us first light."

"Count on it, Rafe. I told Birdy to check the jeep." Ted sounded upset and worried. "Seein' Ally's always takin' it out."

"She'd have trouble changing a tyre," Rafe responded a little grimly. "Don't worry, Ted. It's hardly your fault. I know how stubborn Ally can be. I'll find her." He looked a little impatiently towards the house as Cheryl came flying out carrying what looked like a picnic hamper.

"In case you need it," she called as Ted moved quickly to help her. "Food and drink. Won't hurt if Ally's on her way in."

We should be so lucky, Rafe thought.

Thirty minutes out. No sight of her or the jeep. He had taken a rough track of sorts now he left it, the Nissan bouncing through tall yellow grass and over clumps of spinifex and fallen mulga. He was starting to concede they might have to organise an all-out search for her at dawn. Maybe she had run out of water? Maybe she was thirsty and headed for a creek? wouldn't make Moorak in the light. The sun was already sinking in a great fiery ball. Dusk would be short, a momentary amethyst veil, the vast red earth, the interlocking network of waterways, the crumbling hills, the entire landscape would be blocked out as night fell.

Unbidden but never far from his mind came all the old horror stories. This was killer country if you didn't know it. But Ally did. That gave him great hope. Ally wasn't likely to lose herself in the bush. She would stay by her vehicle even if she ran out of petrol or water or the vehicle broke down.

In the enveloping dusky light he could see the near pyramid form of Moorak. The best course at this point was to head towards it as quickly as common sense allowed. Again unbidden images of Ally. Face down on the red earth. Ally with her head wedged against the steering wheel, the bonnet of the jeep plunged into a crevice that had suddenly opened up for want of water. She wasn't strong enough yet to do the things she did. And yet, wasn't that the way of the bush where everyone was so active.

Stamping down hard on his panic, Rafe began to sound the Nissan's horn, the successive blasts almost painfully loud in the darkening desert. He would have to slow down. He could hit something, put his own vehicle at risk. At least Ally wouldn't be scared like a city woman would be. He'd seen tourists scared out of their wits after they'd been rescued from the waterless wilderness. With good reason.

A kilometre closer with the vehicle's headlights raying out across a night-time scene of aridity and desolation, contorted shrubs and gnarled branches like gigantic bonsai, he heard something.

"Ally!" The deep frown lines etched into his forehead evened out. That was the jeep's horn, answering him. "Keep it going, Ally." He dared to hope she was all right. "Slowly now," he told himself when he was desperate to let the engine rip. This was no smooth city road or even an Outback track full of potholes. This was the unrelenting wilderness. A dying desert oak reared up in the headlights, its twisted upflung branches giving the appearance of a nightmare scarecrow.

He swore beneath his breath, bounced round it, his ears tuned to the S.O.S. of the jeep. "I'm coming, Ally. Trust me. Everything is going to be fine."

But was it? Would the woman he loved with all his heart be forever out of reach. She had told him, in a weakened moment, she wanted to be back in his life. He seemed at that moment he would take her at any price. The Nissan bounced across the mulga plains, riding high across clumps of spinifex and tough twisted fallen branches then dipping sickeningly into narrow crevices and dry shallow gullies.

When Rafe finally caught sight of her she was standing in his headlights, her right arm supporting the injured arm with the cast. God, had she hurt herself? There appeared to be nothing wrong with the jeep.

"Ally?" he bellowed, tremendous waves of love and relief giving way to a crazy anger. Hell, she was even looking back at him like "Isn't this fun?"

It was no surprise then as he gathered her tightly into his arms she laughed aloud, filled with an irresistible happiness he had found her. "You'd better believe this, Rafe Cameron, I knew you'd come for me."

"Did you, now?" He couldn't possibly take it so casually. "I suppose you realise you've had us all terribly worried?"

Immediately she was apologetic. "I'm sorry. Truly sorry. But it's not my fault, Rafe." She pointed to the jeep. "The radiator hose went."

"What a damned nuisance," he muttered shortly. "Isn't Birdy in charge of maintenance?"

Ally flew to Birdy's defence. "Actually he did check it out." Now that Rafe was here, she felt like a kid at a party, no doubt helped along by that nip of brandy. "Isn't this super stuff?" she said blithely, deliberately echoing words she had used so often as a child. "We're going to have to spend a night in the bush together."

But Rafe's emotions were too close to the surface. "What makes you think I won't attempt to drive back. I made it out here, didn't I?" He was aware he was somewhat curt.

"Indeed you did." She stroked his arm. "My hero. Don't be angry, Rafe," she begged him. "All's well that ends well. I'm not hurt. It was my first real chance to commune with the bush at night in years. Look, the stars are coming out." She lifted her curly head. "Millions and millions of them. You never see a sky like that in the city."

He clicked his tongue, looking around them. "We could do with a few streetlights all the same." They were standing in a very small pool of light given off by the Nissan's headlights.

"We are going to stay aren't we, Rafie?"

Her voice, such an instrument of pleasure was pitched low. She never called him Rafie except to tease and taunt. He understood that thoroughly. He looked down at her, seeing she was wearing a little denim shirt with short sleeves and a matching full skirt, buttoned down the front. She was wearing sneakers on her feet. "You're cold," he said suddenly, sounding angry. "You've got a rug in the jeep. You should have put it round you."

"I won't need the rug now. I've got you." She held his stare.

Abruptly he broke away, going to the jeep, and pulled the rug off the front seat. At least she had the sense to use it. "Here, Ally, this isn't funny. Put it on."

She did so immediately, her tone wry. "Aah, we're going to be businesslike, are we?"

"What were you expecting, a party?"

"A party would be marvellous." She stared back up at the blossoming stars. "A party for two. You haven't got any food with you by any chance? I'm starving. All I've had is an apple and a small piece of chocolate."

"Well I can't say cutting back will do you any good. Yes, I've got food. Cheryl put it in. We'll have to make camp for the night. Were you going to stay here?"

Ally nodded. "I wasn't going to move until you came for me. I'm psychic where you're concerned."

"Oh, yes, Ally, you've got all the answers," he groaned. "Get in the Nissan. I'll have to find a better camp site than this. You know damned well how the temperature falls at night."

"So we're going to need to sleep together for body heat."

Her hair fell in a dark cloud all around her face. Her green eyes glittered like a cat's caught in the light. "Full of fun, aren't you?"

She took his arm, hugged it, trying desperately to communicate her deep sincerity for all her covering banter. "Oh, I'm just so happy you're here, Rafe."

"Good." He turned her gently but firmly. "Let's move. Think we can make it back to Moorak?"

"Sure." She walked with him to the Nissan.

"We might be able to find ourselves a small cave."

"As long as you don't mind sharing it with half a dozen rock wallabies."

"Not tonight." He helped her into the passenger seat. "Any wallaby that lives there will have to move on."

They were moving slowing across the rugged terrain.

Ally started to laugh again. "I'm in such a good mood."

"I can see that. Sure you haven't been getting into the medicinal brandy?" he asked dryly.

A fresh bubble of laughter. "I did have a small nip to ward off the cold. I was born in the bush but I still can't get accustomed to the chill of the desert nights. It's so unexpected after the scorching days. What are you doing on Kimbara, anyway?"

"You mean you didn't divine the reason along with the fact I was coming? I collected a bit of mail at McGrath's. Brod's and ours. I decided to deliver it on the way home."

"I hope you intended popping up to the house to see me?"

"I was going to pay you a visit, yes. No mail for you."

"I got mine," she said.

"Who from?"

"Oh, Bart Morcombe." She spoke casually. "He sent a script."

"Which you read?"

"In one long sitting. It's very good. There's a part for Fee if she's interested. Not big but it's important they get the casting right. Heck, what was that?" she cried as the vehicle rocked on its side.

"A blasted boulder," he muttered. "It's a good thing we're nearly there."

They set up camp beside the stream as Rafe couldn't find a suitable cave on the lower slopes. With great efficiency he went about making up the fire, then when it was burning brightly, he rigged a tarpaulin using stout boughs to make it act as a windbreak. Another smaller tarp served as a ground cover, over which went one of the rugs. Station vehicles always carried such equipment in case of emergencies and it worked well tonight.

"Now for the food," Ally said, on her knees busily setting out the contents of the old hamper she and Brod had used as children. "Let's see." She couldn't keep her hunger out of her voice. "Bread rolls." Ally delicately sniffed them. "Nice and fresh. Cheryl must have made them this afternoon. Lord, she's forgotten the butter. A block of cheese. Chicken, a chunk of ham, fruit. No bottle of wine. That's dreadful. We really needed a bottle of wine. And God bless her, nearly half a fruit cake."

"Sounds like a feast." Rafe grinned.

"We could toast the rolls. Burn them to crisp."

"No thanks, Ally. I'll take them as they come. I'm surprised you're so chirpy. I know you weren't lost, but it couldn't have been pleasant."

"I'm normally chirpy," she said. "Have you forgotten? Come and sit next to me. Come on." She grabbed his hand, pulled him down to join her on the rug. "Pretend we're kids again."

"Until you get some of your primitive urges," he said very dryly.

Ally gave a little snort of laughter. "When did you ever need encouragement?"

He ignored that. "So tell me about this new script you've been offered?" He accepted the ham and cheese roll she passed him, wrapped up in a paper towel.

"It's very good." Ally took a bite out of her roll, continuing to talk with her mouth full. "It's an adaptation of Bruce Templeton's novel, 'The Immigrant.'"

"I've read it." Rafe glanced at her clear profile gilded by the firelight. "I suppose you've been offered the role of Constance?"

She was so pleased he knew it. "No, I've been offered the chance to read the script, that's all. Apparently, Ngaire Bell, the New Zealand director, likes my work. Or likes *me*."

"Even I can see you in the part, Ally." He sat quietly. "It might have been written for you, even to the physical description."

It was crystal clear to him now where Ally's future lay. Who was he to deny her the development of her gift? She wasn't any ordinary girl next door. She was immensely talented. She wasn't Lainie Rhodes who would make some Outback man an excellent wife. She was Ally. He might have known her since she was a small child, but Ally had something to offer the world. He loved her. He couldn't change it, only send her on her way. Marriage between them, and he was sure he could get her to marry him, would never work out. They would survive a few years. Maybe have a child, then the same old problems, distance, separation, would erode their love. He wouldn't want any child of his to suffer like little Francesca had.

"Would you like a drumstick?" Ally asked, so happy herself, she was unaware of his sombre thoughts.

"No, I don't think so," he forced a smile.

"Oh, come on! You're a great big man." She put the roast chicken into his hand. "I wish we had a bottle of wine."

"Me, too." All of a sudden he felt like getting drunk. A couple of glasses of wine wouldn't do it. All the alcohol in the world wouldn't numb the pain.

They finished with a piece of fruit each. Ally ate a mandarin, spitting out the seeds, Rafe settled for an apple. "Isn't this beautiful here," Ally said dreamily. "The air is so sweet and fresh we can do without the wine. I love the smell of the bush. It's absolutely unique. I love burning gum leaves. I love crinkling dried leaves into aromatic bundles. I love all the little sounds at night, bush creatures scampering around. I even love the distant call of a dingo. Such a mournful howl." She lay back and Rafe pushed a cushion beneath her head.

"My God, Ally," he said, looking down into her beautiful face, flushed in the coppery light.

"Why are you sounding so regretful?" She lifted her hand, let her fingers explore the deep cleft in his chin.

"Regrets!" He tossed his gilded head away from her like a high-mettled thoroughbred. "I have thousands of them. Haven't you?"

"Of course, I have," she retorted with some spirit. "One can't live without accumulating regrets along the way."

"It's pointless to ask if you're going to accept the role if you're offered it?" He rolled onto his elbow.

She stared up at him. "Even if I got the part I'd turn it down."

"The hell you would," he said in a taut voice, looking down on her broodingly.

"It's very hard for me to get back your trust," she sighed, realising full well words weren't enough.

"It is that. I know you mean well, Ally, when we're alone together but don't you realise…"

"I realise I love you," she cut him off, her voice full of emotion. "I'll always love you. You built such strong defences they won't let you listen. But at some point, I beg you, you've got to believe me."

"Well maybe I do, Ally," he sighed deeply. "Each of us stole the other's heart, but what happens if we marry? Do we bring a tragedy down on our heads."

"Lie down beside me, Rafe," she begged. "Let me show you how much I love you." She fixed her light, sparkling eyes on him, full of entreaty.

His heart was pumping wildly. "No, let me show you," he rasped. Why was life such a mess? Why did love put one at such risk of losing? His arms came under her slender body warmed by the fire, strong enough, tensile as steel, but taking good care not to hurt her. This was the way with them, he realised. No matter the frustrated violence in him, he couldn't bear to hurt her.

He kissed her open mouth that blossomed like a rose, her little moaning breaths gusting back into his. He touched her breast, drew his hand down intimately over her body, bunching the soft denim of her skirt, sliding his hand over a satiny thigh, the length of her leg. The scents of the bush mingled with the scent of her, erotic beyond his understanding. This was how a man and a woman mated, chasing sounds and scents, urgent to know the other's body, as though starved for completion. Two bodies, male and female craving to be one.

"I'm not hurting you," he burst out once, finding her naked breast as delicious as a peach.

"No. I love it." She turned her face into his neck, pressing her lips against his flesh. The damned silly cast on her arm. She was desperate to stroke him as he was stroking her. And yet there was an odd excitement to it, a kind of spice. Gradually, he manoeuvred her clothes away until her body was luminous in the firelight, her blood so heated she felt no chill on her skin. "Ally, are you sure I can't make you pregnant?" he asked urgently, his hand speared into her wonderful hair.

"Make me pregnant," she begged. "Go on, I'd love it."

He stared at her in fascination. "You frighten me. You could lose everything in a minute. Your career."

"No it's an OK time for me," she reassured him. "But I do want your child. Your children. As for my career? Looking back I don't think it existed in the same way it existed for Fee..." She guided his hand down over the smooth curves and planes of her body. "I have something far more important in mind."

He was desperate to believe it. A lie would be fatal. "You can't *do* this, Ally," he said. "I'll never let you go."

She could feel the heat rising from his skin, the male virility, the pounding force of his desire. It was *magnificent!*

"Holding on to your wife is an essential part of marriage," she said with great energy. "How dare you doubt me, Rafe

Cameron. I stopped wanting a career long before tonight. I've tried telling you so often, but if you really think about it, you didn't want to hear. In your hurt you made yourself deaf to me."

It bothered him now that there was a good deal of truth in it. "I must have been completely mad."

She nodded in entire agreement. "The bible refers to the sin of pride," she said severely, then she smiled, the wide luminous smile he adored.

"You mean this, Ally? You know your mind?" He pondered her vivid face so full of eloquence.

"How many times do I have to tell you? I'd give my soul for you."

It sent his confidence soaring. Up and up like an eagle in its powerful flight. "And you are the windows of mine."

A feeling of utter exultation seized him, driving out every last lingering doubt. He felt he would conquer the world for her. Rafe cupped her beloved face with his hands, lowering his mouth passionately to hers.

Around them the bush was utterly still and the glittering stars in all their glory crowded down the sky, scattering diamond dust on a pair of lovers.

EPILOGUE

ON THE MORNING of her wedding day Ally rose early, so full of radiant energy she found she couldn't lie in bed. She dressed in her riding clothes, went quietly through the house filled with wedding guests and out to the stables, saddling up her favourite ride, the beautiful chestnut mare, Aurora, ex-prize-winning racehorse and a present from Brod. Aurora was the ultimate in cooperation or they were perfectly matched, because the mare responded instantly to her lightest instruction.

Twenty minutes later with the dawn wind singing in her ears Ally was galloping across the open grasslands, thrilling to Aurora's speed and power, watching the wonderful glow on the horizon as the sun started into the sky. With the sun came all the glorious rich ochres of the inland. Ever-changing colours that made it such a fascinating place. The pearly grey sky was turning to blue crystal and the birds were out in their millions, every species singing a different melodic line, like instruments in an orchestra, the whole coming together in a perfect, complex, liquidly clear symphony.

Riding was one of her life's greatest pleasures, Ally thought, her mood so buoyant she felt Aurora, like Pegasus might suddenly take wings. She and her horse had developed such a wonderful trusting partnership, a magical harmony. It was far better than driving her BMW but both gave the same feeling of power, of smoothness, of being in control. It was very hard to accept had not some daring Mongolian leapt on a horse's back, the magnificent animal beneath her might have become extinct. Man had to acquire the art of horsemanship before the horse, thought little of eight thousand years ago, was saved from extinction.

She remembered who had taught her to ride as a small child with Brod always a willing helper. It had been Ernie Eaglehawk, Kimbara's finest tracker and horse breaker. The stations owed a big debt to their aboriginal stockmen, the custodians of the ancient land. Ernie had died several years back at a great age but he was one person she would never forget. For his kindness, for the sweetness of his nature, for his natural wisdom. Because of Ernie and his wonderful teaching ability she and Brod were about as good as you get.

She was crossing a shallow home creek when she spotted a rider coming across the plain at a gallop. A moment more and rider and horse took shape. Brod on his majestic Raj. She sat the mare comfortably, waiting for her brother to reach her, saluting him as he reined in alongside.

"Hi, big brother!"

He gave her a brilliant smile. "I told myself that couldn't be Ally. Shouldn't you be in bed resting for your big day?"

"Resting? What are you talking about?" She laughed. "I'm going to enjoy every single minute of it." Her green eyes spilled out radiant light. "Oh, God, I just never knew...."

"I *know*." Brod continued to smile at her broadly.

"Yes, I know you know. You and Rebecca are so close, so much in love it warms my heart to see it."

Brod's expression grew serious. "She was meant for me as Rafe was meant for you. We didn't have much of an early life, Ally, but it's turning out wonderfully now, isn't it?"

"Dear Brod, I love you," she said. "I love the way you and

Rebecca have done everything in your power to make this the most marvellous wedding."

"You deserve it, Ally." Brod gave her a proud smile. "And I love my dual role of giving the bride away and best man. It was the greatest homecoming hearing you and Rafe had resolved all your differences and were finally together again. His joy in you is immense. You know that?"

"He's my man," Ally said, "in every sense of the word. So, we have your blessing?"

Brod gave his white flashing smile. "Ally, so far as I'm concerned you and Rafe marrying is a dream fulfilled." He gathered up the reins, turning the black stallion's head, "What say I race you to the gate of the main compound."

"You're on!" Ally cried. "But don't you dare win!"

"Not on your wedding day," sailed back.

The Outback would long remember the Cameron Kinross wedding, held on historic Kimbara Station, the Kinross flagship. This was the long awaited union of two great pioneering families, and emotions ran high. Guests, three hundred in all, came from every state on the continent, as far away as Texas in the U.S.A. and two of the grand capitals of the world, London and Edinburgh, where both bride and groom had relatives.

As the leading women's magazine reported, the former highly successful TV actress, Ally Kinross, would have four attendants, Lady Francesca de Lyle, her cousin and the only daughter of the internationally famous stage actress Fiona Kinross and Earl of Moray, chief bridesmaid, two of the bride's long-time friends from Sydney, while her sister-in-law Rebecca Kinross, herself not long home from her honeymoon in Europe, would be matron of honour.

The magazine went on to say it had exclusive coverage of the wedding. Their well-known society columnist, Rosemary Roberts, would be in attendance as a guest. The magazine had actually begged to be able to cover one of the biggest weddings of the year. After all, the bride, Alison Kinross, was well-known to the viewing public. The two families were famous in the Out-back. The issue would sell like hot cakes. It was later picked up and subsequently reported the substantial sum that changed hands for exclusive coverage, went to one of Mrs. Cameron's favourite causes, the Sydney Children's Hospital.

Her bridesmaids seemed almost spellbound when they saw Ally dressed.

"Well, don't stare at me as though I'm a creature from some mysterious planet," she laughed, so happy her vitality was like a healing ray of sunshine.

"You look…splendid!" Francesca said for all of them, moving around her taking in Ally's magnificent dress. "Like a young queen."

"That's Fee's tiara," Ally suggested, touching it. "Something borrowed. It's perfectly beautiful."

"So are you." Rebecca went to her and gently kissed her cheek, a feather-light touch so as not spoil Ally's flawless make-up. "That was the most wonderful idea featuring the desert wildflowers on your gown. I'm sure it's going to start a rage."

"Could do." Ally nodded in agreement.

She stood still while all her attendants admired her wedding gown of champagne silk-satin and tulle. It was a wedding dress dreams are made of. Strapless with dramatic swathing of a bil-lowing silk-satin skirt leaving a shimmering tulle centre panel embroidered all over with the everlasting daisies of the desert. Thousand upon thousands of tiny beads, rhinestones and crys-tals had been used to create the small flowers in pinks, white, yellow and gold. The strapless bodice hugged Ally tightly, em-broidered tulle moulding the bust, the draped silk satin defin-ing her narrow torso and tiny waist. It was a stunning gown requiring someone tall with a model's figure and posture to wear it. Ally had it all. Her shimmering champagne-coloured tulle veil matched exactly to her dress stood away from Fee's tiara. A necklet of diamonds, Rafe's wedding gift to her, encircled her slender throat. Diamond studs glittered in her ears.

"Now you can all line up for your inspection," Ally said, thrilled with their appearance and the dizzying culmination of her dreams.

"Just a minute!" Francesca rushed to the mirror to adjust her off-the-shoulder neckline from which each sleeve ballooned out. "Ready." Satisfied she joined the line, a titian-haired beauty with shoulders like cream.

Francesca, as chief bridesmaid, wore the pink of the desert wildflower, a glorious contrast with her hair, Jo Anne, a brunette wore the sunshine yellow of the batchelor's buttons, Diane, the blonde, wore the silvery green of the wildflower leaves, Rebecca, as matron of honour, wore gold.

All wore identical styles, the lovely full skirts flaring to the ground. In their hair they wore a crown of real paper daisies with silk leaves, each crown slightly different as were the small matching bouquets. Around each attendant's neck was an 18-carat-gold bezel-set gemstone on a slender gold chain to match their gowns, a pink tourmaline, a yellow sapphire, a peridot and a topaz, a gift from the bridegroom.

"You all look perfectly beautiful." Ally put her hands together in a little burst of applause. "Thank you so much for attending me."

"Oh, Lord, listen to her." Jo Anne laughed. "We're honoured."

"Now you've got something old," Francesca said.

"Yes, dear," Ally nodded. "You've given me that exquisite antique handkerchief."

"Something blue. What about something blue?" Rebecca fluttered around her.

"I'm wearing it." Ally gave a throaty little laugh. "I won't say where."

"Something new?" Diane completed the traditional requirements.

Ally held out her billowing skirt. "It is a brand-new dress."
Her smile was incandescent.

"Well, there you are then!" Francesca clutched her hands in
delight. "Oh, this is going to be so wonderful. I've got excitement pouring out my ears. I just *love* weddings."

"We'll have to arrange it you're next," Ally told her with a
flutter of mischief.

"That's if Mamma doesn't beat me." Francesca only half
joked then brightened. "Don't forget I caught part of Rebecca's
bouquet, too!"

At exactly three o'clock the ceremony began. Brod guiding his
sister through the smiling sea of guests to where the celebrant
was waiting on the flower-decked dais of Kimbara's ballroom.

"Be happy, Ally," Brod whispered, feeling a consuming rush
of love for her.

Be happy! Ally thought. I'm borne up on wings.

Her hand on her brother's arm, she walked straight to where
her bridegroom was standing, straight and tall, his handsome
head with the glitter of gold. Now after all these years I'm going
to marry the person I've loved all my life!

Rafe and Ally. Mr. and Mrs. Cameron.

* * * * *

The English Bride

CHAPTER ONE

IT WAS GETTING on towards late afternoon when Grant Cameron set the chopper down on the rear lawn of Kimbara as sweetly as a pelican setting down on a lagoon. Winds created by the whirling fanlike rotor stirred up a mini dust storm mixed with grass clippings and a sea of spent blossom from the nearby bauhinias but that quickly abated as the long blades wound to a standstill. Grant completed his interior checks and took off his headset, preparatory to jumping down onto the grass.

This was historic Kimbara Station, desert stronghold of the Kinross family since the early days of settlement; the nearest neighbour to his own family station, Opal Downs, some hundred miles to the north-east.

His older brother, Rafe, much loved and much respected, was currently on honeymoon in the United States with his new bride and love of his life, Alison Cameron, nee Kinross. Rafe ran the station. He, Grant, was making a very successful business out of his own aerial mustering service, operating out of Opal. It had suited both brothers well. Rafe was the cattleman. He was the pilot.

He'd always been mad about aircraft even since he'd been a kid. Even the inconsolable grief of losing their beloved parents to a light aircraft crash hadn't killed his love of flying. With an outback so vast flying was a way of life in Australia. The tragedy had to be survived.

Grant reached for his akubra and slung it on at an unconsciously rakish angle. The sun still had a powerful kick in it and he couldn't altogether forget his tawny colouring, a Cameron trademark. "A pride of lions" was the way people used to describe his dad, Douglas Cameron, and his two sons, Rafe and Grant.

A pride of lions!

For a moment a terrible sadness constricted his chest. He wished with all his heart his dad was still alive. Mum and Dad. They never got to see him make such a success of himself. They would have been proud. He had always been the younger brother, a bit of a wildcat trying to develop in his brother's shadow. Rafe was born responsible, ready to take over from their father.

Out of the helicopter Grant made a quick circuit of the aircraft, his eyes always checking for the slightest sign of possible trouble though the fleet was scrupulously maintained. The yellow fuselage with its broad blue stripe and company logo in blue and gold gave off a crackle as the metal cooled down. He patted the insignia with satisfaction and made off for the house.

It had been an exhausting day driving a whole heap of cantankerous, overheated cattle in from the isolated Sixty Mile out near Jarajara, a single huge sentinel granite dome that marked Kimbara's western border to the camp Brod's men had set up out near Mareeba Waters with its winding water courses. Camp would be shifted as the muster went on. The men were expected to be out for the best past of three weeks. What he needed now was a long cold beer and to feast his tired eyes on a beautiful woman.

Francesca

Not necessarily in that order he thought dryly. Francesca was occupying far too many of his thoughts these days. Lady Francesca de Lyle, first cousin to Brod Kinross, master of Kimbara and brother to Ally, his new sister-in-law. Cameron and Kinross were legendary names in this part of the world, pioneering giants.

Now with the marriage of Rafe and Alison the two families were finally united to everyone's great satisfaction except maybe Lainie Rhodes of Victoria Springs who had nurtured an outsize crush on Rafe since puberty struck her. Not that Lainie wasn't good marriage material but there had never been anyone else for Rafe but his Ally.

The unbreakable bond between them had been forged in their childhood out of tempered steel. Now they were man and wife, deliriously happy from all accounts but Grant realised full well he had better start making plans.

Big as Opal's homestead was he had no intention of intruding on his brother's and Ally's privacy. They would want the homestead to themselves no matter how much they tried to reassure him Opal was as much his home as theirs. A big *share* of Opal Station maybe, which had financed his aerial muster business, but the homestead was for the newlyweds. He was determined on that. Besides Ally had lots of plans for doing the place up and he guessed it needed it.

What would it be like to be married? Grant mused as he strode past the original old kitchens and servants' quarters. Long out-of-date they were perfectly maintained for their historic value. Shrubs surrounded these outbuildings, light filtering trees, the whole linked to the Big House by the long covered walkway he now took.

What would it be like to come home each night to a woman he could take to his heart, to his bed? A woman to share his hopes and dreams, his profoundest inner expectations. A woman he belonged with as surely as she belonged with him.

The first time he met Francesca de Lyle when he was in his teens he had felt an instant click, a deep rapport, now years later he was well into fantasising about her. Why then was he so persuaded an intimate relationship with Francesca could only bring danger to them both? Maybe he wasn't ready for any deep relationship after all. Hell, wasn't he too damned busy to commit. Nothing should be on his mind but work. Building up the business. He had such ideas.

A branch of Cameron Airways was now carrying mail and freight but he'd had recent discussions in Brisbane the state capital a good thousand miles away, with Drew Forsythe of Trans Continental Resources regarding building a helicopter fleet for use in minerals, oil and natural gas exploration.

He'd met the very high profile Forsythe and his beautiful wife, Eve, on several occasions but that was the first time they'd ever got into really talking business. And he had Francesca of all people to thank for that.

Never one, apparently, to let a good public relations opportunity go by, Francesca who had struck an immediate chord with the Forsythes when they had all been seated together at a charity banquet had brought up the idea in the course of an enjoyable evening.

Beautiful blue eyes sparkling she put it to Forsythe: "Doesn't this make good sense to you? Grant knows the Interior like the back of his hand and he's absolutely committed to the big picture, isn't that right, Grant?" She had leaned back towards him then, so heart stoppingly graceful in her strapless satin gown, her lovely cool, clear English voice, full of support and encouragement. Ah, the bright aura of breeding and privilege!

And she was clever. If some sort of a deal ever came off, and he was working on it right now, he owed her. A glorious romantic weekend away together, he fantasised. One of those jewel-like Barrier Reef islands that had those luxurious little self-contained bungalows down near the beach. Though he would have to watch her in the hot Queensland sun. She had the flawless porcelain complexion that so often set off Titian hair. How strange she should want to fit into his background on the fringe of the great desert heart. It was almost like trying to grow an exquisite pink rosebush on the banks of a dried-up clay pan. For all his deep and immediate attraction to her they were an impossible match. And he better not lose sight of it.

He lost sight of it less than two minutes later when Francesca herself appeared, running down the side verandah and leaning over the white wrought-iron balustrade wreathed with a prolific lilac trumpeted vine that gave off a seductive fragrance in the golden heat.

"Grant!" she called, waving happily. "How lovely to see you. Of course I heard the chopper." A singing sweetness showed in every line of her body. Sweetness and excitement.

"Come here," he ordered very gently as he came alongside, reaching up a long arm to pull her lovely head down to him. Despite all the little lectures he gave himself, despite all natural caution, every atom of his being was focused on kissing her. He even murmured her name unknowingly as he put his mouth over hers, sensation beating through him like the powerful whoosh of a rotor. What in hell made him do it? But he was a man and keenly physical.

When he let her go she was breathless, trying not to tremble, a deep pink colour running across the fine skin of her cheeks, sparkling lights in the depths of her eyes. Her beautiful flame-coloured hair had come loose from its clasp and spilled around her face and over her shoulders. "That's some greeting!" Her voice was little more than a soft tremble.

"You shouldn't look at me that way," he warned, still feeling ripples of pleasure moving down through his body, pooling in his loins.

"What way?" She gave a shaky laugh, feeling enslaved by his enormous dash, moving back along the wide verandah as he resumed his journey to the front of the house.

"*You* know, Francesca," he half growled, half mocked. "Lord are you a sight for sore eyes!" He ran his gaze over her, from the tip of her radiant head to her toes. His hazel eyes, which could turn grey or green according to his mood, were now a clear green beneath the brim of his black akubra. They scanned her

face, her swan's neck, the slender body with its willow waist,
her light limbs, a muscle in his hard jaw lightly flicking.

It was impossible to cast his glance away so caught up was
he in her feminine beauty, the soft ravishing prettiness he found
irresistible. She was wearing riding gear. Such riding gear! The
aristocratic young English lady from the grand stately home and
one of the most egalitarian young women he had ever known.

Her short-sleeved cream silk blouse lightly skimmed her
delicate breasts and was tucked into tight-fitting cream jodhpurs. Highly polished, very expensive, tan coloured riding boots
adorned her small feet. There wasn't an ounce of excess weight
on her. She had the neatest, sleekest little butt and good straight
legs. It nearly mesmerised him just to see her move along the
verandah, near dancing to keep up with him. To his overheated
mind, and body, make no mistake about it it thrummed like
electricity, she appeared to be floating, so lightly were her feet
touching the timber floor-boards.

"A hard day?" Francesca asked him as he mounted the short
flight of stone steps to the verandah, excited, not her usual calm,
contained self at all.

He leaned against the rail with slouching elegance, smiling
at her with the unblinking cat's eyes she found so wildly attractive. "I'm over it now I've seen you," he drawled. He was, too.
"What have you been doing with yourself all day?"

"Come and I'll tell you." She indicated the comfortable white
wicker furniture. "I expect you'd like a cold beer? Brod always
does."

He nodded and took off his hat using it like a Frisbee to skim
unerringly onto the head of a wooden sculpture.

"Rebecca will be here in a moment," Francesca slid into the
chair he held out for her. Rebecca was mistress of Kimbara,
Brod's new wife. "We've been organising a picnic race meeting for most of the day. We thought it would be a change from
the usual polo. Rebecca worries about Brod when he plays. He's
such a daredevil. For that matter so are you." She actually shiv-

ered at some of her recollections. Polo was a dangerous game. Especially the way these fellows played it.

"So you worry about me as well?" He held her with his eyes.

"I worry about you *all*," she returned lightly before she drowned in his expression. It struck her more than ever how physically alike Grant and his brother Rafe were. The rangy height, the golden good looks, though Grant was tawnier.

Both had great presence. Both wore achievement like a badge. If there were a difference, Rafe had a kind of courtliness about him. There was no other word for it. Grant showed more "temper" a high mettled energy and determination that didn't sit all that comfortably with everyone. To put it in a nutshell Grant Cameron could be difficult. Add to that, he had a habit of speaking his mind, without holding back. He was full of energy and had a macho quality, an absolute manliness that characterised these men of the outback. In some respects he even seemed like a creature from another world. A creature of vast open spaces with no boundaries. The image of a splendid young lion sat easily on him. He was her first taste of a thrilling excitement that contained a kernel of caution. She knew her feelings for Grant Cameron were getting right out of hand.

Now he knit his dark golden brows together, staring across at her, his strong brown arms on the circular glass-topped table steely with muscle. He was wearing the uniform of his company in serviceable khaki the blue and gold logo on the breast pocket. He looked great, the afternoon breeze ruffling his thick tawny hair with its pronounced deep wave.

"So what's the verdict, my lady?" He came closer to grasping her hand. Never letting her go.

She laughed and blushed at the same time. "Was I staring? Sorry. I was just thinking how much alike you and Rafe are. Growing more so as you—"

"Mature?" he cut in swiftly, his relaxed easy drawl taking on a faint glittery edge.

"Oh, Grant," she said in gentle reproach. Francesca knew

the brothers were devoted to each other, but Grant a couple of years younger must have chafed often under Rafe's authority. With both parents dead Rafe had had to take on almost a parental role from an early age. Grant still had a tendency to chafe if only because of his driving ambition to prove himself, to be the man his father always said he would be. Grant fairly pulsed with raw ambition, undischarged energy. "Actually I was going to say, as you grow older," she told him mildly, watching his tall, super lean body with its athlete's muscles relax.

"Of course you were," he agreed with his charming, slightly crooked smile that revealed perfect white teeth. "Sometimes, Francesca, I've got a perverse devil in me."

"Yes, I know," she told him gently.

"I love Rafe as much as any brother could."

"I know you do," she said with understanding, "and I know what you mean so don't bother explaining." The best of relationships were fraught with little tensions. Like mother and daughter. She turned her head as footsteps sounded in the front hall. "That'll be Rebecca."

A moment later Rebecca appeared like a summer breeze, all smiles, touching Francesca affectionately on the shoulder before speaking directly to Grant who came swiftly to his feet. "Don't bother to get up, Grant," she said, realising he must be tired. "All over for the day?"

"Thank the Lord." He gave a wry grin.

"Then you could probably do with a cold beer?"

He laughed aloud and resumed his seat. "Brod sure has his womenfolk trained. Francesca has just offered me one, too. That'd be great, Rebecca. I have to admit it was long, hard and dusty. I'm parched." He was struck again at how much Rebecca had changed from the enigmatic young woman who had first come to Kimbara to write Fee Kinross's biography. Fee, Francesca's mother, had had a brilliant career on the London stage. The biography was due out any day.

Since her marriage to Brod, Rebecca was all friendliness and

warmth, happiness and contentment shining out of her quite extraordinary grey eyes. This was a marriage that would work, he
thought with great satisfaction. God knows Brod and Ally had
one hell of a childhood with their arrogant bastard of a father.
Such was Rafe's persona even Stewart Kinross had approved
of Rafe, though he hadn't lived to see Rafe and his only daughter, Alison, married.

Grant was certain Kinross would never have approved of
him. "Too much the hothead!" Kinross had once described
him, "with the intolerable habit of expressing his quite juve-
nile opinions." Opinions, of course, that ran counter to the lordly
Kinross. Still the two families, Cameron and Kinross had always been entwined. Almost kin. Now they were.

When Rebecca returned with his cold beer, just the one—he
was too responsible a pilot to consider another—and an iced
tea for herself and Francesca, they talked family matters, their
latest communications from Rafe and Ally, local gossip, what
Fee and David Westbury, the visiting first cousin to Francesca'a
aristocratic father, were up to. The two had become inseparable
to the extent Francesca told them she wouldn't be surprised to
get a phone call to say they'd popped into the register office
that very day. Which would make Fee's third attempt at making a go of marriage.

They were still talking about Fee and the important cameo
role she was to play in a new Australian movie, when they were
interrupted by the shrilling of the phone, the latest miracle for
the outback that had depended for so long on radio communication. Rebecca went to answer it, returning with an expression
that wiped all the laughter from her luminous grey eyes. "It's
for you, Grant, Bob Carlton." She named his second-in-charge.
"One of the fleet hasn't reached base camp or called in, either.
Bob sounded a bit concerned. Take it in Brod's study."

"Thanks, Rebecca." Grant rose to his impressive lean height.
"Did he say which station?"

"Oh I'm sorry!" Rebecca touched her creamy forehead in self-reproach. "I should have told you at once. It's Bunnerong."

The station was even more remote than they were. About sixty miles to the north-west. Grant made his way through the Kinross homestead, familiar to him from childhood. It was amazingly grand in contrast to the Cameron stronghold with its quietly fading Victorian gentility. Ally, of course, would change all that. Ally the whirlwind but for now his mind was on what Bob had to say.

Bob, in his mid-fifties, was a great bloke. A great organiser, a great mechanic, well liked by everyone. Grant relied on him, but Bob was a born worrier, a firm believer in Murphy's Law, whereby anything that could go wrong, would. Equally Bob was determined no harm would come to any of "his boys."

On the phone Grant received Bob's assurance all necessary checks had been made and the chopper had passed the mandatory 100-hour service. The helicopter was to have set down when the stockmen were camped at Bunnerong's out station at approximately four o'clock. The pilot, a good one with plenty of experience in aerial muster had not arrived by four forty-five when Bunnerong contacted Bob by radio. Bob in turn had not been able to contact the pilot by company radio frequency.

"I wouldn't worry too much about it." Grant wasn't overly concerned at that point.

"You know me, Grant, I'm going to," Bob answered. "It's not like Curly. He runs by an inbuilt timetable."

"Sure," Grant acknowledged. "But you know as well as I do things can go wrong with the radio. It's not all that unusual. It's happened to me. Besides it's almost dusk. Curly would have put down somewhere and made camp for the night. He's got all he needs to make himself comfortable. He'd resume again at first light. If he's anything like me he's dog-tired. Besides, he's not actually due to start the muster until morning anyway."

All of which was true. "There's an hour or so of light left," Grant said at length breaking in on Bob. "I'll take the chopper up and have a look around, though I'm coming from another direction. I need to refuel on Kimbara, if I'm going to get close in to Bunnerong."

"I suppose we might as well wait for morning," Bob sighed. "Curly could still turn up. Bunnerong can get a message to us and I'll relay it to you."

So it was decided. "Curly" to all because of a single wisp of hair that curled like a baby's on his bald patch, was a pro. He had food with him. A swag. He'd probably put down near a bush lagoon and set up camp for the night. Nevertheless Grant felt the responsibility to take his chopper up. Initiate a bit of a search before night fell.

Bob's mood had affected him, he thought wryly. Experience told him Curly, though obviously having problems with his radio was most likely safe and sound setting up camp on the ground. Still he liked to know *exactly* where every one of his pilots and helicopters in service were.

Grant walked swiftly back through the house, telling the two young women of his intentions the moment he set foot on the verandah.

"Why don't you let me come with you?" Francesca asked quickly, keen to help if she could. "You know what they say, two pairs of eyes are better than one."

Rebecca nodded in agreement. "I was able to help Brod once on a search and rescue. You remember?"

"That was from the Beech Baron," Grant told her, a shade repressively. "Francesca isn't used to helicopters. The way they fly, the heat and the noise. She could very easily get airsick."

Francesca stood away from her chair. "I don't suffer from motion sickness at all, Grant. In the air. On the water. Please take me. I want to help if I can."

His response wasn't all that she hoped. The expression in his hazel eyes suggested there was a decided possibility she could become a liability. But in the end he nodded in laconic permission. "All right, lady! Let's go."

Minutes later the rotor was roaring and they were lifting vertically from the lawn, rising well above the line of trees, climbing, then steering away for the desert fringe. Francesca like Grant was strapped into her copilot seat, wearing earphones that at least made the loud noise of the swishing blades tolerable. Still she found it a thrilling experience to be up in the air looking down at the vast wilderness with all the rock formations undergoing another change in their astonishing colour display. Even when they flew through thermal cross-winds over the desert she kept her cool as the winds took hold of the small aircraft and shook it so it plunged into a short, sickening dive.

"O.K.?" Grant spoke through the headphones, a deep frown of concern between his eyes.

"Aye, aye, skipper!" She lifted her right hand in a parody of a smart salute. Did he really think she was going to go to pieces like the ladies of old? Have the vapours? She had pioneering blood in her veins as well. Her maternal ancestor had been Ewan Kinross, a legendary cattle king. The fact that she had been reared in the ordered calm of the beautiful English countryside and her exclusive boarding school didn't mean she hadn't inherited the capacity to face a far more dangerous way of life. Besides it was as she'd told him. She had a cast iron stomach and she was too excited for nerves. She wanted to learn this way of life. She wanted to learn all about Grant Cameron's life.

They searched until it got to the point when they had to turn back. When they landed Brod was waiting for them in the brief mauve dusk that in moments would turn to a darkness that was literally pitch black.

"No luck?" Brod asked as Grant jumped out onto the grass turning to catch Francesca by the waist and swing her down like the featherweight she was.

"If Curly doesn't turn up on Bunnerong first thing in the morning we're looking at another search. Bob report in?"

"No news. Nothing." Brod shook his head. "You'll stay the night." It wasn't a question but a statement of fact. "Better you're here anyway. We're closer to Bunnerong if there's any need of a search. I expect your man is boiling the billy now moaning his radio is out of order."

"I shouldn't be surprised," Grant responded to Brod's good spirits. "It's Francesca here who's the real surprise."

"How so?" Brod turned to smile down on his English cousin, as dark with his raven hair and tanned skin as Grant was tawny gold.

"I think he thought I was going to go into a panic when we hit some thermals," Francesca explained lightly, striking Grant's arm in reproach.

"I wouldn't have blamed you if you did," he answered with a faintly teasing smile, enjoying fending her off. "I've always said you're much more than a pretty face." A ravishingly pretty face.

"It would take a lot to put Fran in a tizzy," Brod said with affection. "We've learnt over the years this little piece of English china has plenty of spunk."

Up at the homestead Rebecca smilingly allotted him a guest room overlooking the rear of the house. The meandering creek that ran near and encircled the home compound revealed itself in a silver line as the moon turned on its radiance. Brod walked in a few minutes later with a pile of clean, soap-smelling clothes from his own wardrobe.

"Here, these should fit," he announced, placing the clothes neatly on the bed, a blue-and-white striped cotton shirt on top, cotton beige trousers and underwear that hadn't even come out of its packet by the look of it. Both men were much the same height a few inches over six feet with the lean, powerful physique of the super active.

"Am I glad of them. Thanks a lot," Grant answered, turning away from his own speculation of the night to smile at his brother's best friend. With Rafe and Brod those few years older he'd always been the one trying to catch up, trying to catch them, trying to emulate their achievements, academically and on the sports field. All in all he hadn't done too badly.

"No problem." There was an answering smile in Brod's eyes. "You've saved me dozens of times. I'm for a long, hot shower. I expect you are, too. It's been a thoroughly tiring day." He started to move off then stopped briefly at the door. "By the way I don't think I thanked you properly for doing such a great job," he said with evident approval. "It's not just the way you handle the chopper, which is brilliant, you're a cattleman as well. The combination makes you extraordinarily good."

"Thanks, mate." Grant grinned. "I aim to offer the very best service. And it doesn't come cheap as you're due to find out. What time are we off in the morning always supposing Curly gets a message through he's okay?"

Brod frowned, answering a little vaguely for him. "Not as early as today, that's for sure. The men have their orders. They'll have plenty to do. We'll wait and see what the morning brings. I know bush logic tells us Curly has landed safely, but I'd like to stick around until we're sure."

"I appreciate that, Brod." Grant accepted his friend's support. "A land search in such a huge area would be out of the question. It will take aircraft to find him if he's in any kind of trouble."

"Not that it's odd having problems with the radio," Brod echoed Grant's own previous words, obviously trying to offer reassurance mixed in with the voice of long experience. Brod's expression brightened. "Now, what about a barbeque? I feel like eating outdoors tonight and it gives me the opportunity to show off. I cook a great steak if I say so myself. We can throw in a few roast potatoes. The girls can whip up a salad. What more could a man want?"

Grant smiled broadly. "Go for it! I'm hungry enough to eat the best steak Kimbara can offer."

"You're going to get it," Brod assured him.

A long, hot shower was a wonderful luxury after the heat and uproar of the day. The bellowing of the cattle as they were herded into doing what they clearly didn't want to do; leave the familiar surroundings of the scrub was still in his ears. More of the same tomorrow. And the day after. But he planned on getting right out of fieldwork. He wanted to concentrate on expanding the business. He'd go on building up the fleet and the team but his mind was firmly on extending the range of services.

With time on his hands and glad of the company of such good friends, he used some of the shampoo he found in the cupboard beneath the basin. Kinross sure knew how to look after its guests, he thought with wry admiration. There was an impressive array of stuff to make a guest feel good. Fancy soaps, bath gels, shower gels, body lotion, talc, toothbrushes, toothpaste, hair dryer, electric shaver. Lots of good, big absorbent towels. Man-size. Brilliant!

He stepped out of the shower and wrapped one around himself, feeling the exhaustions of the day slip away. His hair needed cutting as usual. Barbers weren't all that easy to come by in the desert. He shook his wet, darkened hair like a seal deciding he'd better use the dryer if he wanted to look presentable.

Which he did. He was intensely aware of his attraction to Francesca, her marvellous drawing power though he knew how ill advised it was. The Camerons and the Kinrosses had always lived like desert lords but their world was beyond "civilisation" as Lady Francesca de Lyle knew it. No question the call of the outback had reached her. After all she had an Australian mother born in this very house but Francesca was on holiday, taking the rose-coloured holiday view. It was impossible for her to realise the day-to-day isolation, the terrible battles that were fought against drought, flood and heat, accident, tragic deaths. Men could bear the loneliness, the struggles and frustrations, the crushing workload. He knew in his heart an English rose like Francesca would find it all unbearable no matter how adaptable she claimed she was. She simply had no experience of the bush and the hazards it presented.

Grant threw down the hair dryer, thinking he shouldn't have

used it. It made his hair look positively *wild*. He turned to dressing, pulling out the belt of his uniform to thread it through the cotton trousers. No difficulty with sizing. The fit was perfect. If only he were certain Curly was safe and sound he could really look forward to enjoying this evening.

It had been lonely at home with Rafe away on honeymoon. He was looking forward to a letter from them or maybe another phone call. Ally had been so full of their stay in New York. She adored it. The excitement she felt as she "hit the sidewalk" the "thrum" of the place more electric than any other city on earth. "And we've got you some wonderful presents," she'd added. "Really special!" That was Ally and she had the money.

The Camerons had never kept pace with the Kinrosses in the generation of great wealth, though Opal was an industry leader and Rafe was dead set on expansion, building up a chain, just as he, himself, was determined on making his mark in aviation.

The pride of lions! Well he and Rafe had tasted tragedy as had Brod and Ally. At least some things were now working out. Brod had found real love, much rarer than people thought. As for Rafe and Ally! They were like two sides of the same coin. Allowing himself to fall in love with Francesca had to make him downright crazy. Easy enough to get led astray, though, he reasoned. Finding the path back might prove very, very, difficult.

Francesca was crossing through the front hall when Grant descended the stairs. She looked up feeling a sudden rush of blood to her face. He looked marvellous, his strong, handsome features relaxed, hazel eyes sparkling, his full, thick head of hair, obviously freshly washed, settling into the deep natural waves women paid a fortune to achieve. She was astonished at her own desire, so sweet, so primitive like a woman staring at the man she wanted for her perfect mate.

"Hi!" His voice was pitched thrillingly low, stirring her further.

She had to force a flippant tone in case he read what was on her mind and man-like backed off. "You look *cool*."

"Courtesy Brod." He grinned. "He rustled up some gear."

"It suits you." She spoke with a nice balance of admiration and teasing.

"Actually you look very sweet yourself." His eyes gently mocked. She was wearing a sapphire-blue full skirt with a matching strappy little top, the fabric printed with white hibiscus. Blue sandals almost the same shade were on her feet, her Titian hair wound into some braided coil that suited her beautifully. He saw the apricot flush on her creamy skin. He knew it was there because he was coming close.

How did it happen? This longing for a woman that sent a man reeling? He'd been making love to her in his mind at least three times a week for some time now, seriously considering it *had* to happen, shocked because he couldn't seem to come to his senses. But what did sense have to do with sexual attraction? He felt compelled to have an affair. He couldn't make the wider choice, yet he moved right up to her, surprising her and himself by moving her into an impromptu tango, remembering how they had danced and danced at Brod's then Rafe's wedding.

There was music in him, Francesca thought. Music, rhythm, a sensuality that was reducing her limbs to jelly. This man was taking her over utterly, making all her senses bloom like a flower.

"I'm in perfect company right now," he murmured in her ear, just barely resisting the temptation to take the pink earlobe into his mouth.

"Me, too." The words just slipped out, very soft but not concealing her intensity. She hadn't made a conscious decision to fall in love with him surely, but his effect on her was so pervasive she could hardly bear to contemplate her holiday on Kimbara coming to an end.

Rebecca, coming to find them, burst into spontaneous applause at the considerable panache of their dance. "You're naturals, both of you," she cried. "I've never thought of it before but this is a terrific dance floor." She looked around the very spacious front hall, speculation in her eyes.

"Why would you need it when you've got the old ballroom?" Francesca asked, catching her breath as Grant whirled her into a very close stop.

"I mean for Brod and me," Rebecca smiled, still very much the bride. "Come and join us for a drink. I've chilled a seriously good Riesling. It's beautiful out on the back verandah. The air is filled with the scent of boronia. How I love it. The stars are out in their zillions." She came forward very happily to link her arm through Francesca's, her long, gleaming dark ribbon of hair falling softly from a centre parting the way her husband loved it, the skirt of her summery white dress fluttering in the breeze that blew through the open doorway.

They found Brod wrapped in a professional-looking apron, the large brick barbeque well alight, the potatoes in foil already cooking. Ratatouille kebabs prepared by Rebecca lay ready for the grill plate, a leafy green walnut and mushroom salad prepared by Francesca waiting for the dressing.

Grant was given the enjoyable task of opening the wine, and pouring it into the tulip-shaped glasses set out on the long table, while Francesca passed around the crackers spread with a smoked salmon paté she had processed a half hour before. It was light and luscious and the conversation began to flow. These were people, interconnected through family, who genuinely enjoyed one another's company. The steaks, prime Kimbara beef, were set to sizzle over the hot coals and Rebecca decided she'd like a tarragon wine sauce so went to the kitchen to fetch it. While they were waiting, Grant walked Francesca to the very edge of the verandah so they could see the moon reflected in the glassy-smooth surface of the creek.

"Such a heavenly night," she breathed, lifting her head from contemplation of the silvery waters to the glittering heavens. "The Southern Cross is always over the tip of the house. It's so easy to pick out."

Grant nodded. "Rafe and Ally won't see it in the United States. The cross is gradually shifting southward in the sky."

"Is it really?" Francesca turned her head to stare up at him, thrilled because he was so *tall*.

"It is, my lady." He gave a mocking bow. "A result of the earth's precession or the circular motion of the earth's axis. The Southern Cross was known to the people of the ancient world, Babylonians and Greeks. They thought it part of the constellation Centaurus. See the star furthest to the south?" He pointed it out.

"The brightest?"

He nodded. "A star of the first magnitude. It points to the South Pole. The aborigines have wonderful Dreamtime legends about the Milky Way and stars. I'll tell you some of them one of these days. Maybe nights when we're camping out."

"Are you serious?"

A short silence. "I suppose it could be arranged." His voice sounded sardonic. "Do you think it would be a good idea, the two of us camping out under the stars?"

"I think it could be wonderful." Francesca drew a breath of sheer excitement.

"What about when the dingoes started to howl?" he mocked.

"Mournful not to say eerie cries, I know—" she shivered a little remembering "—but I'd have you to protect me."

"And who's going to protect me?" Suddenly he put a finger beneath her chin, turning up her face to him.

"Am I so much to worry about?" She cut to the very heart of the matter.

"I think so, yes," he answered slowly. "You're out of reach, Francesca."

"And I thought you were a man who aimed for the stars?" she taunted him very gently.

"Aircraft are safer than women," he countered dryly. "They don't preoccupy a man's mind."

"So that makes harmless little me a great danger?" Her voice was low-pitched but uniquely intense.

"Except in the realm of my secret dreams," he surprised himself by admitting.

It was a tremendous turn-on, causing Francesca's body to quiver like a plucked string. "That's very revealing, Grant. Why would you reveal so much of yourself to me?" she asked in some frustration.

"Because in many ways we're intensely compatible. I think we knew that very early on."

"When we were just teenagers?" There was simply no way she could deny it. "And now we're to assume a different relationship?"

"Not assume, my lady." His voice deepened, became somewhat combative. "You were born to grandeur. The daughter of an earl. Journeying to the outback is in lots of ways an escape for you, maybe even an escape from reality. An attempt to avoid much of the pressure from your position in life. I'd expect your father will confidently expect you to marry a man from within your own ranks. A member of the English aristocracy. At the very least a scion of one of the established families."

It was perfectly true. Her father had certain hopes of her. Even two possible suitors. "I'm Fee's daughter, too." She tried to stave the issue off. "That makes me half Australian. Fee only wants me to be happy."

"Which means I'm right. Your father has high expectations of you. He wouldn't want to lose you."

Francesca shook her head almost pleadingly. "Daddy will never lose me. I love him. But he has his own life you know."

"But no grandchildren." Grant pointed out bluntly. "You have to give him them. Such a child, a male child, would become his heir. The future Earl of Moray. Inescapably a fact."

"Oh don't let's take that all on yet, Grant," Francesca burst out. She wanted them to be together, with no conflicts between them.

But Grant had other ideas, seeing where it was taking them.

"I have to. You know as well as I do we're becoming increasingly involved. Hell what am *I* sacrificing here? I could fall in love with you then you'd go off home to Daddy, back to your own world, leaving me to profound wretchedness."

Somehow she didn't associate him with becoming any woman's victim. He was too much the self-contained *man.* "I think you have what it takes to resist me."

"Darn right!" Abruptly he bent his head and gave her a hard kiss. "I've seen these patterns before."

"So what's the solution?" She was compelled to clutch him for support.

"Neither of us allows ourselves to get carried away," he said brusquely.

"So much for your behaviour then. Why do you have to kiss me?"

He laughed, a low, attractive sound with a hint of self-disgust. "That's the hell of it, Francesca. Reconciling sexual desire with the need for good sense."

"So sadly there are to be no more kisses?" she challenged with a little note of scepticism.

He looked down into her light filled eyes, aware of the complexity of his feelings. She looked so lovely, very much a piece of porcelain, a woman to be cherished, protected from damage. "Can I help it if I'm continually at war?" he asked ironically. "You're so beautiful, aren't you? You moved into my path like a princess from a fairy tale. I know dozens of eligible, available women. Wouldn't I be the world's biggest fool to pick on someone like you? A young woman who has lived a charmed life? Equally well I don't think your father would get a big kick out of knowing you were dallying with a rough-around-the-edges man from the outback."

It in no way described him. "Rugged, Grant. Never rough. You're a lot more edgy than Rafe, but he's very much your brother and one of the most courteous men I've ever met."

"Free from my aggression, you mean." Grant nodded in wry

amusement. "It's an inborn grace, Francesca, he inherited from our father. I'm nowhere near as simpatico."

Her normally sweet voice was a little tart in her throat, like citrus peel in chocolate. "Well don't feel too badly. *I* like you. Temper and all. I like the way you hit on an idea and go for it. I like your breadth of vision. I like the way you make big plans. I even like your strong sense of competitiveness. What I don't like is the way you see me as a threat."

He could see the hurt in her eyes but he was compelled to speak. "Because you *are* a threat, Francesca. A real threat. To us both."

"That's awful." She looked away abruptly over the moon-drenched home gardens.

"I know," he muttered sombrely, "but it makes sense."

Unlike a lot of men let loose at a barbeque, Brod cooked the steaks to perfection, each to their requirements from medium rare to well done. For all her whirring feelings Francesca enjoyed herself, eating a good meal, warming to the conversation, and afterwards offering to make coffee.

"I'll help you." Impulsively Grant moved back his chair, willing the pleasure of the evening to go on. Brod and Rebecca had shifted seats and were now holding hands. The younger couple wouldn't be missed for a while.

In the huge kitchen outfitted for feeding an army, Grant thought, Francesca set him to grinding the coffee beans, the marvellous aroma rising and flowing out towards them. Francesca was busy setting out cups and saucers then assembling plates for the slices of chocolate torte she'd already cut. All very deftly, he noticed. She was very organised, very methodical, with quick, neat hands.

"You're managing very well," he drawled.

"What is that supposed to mean?" The overhead light turned her glorious hair to flame, giving him a great wave of pleasure.

"Have you ever actually cooked a meal?" he smiled.

"I made the salad," she pointed out collectedly.

"And it was very good, but I can't think you ever have any need to go into a kitchen and start cooking the supper."

She scarcely remembered being allowed in the kitchen except at Christmas to stir the pudding. "Not at Ormond, no." She named her father's stately home. "We always had a housekeeper, Mrs. Lincoln. She was pretty fierce. Nothing casual about her and she had staff, just as Brod's father did, only Brod and Rebecca have decided they want to be on their own. At least for a while. Once I shifted to London to start work I managed to get all my own meals. It truly isn't difficult," she added dryly.

"When you weren't going out?" He poured boiling water into the plunger. "You must accept lots and lots of invitations?"

"I have a full social life." She flashed him a blue, sparkling look. "But it's not an obsession."

"No love affairs?" He found he couldn't bear the thought of her with another man.

"One or two romantic involvements. Like *you.*" Grant Cameron didn't lack female admirers.

"No one serious?" he persisted as though the thought was gnawing away at him.

"I've yet to meet my perfect man," she answered sweetly.

"Which brings me to why you have designs on me."

His effrontery took her breath away. "You can haul yourself out when the going gets tough. Because I'm only following my own instincts. You do have a certain emotional pull and physically you're extraordinarily attractive."

He gave a mock bow, surprisingly elegant. "Thank you, Francesca. That makes my heart swell."

"As long as it's not your *head,*" she retorted crisply.

"My head has the high ground at the moment," he drawled. "But I've enjoyed tonight. Brod and Rebecca are such good company and you are *you.*"

It was so disconcerting, the swings from sarcastic to sizzling emotion. An acknowledgment, perhaps, that their connection was powerful, though he was going to fight it all the way.

"That's good I've done something right," Francesca said in response, trying to keep her tone light, but she was utterly confounded when tears came into her eyes. Being with him made her more sensitive, more womanly with a much bigger capacity for being hurt. For all the calmness of her voice, Grant was instantly alerted. He glanced up swiftly, catching her the moment before she blinked furiously.

"Francesca!" Heart drumming with dismay and desire he reached for her, pulling her into his arms. "What is it? Have I hurt you? I'm a brute. I'm sorry." He could see the pulse beating in her creamy throat answering the pulses that were beating in him. "I'm trying to see what's best for both of us. Surely you can understand that?"

"Of course." Her voice was a husky whisper. She dashed her hand across her eyes. Just like a little girl. Grace under fire.

An immense wave of passion tied to a deep sense of protectiveness broke across him, causing him to mould her into him more tightly, achingly aware of the feel of her delicate breasts against the wall of his chest. He was on the verge of losing it. It was terrible. But good. Better than good. Ravishing.

She attempted to speak but he was seized by the urgent need to kiss her, to take the crushed strawberry sweetness of her mouth, to find her tongue, to move it back and forth against his in the age-old mating ritual. This incredible delight in a woman was something new to him. Something well beyond his former sexual experiences. He wanted her. Needed her like a man needs water.

There was tremendous passion in his kiss, a touch of fierceness that thrilled her because she knew she meant more to him than he dared acknowledge. His hand held her nape, cupped it, holding her head to him. She was almost lying back in his arms, allowing him to take his intense pleasure, and something deep, deep inside her started to melt. She was almost fainting under the tumult of sensation, her own ardent response. She had never known such intimacy, never before revelled in it, knowing it could be a cause of much unhappiness but she was too needy or too stupid to care.

What bright spirit impelled towards delight was ever known to figure out the cost?

They broke apart, both of them momentarily disorientated as though they had been beamed down from another world. Grant, for his part, was profoundly conscious his moods, attitudes and thoughts about this woman were vacillating wildly like a geiger counter exposed to radiation. She set his blood on fire, which greatly complicated their relationship. How could one think calmly, rationally when he was continually longing to make love to her? She might even see his masculine drive as excessive, a kind of male sexual aggression. She was so small, so light limbed, so fragile in his arms, the perfume of her, of her very skin, a potent trigger to desire.

By contrast she seemed shaken, deprived of speech, unusually pale.

"I'm sorry, Francesca." Remorse was in his voice. "I never meant to be rough with you. I got carried away. Forgive me. It's as you say, I lack the courtly touch."

She could have and perhaps should have told him how she felt, how she welcomed his advances with all her heart, but the tide of emotion was too dangerously high. She stood away, putting a trembling hand to her hair, realising a few long, silky strands had worked their way loose. "You didn't hurt me, Grant," she managed to say. "Appearances can be deceptive. I'm a lot tougher than I look."

His low laugh was spontaneous. "You could have fooled me." He watched her trying to fix her hair, wanting to pull it free of its braided coils. What fascination long, beautiful hair had for a man. He could even imagine himself brushing it. God he had to be mad! He forced a grin, the smile not going with the look in his eyes. "I suppose we'd better take the coffee out. It'll be getting cold." He reached around and set the glass plunger on the tray. "I'll carry it out. You relax. Get the colour back in your cheeks." A tall order when he had reduced her to a breathless quivering receptacle of sensation, naked in her clothes.

CHAPTER TWO

FRANCESCA WOKE WITH a start knowing before she even looked at the clock she had slept in. She had set the alarm for five in the morning, now it was six-ten.

"Damn!" This was too awful. She wanted to go with Grant. Francesca flung herself out of bed, glancing through the open French doors that gave onto the verandah. Sun-up four-thirty. The sky was now a bright blue, the air redolent with the wonderful smell of heat. She had even missed the morning symphony of birds, the combined voices so powerful, so swelling they regularly woke her at dawn. Sometimes the kookaburras started up their unique cackling din in predawn and she was awake to hear them, lying in bed enjoying their laughter. But she had slept deeply, exhausted by the chaos of emotion that was in her.

Still she planned to go with Grant and he'd agreed, if somewhat reluctantly. Grant had told them all before retiring he intended to wait an hour for a message to be relayed in from Bunnerong. All stations operated from dawn. Perhaps his pilot had already called in or Bunnerong had notified Kimbara of his arrival? That was the way they did it in the bush.

Hastily she splashed her face with cold water to wake herself up, cleaned her teeth and dressed in the clothes she had laid out the night before to save time. Cotton shirt, cotton jeans, sneakers. She put the brush through her hair, caught up a scarf to tie it back and rushed out into the silent hallway, padding along it until she reached the central staircase. She was almost at the bottom, when Brod came through the front door, surprise on his handsome face. "Fran? We thought we'd better let you sleep in."

Dismay hit her and she sent him a sparkling glance. "You don't mean to tell me Grant has gone without me?" Her emotions were so close to the surface she felt betrayed.

"I think he *intends* to go without you," Brod admitted wryly. "He has the firm idea you're not really up to it. Bunnerong has called in, as expected. Curly still hasn't arrived. Grant has delayed taking off for as long as he can. He's down at the airstrip refuelling."

"So he hasn't taken off yet?" Hope flashed in her eyes.

"No." Brod heaved a sigh, beginning to think Grant was right not to take her. This was his little cousin from England. He valued her highly but she wasn't used to confronting potentially dangerous situations. With no makeup and her long hair floating all around her, her cheeks pink with indignation she looked little more than a child.

"Get me down there," she said, racing towards him and taking him firmly by the arm. Literally a fire head.

Brod resisted momentarily, even though his expression was affectionate and understanding. "Fran, think about this. There's a possibility the pilot has come to some harm. That could be very distressing for you. Believe me, I *know*."

She looked up at him with her flower-blue eyes. "I won't screw up, Brod, I promise. I want to be of help. I completed a first-aid course."

Brod gave a sigh and ran his hand through his raven hair. "I don't want to be alarmist but out here accidents aren't something that happen to other people, Fran. We don't read about it in the newspapers or see it on television. They happen to *us*. All the time. Curly might be beyond first-aid. Think of that. No matter how game you are, how much you want to help, you've led a protected life."

"Most people do. But I'm ready to *learn,* Brod." Francesca caught his stare and held it. "Stop treating me like a pampered little girl. I've had my tough times as well. Now, get in and drive." She ran to the waiting Jeep ahead of him, almost dancing in her desire to get down to the airstrip. "Grant promised he'd take me," she called over her shoulder. "I know it mightn't be good but I'm not going to cave in. I'm half Kinross."

She was, too, he thought with some admiration. Used as a buffer between warring parents. "It sounds to me like you have something to prove, love," Brod said as he started the engine.

"Yes, I have." The great thing about her cousins, Brod and Ally, was they wanted to listen.

"To Grant?" He looked at her with his all-seeing eyes, encouraging her.

"Who else?" she flashed him her smile.

Brod nodded, his expression wry. "He's a helluva guy, Fran, a genuinely exciting personality. He'll go far, but he's very stubborn. Once he makes up his mind you won't change it. Princess that you are you won't wind him around your little finger so be warned. Grant has very strong views. A quick pride. Strength and energy to burn. But he has lots to learn like the rest of us. We know he's deeply attracted to you but you could get hurt. Rebecca and I don't want to see that because we care about you too much."

Francesca's delicately arching brows drew together. "I know and I love you for it but I have to take my own chances in life, Brod. Make all my own mistakes. That's as it should be. My friendship with Grant *has* gone a step further. Everyone is aware of it. We're more involved and as a consequence we're coming increasingly into conflict."

"You know what they say. Life isn't meant to be easy. I can see it happening, Fran." Brod accelerated away from the compound. "Grant has never felt a woman's power. He's had casual affairs but they never burned him. What happens when you go back to Sydney? Have you thought of that?"

"Of course I have!" Francesca exclaimed, trying to push the thought away. "I don't want this time with you and Rebecca to end. I'm longing to see Ally when she gets home. Rafe, too, though I know he has reservations about my friendship with his 'little brother.'"

Brod chose his words carefully, knowing what she said was quite true. "Responsibility is Rafe's middle name, Fran. He damned near had to father Grant when their parents were killed. In his shock and grief Grant went more than a little wild. He was always getting into trouble, always trying to bring some daredevil prank off. That tragedy has shaped him. Put fear in him. Showed him about loss. It might well be to remember it. Grant mightn't let a woman get too close to him. His grief at the loss of his parents was enormous. He was very close to his mother as the youngest.

"They were wonderful people, the Camerons. They took pity on Ally and me and our chaotic home life. They as good as fostered us. Rafe is as close to me as a brother. Come to that I always thought of Grant as a younger brother. To love is to lose. Grant learned that early."

When they arrived at the airstrip Grant was close to taking off. He saw them coming and jumped down again onto the tarmac. There was Francesca looking like someone who should be scattering rose petals at a wedding, Titian hair flying all around her lovely head. He tried to keep a sudden anger down, wondering why he was feeling so angry at all. He didn't want her hurt. That was it. He didn't want her exposed to danger. In short he didn't want her to come.

She was running towards him, crying out in reproach. "You surely weren't going to leave without me?"

He nodded more curtly than he intended. "I don't have a real good feeling about this, Francesca. It might be better if you stay home."

"But you promised me last night." Her churning emotions sounded in her voice.

"You agree with me don't you, Brod?" Grant shot his friend a near imploring glance.

Brod considered a while. "I figure she'll come to no harm with you, Grant. She may see something she's not prepared for but knowing her I'd say she is adult enough to handle it. There may not be much wrong at all. A choke in the fuel pipe, or running too low on petrol to reach the scheduled landing."

"Which places him fair and square in a difficult and potentially dangerous situation," Grant said, feeling the pressure. "The sun is generating a lot of heat." Both men knew a lost man could dehydrate and die within forty-eight hours in the excessively dry atmosphere.

"We're all praying, Grant," Brod said.

"I know." There was tremendous mateship in the bush. Grant turned to see Francesca tying her hair back with a blue scarf for all the world as if she was donning a nurse's cap. She looked achingly young. Adolescent. No make-up. She didn't need it. No lipstick, her soft, cushiony mouth had its own natural colour. What was he to do with this magical creature? But she was game.

A few minutes later they were airborne, heading in the direction of Curly's flight path. Grant pointed to various landmarks along the way, their flight level low enough for Francesca to marvel at the primeval beauty of the timeless land.

Beneath them was lightly timbered cattle country, with sections of Kimbara's mighty herd. Silver glinted off the interlocking system of watercourses that gave the Channel Country its name. Arrows of green in the rust-red plains. Monolithic rocks of vivid orange stone thrust up from the desert floor, thickly embroidered with the burnt gold of the spinifex. The aerial view was fantastic.

Kimbara stockmen quenching their thirst with billy tea waved from the shade of the red river gums along a crescent-shaped billabong. This was vast territory. Francesca could well see how a man could be lost forever.

While Grant spoke to Bob Carlton on Opal, Francesca looked away to a distant oasis of waterholes supporting a lot of greenery in the otherwise stark desert landscape. The sky was a brilliant cloudless enamelled blue and the heat was beginning to affect her.

This wasn't the super aeroplane, the great jet she was used to on her long hauls from London to Sydney. This was a single rotor helicopter she knew little about except it could fly straight up or straight down, forwards, backwards, hover in one spot, or turn completely around. It could do jobs no other vehicle of any kind could do like land in a small clearing or on a flat roof. In many ways, a helicopter was pretty much like a magic carpet and Grant was known as a brilliant pilot. That gave her a great deal of confidence.

A lot of time passed and they saw nothing to indicate closer inspection. Francesca's eyes were moving constantly, trying not to concentrate on the extraordinary surrealistic beauty of the great wilderness, but on spotting a yellow helicopter. Huge flocks of budgerigar, the phenomenon of the outback often passed beneath them, the sunlight striking a rich emerald from their wings. She could see wild camels moving across the red sand beneath them and looking east a great outcrop of huge seemingly perfect round boulders for all the world like an ancient god's marbles.

They were now within the boundaries of Bunnerong with several large lagoons coming up. Fifteen minutes on, Grant pointed downwards then proceeded to tilt the rotary wings in that direction.

They both spotted the company helicopter at the same time. It had come to rest on a small claypan that was probably baked so hard it was like cement and virtually waterproof. Dead trees supporting colonies of white corellas like a million flowers ringed the shallow depression. A short distance off was one of the loveliest of all desert plants the casuarina, a mature desert oak with its foliage spreading out to form a graceful canopy. Beneath the oak Francesca could plainly see the body of a prone man, his face covered by the broad brim of his hat. He didn't rise at the sound of the helicopter. He didn't lift the hat away from his face. He didn't wave. He kept on lying there like a man dead.

Dear God! Francesca felt a moment of sheer terror. She had never seen death before.

In a very short time they were down on the fairly light landing pad, Grant on the radio again to let Bob Carlton back on Opal know he'd found Curly grounded, the helicopter apparently safe. More news would follow.

Outside the helicopter Francesca looked to Grant for instructions.

"Stay here," he ordered, just as she knew he would. "And take this and put it on." He handed her his akubra knowing it was much too big but it would have to do. "You go nowhere without a hat. Nowhere. And you the redhead!"

She took the reprimand meekly because she knew she deserved it. If she hadn't slept in she would have brought one of her wide-brimmed akubras. "Do what I say now," Grant further cautioned. "Stay put until I see what's going on."

It seemed sensible to obey. The birds outraged by the descent of the helicopter into their peaceful territory were wheeling in the sky, screeching a deafening protest before flying off.

She looked at Grant's broad back as he moved off, sharply aware he felt deeply responsible for this pilot. The moment he called back to her, "He's alive!" was to stay bright in Francesca's memory. She ran without thinking towards them, even though he stood up abruptly, holding up his hand.

She hadn't seen the blood. It had dried very dark, almost dyeing the pilot's shirt.

"What's happened. What is it?" she asked in considerable alarm.

"I don't know. It looks like something has attacked him."

Grant strode off to the helicopter, returning with a rifle just in case. Wild boars. Bound to be plenty about. Dingo attack. He didn't think so. Then what? God forbid the attack was human. "Poor old fella! Poor Curly!" he found himself saying.

Francesca went to the unconscious man and fell to her knees. "He needs attention quite urgently. Whatever's done this to him?" Very gingerly she began to unbutton the pilot's blood-soaked shirt and as she did so he started to moan, beginning to come around.

"Here, let me take a look," Grant said urgently, gazing down at the fallen man with perplexity. "He landed the chopper quite okay. He must have become ill. Maybe he's had a heart attack. But those wounds!" Grant looked closer as Francesca working deftly peeled the shirt away. "God!" Grant exclaimed, "It's like claw marks. Feral cats."

"Could they do so much damage?" Francesca asked dubiously, used to the adorable home variety.

"They could slash you to pieces," Grant said grimly. "So many introduced animals do terrible damage to native wildlife and habitats. The camels, brumbies, foxes, wild pigs, rabbits, you name them. I've seen a man gutted by a wild boar. Feral cats aren't like your domestic tabbies. They're ferocious. More like miniature lions."

"They must be if they've done this." Francesca turned her head briefly. "Why don't you get the kit from the chopper," she urged. "I'm okay here. These wounds need to be cleaned. A lot of them seem to be fairly superficial although he's bled a great deal. Others are deep."

"They could start bleeding again," Grant warned, looking at her closely. In the shade of the casuarina she had discarded his hat, which in any case had fallen down over her eyes. She had gone very pale but her hands were rock steady.

"I'll be very careful," she said. "Blood is horrible but I won't faint if that's what's bothering you." In fact she was willing herself to remain in control. "Hello there," she said in gentle amazement as Curly opened his eyes. "Lie there quietly," she bid him swiftly, fearful his wounds would reopen. "You're fine. Fine."

Curly's alarmingly grey face took on the faintest colour. "Have I died and gone to heaven?" His voice was little more than a rusty croak.

Grant moved so he was in Curly's sights. "Hi there, Curly. I'm not paying you to rest easy under a tree."

This time Curly tried a smile. "Hi, boss. I wondered when you'd get here."

"Don't try to speak, Curly. Save your strength," Grant urged, perturbed his man looked terrible. He'd get onto the flying doctor right away. Curly could be airlifted to Bunnerong, which had its own airstrip. The Royal Flying Doctor's Cessna could land there.

"Bloody cats, would you believe it," Curly groaned. "Bloody feral cats, savage little bastards. A whole pack of them came at me out of nowhere while I was off balance being as sick as a dog. Never had such a thing happen to me before. Must have scared them somehow. Reckon I passed a kidney stone I was in so much pain. The radio is out. Needs an expert. I had to land. Just made it before I passed out. Agony I tell ya! Hell wouldn't be too strong a word for it. Now I open my eyes to an angel with eyes like the sky and hair like the sunset."

"Don't talk, Curly." Francesca smiled, knowing it was taking too much out of him. "You've had a very bad experience. I'll try not to hurt you but those scratches need attention."

Curly gave the ghost of a cheeky grin. "Whatever you do to me, I'll love it."

Come to think of it she could pass for a celestial creature, Grant thought as he walked back to the helicopter to put through his calls. She could be counted on, too, to keep her head in an emergency as well. He had to admit he was impressed with her quiet efficiency.

A day later Curly was sleeping peacefully in hospital minus his gall bladder, lamenting the fact the "angel" who had tended his lacerations so tenderly had been replaced by a burly male nurse.

The following week saw the return of Fee and David Westbury, arms full of presents, looking wonderfully rested and increasingly affectionate after a fortnight on a small exclusive Great Barrier Reef island. Both wore becoming golden tans, Fee telling all and sundry she wasn't in the least afraid of the sun, it was "absolutely" essential. Of course Fee was blessed with a good olive skin, well hydrated, well cared for and she'd spent nearly all of her adult life in misty England.

"I'm not like you, my darling!" She looked across worriedly at Francesca. "You've got to watch yourself with that red hair and de Lyle skin. You'd shrivel up if you lived out here," she said innocently.

Well thank you, Mamma, Francesca heaved a small inner sigh. Thank you for confirming Grant's worst fears.

They were all at dinner in Kimbara's truly beautiful formal dining room, Brod, their host at the head of the long, gleaming mahogany table, Rebecca in a lovely aquamarine silk shift with a slightly ruffled hemline facing him at the opposite end. Fee, with David beside her was to Brod's right, ever glamorous in some kind of sophisticated tiger stripe drapery with a deep cowl neck. Facing them Francesca wore a simple shift dress similar in style to Rebecca's but a glowing midnight-blue, with Grant beside her. Their bright colouring was startling under the light from twin chandeliers. Francesca all rosy apricot reds and golds, individual strands of hair glittering like jewellery, Grant tawny bronze, hair and skin.

Brod, sensing Francesca's discomfit, and aware of Grant's misgivings about her, decided to weigh in. "Fee's just having fun, Fran," he told her lightly. "It's simply a question of taking care. Rebecca has perfect skin." Brod raised his wineglass to his beautiful wife in salute, his eyes full of admiration.

"Of course she has, darling." Fee reached out to pat his hand.

"But it's that thick, creamy magnolia skin. My darling girl's is eggshell thin."

"Does that mean it can't wait to crack?" Francesca gave a little wail, her cheeks catching colour as they always did when she was upset. "Anyway eggshell may be delicate, but it's *strong*."

"The answer is as Brod says," Rebecca intervened gently. "Good sun protection and protective clothing plus the essential, wide-brimmed hat. I think Fran could not only survive but flourish out here," she added, earning Francesca's gratitude.

"Becky, darling." Fee finished her wine with amazing speed and no apparent effect. "Don't give Francesca any ideas. She's all but promised to Jimmy Waddington. That's the Honourable James Waddington. His father Peregrine is de Lyle's closest friend. Jimmy was distraught when Francesca quit her job to come to Oz. He's fully expecting her to return. As is her father. Believe me I know my daughter loves it here, but England is her real world."

"What a pity nobody told me." Francesca tried to smile, wishing for the ten thousandth time her mother wouldn't volunteer so much information. But then no one could stop Fee. She had a terrible habit of letting the cat out of the bag and if that didn't go off too well to shove it back in.

"Just knew she'd left a boyfriend behind." Grant turned his head to give Francesca a direct look. "Jimmy Waddington. The Honourable James Waddington. That sounds just about right."

"Breach of privacy, Fee." Brod tapped his aunt's magnificently beringed hand. "Now let's hear Fran's version."

Oh, thank you, Brod, Francesca thought, diving into an explanation. "I think of Jimmy as my friend. I've known him all my life. I love him in that way because he's a truly lovable person. He's decent and kind and he's very intelligent."

"In short someone you ought to marry," Grant inserted in a voice like dark polished silk.

"Except I don't love him in any romantic way. I forgot to mention that." Francesca returned his gem-hard gaze.

"Believe me, darling, liking is much better." Fee of the fantastic love affairs pronounced without turning a hair. "You simply must have things in common. Have the same friends, share the same tastes, the same background. Passion is all very well but unless a man and a woman have similar views of life, things can become very quickly unstuck. Your father for instance was madly in love with me but he should never have married me."

"I can't imagine why he did." Brod gave a brief laugh. "Obviously you were much too hard to resist, Fee, let alone control."

"Well, as they say, it seemed like a good idea at the time," Fee replied. "I desperately want my girl to be happy. I don't want her to make an awful mistake, like me. One should approach marriage in a cool and rational manner."

"That's why you did just the opposite," Francesca pointed out with less than her usual tolerance, causing David to chuckle out loud.

"Fee often says things she doesn't mean," he told Francesca soothingly. "Being in love is the grandest feeling of all. It makes one come alive. It makes one whole. Which brings me to my announcement of this evening." David tapped his crystal wineglass with a spoon and looked around the table. "Fee and I have something to tell you and we hope you'll be as happy about it as we are. We have decided to get married."

Brod was the first to respond, "Now why doesn't that surprise me?" Then everyone stood up at once. Francesca running around the table to kiss her mother, followed by Rebecca, while the men shook hands.

"Congratulations!"

"We're both so happy." A very becoming blush spread over Fee's golden cheeks. "Life is wonderful with David around. Of course he's the man I should have married."

Brod, catching David's eyes gave a sardonic little grin, but didn't point out David was married at the time. "I think this calls for champagne." He looked to his wife, loving her madly, this woman who was making him extraordinarily happy.

"Would it be too much to hope we've got something really good in the frig?"

"If you're into Bollinger." She smiled into his eyes. "Some little instinct told me to put it in."

Afterwards Francesca and Grant chose to walk off the effects of the celebration, leaving Fee to talk further about her plans. The air was filled with all the clean, dry aromatic scents of the bush, the purplish black sky palpitating with the glittering white fire of countless stars. It should have been exciting but there was a kind of estrangement between them.

"So is marriage going to interfere with this movie part Fee's been offered?" Grant asked, more to break the awkward silence than anything else.

"I'm sure Mamma and David have talked it through," Francesca said. "It's not a big role. A cameo they call it. Mamma's thinking of it as a last hurrah."

"Her swan song?" Grant's deep voice sounded sceptical.

"God knows she has enormous energy and a great deal to offer. Anyway David's used to Mamma," Francesca said. "She's right about one thing. They're two of a kind. David has always led a full life, a pivotal member of a very glamorous group, the theatre, the art aficionados. He's very different from Daddy. My father likes the companionship of a few lifelong friends and his own peaceful world of Ormond. He hates leaving it even for a day."

"I expect it's very beautiful."

"One of the most beautiful places on earth." Francesca felt her heart swelling with pride.

"But you won't inherit it?" Grant countered with a kind of disbelief.

Francesca plucked a waxy flower then twirled it under her nose. "No."

"Good Lord!" Grant stared up at the pulsing stars. "Don't you mind, this male of the line stuff?"

"Perhaps." She nodded, in reality deeply attached to her ancestral home. "But I grew up knowing I wouldn't inherit Ormond, just as Ally knew Kimbara would be Brod's."

"A bit of a difference there, I'd say." Grant sounded as if he didn't appreciate the parallel. "The business of running a cattle chain is all hard slog. Backbreaking work, stoic resilience, lots of responsibility. I wouldn't wish the load on any woman's shoulders. The outback is a man's world, Francesca, for all we need our women's love and devotion. You would be in perfect harmony with your ancestral home."

She'd been counting on him to say that. "Only it's *not* mine," she repeated wryly. Hadn't she already moved out, not at all close to her father's second wife, not able to help making comparisons with a beautiful, brilliant Fee.

"That's too damned bad," Grant was saying. "If I were your father I'd have changed things."

"I'm very glad you're not my father," she offered dryly, deeply conscious of his tall, powerful figure beside her, whipcord lean.

He laughed, then suddenly began to croon, taking her by surprise. "You must have been a beautiful baby. You must have been a beautiful child. When you were only startin' to go to kindergarten, I bet you drove the little boys wild...."

Perfect tune. Smooth as honey baritone. It sounded great with a considerable degree of seductiveness.

"I didn't know you could sing," she said delightedly.

"Of course I can sing." The ice broken he pulled her against him, wrapping an arm around her waist. "You should hear me when I'm out riding. When I was a kid I used to sing to the cattle. It used to calm them every time."

"Are you serious?" she laughed.

"Ask Rafe." He launched smoothly into another song. "Home, home on the range..."

His voice came back to them on the wind and Francesca

clapped in appreciation. "From now on you're going to have to serenade *me*."

"Am I?" He turned her, his hands spanning her narrow waist. "So what about this Jimmy?"

She dipped her head. "Daddy's choice, Grant. Not mine."

"You're not running away from them, are you?" he asked as if he were resolved to find out. Holding her, touching her, desire rippling deep inside him.

"In what way?"

"Unwillingness to commit maybe. Your father is concerned with marrying you off properly. He doesn't trust your mother in that regard."

"He doesn't trust Fee at all," Francesca confessed wryly. "He may have loved her madly once but all I can remember is his finding fault. It's not very nice being the child in the middle of a fault-finding divorce and the long aftermath. The physical separation from Mamma. It was like being deprived of the sun. The actor Fee was having an affair with and later married was remarkably handsome and when he wasn't drunk he could be very nice but Daddy *hated* him. He refused to allow me to visit if Fee's 'new man' was anywhere around."

"Well he wasn't around long, thank the Lord." Grant gave a deep sigh. Fee's exploits over the years were well known to all of them. He had a vivid picture, too, of how it must have been for one sad and solitary little girl.

"I can give you some lyrics à la Cole Porter," Francesca offered half in fun, half serious. "'It was just one of those things. One of those crazy things.' Fee can't be without a man."

"Now she's got David, so cheer up." Grant turned her gently so they could walk on.

"And my dear cousin, David, will keep Mamma in line," Francesca said with a note of satisfaction. "He may look and act the perfect gentleman with the Eton accent but he's steel at the core. If he'd been married to Fee in the first place she'd never have shared anyone else's bed."

"Her time with your father could scarcely have been wasted," Grant reminded her. "She had *you*. That alone was a great gift. Anyway she adores you."

"I know." Forgiving by nature Francesca's anger and bewilderment at her mother's abandonment had long since dried up.

"And you're going back to Sydney for her book launch." It was obviously a statement, not a question.

"Of course I have to and I want to. Rebecca as the biographer is going as a matter of course. It's just a pity Ally won't be home. I want to be here when she gets back."

"And I need to be *out!*" Grant startled her by saying.

Anxiety sounded in her voice. "What does that mean?"

He gave a little amused growl low in his throat. "Why, Francesca, do I really have to spell it out? Two's company, three's a crowd. Especially when you're newly married."

She stood stock-still to stare up at him. "But the homestead is so big!"

"What's wrong, love?" Very lightly he pinched that delicately determined little chin. "Don't you like it? Rafe and Ally will want to be on their own."

Privately she thought Rafe and Ally would be very upset if he left. "But where will you go?" she questioned. "I never thought for a minute you'd leave Opal. Apart from the fact it's your home, it's the base for Cameron Airways."

"That can be changed." He sounded as if he'd thought it all out.

"You're serious then?" She was totally distracted.

"Absolutely."

"Do Rafe and Ally know of your plans?" she persisted, so nearly giving herself away.

"Not as yet. Needless to say they assure me Opal is my home as well."

"I should think so." Francesca felt like she was in some trance of non-acceptance. She couldn't lose contact with this man she'd fallen helplessly, probably hopelessly in love with. "Where would you go?"

Grant took her hand and walked on. "Somewhere more central. Even Darwin."

"In the Territory?" She was shaken by the thought. He was talking a thousand miles away and more.

"Gateway to Australia." Grant nodded. "I know of a fine property that could come on the market."

Francesca gave him a dismayed look, unaware her expression was easily readable by the moon. "You've taken my breath away," she told him unnecessarily. "Everyone will miss you terribly." *Me* most of all.

For a long moment he was mad with wanting her. Wanting to crush her to him, feel the softness and smallness of her body against his. Inhale her scents. Instead with force of will he pressed his thumb into her palm, feeling her heat, caressing it with a deep circular motion. What stopped him from making love to this young woman as he was wild to? Other times, other places, other girls, he had felt none of this anguish over lovemaking. The answer was he cared too damned much about her. He couldn't force a potentially disastrous situation. She was Lady Francesca de Lyle, daughter of an English earl and the internationally famous stage actress, Fiona Kinross. If she were any other girl, a young woman of his own circle, he'd have raced her to the altar. Francesca's background reeked of centuries old tradition, a high place in one of the most privileged societies on earth. Even Fee had pushed the fact Francesca was meant for better things.

Finally he managed to say, "I'm not going that far away. Not as a plane flies. I don't aim to stick to helicopters. Dad left me a fair share of Opal even if I'm not Numero Uno."

You are to me, Francesca thought, blindly turning her face away. "Why don't you build a homestead of your own on Opal?" she frowned. "There's plenty of room in a couple of thousand square miles."

His spirits lifted unaccountably. Why hadn't he come around to that? "Opal has only ever had one homestead," he pointed out as if it was written in stone.

She shot him a quick look, aware of his change of mood. "Two Cameron sons who love each other and don't want to be parted? Even if they don't want to share the same house, I would have thought building another homestead would be the obvious solution. And I'll tell you exactly where you should do it."

He was halfway to laughing now, loving the sweet sound of her voice and the surprising authority in it. "Go on. Tell me," he invited, taking the path that led to the walled garden with its pond and winged nymph, glorious scents of roses, jasmine and boronia, herbs crushed underfoot, soft little night wind like music and two carved garden seats.

Peace and harmony by day. Powerfully seductive by moonlight. Maybe he'd been worrying so much he'd suddenly got to the point where he couldn't care anymore. Whatever the reason he led her to one of the benches, sending a few fallen leaves and spent blossoms flying with a lick of the handkerchief from his trouser pocket. Protecting her pretty deep blue dress was a priority. The short skirt showed her lovely legs. The deep oval neck descended onto her breasts, delicate, tantalising, the skin of the upper slopes smooth as silk, white as milk. The rosy nipples he just knew would be like luscious little berries in his mouth, the taste more exquisite than any known fruit.

God the only thing that saved him from ravishing her was he knew right from wrong. Even so his breath seemed to be rasping in his chest. Desire was the very devil. It made an utter fool of a man.

"I would have thought you'd guess," Francesca was saying, making room for him on the bench, mercifully unaware of his unsettled state. "It's extraordinary country and it's only about a mile or more from Opal homestead. Grassy flats, bordered by spinifex and mulga country, then in the distance the rippling slopes of the desert dunes. But what makes it all fascinating is that very strange hill with the perfectly flat top, except for three little peaks around the border for all the world like some ancient crown. It's full of magic. Every time I've seen it, from the distance or the air, it seems to be floating in an amethyst mirage."

Of course he identified the site right away. Francesca was right. There was something about it. "Francesca, you're talking about Myora," he said, referring to the landmark. "There are all kinds of legends attached to it."

"Which makes it all that more delightful," she said happily. "As hills go it isn't high. What would it be…a couple of hundred feet? But it has such an *aura!*" Then she suddenly asked, "It's not a sacred site?" She knew that could change things with aboriginal tribes currently focusing on regaining their sacred sites.

"No—" Grant shook his head, instantly following her line of thought "—but it has associations from the Dreamtime."

"Does that mean you can't build there?" She felt unaccountably disappointed.

"I can build anywhere I want," he told her firmly. "This is Cameron land. We feel we have as much kinship with the land as our aboriginal brothers. The Camerons have always treated tribal people well. We came as protectors as well as pastoralists. As a courtesy I would discuss my plans with the tribal elders. But, Francesca, Myora is even more isolated than Opal homestead."

"You mean the difficulty of getting building materials, etc., to the site?" Immediately Francesca was overwhelmed by the challenges of the job.

"No, I don't," Grant said surprisingly. "Our forebears performed fantastic feats. I mean—" he broke off, rubbing his neck. "Hell I don't know what I mean." When every other thought was given over to placing Francesca, like a jewel, in her proper setting. The middle of the Never Never, for all its fascination, didn't seem the right spot.

"You could *think* about it," Francesca suggested, looking up at his strong profile.

"Wouldn't you be terrified on your own out there?" he countered.

Another rejection. "What should I be terrified of?" She kept her voice composed. "There aren't any bush-rangers anymore. No stockman would dream of causing me harm."

"You know nothing about utter isolation," he said, leaning a little away from her. "When you come out here you stay at one of the grandest homesteads in the country. Kimbara. You're safe and cushioned at all times. I love the bush, Francesca, I have great respect for it but I can tell you even hardened stockmen can get spooked on their own. There are some areas, some places, that have an atmosphere, that can make the hair on the back of your neck stand up. We've all experienced it. This is an incredibly ancient land. We're by way of being very recent newcomers."

Francesca gave a delicious little shiver. "Are we talking ghosts?"

"I'm not talking ballyhoo, my lady," he retorted, giving a lock of her long hair a slight tug. "What I say isn't to be taken lightly. There are certain places even the aborigines won't go."

"On Opal?" She felt as if she was drowning in mysteries.

"Of course on Opal." Grant's voice was matter-of-fact. "Kimbara, too. It's *strange* country in many ways. Our country and not our country. Not the white man's country if you know what I mean. Our ancestors came from elsewhere. The Camerons and the Kinrosses hailed from Scotland. In certain places the Interior seems to be not exactly hostile but not welcoming, either."

"You can't mean Myora?" She'd always thought the land welcomed her on all her visits.

Grant's voice was level. "*I've* never felt it there. But *you've* never actually been there, have you?"

"I'd like to go." She lifted a delicate brow.

"Then this is your chance," he surprised her by answering. "I have a few days all to myself. I can take you tomorrow, though the odds are against my ever building there."

"You might change your mind." She attempted lightness when she was feeling utterly emotional.

"Wishful thinking, Francesca." He turned his hazel eyes on her.

"*What* am I thinking?" Suddenly she could barely breathe. There was humour in his voice but something else that sent a deep pulsing, quiver right through her body.

"An impossible dream."

"What dream," she challenged, softly. "What am I dreaming?"

For answer he bent his head and pressed his mouth to the creamy flesh of her throat.

"Grant!" Even to her own ears she sounded startled.

"You don't really know what you're trying to get yourself into," he said, a shade harshly.

"Can't you see you surprised me?" In fact she was more frightened of her own reactions than anything he might do to her. He was the most beautiful man. Full of a man's powers. Just the touch of his lips against her throat made her head swim.

"You're safe with me, Francesca," he said in a dry voice and stood up, his height exaggerated in the silver moonlight. "As safe as if you were sitting in church."

She, too, came to her feet, humming with tension. "Now I've made you angry, why?"

"I'm not angry with you at all," he said, not really meaning it and not knowing why. "I just don't want you to forget who *you* are and who *I* am."

"Now that's a *message*," Francesca said.

"Yes, it is." Even he grimaced, thinking himself as much a victim of circumstances as Francesca.

"Why can't you get through your head I'm a *woman* not a figurine," Francesca suddenly exploded.

That somehow inflamed him to the point he felt he was burning up. *He* didn't appreciate she was a woman? How could she say such a ridiculous thing, this miracle of femininity.

Before she could take a breath he held her lovely face and kissed her hard and fast. Just seconds to be ravenous. He wanted to plunge his hand into the low, tempting oval of her dress and take hold of her small creamy breasts. Just the thought of it made him wild, but he couldn't do this to her. It was all so damned confusing. One might have thought she was some kind of family, or a little Titian-haired, blue-eyed saint on a pedestal. He should have avoided her right from the start. She was so hopelessly out of reach.

Francesca's own confusion was immense. Grant was breathing heavily. So was she. Both of them filled with a terrible unrequited desire. More than that. Love. She was certain he loved her but instead of helping her it was somehow making him feel guilty. She could have wept.

"Grant, I really care about you," she said, moving close, gripping onto his shirtsleeve with her hand. "Why are you pushing me away?"

"You know very well." That high mettled note came into his voice. "I care about you, too, Francesca. Too much to want to cause you real unhappiness. I can see to the end of this if you can't?"

It was obvious his concerns were real. "You mean you think it inevitable I'll go back to England."

"You'll leave me before I'll ever leave you. England *is* your home. You have a certain position in life. It's not outback wife. Even the heat of the sun can be killing."

She was nearly crying with frustration. "So Rebecca can survive it. So can Ally, so can my mother. Every other woman it seems but me."

He looked down at her, she was totally enchanting and anguish edged his voice. "It's the way you look."

"You think I'm an ice cream that might melt." She made a little sound of exasperation.

"Hell I'm afraid of just that. Look, Francesca, I'm not trying to insult you—" he stroked her cheek "—or anything like that. I'm trying to decide what's best for both of us."

"Which of course is as good as saying *I'm* stupid." She shimmered with sudden temper.

"Far from it." He knew he shouldn't but he laughed, loving the sparkle in her star-struck eyes.

"Then why don't you let me decide what *I* want," she challenged, her blue gaze riveted to his strong handsome face.

"Because it's too dangerous." He bent his head and just brushed the corner of her mouth with his lips. "You're hell bent on a holiday romance."

She heard the teasing note in his voice...of course she did, yet she flinched. "Then it's really astonishing the way *you* keep kissing *me*."

He grinned at her, his teeth flashing very white. "That's what's called turning the tables. I'm sorry, Francesca, you might have started up the saying, you're adorable when you're angry, but I don't want to hurt you. You make me feel as protective as a big brother."

"Oh Lord!" She inhaled the jasmine-boronia filled night air. "So we don't get to take our trip tomorrow?"

He smiled slightly. "Hell you can't go around disappointing me. Of course we will. I wouldn't forego it for the world. You're going to show me where to build my dream house."

"Why should I?" she questioned, turning up her face to him. Why? When he would take to it some other woman as his bride.

"Because you're Lady Francesca de Lyle," he explained in a voice like dark velvet. "And it's your gift to me."

CHAPTER THREE

"YOU'RE GOING TO DO WHAT?" Fee burst out, turning from the French doors and walking back into Francesca's bedroom.

"You heard, Mamma," Francesca continued, brushing her hair at the mirror. It was crackling with electricity, red, amber, rose and gold strands sparkling and flashing. "I'm going over to Opal with Grant. I'm going to help him pick out a home site."

"I don't believe it." Fee's dramatic face wore a worried frown. She slumped into a comfortable armchair imagining she was having a nervous breakdown. "I must ask you darling, is this wise?"

"Of course it's wise, Mamma," Francesca responded respectfully, firmly.

"But you know, darling, your father has big plans for you," Fee reminded her. "I might have embodied his biggest nightmare but you're his dream child. He loves you. He wants to see you happy in your own setting. Married to one of your childhood friends."

"Like good old Jimmy, my ex-boyfriend," Francesca asked wryly, waiting for her hair to settle so she could braid it.

"Not Jimmy if you don't think you could come to love him," Fee told her, reasonably. "But there are others, darling. Roger and Sebastian to name just two."

"Except I don't love them, either. Daddy didn't ask my permission to marry Holly. He just mentioned to me he was thinking of remarrying."

"How extraordinary when he hated every minute of being married to me," Fee said, gazing at her lovely daughter tenderly, maternally.

"No, he didn't, Mamma," Francesca corrected, ever loyal to her father. "He loved you. He would have stayed married to you forever if you hadn't run off."

"It must have been Springtime," Fee said, her face reflective. "Actually I was terribly misled but I was always hotly desired."

"You won't run away from David," Francesca warned.

"Darling, as if I'd want to!" Fee protested going quite pink. "At long last I've got it right. Best thing I've ever done. Anyway it's not me we're talking about, it's you. Don't think for a minute I have anything against Grant. He's a splendid young man, so sexy, he even gives your dear Mamma a funny feeling, but he has his own vision in life. Why only last night he was telling us his plans. His commitment is *here*. The Australian outback."

"Don't you think you're running too far ahead?" Francesca said, making little braids of her front hair.

Fee snorted. "Come on, darling, I know everything there is to know about love affairs. The air literally crackles around you two."

"Holiday affair?" Francesca asked.

"Well if you have to get him out of your system," Fee considered. "I don't see you two together, my darling. I can only see heartache and separation. I know it's not easy but one must try to be wise."

Francesca raised a delicate brow. "Yes, of course, Mamma, but I'm only going over to help him pick out a possible site for a new homestead. Grant doesn't want to intrude on Rafe and Ally."

"Goodness how nice of him," Fee said. "But the place is *huge*.

Besides, why couldn't he buy a property? Douglas would have left his sons very well provided for."

"I'm certain Rafe doesn't want to lose his brother," Francesca said. "They're very close. Closer than most because of the sad circumstances of their life. Why buy another property when Grant could build a second homestead on Opal. Lord knows they've got a whole world to themselves as Brod has here."

"A kingdom at the very least," Fee agreed complacently. "My friends used to find it fascinating listening to stories from my childhood on Kimbara. But don't try to distract me. I'm doing my best to play Mamma. In short, I'm trying to warn you, my darling. You could get badly hurt. So could Grant. I should tell you, too, the Camerons are men of strong passions. And proud. Fiercely proud. You'll have to live with that."

"Actually I like it," Francesca said, her eyes going dreamy.

Fee fell back, unable to keep the genuine worry out of her voice. "Darling, normally I wouldn't interfere but I have a feeling this could be very serious. What have you really got on your mind? Surely as your mother I'm entitled to know?"

Francesca found herself sinking into the armchair opposite her mother. "I've never felt like this before, Mamma," she explained. "I feel like I'm lit up inside."

"You're in love." Fee nodded. "It's just rotten luck you had to fall for Grant."

Instantly Francesca jumped up, outraged. "That's not funny, Mamma."

Fee, too, hauled herself to her feet. "I'm not trying to be funny, darling. For heaven's sake! I'm worried where this might lead. You have *everything* at home in England."

"Except Grant," Francesca said with a touch of fire.

"Maybe so." Fee started to sound doubtful. "But this life couldn't be more *different*, Fran. You've never seen Kimbara under drought. In times of flood. You can't possibly know. You haven't been around when the tragedies happen. Let's face it, darling, do you really want this lifestyle? Can you cope with it?"

"Rebecca is blooming," Francesca told her.

"Rebecca isn't *you* and I expect she'll take up her writing again. She'll have something engrossing to do. She and Brod will start a family. Kimbara needs its heirs."

"What about Ally then?" Francesca challenged, feeling like everyone was against her. "Ally could have had a huge movie career. She knocked it all back for Rafe."

"Oh, darling." Fee returned to her chair looking at her daughter with pity in her eyes. "Ally is that little bit older than you, and she's had longer to consider what she really wants out of life. Then there's the fact, good actress that she is, Ally wasn't really dedicated as one has to be. The theatre was *everything* to me. That's the difference." But there had been a devastation to it, Francesca thought, but was too tender-hearted to mention. Her mother had been a wonderful actress but she hadn't been the best of mothers.

"A career isn't the only way to happiness and fulfilment, Mamma," she said quietly, sitting on the edge of the four-poster bed. "It's a big job raising a family and I want children. I'd rather find Mr. Right than be a huge success in the business world though most people would tell you I was very effective at P.R."

"And it didn't hurt to have an earl for a father," Fee pointed out dryly.

"That doesn't give me a warm glow, Mamma." Francesca couldn't help but speak a little sharply. "In many ways your view of me seems to be as a *child*."

It was true. "Ah well, you are very young, darling," Fee sighed. "Moreover you're the bearer of your father's dream. You're bright, beautiful, charming, so clearly destined for big things. You must realise, too, your son could become your father's heir."

Francesca looked at her mother levelly. "Even Grant has pointed that out to me."

Fee nodded. "I'm sure it concerns him. Whatever his feelings for you he must be aware of the situation."

"*What* situation," Francesca burst out in pure frustration. "Anyone would think I was a member of the Royal Family. Grant and I are equals. Come to that you always had more money than Daddy. I know you helped extensively at Ormond."

"You can say that again!" Fee breathed. "But I don't feel at all bitter about it. It's as I say, one day my grandson might occupy it. I don't want to be disagreeable, darling. I don't want to upset you. I know the wonderful feelings that come with thinking oneself in love but I have to help you to look steadily to your future. I feel a great affection for the Camerons, Rafe and Grant. Grant is an admirable young man. There's no question he's going places. He's masterful, aggressive, assertive and very hot-headed from time to time. You may find it exciting now but as he develops I think he'll turn into a real dynamo. Dynamos in a way are dangerous people. They're high risk."

"I'm not afraid of anything about Grant, Mamma," Francesca said very seriously, twining her arms around the polished mahogany bedpost, all rose and cream and blue sheened eyes. "I think he'd die rather than hurt me. What makes me fearful is the thought he could turn me away thinking it was for my own good."

Fee gave an uncomfortable little laugh. "Darling, have you considered he might be right?" Breeding showed in every line of her daughter's petite, slender body, breeding and what Fee interpreted as a certain fragility, an inability to withstand rigours.

Her mother's seeming opposition was like little barbs to the heart. Francesca moved off the bed so quickly her thick braid swung against her cheek. "Except if I lost him I know I'd be sorry for the rest of my life."

They landed on Opal's front lawn while the hot humming earth sent up spirals of dried grass, bleached bronze and gold leaves. When the air was still they alighted, Francesca looking with great pleasure towards the huge, rambling old homestead with its gables and verandah bays, the pedimented porch and the white wrought-iron lacework that matched the timber fret-work. Opal lacked Kimbara's conscious grandeur but it was a fine colonial homestead by anyone's standards. Cascading bright red bougainvillea made a glorious show falling from the slate roof of the east wing, down the white pillars to the ground, as did the deep hardy border of agapanthus with huge hyacinth and white heads right along the front of the house, but it was evident not a great deal of time had been spent on the once extensive home gardens. The lawn not shaded by a giant magnolia and a row of classic gums, was yellowed by the heat of the sun and the central three tiered fountain that once had played was now dry and dusty. Nevertheless it was an amazingly attractive building and Francesca knew Ally would have the most wonderful time bringing the homestead and its home grounds back to their former glory.

"Come up and look around," Grant said, taking her by her silky arm, feeling the sizzle in his fingers. "It's very quiet with no one around. As you can see, the gardens of my mother's day have gone, neither Rafe nor I have had the time to look after them. Not that either of us know much about gardening but we surely miss what it was like with Mum around. That wonderful feminine grace went out of everything. But Ally will bring it back."

Francesca looked up to smile into his face, feeling so happy it was like her blood was filled with bubbles. "And have a marvellous time doing it. I *love* the homestead." Her eyes shone. "It's extraordinarily picturesque. As a matter of fact now I look at it, it would be the ideal outback setting for Mamma's new movie?"

"What are you saying here?" Grant cocked a brow. "I thought the woman director was coming out to take a look at Kimbara? Surely Fee said so at dinner last night?"

"Actually, Mamma did that without asking," Francesca confessed. "Something she has a tendency to do. Not that Brod would refuse her and Rebecca would take pleasure in it but I've read the screenplay and Kimbara homestead is too...too..." She sought the right word.

"Teetering on grand?" he suggested dryly.

"In every way. Uncle Stewart spent a fortune on its upkeep and it shows."

"While the Camerons did not." He looked her straight in the eyes, loving her sudden flush, a rosy pinkness that wasn't there a moment ago.

"I don't mean that." Francesca shook her head. "I mean Opal has a soft well lived in..."

"Faded charm?"

"Are you going to finish all my sentences for me?" she demanded.

"If we want to get to the nitty gritty." He grinned, moving her into the shade of the verandah.

"If you read the screenplay you'd know what I mean."

"Francesca, I'm one up on you." His smile mocked her. "I've read the book."

"*Have* you?" She sounded delighted.

"Outback people are great readers," he told her. "Didn't you know?"

"As a matter of fact I do." Reading was a big part of entertainment. "Opal homestead is really what they're after."

"Maybe, but who would need all those film people around?" He opened the front door, turning to look at her in her simple cotton shirt and jeans. Who said a redhead couldn't wear pink? He'd never seen a pink shirt look so good.

"You said yourself it was very lonely on your own." Her eyes were alive with ideas. "I expect the outback scenes could be shot in a month. Riversleigh, the Sydney colonial mansion is the setting for most of the action. Anyway it's just a thought."

"Then why are those blue eyes so bright and alive?" he retorted with amusement. "The last time they sparkled just like that you were doing an excellent P.R. job on Drew Forsythe from TCR."

"I'm always full of ideas," Francesca said, moving into the spacious hallway and looking around.

"I can see that," he commented, captivated by her presence.

"So am I allowed to discuss it with Mamma?" She twirled her small supple body. "The director and script writer will be here in a couple of days."

"You're kidding?" In a way he was utterly taken aback.

"No," she answered simply. "It would be lovely to see Opal up on the big screen. It's not the first time a colonial mansion has been used in an Australian movie. I think it would be brilliant! Moreover you have such enormous interest in everything you'd probably enjoy it."

"Well I might," he admitted, "but, Francesca, I'm not around much during the day. I have a business."

"All right. So no one would bother you. There would be good company for dinner. You would want to speak to Rafe and Ally?"

He laughed. A mocking sound, slightly awry. "Darling, are you reminding me of my obligations?"

The way he called her "darling" nearly took her breath away. "Really I'm just having a bit of fun," she wavered.

"No, you're not." The laugh turned indulgent. "You want me to take this seriously."

"I swear I never thought of it until five minutes ago," she said sincerely. "I looked up at the homestead and there it was! The setting right under my nose, so to speak."

"They pay well I imagine?" Grant the business man was considering.

"I'm sure they would."

"In that case Rafe is involved in a programme for rehabilitation for troubled youth, a kind of bush rescue scheme. I'm interested, too, but as Rafe runs the station it's mainly his concern. The Trust could do with the money."

"What a good idea." She felt a real flutter of excitement. "I've heard about the scheme from Ally. I can see, too, the bush has great healing powers.

"Nature's cathedral," Grant said. "God can speak very clearly here. But hang on, Francesca, your mother has other ideas."

"Not by the time I've spoken to her." Francesca gave her lovely endearing smile.

"I believe you, but you'll have to hang on until I speak to Rafe and Ally. They mightn't want any part of it."

Francesca lifted her face to him. "I'm not exactly sure about Rafe, but I know Ally will be intrigued. She might even want to be home when they shoot the scenes. We'll all enjoy watching Fee. She becomes so much the part she's playing, it's shivery. As soon as the makeup goes on, the dress, she's that person."

Grant could well believe it. He'd seen Fee transform herself into any number of people in the space of telling a story. "You've never thought of acting yourself?" he asked Francesca.

"Believe it or not I was considered quite good at school."

"So did Fee go along to see you? Tell you how wonderful you were?"

The smile faltered slightly. "She was so busy at the time she missed all of my performances, but Daddy came."

"Hell I put my foot in it," he groaned, so much in empathy with her he felt her old pain.

"It doesn't hurt anymore."

"Sure?" He badly wanted to kiss her, hold her in his arms, comfort her, only he was too keenly aware it could all get out of hand. She made his blood soar, this exquisitely fashioned young woman. Not a figurine. She had far too much intelligence, humour, radiance to be that.

"I don't think I could love Mamma any more than I do. I *know* she's not ordinary but I have missed her terribly many times in my life." Read years, Francesca thought but would never say. Not now when the estrangement was over.

"It could have ruined your relationship forever," Grant considered broodingly, "but you're far too compassionate for that. Fee was perfectly charming to me when we left, but I got the feeling she's afraid of something."

"Oh, Grant, don't talk about it." She came to him and took his hand, trying to distract his attention. "I feel like a cup of coffee and I want to look over the homestead."

"You know you're safe with me, don't you," he said, not to be deflected.

She stared right into his eyes. "To me you're the most honourable man on the face of the earth."

"Francesca!" He couldn't help it, he pulled her into his arms as his emotions took control. "I have to tell you I'm suffering for it." His tone was self-mocking and dry.

"What could be wrong about falling in love?" she whispered rejoicing in being within the circle of his arms.

"Falling in love is wonderful, Francesca," he agreed in a low feeling voice. "The world is a lovely, romantic place, but there's no question falling in love with the wrong person can wreck lives."

"Then why don't you let me go," she taunted him very gently, lifting her head.

His expression was wry. "It seems my arms have a life of their own."

"So you are happy to hold me?"

"I love holding you," he said and meant it. "I could hold you like this forever. I could spend eternity looking into your eyes. I could run my mouth over that little pulse in your throat. I could open that pink shirt and caress your breasts. I could topple you into my bed. But that wouldn't get the coffee made." Determinedly he bent his head, kissed her cheek and swiftly turned her about. "Do you like it black or white?"

"You're a devil," she said. So he was for tempting her so richly.

"There's a devil in every man," he warned her, his eyes glinting," but depend on it I'll keep him well hidden around you."

* * *

They took the horses along the long, twisting trail of gullies and billabongs that led to the ancient flat-topped hill the aborigines named Myora. At intervals they came across stockmen leading herds of cattle to camp, stopping briefly to watch an aboriginal stockman breaking in a silver-grey brumby obviously descended from station stock. The stockman's movements were filled with a kind of exquisite grace and Francesca was reminded Australian aborigines were among the finest natural dancers in the world. Overhead legions of birds flew like bright flags in the sky and there was music, too, from thousands and thousands of tiny throats with occasionally a wonderful cello solo from some bell-toned bird in the furthermost branch of a towering gum, or deep in the swamp.

There were kangaroos of all sizes, a marvellous sight when they bounded away across the flats, endearing standing stock-still by the water as they picked up their scent, ears pricked, pointed noses quivering, a curious look in their large, bright eyes. Through all this wonderful ride, Grant kept exclusively to the shade, following the tree-lined creeks that were scented with acacia and some kind of little lilies that grew thickly guarded by grand old coolabahs and ghost gums. At one of the many reed fringed billabongs they saw masses of waterfowl, and several times the wonderful blue cranes, the brolgas, making a striking picture as they fished among the waterlilies. Pink in this lagoon, blue in another, sometimes a mixture of blue and cream. Francesca, the nature lover, was utterly enchanted, thinking as she always did, the bush was a place of great magic. Her mother's blood truly spoke to her. She had absorbed it into her soul.

By the time they reached Myora there was a taut expectancy in the air. Because of the extreme flatness of the vast open plains even an elevation of a few hundred feet took on a considerable aura. Today as she had seen it from the air Myora's base was floating in a sea of amethyst mirage giving the impression the ancient eroded mesa was anchored to a cloud. To north, south, east and west the plains ran on for endless miles. In fruitful years wildflowers bloomed in their countless millions, way out to the far horizon but even in the Dry it was a magnificent sight.

"You're really enjoying yourself, aren't you?" Grant said with immense satisfaction, keeping a sharp look out for anything to startle her, a large goanna, a prowling dingo, the frilled lizards that came at a lightning rush but were harmless, some slight movement at the base of a bush that could only be a snake trying to escape.

"This is a special place," Francesca breathed, watching as Grant hitched the horses to a huge fallen tree limb for all the world like a massive sculpture. "This is where you should build your house. Right in the middle of the sweeping plain with Myora as a backdrop. It must be an incredible sight when the great inland blooms. I've missed it on every visit."

"You'll have to come back when the time is right," Grant managed to say in a casual voice, at the same time feeling a deep ache that took a moment or two to pass. "Flowers as far as the eye can see," he continued. "Mile after mile, the flowers go on. Over the graves of the pioneers. Over the graves of the lost explorers. The flowers are fragrant as well so the air might be blown in from heaven. Last year after the winter rains the country around here was smothered in yellow and white paper daisies, golden craspedia, green pussy tails, poppies and firebush, hopbush saltbush, yellow top carpet of snow, you name it. Though I've witnessed the flowering of the desert gardens all my life in times of drought even I can't believe the flowers will ever rise again. Yet they always do."

"A miracle," Francesca said quietly, still badly shaken by his casual acceptance she would be returning home.

He walked towards her, tall and powerful. "It sure seems like it. Experiments have been done on the remarkable desert seeds. Apparently they contain chemicals that prevent germination until the optimum time. Nature's green light. They don't spring to life for example after a brief shower only to quickly die back. The right timing ensures the seed crop for future generations." He pointed upwards to the ancient glowing hill.

"At the right times, there are beautiful blooms hidden away up there on Myora. Tucked into all sorts of places where the wind has blown the seeds. Fan flowers, wild hibiscus, little lilies, Lilac Lamb's Tails literally covering the rubble down the hillside, all waving in the breeze. Anyway, come along." He took hold of her hand. "I've something special to show you. Something we don't talk about a great deal on Opal mainly for protection."

"That's exciting! What is it?" She stared up into his golden-skinned face, his iridescent eyes shadowed by the broad brim of his akubra.

"All in good time." He stopped, touching a gentle forefinger to her chin. "God, you're beautiful!" He truly didn't mean to say it but it just popped out. Why was he sending out all these dangerous, conflicting, messages? Only her lovely face looked so rapt.

"I'm happy," she told him.

"That's what I want you to be." He spoke quietly but something in his voice turned hard. "Let's climb to the summit." He drew her on. "It's not that far and it's amazing the view of the surrounding countryside.

Despite his contradictions, a not to be denied exhilaration took hold of Francesca. It lent wings to her small feet. She was like a gazelle going up the rocky slope, foot sure, keeping hold of his hand but making her own confident ascent.

"Oh, this is marvellous!" she announced, when they finally reached the plateau.

"Get your breath," he advised, knowing he was being over-protective.

"I'm not out of breath." She showed a radiant smile to him.

"No, you're not," he admitted.

"It's all so vast!" She turned away from him and threw up her arms. "Overwhelming. I love the colours of the inland. All the ochres. They're so deep and weathered yet they *vibrate*. And the sky's so blue. Not a cloud in sight. The European explorers must have thought they'd ventured onto another planet. Thousands of square miles with not a soul in it except for nomadic tribes. And that sea of red sand dunes on the horizon sweeping on and on forever."

He went to her and checked her progress towards the rim. "Deserts are powerful landscapes. They're also death traps, so don't forget it. Knowledge is the thing. Modern transport, equipment. Even then things go wrong."

"Hey, Grant, you can't put me off," she warned gently.

"I can see that."

"Besides the Channel Country is a riverine desert," she pointed out. "All this wonderful network of interlocking rivers and creeks. The billabongs and lagoons."

"In drought except for the permanent billabongs they go dry," Grant told her. "In flood the rivers run for miles across. That's what the Channel Country *is,* a vast flooded plain. It covers a good five percent of the continent. During the monsoonal months the deserts to the north and here can be hit by fierce electrical storms. One claimed Stewart Kinross's life. Almost claimed Rebecca's. The roars of thunder are quite terrifying and they're accompanied by tremendous flashes of lightning. When lightning hits the inflammable spinifex we can have grass fires for days."

"So you're telling me it's a beautiful savage land."

"One has to remember that at all times."

"Yet it's so incredibly peaceful." Francesca looked out over the endless open vista. "Man needs the wilderness. These vast, open plains. There's such dignity about the outback. So much character. When one loves city life, cities are the place to be. I've always been a country girl at heart. I'm like my father. I love the land."

"This is a far cry from what you're used to, Francesca." He felt driven to keep repeating it.

"Certainly," she agreed. "Sheer *size* alone. It's a strange beauty. Primeval. One is constantly aware of the land's great antiquity but it's not alien to me. Don't you see that?"

"Francesca, you're classic English," he pointed out bluntly.

"And you just could be a classic stubborn Scot," she returned with a touch of fire.

He inclined his head in wry acknowledgment. "Anyway I love your company. I love your calm, your patrician elegance and that little fiery streak that shows itself now and again."

"But you're discouraging anything beyond close friendship?"

"Actually I think I'm behaving impeccably while we sort something out."

"I'll remind you of that when you're married, secure and settled." She managed a smile. "But you haven't told me. What do you think of my idea of Myora for a homesite? It's spell-binding country."

"Don't you think I should consult my future bride?" he asked, a sardonic note in his voice.

"Not necessarily. Opal homestead has been lived in for generations. I'm part of everything. I'm descended from Cecilia Kinross who married her kinsman Ewan Kinross when she really loved Charles Cameron."

Grant groaned. "That story has been around for a long time."

"It must have been true. What do you think? There must have been some reason for Cecilia to turn her back on the man she loved? Then there was the famous opal-and-diamond necklace. Cecilia's Necklace. Both men Kinross and Cameron gave it to her."

"I love your accent." He digressed knowing where this was heading.

"I love yours, too." She barely paused. "The deep drawl until it gets very clipped. Anyway to continue the conversation maybe your ancestor allowed my ancestor to outmanoeuvre him. Maybe your ancestor tried to talk Cecilia out of staying in this country. It would have been hard indeed in the early days. He must have felt obliged to warn. He may have even urged her to go back to Scotland for her own good."

"Now why aren't I surprised you'd get around to saying that?" he asked a little caustically.

"I wonder what did happen?" She moved away a few feet, staring down at the spinifex-covered plains. The mirage was abroad, creating phantom hills, lakes and tall, sticklike nomads.

"My family believes there was a trick," Grant admitted after a pause. "Kinross managed to convince Cecilia his friend was promised to another woman, a woman far more suited to his way of life. The woman, in fact, Charles Cameron eventually married. But what does it matter now? Eventually the two families were reunited but the two men were never close again. It happens like that with betrayal. God knows a man like Stewart Kinross could have played that role." The accusation surged out, borne of many old resentments and griefs.

"But my grandfather wasn't like that," Francesca protested, recognising the hard kernel of truth in what Grant had said of her uncle Stewart. "Sir Andrew was greatly loved and respected."

It was perfectly true. "Sorry. I'm sorry, Francesca," Grant apologised. "Sir Andy was a fine man. Don't let's talk about ancient history anymore."

"It seems to me it has repercussions to this day," Francesca sighed. "Everyone gets stirred up when they talk about that old love affair."

"A love affair gone wrong." He spoke briskly. "Come back from that edge, there's a lot of loose shale."

"I'm no daredevil." She obeyed at once. "But it does have a compelling fascination."

"Tell me have you seen enough?" He was moved by her reactions, the great pleasure she had taken in their trip.

"For now. But you promised me a surprise."

"And I'm going to show it to you." He captured her hand again, so small in his, fingers so delicate. "We'll take another route down."

She would have missed the dome-shaped entrance to the cave guarded as it was by a desert grevillea in full orange flower that appeared to grow out of sheer rock.

"We're here." Grant steadied her, though the ledge was fairly wide.

"Oh my goodness!" She felt a surge of excitement and anticipation. "Don't tell me, rock paintings?" She looked at him, willing him to say "yes!"

"This isn't a recorded site." He smiled at her enthusiasm. "There must be thousands all over the country. We like to keep ours a secret. It's not an important site but it's fascinating and it's been here since God knows when. The aborigines love to give colour and life to all of their shelters and caves. Inland hills, rocky outcrops, anywhere they can execute their art. A great many are in inaccessible places. It would be very easy to miss this. The family didn't know about this particular cave until fairly recently. Of course the local aborigines knew of its existence. Apparently they decided by my grandfather's time the Camerons had sufficient respect for traditional aboriginal culture to be told of its location."

"Why haven't I heard of this?" Francesca's expression was a mixture of awe and animation.

"You might have repeated the story all over." Grant drew back a large sage-green branch with its long, slender spines and masses of curly orange brushes exposing the wide, shallow entrance.

"Heavens you could have trusted me," Francesca said, peering in.

"I'm trusting you now," Grant's tone was dry. "I also want that ribbon you've got in your hair."

"Really?" She turned in surprise, standing stock-still as he reached out and pulled the ribbon from her thick upturned braid.

Immediately the plait began to unravel and he smiled in be-
guilement, thinking she had the most wonderful hair he had
ever seen. "Don't worry, Francesca, I'll give it back. For now I
want to tie up this branch and let a bit of sun into the cave otherwise we won't have sufficient light."

"Keep the ribbon. A memento." It was a throwaway line but
she found herself quivering at the look in his eyes, utterly brilliant, utterly desirous. She could not look away. She felt powerless to move. He tied the branch back, then he took her arm,
moving her away from the neck of the cave. "Just stand out of
harm's way for a moment while I check the interior. Some animal might have made the cave its home."

"As long as we're not talking bats." She gave a little shudder.

A moment more and he returned, so masculine, so vibrant,
he stirred every deep feeling in her. "All clear. Actually I've
forgotten how marvellous it is."

The instant they were inside the sandy-floored cave Francesca straightened up. Her eyes flashed around the ancient gallery that was covered in drawings. So many! The stone mass
of the rear wall displayed highly stylised designs Francesca
couldn't understand but found very attractive, executed in
ochres, red, yellow, charcoal, black and white. On the ceiling,
the highest point of the dome some eight feet, the designs were
quite different. She understood immediately that they were male
and delicate female figures in different aspects of making love
watched over by what appeared to be totem beings or spirit
figures. On the end walls were drawings of kangaroos, emus,
mammals, reptiles, fish, birds and what seemed to be giant insects. Simple linear drawings but accurate and charming, the
whole framed by impressions of human hands like a decoration.

"I can't possibly see this all in one day," she said her voice
instinctively pitched low in deference to all these ancient sym-
bols and ancestral beings. For all the drawings' simplicity this
wasn't doodling in any shape or form. The rock paintings had

a definite mystical power. The paintings relating directly to sex were even bringing the hot blood to her cheeks.

"So what do you suggest?" Grant's voice too was quiet with a faint shivery ring caused by the acoustics of the cave.

"Oh, God, I don't know! These are wonderful. Who else have you brought here?" She was aching for him to touch her, as sensations flashed through her body like so much sorcery. Weren't all those paintings supposed to mean love magic? Now there was a light wind blowing through the neck of the cave, adding its own hollow drumming, deep, soft notes reminiscent of the native didgeridoo, the wind's movements rippling the burnished sandy floor that she now saw had delicate, unusual patterns all over it. Spiders or little dragon lizards, she thought. Tracks recorded on the fine sand. Their tracks as well. Hers and Grant's. Her foot so much smaller.

"I expect a hundred girls," Grant said with a faint rasp.

"All of them in love with you?" She turned quickly, knowing without being told that she was the first woman outside family, except she was sure her cousin Ally, who had ever been brought here.

"I've never been in love in my life," he said, "except I'm afraid with *you*," he admitted almost roughly, a certain tension coming into his high-mettled face.

She had to clear her throat to speak. "And that's taboo?"

"That's how it is, Francesca."

One hand unconsciously went up to lie between her breasts. "You mean my title is a terrible constraint?"

"Your title is the smallest part of it," he said. "The *implications* of your title stronger, but overriding everything the near impossibility of transporting someone as delicate as you into a baked, red-glowing soil. It would take a miracle for you to survive."

His rejection was shattering. "So falling in love isn't enough?"

He groaned. "Think about it, Francesca. I beg you. Falling

in love is agony. Allowing a woman to reach far into your mind and your body would be to give her all the power in the world."

She looked at him out of sparkling eyes. "So it hasn't happened yet?"

"I'm not going to let it get the better of me, Francesca," he warned.

Her heart was beating swiftly, to the point of pain. "So you think rules apply to people like me and you're not going to break them?"

He held up his hands, palms forward like a supplicant warding her off, yet his glance was magnetic, luring her on. "Don't look at me like that."

"Do you think I wanted this to happen, willed it to happen?"

"You couldn't have." He shook his head. "It happened all at once. Years ago when you were just a sweet little teenager."

"We were close then." Nostalgia was reflected in her voice.

"Aren't we closer now?" His own tone was regretful.

"But you want me to go?"

"As things are—" He broke off, intensely confused. On the one hand he was trying to do the right thing, on the other he was mad to take this woman and make her his. It had got to the point when he couldn't imagine life without her. It wasn't meant to happen like this. Not at all.

She gave a little cry that startled him. Then she was flinging herself backwards as a small brightly patterned dragon lizard lifted itself out of the deep sand, every spine on its head and back upraised, a fearsome little harmless thing, still with the ability to give an unsuspecting person a fright. It dashed at breakneck speed, across Francesca's foot and outside the cave.

"God, Fran, here." He caught her as she stumbled, sinking, sliding to the cave floor. "It's only a lizard. It can't hurt you." But he could. The fragrance of her body, that unique rose scent was everywhere. He thought constantly about making love to her. Now here she was in his arms, a featherweight, so utterly beautiful inside and out.

"I'm sorry. Sorry." She gave a little laugh that wasn't a laugh at all. More like a sob because it was all so sad, so ridiculous, so cruel.

Desperate for her now, Grant caught her up strongly, experiencing such passion he was drawn to cover her mouth fiercely, voluptuously, feeling it open...open, her breath as sweet as the desert breeze. The tip of her small tongue, barely lapping, danced around his, inciting him until he felt he couldn't stand it. He was hard with desire, bearing her slender body down onto the soft sand as if he had been waiting for this all his life.

"Francesca!" Everything about him was doing a slow, sizzling burn.

"Don't talk." Her white fingers came up to his lips. "Don't talk at all."

She allowed him to slip open the small pearly buttons of her pink shirt. He had never known such exquisite anticipation. He moved his hands over her small breasts, the rosy nipples already bunched tight to his touch. She was wearing some kind of white lacy thing like a little singlet beneath her shirt. Nothing else. Her breasts were perfect, small, taut, high, the skin like satin. He lowered his head and took first one nipple then the other into his mouth, hearing her soft, urgent moans, the most exciting and dangerous little sounds in the world.

Exactly what he feared was happening. He could get her pregnant. This beautiful creature. Yet his hand found the zip of her cotton jeans, drawing it down. His fingers moved in desperate caressing patterns over her velvet stomach to the apex of her body, a point he knew he shouldn't cross, but he did because he couldn't summon enough will to turn back.

Wonder. It was wonderful. And now he was quite, quite certain of what he had only suspected.

All the while he caressed her, his ministrations causing her to writhe, he studied her lovely face. Her eyes were closed, her head turned sideways, her hair a fiery bolt of silk across the sand.

Take her, he thought. Just take her. Give in to your greatest desire. You're both young and so much alive. So much in love. He couldn't deny it. She was too honest to try.

"Francesca, Francesca," he muttered in a mindless ecstasy, his mouth closing over hers again. She was extraordinary. A dream. He never imagined a woman could be so beautiful. He wanted to cover every inch of her with kisses. Kisses like little indelible marks that would stay on her body forever.

He smoothed his palm across her satin-smooth stomach. So flat. He imagined her having a child. His beautiful child. Boy or girl he wouldn't care. Such a child would surely have red-gold hair. A little innocent. Perfect in their eyes.

But seeing that child in his mind's eye brought him back to his senses at a powerful rush. Her slender white arms were thrown back, fingers digging into the sand. She couldn't stop that soft, little moan as his hunger had taken him deeper and deeper into exploring her body.

His hesitation was minimal but deeply painful as if he was gripped by cramps, but by sheer force of will he managed to move, retrieving the pink shirt he had thrown away, getting a handle on the deep clashing tumults inside of him.

"Francesca. Please. Come on." He coaxed her urgently but she kept her eyes shut, not responding. Somehow, unaided, he fixed the little singlet, got her shirt back on and buttoned, rezipped her jeans.

She didn't help him at all as if she had loved the way she was, half-naked and lost to him.

"You don't think this is easy for me, do you?" he pleaded, half-cursing his own principles. "This is harder than you'll ever know. But I have to stop, Francesca."

At last she showed some reaction by shaking her head. "Why?"

"How can you ask? How can I possibly know if the time is right for you?" he asked tautly. "Are you on the pill or don't you care if you fall pregnant?"

She sat up immediately, clenching her small white teeth.

"I'm going to get a prescription right away." She was howling inside. Full of frustration.

"You have your virginity to bring to a man as a gift," he pointed out quietly.

"Damnation to that!"

He had to laugh, though the laugh went awry. "I like it. It's pretty unusual these days."

"It's the way I've chosen to live," she said, averting her head. "I've never cared enough about anyone to let them get to the stage where they *know* me."

He held her face between his hands and kissed her. "So whatever happens some part of you will always be mine. Could I have made you pregnant today?"

A wild rose flush mounted her cheeks. She looked across the silent cave, her blue gaze falling on ancient couplings. "I was too far gone to make notes." She tried a sad little joke. "I suppose you expected better of me?"

Her expression was so poignant he reacted strongly. "*I'm* the guilty one here, Francesca. I found the way to seduce you."

"And you would have only you're blessed with an exceptionally strong will."

"A year from now you might thank me." He stared into her face intently, committing every single feature to memory.

"I don't think so." She shook her head firmly, pushing her long hair back over her shoulders. "I don't regret any of this, Grant Cameron. What I feel for you is in very short supply."

CHAPTER FOUR

FOR DAYS AFTER Grant drove himself so hard, Brod, all his life honorary big brother, began to feel a niggling concern. There was no question Grant was splendidly fit, physically very strong, with nerves of steel, but it seemed to Brod he was putting himself under too much pressure without a safety valve. Cameron Airways now had sufficient pilots able and experienced enough to take over the big mustering jobs, but Grant was handling too much himself. It was a day in day out, dawn to dusk routine and not without its dangers especially for the helicopter pilot manoeuvring in difficult situations.

There was an undercurrent to all this. Brod was sure he knew what it was. *Francesca*. Grant had fallen very deeply in love with her but it was obvious to anyone who knew Grant well, he was taking it hard. It wasn't just a question of a young man used to a high level of self-sufficiency and freedom, fighting love's lasso. Grant seemed to be in genuine fear of hurting both of them by allowing their relationship to deepen.

Whatever happened the day he took Francesca off to Opal to see the cave—both had confided in him and of course as Rafe's best friend he had seen it—had been pivotal in their relationship. Of that Brod felt all but certain. There was a kind of shining innocence about Francesca, a definable purity that remained. But something fairly traumatic had happened.

Midafternoon when the men were relaxing over billy tea and fresh damper, hot from the coals, Brod drew Grant aside.

"Why don't we go down there?" He indicated a fallen log like a giant bonsai on the sandy shore of the creek, with its spreading green signifying the return of the good seasons.

Grant followed him gratefully. Rarely tired, he found himself curiously drained. "All right with you if Jock McFadden finishes tomorrow?" he asked, as soon as they were settled, a fragrant mug of tea in hand, a couple of the cattle dogs, Bluey and Rusty, curled at their feet.

"No problem at all." Brod pushed his akubra back on his head, turning to look at his friend. "Is everything okay?"

Grant smiled wryly. "Now why do you sound like Rafe?"

"Do I?" Brod's grin displayed his beautiful white teeth. "Well, Rafe's away."

"So you're his deputy. Anyway I meant to tell you—" Grant swallowed a mouthful "—had a phone call from them last night. Early hours of the morning actually."

"Both well?" Brod watched him expectantly.

"On top of the world. They're on the West Coast now. Los Angeles. And guess who they met up with in the street?" His hazel eyes sparkled with amusement and pleasure.

"Any clues?"

"One." Grant nodded. "When we were kids he was considered an even bigger rebel than me."

Brod laughed. "In that case it would have to be your cousin, Rory."

"Got it in one." Grant took another deep gulp, realising he was parched. "Rory Cameron."

"Would have been at Rafe's wedding only he was taking a little hike up Everest wasn't he?" Brod asked.

Grant nodded. "What words can you use to describe that? He's fearless, Rory. I'd love to do it myself. He went up with a

New Zealand party. Rory's a real adventurer. There's nowhere he hasn't been from the Himalayas to the Amazonian jungle. His dad thinks he'll never settle down."

Sammy Lee, part aboriginal part Chinese camp cook arrived with slices of damper and jam, which both took.

"It's a good thing then Rory has an elder brother to take over the running of Rivoli," Brod remarked dryly after Sammy had gone. Rivoli was one of the Northern Territory's biggest cattle stations owned and run by Grant's uncle, stepbrother to his late father.

"Josh is a great guy," Grant agreed, "but he hasn't got Rory's enormous *zest*. There's a guy who's brimming over with life. Anyway would you believe it, he's coming home?"

"Lord, he's been away years. He's going to find it tame, settling in the one place, if that's what he intends to do."

"Don't spread it around but I aim to talk him into joining me," Grant told Brod confidentially. "I got to thinking about it last night after the call. Rory's a great pilot. Every last Cameron has a head for business. I could use a man like Rory."

Brod shook his head doubtfully. "No way he'd come into anything without being a full partner."

"You're not wrong! But no harm in discussing it. Rory's my cousin, a Cameron. I know for a fact he got all old Digby Cameron's money. That makes him a rich man. Anyway we'll see. Needless to say Rafe and Ally send you and Rebecca their love. I spoke to Rafe too about Francesca's idea of doing those outback location shots on Opal."

Brod finished off his mug of tea and signalled for another. "What did he say?"

"He doesn't mind. In fact he supports it if I negotiate a good deal and the money goes to the Bush Rescue trust."

Brod nodded his approval. "Rafe's doing a wonderful job with that. Now that Dad's gone Kimbara will enter the scheme. Rafe and I discussed it. Even if we save one kid and put them on the right path it's worth it."

"Well it's working." Grant paused to thank Sammy who was back pouring fresh tea.

"So what are you going to do tomorrow?" Brod returned to his main concern. "Take some time off. It seems to me you've hit a cracking pace."

"I won't have Francesca over to visit if that's what you mean." Grant shot him a sidelong glance.

"What's the problem?" Brod was equally direct. "Aren't you two in love?"

"God, love! What *is* love?" Grant muttered in a kind of anguish.

"I'd say what *you feel*," Brod responded. "You're not just in love with my cousin. You love her. You're tormenting yourself with what you consider is appropriate."

"It shows?" asked Grant, not smiling.

"Hell, Grant, I've known you all your life. I know how a man feels, when he's faced with a big emotional decision. I know you're a man of integrity. I know I can trust you with Francesca. I know you would never consciously hurt her."

Grant gestured wearily. "I'm wrong for her, Brod."

"Why?" Brod damned nearly shouted. "The consensus of opinion is you're an exceptional young man. You have real standing in the outback community. That's not all that easy to earn."

"Down here. Down here, I'm worried." Grant struck his chest. "If she were any other girl! I want her as much as it's possible to want a woman, but she's like some enchanting creature from another planet. Even her colouring scares me."

Brod shook his head, halfway between disbelief and understanding. "Grant, get a balance here. Your own father had red hair. Your mother was very blonde. Look at you and Rafe. Don't all the girls call you the golden boys?"

Grant studied the glint of hair on his forearms. "We've had generations to acclimatise. We've grown hardy. We're *natives*. Francesca is like some rare exotic no one in their right mind would plant here. She can't survive. The big heat is ahead. You know as well as I do, Brod, the mercury can hit forty-eight degrees!"

Brod looked up at the cloudless, peacock-blue sky. "We don't expect our womenfolk to go out in the midday sun, whatever Noel Coward had to say. Times have changed greatly. We have so much now, so many aids we've never had before. It's been a technological revolution."

"Maybe. But the fact remains no one is going to be able to change the desert environment."

"Between the two of us," Brod said wryly, "I don't want to change it. I love my home like no other place on earth."

Grant responded with a sudden spurt of passion. "Don't get me wrong. I love it, too. We've learned to love it. We thrive on it. But Francesca is a very special person. I'm determined to protect her."

"Hell, Grant, if you keep this up you'll drive her away," Brod warned. "You'll lose her. Are you prepared to risk that?"

Grant's handsome, determined features tautened. "I'd rather lose her now than lose her later on. That would kill me. What if we were married and she decided one day she longed for everything she had lost? Everything she had ever known and understood? She's no *ordinary* girl."

"An ordinary girl wouldn't suit you, Grant. Have you thought of that?" Brod suggested dryly.

Grant shook his head. "I don't know any other girl of her particular background. Surely it couldn't be more different from ours?"

"So you don't think she's adult enough to make up her own mind?" Irony crackled in Brod's tone.

"You realise any son she may have could be her father's heir?"

Brod gave a faint smile. "So what? As far as I know, Francesca's father is having the devil of a job trying to keep Ormond intact. The upkeep must be crippling. Especially without Fee's money. Fee was the heiress. For that matter, still is."

"You don't see anything tremendously threatening about our relationship?" Grant asked, realising this conversation was going some way to easing his mind.

Brod took his time replying. Then he spoke very seriously, from the depths of his soul. "I think when you find someone you truly love you never let them go."

In amongst all his thinking, and he had lots on his mind—an upcoming meeting with Drew Forsythe of Trans Continental Resources for one—he kept drawing mental plans of his dream homestead. Of course he'd need an architect to walk the site, gauge just the right spot for the house to go. There were vast, sweeping views from everywhere nevertheless siting the homestead properly would present a challenge. Without fully realising it his mind was extraordinarily visual so his intermittent daydreams really came alive. He wanted the house set on low pylons like Opal but there the similarity ended, except for the mandatory wide verandahs to shelter the core of the house from the heat and sun at the same time as providing deep shade and cooling breezes.

He wanted his homestead radically different. He wanted a completely contemporary structure using a mix of materials: stone, glass—lots of glass, floor to ceiling—steel to support the long spans of verandah, the polished timbers he loved, local stone with all its wonderful ochres, especially for the fireplaces. The really hard thing would be to come up with a design worthy of the great wilderness bounded as it was by the great rolling parallel waves of the desert, unobstructed views over the plains to the horizon with the legendary Myora for a background. How many people had an awe-inspiring prehistoric monolithic rock in their backyard. A backyard that ran on forever.

He had visited the island of Bali many times, loved it, and found Balinese influences creeping into his thinking, though the lush jungle settings could scarcely be more different from Opal. But the harmonious feeling of timbers, open spaces, high tentlike ceilings, open pavilions was the same. Like Bali, too, nights in the Dry could be surprisingly cold as the desert sands lost their heat. He would need those couple of huge, inviting fireplaces. In every room he saw Francesca, however much he tried to picture some other woman.

Lord knows he knew enough attractive girls. They swarmed to the polo meets. There was a time he felt quite happy with Jennie Irvine. Her father, Tom Irvine, the well-known pastoralist, had been a good friend to his own father. Jennie was good-looking, well educated, easygoing, fun to be with. He knew he could get Jennie to marry him. He knew her parents would be really happy about it but someone called Francesca de Lyle had put paid to that. By Brod's wedding he had really known Francesca had stolen his heart.

She was like some irresistible fragrance. All those silly ads he had seen about perfume and the way they enticed a man weren't so silly after all. Francesca was a rose, to him the most beautiful, the most fragrant of all flowers.

Even his dreams were set at this homestead that had yet to be built. Vividly he saw Francesca at the breakfast table, having a cup of coffee with him. Francesca in the glowing panelled dining room playing hostess to family and friends. Francesca in the study reading over his shoulder as he drafted an important letter, welcoming her input because he valued her opinion and good business sense. Most of all he saw her in the bedroom, lying on top of their huge bed, a modern four-poster hung with curtains of white netting against any little insects that might fly through all the open doorways. For some reason he never saw his Francesca naked. She was always wearing the prettiest, beribboned, most feminine nightgown, a swirl of peach silk, he would lovingly peel off.

What a fool! At this point he always woke himself up. Falling in love with Francesca was bliss and despair. Her destiny like his was already written. Dreams had little to do with real life. That was the unpalatable fact. The reality of the situation was, he was acting out a fantasy and heading for disaster. Love had to be matched by other factors that would make a marriage survive.

Francesca was a beautiful, bright superior creature, carefully guarded by her father and clearly destined for a privileged life similar to the one she had led. How could he hold such a woman in isolation? The polar caps could melt before he tired of her but what if she found his way of life far too lonely and distant from all she had known? Despite his conversation with Brod he still was deeply affected by practical constraints as a man who was making a decision that would affect his whole life had to be.

He didn't need to be a mind-reader, either, to guess Francesca's father would be utterly and completely against such a marriage and why not? It would take his only beloved child away from him. Halfway across the world. As far away as she could go. Shatter his plans. Fee had all but admitted that. So problems continued to beset his euphoria. Women seemed conditioned by nature to take great leaps into the unknown. For a man it was different. A man's duty was to keep his feet on the ground.

The film people arrived at the weekend, staying over at Kimbara, which with its many guest rooms at the ready was far better suited to accommodating guests than Opal; Ngaire Bell, the New Zealand born director, who was making quite a name for herself internationally, accompanied by long-time associate and script writer, Glenn Richards. Grant was kept busy all day Saturday working out schedules for incoming jobs, double-checking maintenance, arranging freight pickups, a workload that kept him on Opal but sunset found him landing on Kimbara preparatory to meeting Brod and Rebecca's guests at dinner.

Francesca was there to greet him, dressed in jeans and a yellow T-shirt, her hair burning like flame in the incandescent light.

"Hi, this is nice!" He bent to kiss her cheek, thinking "nice" was a ridiculous word. He was just plain thrilled to see her. She made his heart run hot.

"It's lovely to see you, too," she responded. "It's been a very long week."

"Lots to do." He spoke casually, throwing his hold-all in the back seat of the Jeep, not mentioning he had found the time away from her a near eternity. "So what are the guests like?" he asked as they got under way, Francesca at the wheel, small hands but capable and confident.

"I know you're going to like them." Francesca turned her head half-laughing now with pleasure. "Ngaire is a very interesting woman. She and Fee are getting along famously. Glenn is good company, too. Rebecca and he have a lot in common."

"And what about you?"

"I'm happy. I'm really happy," she said, eyes alight. "We're all getting along well but of course the others have special interests in common."

"How old, I wonder?" He spoke lightly, companionably when all he wanted to do was wrap her in his arms.

"Ngaire, late thirties, early forties. Naturally I didn't ask. Glenn would be around thirty-five."

"Married?" He wanted this guy married. He refused to confront why.

"Neither of them are married," Francesca said. "They're great friends and colleagues but I wouldn't think they were romantically involved. Of course I could be wrong. You didn't want to kiss me?"

Because if I did I wouldn't stop. "Kissed your cheek, didn't I?" he said.

"So you did. It was nice, too. How glorious the sunsets are out here," she said, examining the sky.

"Like your hair." He successfully resisted touching it. "If you want to see a sight, cut off the track now and head north-

west for about a mile. The black swans should be heading in
for their roosting sites at dusk."

"So where are we going?" Where the heck *is* north-east, she
thought. She'd have to ask him to show her.

"Here, let me."

They stopped to swop positions, Grant driving, Francesca
in the passenger seat of the open Jeep. "Kingurra. You must
know it," Grant said a few moments later, the Jeep exploding
into action.

"Lake Kingurra?" She cast a glance at his golden profile.
Like Rafe he had a cleft chin, the cleft not so deep but vertical.

"The very one," he teased. "Kingurra means black swan.
Didn't you know that?"

She shook her head. "The straight answer is no. There's so
much *to* know. It would take a lifetime. Even learning all the
aboriginal names."

"They're the ones I like best. Our aboriginal brothers have
been custodians of this country for over sixty thousand years.
Kingurra is a very old lake, a real oasis of wildlife."

"Of course I've seen it," Francesca said. "It's astonishingly
beautiful especially with the area all around it so arid."

"Listen *now*." Grant leant towards her, his expression full of
the pleasure of sharing.

They heard the birds before they saw them, the sound carried on the sweet evening breeze. The dark shadows became
hundreds of black swans skeining across the darkening mauve
sky still banded with the brilliant rose, gold and scarlet of the
desert sunset.

"What a sight!" Francesca lifted her head, staring, fascinated
by the pure white underwings of the ebony birds, the little band
of turquoise, the red beaks. The *S* bends of their beautiful necks
were fully outstretched, straight as arrows.

"We've got time to take a walk down to the water," Grant
said, picking up speed and heading away from the mulga scrub
to the lake.

A little bit of excitement went a long way. "It might sound extraordinary but I'm rarely away from the homestead at this hour," Francesca explained, her cheeks pink. "If I go riding or driving around the property Brod likes me home before dusk."

Grant shot her a shimmering glance. "So would I if you were on your own. Night falls as dramatically as a black curtain. But this is worth seeing and I'm with you."

He held her hand all the while they descended the sandy track crisscrossed with the prints of kangaroos and smaller creatures. Quietly, quietly, they kept to the cover of the trees so as not disturb the birds.

There were hundreds of them! Squadrons splashing down on the silver lake, while others circled just like aircraft waiting for landing. Two hundred or more stately pelicans had congregated at the far end of the lake, keeping their distance from the common ducks, the cormorants, egrets, banded stilts and so many species Francesca couldn't possibly identify them. As the swans landed, they sealed off their white underwings, bending their long necks into the beautiful curves of legends. They remained, united by their great pleasure in the scene, familiar to Grant all his life, though he never tired of it, a rare enchantment for Francesca.

The outback *was* birds. She adored watching the great flights of budgerigar, the parrots and galahs, the flocks of white corellas that literally covered the trees, but she had never seen so many water birds congregated in the one place. It was like some wonderful harbour, the waters that swirled with birds gradually blanketed in feathers.

"This is wonderful!" she whispered.

"I agree." His head was bent over hers, his breath warm against her ear.

"Thank you for bringing me here."

"I'm amazed you've missed it on your visits."

Not so many, she thought with regret. She'd first come to Kimbara at the age of ten. Her father didn't want her to come.

He told her Australia was a far country. *Strange*. He told her her mother's people lived in the desert. Were barely civilised. Yet her mother was the most beautiful most glamorous creature she had ever seen.

When she arrived on Kimbara it was like coming home. She wasn't drawn to it. It didn't take time. She loved it at once. It was almost like her spirit had been unleashed. She was a very lonely little girl. Although her father tried to do everything he could, when she wasn't away at boarding school, she was left to her own devices a great deal.

"Coming to Australia was the greatest adventure of my life," she murmured aloud. "Still is for that matter."

"What about the heat, little Titian head?" he gently mocked.

"The heat could never exhaust my excitement. Not now. Not then. It's *dry* heat, isn't it? Not steamy, enervating heat."

It was true she always looked as cool as a lily. "Well, I'm glad you enjoyed your visit," he said lightly, "but we'd better go." Before I give in to the desire to kiss you until you're panting and incoherent.

They crouched low beneath some overhanging branches, finding their way back up the slope, Francesca forging ahead with a buoyant step. They almost arrived at the top when suddenly Grant grasped her firmly from behind, locking an arm around her waist, stopping her short.

"What is it?" Now he lifted her clean off the ground, holding her with one arm as though she were still a ten-year-old.

He didn't answer for a moment, then he set her down again with a nonchalant, "Nothing!"

She had to lean back against him momentarily unsteady. "You gave me such a fright."

"Better that than let you tread on a snake," he drawled. "There it goes. Off by the rocks."

"Lord!" Her expression sharpened with dread, as she strained back against him.

"Harmless, that one," Grant told her. "It was only trying to

get across the track. Snakes flee man in general. It doesn't do
to step on one all the same."

She gave a little shudder, turning within the circle of his arm,
banging him on his chest in an instinctive response to fright.
"I suppose you think I'm silly?"

He slipped his hand around her wrist and felt the delicate
bones. "No, I think you're enormously brave." He gazed down
into her eyes, eyes that seemed to see further into him than
anyone else. "I'm sorry I scared you."

"I'm not scared," she breathed. And now she wasn't. "I'm
here with you."

Inside he fought a violent struggle but he lost it. He lowered
his head blindly, ravenously, taking her sweet gorgeous mouth,
devouring it deeply, hungrily, luscious as a peach.

My God, I love her! he thought, abandoning himself to the
ecstasy. Why the hell didn't he just hang on to that instead of
making a terror out of all their difference.

"At least we've got one thing in common," he muttered, when
he found the strength to lift his head.

"Lots!" She could only manage one word, her heart hammering, her breath drowned in her throat.

After a minute she was able to open her eyes. "We've got
lots of things in common," she protested with soft vehemence.
"Don't push me away, Grant," she warned, and he had never
seen her more serious. "I've been pushed away all my life."

The next moment she turned, straightened the T-shirt his
caressing hands had somehow pulled askew, and ran from him
leaving him utterly sobered, staring after her.

Pushed away all her life! How was that possible? From all
accounts her father adored her. He had big plans for her. Fee
was Fee. Not the most maternal of women but it couldn't be
plainer she loved her beautiful daughter. It struck him like an
actual blow Francesca could ever feel rejected. Francesca was
a miracle. She touched his mind, his body, his heart with her
exquisite grace.

* * *

They all came together in the very grand drawing room for a predinner drink, Brod introducing Grant to his guests.

"My God!" Ngaire Bell thought as they shook hands. These cattle kings are something else! A distinct breed. To begin with they had such an aura of masculinity they really made a woman *feel* like a woman. Moreover they made direct eye contact with far-seeing, delightfully sun-crinkled eyes. Broderick Kinross was an extraordinarily handsome man. She truly hadn't expected anyone else to match him yet here was this fabulous-looking man with the rarest of colourings.

On their looks alone she could make stars of them, she thought wryly, only it couldn't have been more obvious they exactly matched their setting. They were outback men yet they lived in great style.

Kimbara homestead was splendid, meticulously maintained, but too grandly furnished for the homestead of her new movie. It had been suggested to her by Fee Kinross's beautiful daughter, Francesca, the homestead at Opal Downs would fit readily the description of the sprawling, elegant old homestead of the novel, its Victorian furnishings still largely in place, the atmosphere retained. She was dying to see it. Couldn't wait. This wasn't the first historic mansion she had been invited to but this was the furthest into the continent's Wild Heart. It fired her already fertile imagination.

Glenn Richards, drink in hand, was thinking much the same thing as his friend and colleague. These Kinross-Camerons were an extraordinarily good-looking bunch. He had to put it down to the desert air. Even Fiona Kinross, who had to be in her sixties, looked marvellous. In the flattering light no more than forty-five. Of course she could have had cosmetic surgery, but he didn't think so. Nevertheless her skin was unlined, her jawline firm, her figure in a neat jade knee-length dress, excellent. She cut a glamorous figure as did they all, including Fiona's brand-new fiancé, David Westbury, tall, distinguished, pewter haired, very upper class English. As far as Glenn could make out, Westbury was a relative of sorts, and he was a touch overawed, trying to click in all his various impressions.

But the one who really took his eye and had from the very first moment, was the Lady Francesca. As far as he was concerned she was quite lovely. He adored her soft, dreamy looks, the uncontrived sensuality that made a man drool. And that colouring. He couldn't think of a more heavenly combination than red-gold hair and sky-blue eyes. Not a freckle in sight. Not even a gold dusting across her nose.

It struck him she would be perfect in the movie as the hero's tragic first wife. What made it even better was she had the authentic English accent. Maybe a bit too cut glass but that could be modified slightly. It was only a small part. They had more or less settled on Paige Macauly but he was certain if the girl could act at all she would be perfect in the role. And why wouldn't she be able to act with Fiona Kinross for a mother, let alone her cousin, Ally, who proved she didn't have what it took to make the big time by going off and getting married. What a waste!

Still, their leading lady Caro Halliday, wife number two in the film, who didn't feature in the early outback scenes, was beautiful, talented and almost as charismatic. As they went into dinner, Glenn began to turn over ideas in his mind. He'd put a lot of hard work into the screenplay. A lot of his own money went into the backing. It was crucial the film do well not only as an "art" film but as entertainment for the masses. The English rose, Francesca was enormously appealing, beautiful but nonthreatening. She had as much appeal as her far more exotic mother.

Grant, as sensitive to Francesca as it was possible to be, honed in immediately on Richards's interest in her. It was all managed with charm and a certain suavity but Richards couldn't keep his eyes off her. Not that Grant could blame him no matter how it made him inwardly bristle. Francesca looked ethereal in a delicate lace dress, the soft apricot of his dreams. She had left her hair out, too, in the way he loved it, long and flowing.

It wasn't the first time he had seen Francesca capture a whole lot of male attention but it was the first time another man had provoked his male aggression. Francesca was *his*. Immediately, as he thought it, he was forced to confront his own contradictions. He had no rights where Francesca was concerned. She was a free agent. As was he and apparently Glenn Richards. But no question about it, Richards's eyes on Francesca had set him off. Richards wasn't even being terribly discreet, his dark eyes savouring Francesca's appearance and the quality of her conversation. Which seemed reasonable enough given Francesca showed her intelligence and breeding, but he was starting to fill Grant with an odd hostility he tried to fight down.

Richards was an attractive man—dark curly hair, deep brown eyes, quirky eyebrows, an easy, friendly smile, midheight, well dressed, well-travelled, clever and articulate. Nothing there to dislike except he was taking far too much interest in Francesca. Grant felt a need to sort out his emotions before they got out of hand. He knew he had an aggressive streak. He knew he had to keep it under control.

They were seated in the formal dining room with its fine paintings and furnishings. Ngaire started out by commenting on the exquisite floral arrangement at the centre of the table, and reached to stroke a petal. Rebecca smiled her pleasure. "Francesca must take the credit. We spent some time over the arrangements, experimenting with containers and the various shapes for the flowers."

"Yes, I noticed," Ngaire said as indeed she had. "The arrangement in the main hall is quite dramatic."

"I'm afraid we robbed the Golden Shower tree." Francesca smiled. "A few palms, gold ribbon. A wonderful big Chinese vase. We had a lot of fun."

"Ikebana isn't it?" Ngaire asked, thinking how beautiful and stylish all the arrangements through the house were.

"I actually took a course with a master teacher a few years

back," Rebecca said. "I must say Fran is an apt pupil. The centrepiece is inspirational."

"I agree." Brod looked like he thought his wife and cousin could do anything they turned their hand to.

"A mangrove root, dracena and a couple of sprays of white butterfly orchids, plus some red wire for a bit of dash," Francesca said, identifying the materials she had used. "It means something, too. I quote from I don't know where. Probably anonymous. 'Happiness is like a butterfly. The more you chase it the more it will elude you, but if you turn your attention to other things, it will come and softly sit on your shoulder.'" Somehow it seemed appropriate. Her gaze met Grant's enigmatically across the table. "Of course, too, it's a symbol of welcome."

"Yes, indeed. Welcome to Kimbara, Ngaire and Glenn." Brod raised his wineglass and the others followed suit. "Tomorrow you'll see Opal, my sister Ally's new home. It has its own wonderful appeal as you're due to find out. In our childhood Opal was Ally's and my second home."

"In fact we were all so close we were family." Grant gave a truly illuminating smile. "Now we are family. The Camerons and the Kinrosses united at last."

"There's such a fascination about your stories," Ngaire said. "Two great pioneering dynasties. I can't wait to read your biography, Fee."

"Don't worry, darling," Fee said in her deep sexy voice. "You and Glenn are invited to our preview party. It was a brainwave on Fran's part thinking of Opal for the colonial outback scenes. I was re-reading *The Immigrant* last night. The station is close to perfect for Bruce Templeton's book."

Grant nodded. "I've read the novel as well and thoroughly enjoyed it. With a few minor changes the homestead will serve you well. You're lucky Ally hadn't got started on all her refurbishing. My mother intended to make them but never got the chance."

"I'm so sorry, Grant," Ngaire murmured, aware his parents

had been tragically killed in an air crash. "I can't wait to visit tomorrow," she added gently.

The meal Rebecca and Francesca had worked on for a couple of days before the guests arrived, progressed splendidly with help in the kitchen: crab cream for starters, with crisp fried vermicelli followed by tournedos of Kimbarra beef with roast parsnips and potatoes, fresh green beans and two sauces, madeira and béarnaise. The conversation flowed over a wide range of subjects: the movie, Fee's role in it, Fee's and David's impending nuptials, Grant's vision for Cameron Airways, outback life, Rafe and Ally's overseas honeymoon, domestic politics, world politics, a smattering of gossip, books that had not made an easy transition into movies.

Everyone took part, full of animated interest as the wineglasses quickly emptied. Francesca, as usual, limited herself to two. She noticed Rebecca did the same, but Fee sipped her wine quickly, glass after glass, showing no effects except her beautiful, slender hands moved even more expressively and her green eyes glittered with great good humour. This was an area where Fee shone, and David looked on, his heart swelling with pride. After the last few sad years Fee was a positive joy to him.

There was a choice for dessert—chocolate sorbet and orange ice-cream or an Old English apple pie, richly flavoured with dark brown sugar, nutmeg, cinnamon, orange and lemon zest, raisins and sultanas, served with double cream. This was David's contribution to the meal from a family recipe he had enjoyed from childhood. He knew all the ingredients, even if he didn't know exact quantities. He even stood beside Francesca in the kitchen while she made it saying he always liked his with cheddar cheese.

Mellowed by such a wonderful meal, Glenn took the opportunity to say what he'd been thinking for the past two hours.

"It was a wonderful coup securing you for a pivotal role, Fiona—" he deferred to her "—you'll bring great presence and credibility to the role, but I can't help thinking your beautiful daughter, Francesca, would make a marvellous Lucinda."

"Hey, that's amazing!" Ngaire burst out, but Fee stared at Glenn in astonishment, her spoon frozen in midair.

"Fran doesn't *act,* Glenn," she said as though it were completely out of character. "She's had no training whatsoever. Ally is the only other actress in the family."

"And she's marvellous, too," Glenn said, still getting over his disappointment Ally Kinross had rejected the lead.

But Ngaire waved a hand. "Training is important, of course, Fee, but I know for a fact some people are naturals. The fourteen-year-old I had in my last movie was sensational. Straight from school though she was learning drama and art of speech."

"But Fran has no interest in acting, have you, darling?" Fee looked down the table, clearly unable to picture her daughter as an actress. "She's much happier with her drawing and her music. She's very good at both. Francesca is the product of a very good school."

Grant turned his iridescent eyes on Francesca. "I didn't know that," he said, sounding like he wished he had.

"Now that we've settled down I'll get a good piano sent out here," Brod said briskly.

"Make it a Steinway." Francesca smiled at him.

"Then a Steinway it is." Brod was quite serious. "I know you *draw* extremely well."

"What about acting?" Glenn persisted, fingering his wineglass. The sauterne was wonderful. "Surely they put on plays at your very good school?"

Francesca nodded her head. "Of course they did. Mamma's going to be amazed but I was very much in demand. A lot of Shakespeare. I was a fabulous Juliet," she joked, "to my friend, Dinah Phillip's Romeo. Pity you didn't see us."

"*Why* didn't I see you?" Fee demanded.

"Ah, Mamma," Francesca murmured, rolling her eyes.

"You mean I wasn't around?" Fee gazed off into the middle distance remembering how it was.

"You were lighting up the London stage," Francesca reminded her.

"Now I think about it you *could* play Lucinda." Grant's voice had gathered conviction.

"I agree," Ngaire murmured.

"You really think Francesca could handle it?" Fee stared at Ngaire as though she had gone mad.

"I'd love to," Francesca said

"You could handle it, I know you could." Grant looked across the table at Francesca thinking Fee was the last straw. "It would be good for you. A bit of fun, widen your horizons."

"Surely, darling, you wouldn't entertain the idea of acting as a career?" Grant might as well have suggested prostitution.

"No, Mamma, I wouldn't." Francesca shook her head, her manner gentle but firm. "It's more as Grant says. A bit part. A bit of fun."

"A challenge." Grant smiled, always one for a challenge, good, too, at encouraging others. "You're full of surprises, Francesca. Full of refinements. I'd *love* to hear you play the piano." No wonder he always heard music flow around her.

"So you shall," Brod promised. "There was a grand piano here in my mother's day. She played beautifully, but my father got rid of it. He wouldn't let Ally learn, either," he added a trifle bleakly, "though she wanted to."

"I expect it was too painful," Ngaire murmured, not knowing the full story.

"But surely you have that NADA graduate, what's her name, Paige something?" Fee carried on with her objections.

"Paige Macauly," Glenn supplied. "Yes, Paige was well in the running but we've made no final decision, have we, Ngaire."

"I thought we had, dear," Ngaire said wryly. "But I quite share your vision of Francesca as Lucinda. One can see her in the part."

"I get killed off early," Francesca said. "I could do a good job of pining away. Isn't that what I'm supposed to do. Pine away in a strange new country?"

Glenn smiled. "Of course your character was never very strong. Physically you suggest fragility, sensitivity."

Francesca didn't see herself as quite the marshmallow. "Ballerinas are very fragile looking," she pointed out, "but they're very strong. I'll have you know I play an excellent game of tennis. There was a time I was good at archery. I'm a very good rider, aren't I, Brod?" She appealed to her cousin who was always on her side.

"A lovely seat on a horse. Sweet hands," Brod agreed. "A woman's looks can belie her strengths."

"So what about reading for the part?" Glenn pressed on as keen to get to know Francesca better as to have her in a role that would keep her in daily contact.

"I must say, Glenn, I think you're going too fast," Fee protested. "Francesca's father wouldn't be at all happy about another actress in the family. One was more than enough."

"It's only a bit part, Mamma," Francesca said reassuringly.

"Yes, but you might get the bug."

It was hard to say what was really bothering Fee, David thought. Fear Francesca could cause herself some embarrassment? He couldn't see *how*. Or fear of de Lyle's wrath. As far as he was concerned his cousin was of an age she could do as she pleased. Probably very well.

It was difficult for Grant to get Francesca alone until well after eleven when Brod excused himself from the conversation saying he had a dawn start. Station work went on seven days a week and though the staff had a roster Brod did not. Rebecca, too, excused herself with a charming smile leaving Fee to carry on with the conversation, which reverted to an in-depth discussion of the film, characterisation and so forth.

It was time to grab Francesca and run, Grant thought, aware

of Richards's acute disappointment when she left the charmed circle, though Fee talked on, her chain of thought unbroken.

"I think you've won yourself a heart," Grant commented dryly as they walked down the front steps to take a short stroll.

Francesca ignored that, picking up on what really concerned her. "Mamma didn't sound too pleased with Glenn's suggestion," she said, her own pleasure eroded by her mother's reaction.

"I think you're going to be brilliant," Grant said, mutually upset by Fee. "You're vibrantly artistic. I don't like to say it but Fee seems to be devoid of sensitivity sometimes."

"She isn't always tactful," Francesca was forced to agree. "Maybe she thinks I'm going to make a goose of myself. Or worse a goose of her."

He drew her to him, one arm lightly around her waist. "You want to do it, don't you?"

Francesca felt a lot easier in his company. "Yes, but not if Mamma would rather I didn't."

"You're a big girl now, Francesca," he pointed out, his voice oddly tender.

"I've never been much good at upsetting people."

"Don't feel guilty about Fee," he warned.

"So what do you think I should do?" she spoke softly, but sounding pained.

"I've told you. Go for it. You'll enjoy it." His arm tightened in a hug.

"And what if I get bitten by the bug as Mamma seems to think?" She knew she wouldn't. Her priorities had been long since fixed.

"If you get hooked, you get hooked," Grant answered lightly, thinking it unlikely. "It's your life. Just don't move away too far. I'd miss you too much."

"So you don't care if I turned into another Fee?" she stopped dead, rounding on him, heart high.

"You won't, Francesca." He couldn't resist it. He bent his

head and briefly brushed her velvet mouth. Fast and light, still consumed by the pleasure of it. "Remember all the heart-to-heart talks we used to have when we were kids. You want home and family. A man who loves you. A man who is fully committed to you to share your life. And what was it? Four children. That's a full-time job," he added with a sympathetic laugh.

"That's what comes of being an only child," she said as he steered her onwards. "My growing up was painful. I'm not going to let that happen to my children."

"But you still need your mother's encouragement and approval?"

"That's normal isn't it? It's what we all hope for. Parental approval?"

He nodded gravely. "Our parents were one hundred percent behind Rafe and me. Brod and Ally endured a kind of hell. I didn't fully appreciate how deeply your parents' separation affected you until recently. While we're on the subject, what about your father? Would he object so strenuously to your becoming an actress if it ever turned out that was what you wanted?"

"Wow!" Francesca's exclamation said it all. "Actually he'd be *shocked*. Depend on it."

"Because he has big plans for you?" Definitely. It was an inexorable fact.

"They won't work, Grant, if they're the opposite to mine," Francesca murmured, in the fierce grip of sexual longing. "I don't want to disappoint either of my parents but as you've just pointed out my life is my own. That's what makes your pushing me away so peculiar."

"For pity's sake, Francesca. That's not what I meant at all." He stared down at her, her beautiful skin silvered by the moonlight.

"But you won't allow I know my own mind?" Her response was swift.

"What *is* your mind, Francesca?" He made a little grimace, taking her firmly by the shoulders and turning her to him.

"Are we allowed to use the word love here?" A flush of colour had appeared on her cheeks. Even by moonlight he was able to see it. "You hold so much back."

He was haunted by the truth. "There's no way ever, Francesca, I'd hurt you. I'm in love with you," he admitted freely. "You know that. You're in my mind all the time, let alone my dreams." How intoxicatingly erotic he didn't tell her.

"You care a lot but you won't take me seriously." She couldn't control the wave of resentment that welled up.

"That's ridiculous and you know it."

Her chin came up. "Then maybe there's some part of you you don't want me to share. A man like you would worry about loss of liberty, loss of freedom."

He was shocked she thought that. "So what do you want me to do? *Marry* you?" he demanded of the embodiment of his dreams.

"I'm sorry, sorry." Suddenly Francesca broke away feeling utterly humiliated. Where was her pride? Did she really have to force his hand?

"Francesca." He came after her, wrapping his arms around her. "It's never been like this for me with *anyone*. I want you desperately. So desperately I can't really understand myself. That day in the cave, I wanted to take you then. I was a hair's-breadth away from messing up your life. My life. It's not as easy as you're saying. You can't know what's involved."

"And you won't let me learn?" The strong passion in him communicated itself to her.

"I'm trying to think what's best for both of us. God, do you think I'm so utterly selfish I'd trap you in a cage?"

She broke away again, moving like a shadow into the swaying sheltering trees. "I don't want to hear it."

"You've got to hear what I'm saying." He found her easily in the velvet dark, following her fragrance. "I take the idea of marriage as a very serious business. I'm like the black swans. I'm going to mate for life. If you'd had my own kind of background I wouldn't hesitate for a minute but you were reared to the high life. Do you really think I'd ever let you run off? Do you think I'd ever let you get away from me with another man?

Tears sprang to her eyes at his forcefulness. Didn't he know she loved him? "I don't know what you're talking about," she said, her agitation apparent.

"But it happens, Francesca," he groaned, trying to get a handle on an emotional situation that was gaining swiftly in intensity. "It happens all the time. Not every woman can stand the isolation, the lack of entertainment, theatre, ballet, concerts, art showings, all the things you've been used to, being on your own when your man's away. I have to point out these things. I'd be painting a false picture if I didn't."

Even as he spoke, trying to warn her, prepare her, he didn't know which, shards of desire were piercing him through, sharper and sharper as she stood quietly under his hands, her long hair rippling over them like skeins of silk. He was desperately afraid of his own driving male hunger so fierce it could frighten her. "Hell I'd take the all-for-love gamble if you could pay the price. If I married you I'd never let you go," he exploded. "Can't you understand all this loving, this passion is dangerous?"

His hands were sending electric currents through her. She loved his hands, the shape of them. Hands were important to her.

Francesca bowed her head in acknowledgment, knowing her feeling for him had not only coloured her world, but turned it on its head. There was a Before Grant and After Grant. What else was Fate for? Nevertheless she turned away saying poignantly. "I won't bother you again."

"Francesca!" he moaned aloud his frustration, torn between stifling her mouth with kisses and letting his ardour cool. Love. This kind of love was like jumping off a cliff.

"It's depressing coming down to earth with a crash." She made a gallant attempt at humour, almost reading his mind. "You're quite right, Grant. We don't have enough in common."

Nothing would work without a solid base of trust and hope.

CHAPTER FIVE

THE WEEK THE film people moved into Opal, Grant had to fly to Brisbane for a meeting with Drew Forsythe, set up some time back. A meeting that went so well, it spun out to intensive discussion over a period of three days as Forsythe found time out of his hectic schedule. Both men clicked, sons of dynasties, full of vision, energy and ambition with the brain power to make it all work. So it was working out deals by day, getting the go-ahead from his own financial advisers and at night Drew and his beautiful wife, Eve, made it their business to see Grant enjoyed himself.

They organised a dinner party one evening, and tickets to "Pavarotti and Friends" in concert, the next. They even rustled up a very attractive young woman called Annabel to make up the numbers, dark brown hair, big brown eyes, a head-turner in her own right, but Grant couldn't get Francesca out of his mind. Such was the depth of his feeling for her, she was a constant "presence." Before he'd left she had already been accepted for the role of Lucinda despite Fee's stated qualms. Ngaire Bell and Glenn Richards had swept Fee before them after hearing Francesca read.

"No shortage of talent in this family" was Ngaire's comment, breaking into a big smile. "With Francesca's looks and voice she would never be out of work. With no experience at all she understands the part thoroughly."

"Audiences will weep for her," Glenn Richards added, looking spellbound. Francesca got such "agony" out of his lines. It was very gratifying.

It struck Grant as ironic Francesca was playing a part that had some relevance to their own situation, however slight. The character in the book, Lucinda, a gently bred English girl migrates to Australia with her handsome, vital, adventurer husband, loving him so deeply she is prepared to give up everything, homeland, family, friends to share his life. Eventually the rigours of trying to survive, let alone cope in a harsh new land with no one outside her husband who thrives in his new environment, to turn to for comfort or advice, wears her down. Never strong, painfully aware of her husband's disappointment in her, his expectations so much more than she can give, her inability to conceive, Lucinda sinks into a depression that ends in tragedy.

"Don't come without a box of tissues," Ngaire warned, using one herself. She was enormously encouraged by Francesca's ability to win sympathy for her character without portraying her as in any way wimpish. Francesca delivered her lines movingly, and with great sincerity bettering the very talented Paige Macauly.

Even Fee had been impressed, in fact her little girl took her breath away. Perversely Fee was hurt. Francesca hadn't asked her to run through her lines with her, or even offer a few words of expert advice.

"Brought it all on your own head, Fifi," David told her. "Francesca wants to contribute. Let her."

Whilst he was in Brisbane, Grant decided to take the opportunity to speak to an architect about his proposed homestead. Drew recommended an excellent man and an appointment was set up by Drew's secretary. The homesteads of Opal Downs and Kimbara appeared in a number of editions of *Historic Home-*

steads of Australia and when Grant arrived at the architect's office he found the best coffee table edition lying open on the desk. They talked for quite a while about family influence and inheritance, the marriage between architecture and environment, while Grant revealed the sort of thing he wanted.

He expected the architect, Hugh Madison, a handsome clever-looking man in his late forties to pick up a pencil and tracing paper, instead he went to the computer and immediately began drawing up concepts. It was fascinating watching a wonderful kaleidoscope of graphics, but Grant still preferred drawings like the framed architectural drawings that hung on the walls of Opal. Drawings he had loved all his life. It was agreed Madison should visit the proposed site and a tentative date was set towards the end of the month. Madison would travel to the nearest outback domestic terminal and Grant would pick him up from there and ferry him back to Opal.

"I feel quite excited by the prospect," the architect told Grant as they parted. "It will be a joy! It's not often one gets the chance to design a major contemporary homestead. The powerful mystique of the outback will be inspirational. It will fully test what gift I have." As it would have to, Madison privately thought. This young man radiated purpose and energy. He was also very definite about what he wanted. He would be an exacting client but a very appreciative one if Madison could deliver his dream. Madison was confident on both scores.

Back at the Opal homestead, Francesca was finding filming wasn't as easy as she supposed. As a novice she had so much to learn, even how to turn her head but Ngaire, the guiding hand, was very patient with her, taking her steadily over her scenes. They didn't amount to many—Lucinda disappeared early—but they were essential to the story. They were shot to surprisingly few takes, sometimes four or five, never as many as Francesca feared might be necessary given her inexperience. But she made sure she came well-prepared—as well-prepared as Fee, who continued to show her amazement at this new side to her daughter.

Ngaire seemed delighted by both their work. She even listened to Francesca's input regarding her own character, a delicate young woman but still possessed of courage, struggling to survive in a world radically different from everything she had known. For all Ngaire's demonstrated brilliance, Francesca found she was remarkably kind and easy to get on with, never once giving way to temper when sometimes, as could be expected, things went quite wrong.

The lights were hot, cords trailed all over the floors. The make-up was just awful. It took such an age to put it on let alone get it off. Wearing the costumes in the sweltering heat. But Francesca found herself having a very good time. The trick was to forget Francesca de Lyle completely. She was Lucinda who loved her husband desperately, knowing each day she was losing him to forces outside her control. A young woman's dreams shattered. A young man's vision rewarded. Francesca was stunned to finish a particularly poignant scene only to see her mother and Ngaire bunched together with tears pouring down their cheeks.

"Oh my God, darling, you could make your mark!" Fee cried emotionally, neatly evading a whole lot of equipment to take Francesca in her arms. "You do have a lot of your mother in you after all."

Each night when they watched the day's scenes reeled off, Francesca couldn't believe it was herself she was seeing on the screen. It gave her an actual frisson seeing her own face as she had never seen it before. She couldn't help but know her looks were out of the ordinary but the young woman on the screen was lovely in a way she hadn't fully appreciated and she had a way of speaking with her eyes and her hands. It cheered Francesca enormously to know she was acquitting herself rather well. It affirmed her value, reinforced her confidence in herself.

"And with absolutely no experience!" Fee exclaimed, still struggling to come to terms with this unexpected side to her daughter. "Just goes to show the power of the gene. Ally will marvel at this when she sees it."

Except Ally always knew I was a closet actress, Francesca thought. It was different with her mother who viewed her as much more a de Lyle than a Kinross.

Glenn was always there at her shoulder, ready to offer help if she needed it, ready to explain, to instruct, to admire. Glenn was very much part of everything, not only the screenwriter, but Ngaire's much valued colleague. Ngaire and Glenn took their lunch break together, heads close as they got into intense discussion about how things were progressing. In the evening Glen had taken to asking Francesca to go for an after-dinner stroll with him. Francesca didn't know quite how it happened. Certainly she hadn't initiated anything but she found Glenn attractive, his personality easy yet stimulating. There was a depth to him she liked and they had the film in common as a constant subject of conversation.

"So when is Grant coming home?" Glenn slid the question in neatly the third night out.

"I don't really know." Francesca shook her head desperate for Grant to return home.

"Really? I thought you two were very close." Glenn stared down at her, attracted to her strongly but unsure how to proceed. It wouldn't take a rocket scientist to discern something intangible but very powerful between Cameron and Francesca.

Yet Francesca was startled by the question, not thinking herself and Grant so transparent. It wasn't as though there was any kissing or touching or telling conversation in front of other people. "Surely you've had very little time to see us together?" she parried.

He gave a faint laugh. "I'm someone who notices things, Francesca. I'm a writer. It's my training and my nature."

"So what have you noticed?" She tried to speak lightly.

"I would say you two had a special understanding."

Francesca stopped to shake a tiny pebble from her sandal. "I'm not sure what you're getting at, Glenn?"

His voice was wry. "I suppose what I really want to know is are you spoken for?"

She knew she blushed, grateful he couldn't see it. "A writer must be noted for getting to the point."

"It's not every day I meet someone like you, Francesca," he said. "I don't think it's a secret, either, that I find you very attractive. I would like to get to know you better. But maybe that's not possible?"

How to frame a response? As though it were any of his business anyway. "Grant and I are very good friends." Francesca lifted her head to stare up at the glittering desert stars. Friends? When he filled her with the most wonderful sensation of "coming home."

Glenn evidently wasn't impressed. "Don't you just hate that," he mocked. "Very good friends."

"Well that's all I'm prepared to say."

"Actually I am rushing it," Glenn apologised, shaking his head ruefully. "But a man's a fool if he lets someone wonderful like you pass him by. You're beautiful, Francesca. You're also very talented."

"I'm sure Mamma's surprised," Francesca answered lightly, trying to turn the conversation. She did find Glenn attractive. In some ways he charmed her but there was only one man she wanted and perversely he was trying to push her away.

"Would you think of repeating your experience?" Glenn asked, warmed by the silken brush of her arm.

"You mean consider acting as a serious career?" She sensed he was very interested in her answer.

"There would be much to learn, Francesca, but there's no doubt you're a natural and the cameras love you. It doesn't love everyone no matter how good-looking. I've seen beautiful people film as quite ordinary."

"Strange, isn't it?" Francesca mused. "I suppose it's all about photography. I've always taken a good picture. But to answer your question, I don't want to be a film star, Glenn. That's not my dream at all."

It was absurd to feel such disappointment. "And what is your dream?" he asked, looking down at her silken head.

"In some ways the hardest thing of all," Francesca responded. "To have a happy, lasting marriage. To raise a family. Bring all my children up with the right values. Help them to become people of confidence and accomplishment. I want to *love* them. Have them love me. I never want discord or alienation. I fear conflict."

This girl had been hurt. Deeply hurt, Glenn thought.

"No easy ambition," he murmured

"I know." She looked back at the purple sky. "But I want to focus all my energies on family. If one is in the fortunate financial position to do so being a wife and mother is a full-time job."

"Fee's career would have taken her a lot away from you?" he said with sudden realisation.

"Yes." Francesca nodded not wanting to discuss the breakdown of her parent's marriage, her father's custody of her which Glenn didn't know.

"But I understand from Rebecca that you had a first-class P.R. job in London?"

"That's true. I was competent but I've said my goodbyes. It didn't make me feel I was doing anything terribly important. There was no *charge*. I wanted to have a musical career at one time but my father vetoed that. It wasn't quite the thing."

"I expect your father wants what you want. For you to marry well and happily."

Though Francesca laughed, it sounded a little hollow. "He has my future husband lined up."

"Good grief you're surely not going to let your father pick your future husband?" That would ruin everything, Glenn thought.

"Of course not," Francesca answered calmly. "But there's been a bit of pressure there. From my side of the family and his."

"Your suitor's?" Glenn was totally distracted.

"It's a class thing, Glenn, being an Australian you mightn't understand. I'm a 'today' person. My father definitely isn't. Being an earl has a lot of implications."

"I would imagine," Glenn agreed dryly, his quirky eyebrows going up. "And being an earl's daughter has its responsibilities, I take it?"

"They do have an effect on me." Francesca remembered all the times she had suffered inner qualms and discomforts, aware of her father's plan for her. "I can't overlook them but my parents had their life. Surely I must have mine."

"I should jolly well say so." Glenn was thinking too much parental involvement was a terrible intrusion on a person's life. "Surely this chap knows you don't love him?"

Francesca's voice was gentle, almost resigned. "I do love him. I've known him all my life. He's counting on that. But it's not that kind of love. That *one* person."

That one person! It sounded very much like she'd found him. "Does Cameron have any idea about all this?" Glenn asked. Cameron was in love with her. He was quite sure of his own radar.

Francesca answered with some irony. "Grant seems to be on side with my father's master plan."

Glenn turned his keen, intelligent brown eyes on her. "I find that very hard to believe. I see Grant Cameron as a tough, very determined young man in a man's world. He wouldn't knuckle down to anyone."

"Except maybe himself," said Francesca.

His father had always told him, especially when he was a headstrong kid. "Don't *do* things, Grant, without thinking them through. Hell, hadn't he learnt? Yet he couldn't wait to get back to her, every day bringing him closer to asking her to marry

him and to hell with the rest. Why not let it out? Let his feelings go free? Tell her exactly what he felt for her. Why didn't
he simply cry out, "Now I've found you I'll never let you go!"
Why! Did his love for her run to self-sacrifice? Was that what
love was? Putting the loved one's welfare before one's own?

In his business he had grown into the habit of setting down
all his concerns, identifying them by putting them in print.
Then working out solutions from there. Even as he was hiring
an architect to draw up plans for the new homestead his mind
was ranging over other options. Other places from where he
could operate.

Places where Francesca wouldn't feel quite so isolated and
the climate would be kinder. Maybe most of the Camerons
from the beginning had been blondes or redheads? They'd had
time to acclimatise over the generations. He was as genuinely
fearful for Francesca's beautiful skin as a collector would be
fearful of hanging a fine painting where it received too much
strong daylight. Francesca was taking up so much of his head
space he felt he was never without her.

He was flying in over Opal, on a hot clear day, looking down at
the great maze of interlocking billabongs and creeks, marked
by narrow bands of verdant green on both sides of the water
channels. The mulga, the vast region where acacias predomi-
nated, spread away to the horizon, bridging the gap between
the hardiest eucalypt country and the true desert with its golden
plains of pungent, pointed, spinifex and saltbush, its glittering
gibber-stones and rolling dark red sand-dunes.

How he loved it! His home. It called to him as it always did
when he went beyond its boundaries. The Dead Heart. Only it
wasn't dead at all. It was beating, magnificent, unique; the flora
without parallel for its adaptation to such a harsh environment.
Even the ghost gums grew out of sheer rock where occasional
storm waters had flowed and the barren interior became an
ocean of wildflowers that gloried in its short, breathtaking tide.

Flowers! The fragrant flowers of the inland. Blazing on and on. Mile after mile. In such a harsh land none had thorns. Neither did the trees and bushes of the desert. Nothing to protect themselves. The exquisite roses had thorns to protect them. In other parts of the world thorns were the rule rather than the exception. Grant went with his stream of consciousness, which always carried images of Francesca. She might have been the only girl left in the world so obsessed was he with the thought of her.

The fair Francesca! A pink rose with satin petals. A rose in the wilderness. Once this wilderness, this great savage land, the parched deserts and plains formed the bed of the Great Inland Sea of prehistory. Twenty thousand years ago the vast Interior had been clothed in luxuriant vegetation to rival the paradise of the wild, the tropical rainforests of the Far North. Crocodiles had once thrived as they still did north of Capricorn. There were many drawings of crocodiles recorded by the aborigines in the rock paintings in and around the Wild Heart. A remarkable witness to the length of time the aborigines had roamed Australia. One of the rarest trees in the world, the Livistona, a tall, graceful tropical "cabbage" palm he had seen growing in pockets in the heat of the desert. A microclimate created by a river gorge.

An oasis in the desert. Ferns and palms and the ancient cycads, their emerald-greens contrasting with the fiery red walls of the cliffs and the deep sapphire sky.

An oasis. Lushness in the arid spinifex plains.

It mightn't be the natural environment for a rose but roses survived and flourished in the sheltered gardens of Kimbara, which relied on bores that had been sunk deep in the Great Artesian Basin. It had taken generations for the gardens at Kimbara to flourish. Generations, a great deal of time and money, a dedication that had filled Kimbara's women's souls.

In his grandfather's day the gardens at Opal had been significant though they had never rivalled Kimbara's. He remembered his mother working hard to keep the gardens going. He remembered her talking about the difficulties. It had taken such a short time for Opal's gardens to die after their mother had been taken so cruelly from them. But Ally would bring them back. Ally was a doer. Ally and Francesca. Cousins. And great friends.

He began to imagine Francesca walking through the gardens love would create in the desert. Francesca in a microclimate. In an oasis of fragrant flowers. Surely if he could create an oasis for her she could not only survive but thrive. Go forward, a voice in his head told him. You can only go forward. You can't go back.

The cast and crew were taking a break from filming when he arrived at the homestead early midafternoon. All these strange people in his family home. But they were paying well and Bush Rescue would get a very welcome injection of funds. Fee saw him first as he pulled the Jeep off the circular driveway into the shade of the trees, waiting for him at the top of the steps.

"Hello there, Grant, darling," she called, the incomparable Fee completely at home in her elaborate get-up that had to be stifling in the heat. "We've missed you. How did it go?"

He bent to kiss the cheek she extended to him, a thin layer of the heavy make-up used for filming smearing his lips. "Sorry, darling." Fee produced a handkerchief from somewhere in her deep violet costume, dabbing at his mouth.

"It's all right, Fee," he reassured her casually. "It'll come off. In answer to your question, things went well. TCR and Cameron Airways are not far away from signing a deal. The lawyers will work it out. Where's everybody?"

Fee gestured gracefully towards the house. "Taking a break. It's hot work as you can imagine, consequently tempers are getting a little frayed. I came out to catch whatever breeze there is. Apart from that things are moving along nicely. Francesca has been the truly big surprise. She's amazingly good."

"Why wouldn't she be?" Grant countered breezily, feeling Fee hadn't been giving Francesca enough credit. "She *is* your daughter."

They were all over the main reception rooms so Grant decided on going immediately to his room, changing his clothes, then looking in on Francesca and Ngaire on his way back. He sent a searching glance through the drawing room nevertheless hoping to catch a glimpse of Francesca. He wondered what she would look like in period costume. That tiny waist his hands could span, her beautiful hair dressed in unfamiliar fashion. He couldn't wait to see her on the footage they had shot. It was a pity he'd had to go off as shooting started but he couldn't have cancelled his meeting with Drew. It was too important.

They were sitting side by side on an old Victorian love seat. Richards obviously feeling the need to hold Francesca's hands in his. He had his dark head bent to her, speaking earnestly, while she listened as attentive as any man could possibly wish. She was the embodiment of Lucinda in her dark grey gown, the bodice tightly buttoned, a show of cream near the throat, the heavy full skirt spread out across the rose velvet. Her glorious Titian hair was drawn back severely from her face from a centre parting with some kind of thick roll at the back. The hair style and get-up reminded him of how they had tried to make Olivia de Havilland plain for the part of Melanie in *Gone with the Wind.* Never succeeding. Both de Havilland and Francesca had such sweetness of expression quite apart from the lovely features that could never be denied.

And just because he was the screenwriter did that give Richards the right to go into a huddle with Francesca? Surely Ngaire, who was nowhere to be seen, should be handling the direction? Grant had thought he would be overjoyed to see Francesca again, thought they would greet each other like they'd been parted for years. Instead here she was lifting her head to stare soulfully into Richards's eyes while Richards stared back at her, clearly under her spell.

What the hell was going on? Grant fumed. Whatever it was it ripped the heart out of him. He broke his glance, striding off towards his bedroom, his earlier mood of excitement and anticipation replaced by one he barely recognised as jealousy. Not that he had time for any of it, he thought grimly. He had work to do. Bob Carlton was a tower of strength to him but he couldn't leave him carrying the load. Also Bob would be anxious to hear all about his meeting with Forsythe.

Dressed in his everyday uniform of khaki bush shirt and trousers, he went back through the house, hearing voices from the formal dining room he and Rafe never used while they were on their own. Obviously they were back at work. Not that he was about to interrupt. Not now. In his absence he had arranged for one of his men to ferry Francesca, Fee, Ngaire and Richards back to Kimbara at the end of the day's shoot and the leading man when he arrived—he could have for all Grant knew. The male film crew elected to stay close to their equipment, bunking down in the stockmen's quarters, and taking their meals there.

The women, four in all, wardrobe and make-up had taken over a bungalow, which had been made as comfortable as possible by a couple of the station wives. Over the period of time it took to finish the outback scenes, the wives were assisting the camp cook who could produce dishes every bit as good as those many city chefs could offer. Opal staff worked very hard. Opal staff deserved to be fed very well. It was essential to keep up their energy level and good spirits. It was mandatory as well, to ensure station guests were well catered for.

Grant stalked off realising he had to return before sunset if he wanted to see Francesca at all. He had planned on ferrying them back to Kimbara himself but something about Richards's proprietorial attitude and Francesca's seeming quiescence had set him off. It shamed him and made him angry he could be so jealous. A feeling entirely new to him and something he didn't want to accept. He realised with a kind of despair this was another thing that went along with passion. He didn't like Richards's intimacy with *his* girl!

* * *

Fee waited until she and Francesca were getting out of their heavy costumes, handing them over to Liz Forbes, from wardrobe, before she mentioned Grant had arrived home.

"You mean he never came in to say hello?" Francesca turned sharply towards her mother, feeling a clutch of dismay on two accounts: Fee had neglected to tell her and Grant hadn't called in.

"I thought he would," said Fee taking off her wig and placing it carefully on the dummy.

"Perhaps he didn't want to interrupt us," Francesca suggested, trying to rid herself of the notion Grant hadn't missed her as much as she had missed him.

"We were taking a break at the time," Fee protested. "Don't be upset, darling." Fee began to brush her own hair out. "He's probably had lots to attend to. The meeting in Brisbane went well."

"Couldn't you have told me earlier, Mamma?" Francesca asked reproachfully, not appreciating the fact Fee seemed to be working underground to drive a wedge between herself and Grant.

Fee shook her head. "Darling girl when you're in character it's best not to have any outside distractions. I'm proud of what you're doing. You're very good you know."

But Francesca wasn't to be diverted. "I think you planned it, Mamma." She looked her mother in the eye, seeing no sign of apology on Fee's still stunning face. "You like Grant. At least I thought you did but you're doing your level best to create divisions."

"Darling girl, I'm not the enemy here," Fee exclaimed. "I don't want you to ruin your life." Tears suddenly filled Fee's eyes and she made no attempt to blink them away. "I do like Grant. He's an admirable young man but I just can't see he's for you."

"Okay so who is?" Francesca challenged, more aware than anyone her mother could call up tears at will. "Don't leave it up in the air. Who?"

"Jimmy," Fee's response was instantaneous as though she'd come up with a crucial piece of information. "Jimmy Waddington. Surely you can't have forgotten him? Jimmy will make you happy."

Francesca concentrated hard on not getting angry. "How's that?"

"Darling, he knows you so well," Francesca cried with more than a touch of theatre. "He *understands* you. You've been great friends since you were children. Be honest now, weren't you in love with him?"

"I didn't know what love was." Francesca shook her head. "I'm very fond of Jimmy but fondness isn't what changes your life."

"Maybe not," Fee admitted. "Being in love is wonderful at the time but it doesn't last. Lord, child I should know."

It had to be said. "I'm not frivolous like you, Mamma."

Fee opened her eyes wide. Francesca didn't realise it but she sounded exactly like her father. "Darling, couldn't you be more respectful?"

"I'm surprised you don't agree. Anyway Jimmy *doesn't* understand me. He doesn't think I have a serious thought in my head."

"What nonsense!" Fee gave the impression she was shocked. "You know perfectly well he thinks you're a wonderful girl. More importantly you have the same background. Your father has hand-picked Jimmy for your husband."

"Father's not the expert on marriage, either," Francesca said. "Anyway fathers have no right to do that."

"You can face him with that?" Fee challenged, locking her daughter's gaze.

"It wouldn't be easy, but yes." Francesca gave a long-suffering sigh. "What are you trying to suggest anyway, Mamma? In refusing Jimmy I'm betraying Father. Is that what you're saying?"

Fee stared off for a moment. "Please don't raise your voice, darling. Ngaire and Glenn are still about. I'm the last person in the world to want to upset you. I love you, but I must point out Grant in many respects is an unknown entity."

"After all these years?" Francesca gave a wry little laugh.

"Darling, you met him briefly when you came for visits," Fee pointed out. "You didn't really get to know one another until recent times."

"So you don't recommend him as a husband?" Francesca said. "Be frank."

Fee reached into her handbag and pulled out her eau de cologne. "I'm sure he'll make a delightful husband but maybe a difficult one, too. He's very ambitious. Hungry for success."

"He's a success already, Mamma," Francesca said in a pained voice. "Grant told me he wants to give something to his country, to his community. I believe him. The Camerons have money already. Money isn't the motivating factor with Grant."

"Don't be ridiculous, darling," Fee said with hard irony.

"I'm not being ridiculous." Francesca shook her head. "Money is fine. Everyone welcomes it but I know Grant means what he says. He wants to do things. He has a vision. Don't please tell me Jimmy has one."

"At least you'll be able to handle him," Fee said in a voice that suggested Francesca wouldn't be able to handle Grant. "Come on, darling," she coaxed as Francesca turned away from her. "I'm sorry if I'm upsetting you but I'm trying to do the right thing. At least give yourself *time*. I know all about dynamic men. They sweep you off your feet, but before you know where you are—"

"Please, Mamma." Francesca signalled she had had enough. "You're so used to thinking of me as your little girl...you can't see I'm an adult. I can't depend on you or Father to make my decisions for me."

"Even when there's so much at stake?" Fee pleaded, using her full voice. "Your happiness? Your well-being?"

"May I speak now, Mamma?" Francesca asked. "Even then.

This is the most serious relationship of my life. If I'm ready to take the leap Grant is reflecting on things long and hard. In fact it might ease your mind to know he, too, is considering our relationship might be dead wrong."

Fee frowned deeply as though no one was permitted to think such a thing of her daughter. "My darling, don't you see you could fight about everything! I see a huge contrast between you two," she said.

"Then you don't know Grant or me as well as you think," said Francesca.

Grant did return to ferry them home but Grant and Francesca never had the chance of a private word until they reached Kimbara homestead and the others had gone inside.

"Couldn't you stay, Grant?" Rebecca, who had been standing with them on the verandah asked. "Do you have to rush away?"

"Actually I do, Rebecca." Grant softened his refusal with a smile. "I have to be ready for a big job on Laura tomorrow. Thanks anyway. Give my best to Brod when he comes in. Tell him everything went well."

"That's great. I know he'll be thrilled for you." Rebecca smiled, a sparkle in her eyes. "I'll leave you two to catch up. You're coming to Fee's book launch aren't you?"

"Well I'm thinking about it," Grant said.

"You *have* to!" Rebecca insisted. "It'll be lovely for the four of us to go out together one night while we're in Sydney. You and Fran. Brod and I. See if you can pull out all the stops."

"I'll try!" Grant sketched her a salute. "Rebecca is looking radiant," he said, when he and Francesca were alone.

Francesca raised a delicate eyebrow. "Is that really so surprising? She's head over heels in love with her husband."

"Then she has excellent taste." Grant allowed his eyes to dwell on her. The slant of her blue eyes, the curve of the lid, the line of her cheek, the clean cut of her jaw, the exquisite shape of her mouth. She'd creamed off all the heavy film make-up and her beautiful skin had a slightly shiny lustre. "How are you?" he asked, wanting to tilt her face to him and kiss it. Amazed he didn't.

"A bit down in the dumps," Francesca admitted. "Why didn't you come in and say hello when you arrived?"

He raised a sardonic eyebrow. "Because I didn't want to interrupt your little coaching session with Richards."

"You're kidding!" Whatever she imagined, it wasn't that.

"Never more serious actually. I glanced into the drawing room only to find the two of you on that old love seat, tenderly holding hands."

"Could it be your eyes were deceiving you?"

"No."

Francesca glanced up at him quickly, her eyes searching out his mood. "If it were anyone else but you I'd say you were jealous."

"Not overly. You don't think I'm capable of being jealous?" he asked, iridescent eyes narrowing over her.

"You wouldn't allow yourself to go so far. Now let's see. We were sitting on the love seat. I'm trying to cast my mind back."

"Cocooned in your own little world," he prompted. "Richards has his head bent to you. You were staring up soulfully at him. It was one hell of a scene!"

It must have been to cause such a reaction. "Now I remember. I'm just a beginner, Grant," she explained patiently. "Green as they come. There's so much I don't know. Practically all of it. Glenn has been very kind to me."

"Kinder than Ngaire?" he asked suavely. "I thought she was the director. Isn't it her task to correct any mistakes? Smooth over all the little rough bits."

"Ngaire helps me as well," she told him briskly. "Everyone does. They give me all the support I need."

"So you're loving it then?" Because I missed you like hell.

"I think I'll look back on it as a very worthwhile experience," Francesca said. "But I'm not taking it too seriously. And what about you? I want to hear all about your meetings with Drew. How's Eve by the way? Did you manage to see her?"

He nodded. "Eve's fine. She sent her best regards. They entertained me royally. Two nights. A dinner party at their beautiful home. Then Pavarotti and Friends in Concert. Our meetings went very well. Drew and I are on the same wavelength. Let's walk down to the chopper?" He took her arm, wondering how things could go so easily wrong, when he desperately wanted to hold her close. "I called in on an architect while I was there. Drew recommended him."

Her head seemed to explode with stars. "Really? Now you know something funny? I dreamt that you did."

He squeezed her delicate upper arm. "Francesca you're not *acting?*"

"No I'm not. I don't tell fibs. I actually did dream w—" she could hardly give herself away "—you and an architect were speaking together. It was quite a vivid dream. I've thought about it a lot. As a matter of fact I've had a lot of fun sketching some designs. You might like to see them some time."

"Run and get them now," he said. "I'll wait."

The high colour of excitement came into her cheeks. "I want us to look at them *together.*"

"Then come back to Opal with me tonight," he said with quiet intensity. "I want to be near you. Make love to you. Open all the doors and curtains so the moonlight will fall on your beautiful, luminous skin."

She hesitated, half-poised to run back to the homestead. "Sometimes you're crazy."

He gave her an ironic look. "You don't want to come?"

"You know I do." Her breathing softly rasped. "I missed you terribly."

"Did you?"

"Yes."

He took her chin and tilted her mouth. "Poor, poor, Francesca," he said very softly. "It was no different for me."

She stood very still while he kissed her, feeling the force of his desire held on a tight leash. "What is it you want?" she whispered into his mouth, half-closing her eyes.

He wanted to slide his hand down over her swan's neck, cup her smooth, creamy breast, feel it swell to the tenderness of his fingers. He wanted to let his hand descend...

"Just one word, Francesca," he said huskily. "*You.* There's so much I want to tell you."

"So much I want to hear."

Anything might have happened next, so closely were they drawn together in heart and mind, only Fee chose that very moment to come hurrying out onto the verandah, walking to the balustrade. "Darling, Ngaire wants to show us today's rushes. Sure you can't stay and see them, Grant?"

Grant's smile was openly mocking. "I really have to get away, Fee." Of course she knew he did, if he wanted to be on Opal by nightfall. "You'd better go, Francesca," he told her dryly. "Fee's full of surprises. Now she's applying a bit of maternal pressure."

Goddammit, yes, Francesca thought in amazement. The phantom mother of her childhood, the brilliant shooting star, was now siding of all things with the ex-husband she had so capriciously cut out of her life. Nevertheless Francesca sprang to Fee's defence so deeply was the habit ingrained. "Mamma only intends to be..."

"Please don't say kind," Grant warned, his strong, handsome face showing its high mettle. "I think Fee could be a ruthless opponent. What she doesn't intend is for you to be buried away in the wilds. Not that I blame her. God knows I can see both sides."

Gently, conciliatory, Francesca touched his hand. "I'll bring my sketchbook over tomorrow. I so much want to show it to you. Another part of my dream—" the *same* part...she didn't tell him in her dream the homestead and the garden merged "—we were planning an oasis in the vast landscape. It would be impossible to conquer such immensity but one could devise a sort of sweeping Australian garden landscape. Something on the grand scale to live in harmony with the unique environment and survive drought. I suppose it's far too ambitious, but one could landscape some of the watercourses. Indigenous trees of course but massed plantings. And there could be a polo field with lots of shade for the ponies, the spectators and their cars. It would be an enormous challenge, probably daunting, but so exciting. We could create our own vision rather than going along with existing..."

He interrupted her almost fiercely. "We? You did say *we*, didn't you?"

Francesca didn't falter, even with her mother waiting anxiously for her up on the verandah. "Yes," she answered, her heart in her eyes.

CHAPTER SIX

NEXT DAY HE couldn't get away from Laura Station until after the midafternoon break. He had a new recruit on roster, a man the same age as himself, Rick Wallace—an excellent helicopter pilot with more than enough qualifications and flying hours to warrant his inclusion in the team, but a mite short on actual experience in aerial mustering. It was his first priority as boss of the team to make sure Wallace was handling the job properly. He always conducted a premuster briefing, always took aerial shots, pointing out possible dangers on the site, sometimes acting as copilot to continue with the first-hand instruction. By smoko he was sure he was leaving the rest of the day's work in Rick's gifted hands. Rick was well on the way to having the same sort of skills as himself and he, too, was mad on flying. They would be friends.

When he arrived back on Opal it was to find the leading man had arrived to film his scenes; Ngaire introduced them, pleasure in her eyes. Her hero was an up-and-coming young English actor unconventionally handsome, dark-haired, light-eyed, with reputed considerable sex appeal for women and the ability to get male audiences onside. Grant knew the role called for a genuine English accent rather than an assumed one, which could slip from time to time, as well as a male lead with an international "name." The name was Marc Fordham. He had a friendly manner and a firm hand shake. Grant liked him.

Marc was dressed in part in a stained and dusty rather billowy white shirt and tight dark brown trousers and a wide silver buckled belt. His dark curly hair was shoulder-length and tousled, a few days growth of beard on his face. He looked great, every inch the dynamic hero of the novel. The women wouldn't be able to take their eyes off him, Grant thought, amused the dark tan—dark as Brod's that went so extraordinarily well with light eyes—was courtesy of the make-up department. Someone would have to warn him of the dangers of the outback sun. Though he tried not to make it too obvious his own eyes were going in search of Francesca. Finally when she didn't appear and he couldn't sight her, he was forced to ask Ngaire where she was.

"Out riding," Ngaire volunteered, as though it was her own greatest pleasure to be in the saddle. "With Marc here we thought we'd go ahead with his scenes with Fee." Fee played the hero's distant relative, the wife of a powerful Sydney landowner keen to recruit the hero to his interests. "Francesca wasn't needed so she and Glenn decided to go for a ride. Glenn is a weekend rider," Ngaire laughed indulgently. "Francesca, I believe is a brilliant horsewoman. One of the many reasons she got the part of Lucinda. She has that mad, suicidal ride in her final scene. We'll leave that to the last days of shooting. We were even going to ask you if you could line someone up for the long shoots. Someone who could pass for Marc. Marc has had to learn to ride a horse of course, but he's no expert. If you could come up with a stand-in?" Ngaire looked winsome, clearly hoping or counting on, either he or Brod would do it. But he couldn't answer for either of them.

Instead he nodded noncommittally. "Any idea where they're headed?"

"Oh, not too far I would imagine." Ngaire started to lose interest, keen to get on with filming. "Francesca said you liked her to stay close to the home. I think she left a note for you." She cast her eyes around, saw nothing, fluttered a hand. "She was sitting out on the side verandah, sketching as I recall. Maybe it's out there."

No note. A number of sketchbooks tidily stacked on the circular table, a leather case full of pencils, charcoal sticks close beside. He was finding out something new about her all the time. It was absurd to be jealous of Richards. Beautiful as she was, Francesca as a femme fatale he couldn't buy. Francesca was honest and true. She had gone for a ride and she would be back soon. Grant sat down taking the sketchbook from the top of the pile, conscious of a swift emotional response as his eye fell on a drawing of...

Himself. Or himself as Francesca saw him. He stared at it for a long time thinking she had made him look a whole lot better looking than he was, maybe a touch arrogant with the lift of his chin and the angle of his head. But it was undeniably him and it was very good. He turned more pages marvelling at the drawings. Himself again and again. Members of the family. There was Brod, a genuinely handsome devil. Beautifully lily cool Rebecca in any number of poses. Fee in an armchair, Fee reading a script, Fee and David, numerous sketches of Ally, a few of Rafe looking like a medieval knight. Perhaps that was the way she saw him.

Other books were devoted to animals, beautiful drawings of horses, cattle, kangaroos, emus, brolgas, swans, pages of the giant wedge-tailed eagle with detailed inserts of wings. She was wonderful at capturing animals in action. She must have sketched at the instant it happened. Other sketchbooks contained Kimbara landscapes, with stockmen at rest, or driving herds of cattle. There were innumerable little sketches of wildflowers, lilies, ground orchids, boronia, flowering vines.

Another couple of sketchbooks were devoted to studies in anatomy the structure of the human body. They appeared to be absolutely accurate. Other exercises fleshed out the skeleton. Obviously Francesca had received a good deal of training. He'd no idea she was so talented in this way. He wondered if she painted in other media—watercolours, pastels, oils? He would love to see what she could do. Talent like this deserved the greatest encouragement.

The very last book in the pile, almost hidden, contained what he was so desperate to see. Francesca's visions of his dream homestead. The first sketch was front on. So real he felt he could reach out and open the front door.

Francesca! He loved what he saw. She drew effortlessly as if she loved it. The facade was completely modern, huge areas of glass that could be opened to the desert air. The central core of the homestead enclosed front and sides by sweeping verandahs, no flamboyant classical columns but representations of narrow steel supports running the entire length of the facade. A concession to tradition a double height entrance but what totally blew him away rising behind it a three-story open bell-tower, modelled on a Spanish mission tower from where bells would call and one would have a fantastic view of the desert landscape.

Other drawings followed, different aspects, different angled facets, various sketches of the tower, all a little different, open views down into the interior with the layout of open-plan rooms and an enclosed central courtyard with a tall fluid water sculpture instead of the traditional fountain. But what was so fascinating was Francesca had put splashes of colours—yellow ochre, burnt umber, raw sienna, ultramarine blue, cobalt blue, cadmium yellow and red, lamp black, he read them off—down the side of the pages along with specified materials, stone, glass, steel, richly grained timbers, different shades and textures of granite.

Obviously their minds worked in the same way. Working quite independent of him, with her own background of a jewel-like English country home, she had come up with a design structure little different from his own except for the novel addition of a tower.

It was downright uncanny. Her vision reflected his own. A

graceful house for all its modernist approach. She had even sketched entrance gates to the main compound. Not high to restrict the uninterrupted views but substantial, making a statement, two low pillars of desert rocks anchoring bronze gates depicting two magnificent rearing horses, the whole shaded by an A-framed roof from which hung the legend, Myora-Opal Station.

There weren't words for what he felt. He only knew he wanted to live there. With the girl of his dreams, Francesca.

This was the kind of thing he had wanted from the architect but he realised in that he was being too simplistic. Madison had picked up on all his basic cues, his vision a striking contemporary version of the traditional homestead but Francesca with her knowledge of the site had worked from the imagination. Clever, clever, girl.

From his vantage point on the verandah he was the first to see the grey gelding come in, disconsolate, head down, reins trailing.

God!

Grant vaulted up from his chair, taking the steps at a single leap, running across the garden to the open grasslands. The horse heard his repeated whistles, carried on the wind. It pricked its ears in the direction from whence they had come, then adjusted its direction. Minutes later Grant had it by the reins. The grey's coat was covered in sweat. It was obvious it had bolted, only slowing its flight when it was in sight and sound of the homestead. It gave Grant considerable comfort to know Francesca was a fine horsewoman with hands like silk. But Richards, according to Ngaire, was an inexperienced rider. He only hoped if it was Richards who had become unseated he'd been wearing one of the light weight helmets the station insisted their guests wear. Galloping across the plains with only an akubra to protect a fragile skull was only a romantic notion for anyone but a skilled rider.

A young aboriginal boy came running as he approached the

stables complex, taking the grey's reins. "What'sa matter, boss?" Bunny so called because of his prominent but dazzlingly white, front teeth stared up at him with black, liquid eyes. "Where this one come from?"

"You tell me, Bunny," Grant responded grimly. "Were you on hand when Miss Francesca and her friend went out?"

"Sure was, boss." Bunny was happy to confirm it. "Saddled up for them. Miss Francesca picked out Gypsy. A bit frisky but I reckon she can handle 'im. The guy settled for Spook. Nice and quiet." Bunny ran an ebony hand over Spook's side. "Though with a horse you never to know. Reckon he's come a way. Sweatin'."

Grant looked as if he was about to curse but didn't. "So someone has taken a tumble I just hope to God, Bunny, you gave him a hard hat?"

Bunny looked him straight in the eye. "I was goin' to, boss, but Miss Francesca insisted on it right away. Wore an akubra herself like the rest of us. Talk about bushie!"

"You know she's half Australian. Get the saddle off him, Bunny," Grant said. "Any idea where they headed?"

Bunny waved a hand. "Miss Francesca didn't say and I didn't think it my place to ask."

"That's okay," Grant said. "See ya, kid. From now on you have my permission to ask everybody where they're headed. So don't have any qualms. I'll go back to the house and check. Miss Francesca was supposed to have left a note."

Fee as it turned out had it, which struck Grant as odd, given Fee appeared to be against his and Francesca's deepening involvement. She apologised profusely when Grant told her crisply she should have handed it over once he returned.

"One of the horses has returned without a rider," he told her, grey-green eyes glinting. He took the note from its unsealed envelope and opened it. "Don't panic, it's not Francesca's horse," he had the grace to reassure Fee. "She was riding Gypsy. Richards was riding the grey gelding, Spook. It's a quiet work horse, but like all horses it's unpredictable." As he was speaking he was reading swiftly. "They've headed out to Blue Lady Lagoon. An easy trail. I'll get going."

"I do hope it's nothing serious." Fee was looking unaccustomedly chastened. "I understand Glenn was little more than a beginner. He couldn't handle anything at all lively. And Francesca! I know she's got a lot of common sense but I hope she gave that serious consideration."

"I only hope we're not looking at broken bones. Just in case I'll have to put out a call to the Royal Flying Doctor."

"Glenn wouldn't have a clue about roughing it," Fee said.

"Would Francesca?" Grant countered briskly. "Anyway I must go. There's only so much daylight left."

He took the four-wheel drive, heading out across the plains country to a favourite haven for all the station, black and white. Blue Lady Lagoon. All the stations in the Channel Country had similar flowering waterholes, filled with beautiful waterlilies, the sacred blue lotus, the pink, the cream, the rarer red lotus and the giant blue waterlily of Blue Lady Lagoon with its spectacular flowers growing up to a foot across. No matter how hot it was Blue Lady Lagoon with its tall trees, numerous golden grevilleas and native hibiscus, its understorey of mosses, vines and ground orchids offered an almost junglelike cool. He could understand why Francesca had headed there. He didn't realise it but he had tightened his jaw until it ached. He wouldn't accept Francesca was perfectly all right until he laid eyes on her. At least they couldn't get lost. They had only to follow the chain of billabongs home.

Ten minutes out he was confronted by an extraordinary sight. In the shimmering, dancing light of the atmosphere a small figure appeared out of the near distant mulga. The figure was on foot leading a black horse that could only be Gypsy. Hunkered down over the horse's back was a far more substantial figure. Richards.

Without further ado Grant tore off across country, angered

beyond words—Francesca was walking in the heat. No way to travel! God she could have been walking for miles! If so she would be parched. A wave of hostility towards Richards swept through him, rivalled by his great sense of relief. Richards had to be in a bad way if he had consented to do the riding while Francesca walked.

Closer he saw Francesca had come to a standstill, holding firmly to Gypsy's reins, looking up at Richards probably asking him how he was. Moments more and he brought the Jeep to a halt, jumped out and moved towards them with all the speed and purpose of a big cat.

"What's happened here?" His intense scrutiny devoured Francesca as he checked to see if she was all right. Only then did it move on to Richards as he tried to neutralise his anger. "Are you okay there, Glenn?" he asked, moving alongside Gypsy soothing him.

Richards managed a smile, trying to straighten. "Afraid I took a tumble." That was clear from all the grazing down one side of his face and the condition of his clothes.

"No bones broken." Francesca came to stand at Grant's shoulder. "He's concussed, I imagine. Very groggy."

"So you let him up on your horse?" He all but accused her in a display of perverse male emotion.

"Come off it, Grant. I had to," she answered in a mild voice. "He's in no condition to walk."

"And *you* are?" He stared down into her lovely, sensitive face. She was wearing her wide-brimmed akubra with a light blue bandanna protecting her nape, but her face was very flushed and beads of sweat had gathered across her forehead at her temples and beneath her eyes. Sensibly she had let down her long hair as a curtain and had rolled down the long sleeves of her yellow cotton shirt but he could plainly see a runnel of sweat moving down between her breasts with damp patches all over the blouse and waistline. "The first thing we've got to do is get you a drink of water," he said harshly, starting back to the four-wheel drive.

"It's all right." She came after him to lay a reassuring hand on his arm. "I made sure we didn't set off without water. I stopped to give us a drink just before we moved out of the scrub."

"So you can drink some more now," he said, making short work of pouring out some water from the supply in the vehicle.

"You're not going to stand over me while I drink it?" Francesca asked wryly.

"Yes, I am," he answered firmly. "Something else I want you to do while I get Richards is put this towel over your face and neck." He started to saturate a small hand towel with water, not content with handing it to her but taking charge himself. He swept her akubra off then began sponging her hot face with the cool, clean water easing part of it around her throat. "What boots have you got on?" he demanded next, his brow knotted.

"Good ones," she gasped as he ceased mopping her up. But her sense of being dreadfully overheated had eased.

"So get in the vehicle," he ordered briefly. "I'll attend to Richards."

Francesca did so gratefully, making a real effort to appear sprightly though it cost her a lot. Glenn might be very gifted in his own area but a man of action he wasn't. The last hour had been fairly ghastly as she made their way out of the rough country where the gelding's startled gallop had ended, and found a track through the mulga until they reached the open plain. Nothing had spooked the grey gelding outside its rider. Glenn simply didn't have sympathetic contact with the horse. In fact he had all the common faults, especially with his hands. A horse's mouth was soft and sensitive. Glenn's handling harsh and unencouraging. She'd even been giving Glenn riding instructions as they went, realising he'd never been taught, much less got to the point where he understood horses. Nearing the lagoon despite her objection, he had resorted to force instead of hands to change the gelding's direction, kicking the heel of his boots into its side.

Spook didn't like that. Francesca the horse lover didn't blame him. With Glenn's armchair seat and his bad leg position it was inevitable he would be thrown. To make matters worse he had complained about wearing the helmet from the outset saying he found it much too hot when he really wanted the breeze through his hair. Somehow she had persuaded him to keep it on until they reached the green shade of the red river gums. There he had whipped the helmet off with a kind of bravado, ignoring her pleas to keep it on.

The miracle was she didn't have to pick up the pieces after he'd been thrown. Some facial grazing where he'd hit the ground hard. A large lump on his head, all the symptoms of concussion, blurred vision, grogginess, some retching. She'd had the devil's own job getting him up on Gypsy, finding the right boulder to use as a mounting block, then using her own weight on the other side to counteract his. Finally it had all come together without strain to the horse. Gypsy, the ex-racehorse, had been very, very good while the inferior hack, Spook had taken the rare occasion to play up.

Her clothes felt terribly damp and heavy on her, her shirt soaked from Grant's ministrations, her hair slick with sweat in need of a shampoo. She turned back the cuffs of her shirt, rolled them up then she whipped off the wet blue bandanna. Her heart was still thudding in her chest after her long walk but she just had to grit her teeth and bear it until she could get under a lovely cold shower. Originally she had wanted to ride to the homestead for help but Glenn though disorientated had been adamant she didn't leave him. She might be getting used to vast distances and life in the wild but Glenn appeared to be genuinely intimidated by the bush. In his altered state he gave the impression he really believed if she left him he'd never be found again or dehydration would claim him.

With Glenn comfortable in the back of the vehicle, Francesca wasn't surprised when Grant shot her a rapier glance. "Why didn't you ride for help, Francesca? You made it so hard for yourself walking in." He noted with relief the high colour of exertion had faded a little from her face. In fact though she was uncharacteristically dishevelled she was looking remarkably calm and composed.

"My fault, I'm afraid," Glenn mumbled from the back. "I wouldn't let her go. I don't mind telling you I find the bush extremely intimidating. It's great size! A man doesn't realise until he gets out here."

"You're sounding better, Glenn," Francesca said with satisfaction, turning her head with its dark curtain.

"What a fool you must think me."

Why not? Grant thought with strong disapproval.

"I have to say you did give me the impression you were a better rider," Francesca pointed out in a wry voice.

"But, Francesca, I thought I *was*. Just goes to show how much I'm out of my element here. I've been on horse riding trails. Come to think of it, it was mostly in a straight line and always with a party."

"And what became of your helmet?" Grant asked gratingly, trying to push his extreme irritation with Richards to the back of his mind. Not only had Richards expected Francesca to sit and hold his hand, he had expected her to lead him seated on the horse across the spinifex belt in the heat of the afternoon. He'd never have allowed a woman to undertake such a long, hot trek. This was rough open country not a jaunt through a tree-filled city park.

"It came off in the fall." Francesca aware of Grant's anger risked a fib. "The safety harness must have worked loose."

Grant sighed. "Tell me another one."

"Sorry. I'm ashamed of myself. Glenn was feeling the heat. He took it off briefly to cool down."

"And what spooked the gelding?" His eyes sparkled. "Make my day and give me a straight answer."

"It was the darnedest thing." Glenn found his voice from the back. "Such a tame horse yet it cut up a treat. I gave it a little bit of a kick in the sides to make it change direction and ended hanging on for dear life. It bolted into the scrub. I felt a branch might take off my head."

"Especially without your helmet," Grant murmured dryly. "They say all's well that ends well, but I don't suppose you'll be interested in going riding again." He mightn't have put it into words but *not with Francesca* came over loud and clear.

By the time they got back to the house everyone had been alerted to the situation, swarming out onto the verandah as Grant drew the four-wheel drive up at the base of the front steps. There were hugs and kisses all round. As the injured party, however self-inflicted, Glenn came in for the lion's share of attention but as Fee drew her daughter away her face revealed the strain of the past half hour.

"My darling!" One good look was enough for Fee. Embarking on a horse ride with Glenn Richards had not paid off. She could see Francesca's pink shirt was drying quickly in the heat otherwise she looked as if she'd been dunked, her beautiful long hair pressed flat against her skull her face carrying an expression Fee remembered down the years. Francesca trying very hard indeed to be a good little girl and not cause any fuss.

"It's all right, Mamma," she was saying now, anxious to offer reassurance. "Glenn took a tumble but no bones broken. A bump on the head and a modicum of hurt pride."

"To hell with that!" Fee laughed shortly, looking back over her shoulder to where Glenn was seated on a verandah chair with Ngaire and the crew in attendance. "I don't know why you took him in the first place. All Glenn knows about horses is what he's learned in the movies."

Grant pondered that. "I've never seen the hero look for the little lady's help. He *rode. She* walked," he said, trying with some difficulty to lighten his own expression.

"For crying out loud." Fee shook her head in a flurry of ringlets. "Look, I've got to have that out with him." She made to stalk off with a considerable air of majesty, only Francesca caught at her arm pleadingly.

"Please don't, Mamma. It wasn't as though Glenn was himself. He'd taken a tumble. I expect quite a lot of bumps and grazes will appear overnight. "He was far too groggy to walk. The gelding simply bolted for home.".

Outback-bred Fee stared at her perplexed. "But my darling child, why didn't you simply leave him there and ride for help?"

"Because he got quite agitated when I tried to leave."

"A case of a city man behaving rather badly in the bush," Grant offered in a sardonic voice. "Leave it, Fee. Glenn has a nice little story for after dessert. Right now Francesca should get under the shower and cool off. She had quite a trek in the heat."

Fee knitted her brow very delicately to lessen the chance of wrinkles. "There are things that *need* saying, Grant."

"Don't be upset. Forget it, Mamma," Francesca begged, hearing another wave of laughter at Glenn's droll account of his tumble. "It was all my fault. I knew almost from the outset Glenn had little experience. I should have abandoned the ride altogether."

Grant agreed with a single, very definite nod. "By the same token a man of sense would have told you how little experience he'd had." He reached out and encircled Francesca's fragile wrist. "I can find you a clean shirt of mine to put on. Sorry about the jeans. You can use either the bath or the shower in the master bedroom. I'll find you some clean towels. Richards can use the shower room off the storeroom at the rear of the house. There are clean towels there. I'll get Myra up to take a look at him." Grant referred to the wife of Opal's overseer, for years a qualified nursing sister. "I don't think there's much the matter with him if he can sit around spinning yarns."

"I'm going to make it my business to put them all straight later," Fee promised. "I'll come with you, darling," she said to Francesca, feeling for once extraordinarily useless.

"No, Mamma, I'm fine!" Francesca shook her head. "I just

want to cool down. Thank the Lord I was wearing a good sun block. Glenn will find himself with a bad case of sunburn, but I'm afraid he was too careless for comfort." She glanced at her watch, then back to her mother. "You're not finished for the day are you?"

"We'll see, darling." Fee glanced around. "We were doing some lighting set-ups when that wretched horse came in. But now that you're both home safely I expect Ngaire will want to finish the scene. Marc and I are ready. He's a pleasure to work with. So professional."

"Can you pass on that message to Richards, Fee?" Grant asked, as Fee started to move off. "I'll put a call through for Myra to come up to the house and take a look at him. She'll find him a good spray for that sunburn. It doesn't matter how many times you warn people of conditions out here they don't seem to take much notice."

All the rooms at Opal were of a generous size but the master bedroom was huge, dominated by a beautiful satinwood four-poster the floral pelmet of the elegantly decorated canopy matching the chintz of the ruffled bed valance that fell to the carpeted floor. All the furnishings were instantly familiar to Francesca's English eyes, the George III giltwood mirror, the mahogany chests, the scrolled day bed near the French doors, a pair of Regency chairs. All of it could have come from Ormond even to the side cabinet painted Chinoiserie panels and the English needlepoint carpet. Obviously the Camerons had gone "Home" to do their buying or had the furnishings and all that went with it shipped out.

"The bathroom is through here," Grant said, leading her through the dressing room to a very large bathroom, which had been modernised without losing its sense of the traditional.

"You wouldn't have anything like shampoo?" Francesca asked hopefully, realising the master suite hadn't been used for some time.

"I wouldn't think here," Grant said doubtfully, looking towards a wall of handsome timber cabinets and matching wall cabinets complemented with brass fittings. "But let's see, Rafe and I didn't want a live-in housekeeper like the old days. A couple of the station wives, headed by Myra, keep an eye on the place for us." As he was speaking, Grant walked to the line of cabinets trying the wall fixtures first.

"It's your lucky day," he announced, full of satisfaction. "There's a whole range of stuff here. There could even be towels in the linen press. Myra must be anticipating the day Rafe and Ally get home."

That was evident judging by the contents of the tall linen press that flanked the cabinets. Francesca saw two of the deep shelves held bed linen, others a selection of towels in three colours: white, pale yellow and apple-green.

"I don't know what we'd do without Myra and her crew," Grant said gratefully. "They're downright motherly. I expect Ally will change things but she'll always have their support. So what's it to be." He turned to Francesca as she stood staring around her." Bath or shower? I can run the bath for you if you like? You might relish a soak."

Francesca raised her eyes to his, finding them electric, sparkling with erotic fantasies that rivalled her own. "I would but I think I'd better settle for a shower," she said as calmly as she could. "Easier to shampoo my hair. Besides you'll want to get everyone home before sunset."

"I find I'm more concerned about you," he said, still gazing at her with those gold-flecked eyes.

"The shower is fine, Grant." It shook her that she was wishing he could join her, her whole body, tired as it was, vibrating with awareness, her pulses speeded up.

"All right I'll leave you to it." Grant moved abruptly, prey to his own wishful thinking. "Thanks to Myra everything you need is there down to new combs. Take your time. Some of those towels would be bath sheets. Rafe and I hate those little bits of things that would only go once around you. You'll be able to wrap yourself up."

Without a backwards glance he moved off, closing the bedroom door after him with a soft thud. Alone Francesca shook her head, trying to clear it. It was truly extraordinary the way he affected her. She had never in her life believed herself to be highly sexed. Now she realised it was only because she had never met the man who could deeply stir her. The master musician who could play her like golden sounds.

Quickly Francesca stripped off her clothes and wrapped herself in a huge yellow towel. Then she walked out to the enclosed verandah off the bedroom where she lay her clothes over a couple of chairs that still received hot rays of sunshine. That should dry them off! Back in the bathroom she flung off the towel stepping into the large shower enclosure that would easily accommodate two people with its frameless translucent walls and porcelain fittings. She turned on the taps, keeping the temperature initially lukewarm. The shower cascaded like a waterfall from a very effective wide nozzle producing a wonderfully, sensual, soothing effect. She held up her face to it letting it splash all over her skin. She really needed this. She had come over really rough terrain on foot and no one could understand the effects of the blazing outback sun, the dazzling quality of the *light* unless they had experienced it.

She reached for the shampoo and conditioner in one, lathering her hair twice then rinsing off. Only then did she start to feel the effects of her trek or maybe it was the alternate play of warm then cold water. A faint mist, like a veil, seemed to rise before her eyes and the legs that had pumped so strongly across the spinifex plains began to feel extraordinarily weak. She made a big effort to pull herself together, lurching forward to grasp the porcelain controls. The mist wasn't clearing. It was turning into a fog. Surely she wasn't going to do something silly and faint? She hadn't done that since childhood when she had taken a nasty fall from her pony.

Moaning aloud, Francesca made another attempt to get out of the shower enclosure, only barely aware of a tall figure that loomed up outside the glass door.

In the west wing of the house, Grant had put a call through to the overseer's bungalow, glad Myra was around to pick it up. Quickly he explained what had happened to Richards asking her to come up to the homestead and check him over. That out of the way he thanked her for looking after the homestead so well, particularly for stocking the bathroom in the master suite. It had proved a godsend.

Afterwards, with Myra's bubbly, pleased laugh still in his ears, he hunted up a fresh shirt for Francesca to put on. He understood she would be the most fastidious of young women. Of course he was a good foot taller and maybe four stone heavier but the shirt would be clean and fresh and she could turn up the sleeves, tie up the tails, whatever women did with men's shirts. Difficult to fit her out with jeans, he thought with a wry grin, but her pink shirt had taken the worst of it.

A soft collared white cotton sports shirt with a blue stripe through it came to hand. He couldn't remember the last time he had worn it if he'd worn it at all. Either way it looked pretty new or it had been beautifully laundered and pressed. It would do nicely. He had a clear mental picture of how Francesca would look in it. *Only* it. An image that caused him to take a deep, whistling breath. He tapped on the master bedroom door and received no reply. Unless she'd been very slick about it, Francesca would still be washing her hair. The shirt over his arm he trod quickly to the foot of the canopied bed, intending to lay the shirt on the quilted damask coverlet before beating a retreat when he heard to his alarm the most piteous low moan.

The hair on the back of his neck literally stood up, his stomach muscles contracting sickeningly. For God's sake what was the matter? He shouldn't have left her. He should have sat right outside the door.

"Francesca?" Grant strode to the entrance of the dressing room, noting the sliding door to the bathroom wasn't fully shut. "Francesca?" His voice had picked up considerably in volume and intensity. What the hell *was* this? She had to hear him.

No answer but he could hear the water running. He called her name one more time coming right to the sliding door. Another of those moans saw him flinging it back so hard it rocked in its tracks.

Her naked body was even more beautiful than his imaginings, the curves and the contours, the breasts like fruit. She was hunched over the taps, slender arms extended to turn them off, fingers tightening but ineffectually.

"All right, I'm here!" Grant moved with speed, opening the shower enclosure, catching the spray, grasping her with one arm while the other made short work of turning off the taps. "Francesca!"

She slumped against him causing a great surge of desire he couldn't possibly control, her lovely creamy flesh under his hands, breasts so pretty they left him breathless, the lick of red-gold at the base of her body. Desire he was immediately ashamed of. She was fainting right under his eyes.

A long arm with its whipcord muscles shot out and grabbed a yellow towel. With the utmost dexterity he wound it around her as carefully as if she were a newborn babe, cradling her, before he lifted her completely into his arms, carrying her back to the bedroom where he sat her upright on the side of the bed.

"Francesca, sweetheart!" Quickly he pushed her head to her knees, one arm around her strongly and within moments he was rewarded by the little sounds she made as she came around fully.

"I nearly fainted." Her voice was weak and husky.

"Don't talk." A few moments more and he let her head come up slowly, her long hair hanging in dripping coils. "I'm furious with myself for leaving you," he admitted. "Thank God I came back. How do you feel?"

The first shock over, Francesca started to realise her situation. "Still a bit giddy."

"Hell!" he said quietly. Now that she was recovering he was back to being excruciatingly aware of her nakedness, trying to keep his eyes on her beautifully shaped legs, imagining his hands stroking their satin length. Petite, she was perfectly proportioned, the most graceful nude a master such as Renoir might have painted, though there was far less of her than his usual voluptuous young models. But the red-gold hair, the extraordinary luminescent flesh, the rose tips of her breasts gave off the same erotic charge. The yellow towel had slipped almost to her waist and he pulled it back up with great delicacy, his sense of touch never more pronounced, never more sensuous, her free-flowing hair fell forward over her shoulders and down in the curve of her back, so richly coloured it lit her skin.

"Myra is coming up to the house to take a look at Richards," he told her gently. "I think I'll ask her to also take a look at you."

She was trembling slightly, a mixture of emotions spiralling through her, not able to handle any of them. "I'm all right," she protested, shaking her head a little so spray fell on him.

"I'll get her to come all the same. It won't hurt." Grant stood up and walked through to the bathroom coming back with a fresh towel. "Here, let me dry your hair."

She held the towel tight against her breasts. "I'm dripping all over the coverlet."

"Who cares! You don't suppose Ally is going to leave any of this intact?" he asked wryly. "Sing out if I'm hurting you."

Hurting her? Every sexual nerve end was screaming into life.

Yet she sat quietly, the yellow bath sheet wrapped tight around her while Grant drew her hair back over her shoulder and mopped up the long ends. Then he applied the towel with a more vigorous motion until it was ready to comb. He might have been doing this all his life so efficiently he went to work drawing the wide-toothed tortoiseshell comb down the full length of the strands until the job was done.

"Have you any idea how young you look?" He forgot every-thing and put his mouth to her tender nape.

Her whole body began to tingle, responding irresistibly, caus-ing her to lean in against his lean powerful frame.

"What are we doing here?" he whispered into her ear, one hand coming down to cup the delicate mound of her breast. "You should be getting dressed. I should be going for Myra." His head dipped further, his mouth against her ear, the top of his tongue flickering over its shell-like shape. "Francesca!" He began whispering things, endearments that turned her heart over, his breath warm and clean going deeper and deeper into her, like a tunnel that reached into her soul. "You taste of fruit," he marvelled. "A delicious white peach."

She thought she would faint again with the pleasure of it. The ravishment.

"God, what's the matter with me?" he whispered hoarsely something about the attitude of her body concerned him. He lifted his mouth away from her with a remarkable effort. "I'm sorry, you need care not hungry kisses." His voice was so low and seductive before it turned brisk and businesslike. "If you hold the towel around you I'll help you get into my shirt. That's what I came for. Here, Francesca." He reached for his white shirt, slid it on one slender arm, fixed it around her back, then pushed her arm into the other sleeve.

She didn't feel able to help him and he seized her hand and kissed it. Then he went down on his haunches in front of her, beginning to do up the buttons, hazel eyes smouldering as his hands skimmed her breasts, slid along the smoothness of the fine cotton, lingered in her lap, the warmth of her, the place where he wanted to be.

"Well that's done!" Her weakened physical condition was the only thing that saved him. He wanted her so much he could feel his own head swimming. Only then did she make eye contact.

"I love you, Grant," she said, more sweetly he thought than any other woman would have said it before.

"Will you say that when you're ready to say your goodbyes to me?" he asked her tenderly, his whole soul crying out for her. "I bet you never even told your father about me."

It was true. It never seemed to be the right time when she rang home. Her letters contained a lot of news: people, places, families, her own family the Kinrosses, and their neighbours the Camerons. But unless her father was excellent at reading between the lines he would have little idea she had fallen madly in love with Grant Cameron. Why didn't she tell him? Was she a coward? She only knew her father had always been there for her when her mother wasn't. She dreaded the thought of hurting him, a beloved parent, shattering his dreams.

"Somebody ought to tell him, Francesca," Grant warned. "Tell him straight, you owe him that. If you can't. *I* can. Then you'll really know what to expect."

Her delicate fingers touched his face, tracing the cleft in his chin. "How would you tell him?" Was he offering a magical solution?

He made a little sardonic grimace. "What do you think, flower face, I'd hop on a plane."

"Just like that?" His decision seemed to galvanise her.

"Why not?" Your father doesn't bother me. He bothers *you*. He even bothers Fee who doesn't give a damn about anyone. I suppose that's what comes of being a belted earl." Grant stood up determinedly. "Now I'm going to get Myra to take a look at you. Why don't you lie down while I'm gone."

"I'll take the daybed near the door." Francesca made an attempt to stand up, Grant assisting her until she was upright. Her feet were aching, she realised without surprise. But what about her neck and her back? How had she hurt herself? The answer was obvious, struggling with Glenn, first to get him off the ground then mounted on Gypsy. Strangely she hadn't felt much of anything at the time. She was going to have to suffer for it now. But she had no intention of complaining. It wasn't her way and she had brought a lot of it on herself. She should have left Glenn to go for help. Even as she thought it she knew she would do the same thing all over again. Ally always told her she was a softie.

She looked utterly adorable in his shirt. It was miles too big for her, but for all that or maybe because of it she looked as innocent as a child. Yet incredibly sexy. The flame-coloured mane he had combed back from her face and over her shoulders was drying in the late-afternoon sun. It radiated light, the perfect foil for the creaminess of her skin. She touched every part of him, the sight of her an actual hand squeezing his heart.

He took her chin between his fingers, tilting her face to him, staring into those starry eyes with a very serious expression. A total acceptance of his role. "I want you more than I've wanted anything in my whole life," he told her, his voice harsh with emotion, but reverent. "I've dreamed about you. Night after night after night. I want you in my bed. I want to take your precious gift of virginity. And it is a gift, Francesca. I want to be the only man in your life. *Ever.*"

The whole room seemed to be filled with the fabulous colours of the sunset. Tears came from a deep place inside of her. "And I'm yours to keep. To have and to hold."

Triumph blazed in his eyes. His arms closed around her so strongly they almost lifted her from the floor. He found her upturned mouth, a smile of utter bliss at its corners, her tongue feverish to mate with his. The kiss went on forever. "Do you love me?" she whispered frantically, twisting away from him for a few seconds. "Say it. Say it."

"*Say* it? I'll show you." His whole body was reverberating with passion. There was no alternative left in the world for them but marriage. And God how he wanted it. He would do anything for her. Fly to England. Seek out her father. Speak to him. Ask for his approval. He owed him that courtesy. With Francesca by his side he could build something of great value. She needn't jettison her old life altogether. He would always allow her to visit her father, her homeland, her friends. Hell he'd find time to go with her. She was the only woman who would make his life right and he was drunk on her love.

Fee calling in to see how her daughter was, found her and Grant locked in a kiss so passionate she felt no one had the right to intrude on such intimacy. But disturb them she must, discovering in herself a great rush of regrets. Although she had known Francesca and Grant were in love she'd had no real inkling of the depth of their feelings.

What she was witnessing was something irrevocable. Something that would work. A cataclysm of desire the likes of which she had never thought her lovely young daughter capable. Francesca was so young, so inexperienced, sheltered all her life. Now it seemed Grant Cameron had taught her all about her own sensuality. This wasn't the holiday affair she had feared. Francesca's loyalty lay with Grant Cameron when Fee genuinely believed it lay elsewhere.

While Fee stood rigid, unable to move, Grant and Francesca finally became aware of her presence. They didn't spring apart. They didn't act in the least guilty. They broke apart slowly. Francesca shook her long hair back from her face and Grant gave his white mocking smile.

"Fee, you've made an art form of exits and entrances."

If she'd been thirty years younger Fee would have blushed. "Sorry, I didn't mean to intrude but I thought at least Francesca you'd be lying down. And what on earth have you got on?" She peered at her daughter's petite figure, astonishment on her face.

"Goodness, Mamma, can't you see?" Francesca came forward for inspection, the most beautiful smile blooming on her face. "It's a man's shirt. Grant's."

"And it looks very fetching," Grant remarked, reaching for Francesca's hand, a unity of two. "Actually, Fee, we made a mistake leaving Francesca. She all but fainted under the shower."

Fee who couldn't even remember all her lovers' names looked and sounded aghast. "And you rescued her?"

"Thank God I was on the spot," Grant answered very seriously. "I returned with the shirt and heard Francesca's moans."

If it hadn't been her own daughter, Fee would have come out with something possibly caustic, instead she rushed to Francesca's side. "Is this true, darling? You're such a delicate creature."

"Even Ally might have fainted after a trek like that," Grant offered dryly.

"I don't think so, dear," Fee said. "Ally wouldn't have been fool enough to take pity on the man."

"Lucky Ally to get your approval, Mamma," Francesca said with a gentle touch of censure.

"Oh, you know what I mean!" Fee cried. "Don't be miffed at me, darling. You're such a tender-hearted little thing."

A wry smile spread across Grant's face. "And there is the shining fact, she makes no fuss. None of us have heard a word of complaint from her. Francesca may be tender-hearted and I love her for it, but she knows how to handle herself. Tell you what. You two have a talk. I'll go fetch Myra. Francesca is looking a vision at the moment but we can't overlook the fact she did go into a faint."

"For a girl who nearly passed out you're looking the vision Grant said," Fee commented, looking into her daughter's eyes. "You've come to an important decision, haven't you?"

"I knew right from the beginning," Francesca answered simply. "Grant had certain fears for me. As you did, Mamma, and probably still have. But ours won't be a marriage between two very different people. A marriage between two cultures, two different lands. Grant and I are soul mates. We agree on mostly everything. All the important things anyway. Now he's finally realised I will be able to adapt to his world. Something I've known for years. I've loved my mother's country since I was ten. It speaks to me, too."

Fee thought for a long time. "I should have seen that, darling," she said, "but as usual I was too self-engrossed."

"I know in my heart, Mamma, this is right. Grant and I will

aid each other. He trusts me. He respects me. He knows I can help him. That's the way of a real marriage."

Fee touched her daughter's cheek with love and un-characteristic humility. "Do you realise how lucky you are, darling? It's taken me half a lifetime to find my other half. David loves me just the way I am. Your father desperately wanted me to change. Still he mattered a great deal to me at one time."

"He loved you, Mamma," Francesca pointed out gently, ever loyal to her father.

"They all did, darling," Fee argued, juggling all her memories, "if I say so myself I was very hotly desired."

"So am I." Francesca gave her enchanting smile, moving over to the daybed near the French doors and sinking back on it. "I want Father to give me away. I want to go forward to my new life with my hand on my father's arm."

"Of course, darling," Fee agreed. "But you must tell him about Grant without delay. Once he sees how happy you are I'm sure there will be no anger, no pressure." Fee sincerely hoped not, finding solace in the knowledge the earl doted on his daughter. Besides, stacked up against Jimmy Waddington, Grant would emerge the overwhelming winner.

"As it happens, Grant wants to fly home to see Father," Francesca was saying, sounding as though her own resolve had firmed considerably. "He wants to speak to Father himself. I'm not afraid they won't get on. In many ways Father and I are very much alike."

"You do show your lineage," Fee agreed. "Little bits of us both you carry around with you."

"And I'm going with him," Francesca said. "There are many things I want to explain to Father. Many things to thank him for. As for Father and Grant! I think they'll find plenty to talk about," Francesca said prophetically. "There's nothing to stop him coming to see us from time to time."

"My darling, count on it," Fee said. "Especially when you have your first baby."

Both women laughed, a wonderful companionable sound.

When had her daughter turned from a charming child into a woman ready to take on the biggest challenge in life, Fee thought. Quite obviously when I wasn't looking.

CHAPTER SEVEN

TEN DAYS LATER with the outback location shots completed and Francesca's small part in the film over, Ngaire, Glenn and the crew, returned to Sydney taking Fee and David with them. Fee still had some scenes, shot in and around Sydney, to go and she needed to prepare for the big party she was throwing to launch her biography. That was set for the end of the month.

"Thank you for saving my life, Francesca," Glenn exaggerated suavely on departure, taking her hand and pressing a lingering warm kiss on it. "I can't wait to see you again at Fee's party. You were absolutely perfect as Lucinda. The best we could have hoped for."

Ngaire agreed with a hug and a kiss. "Let's face it, darling, you could have a career if you wanted it."

Not when I have a better one in mind, Francesca thought, keeping her own big news for the time quiet.

Grant watching Richards turn on the charm had the satisfaction of knowing by the next time Richards saw Francesca she would be very much engaged. He had the ring in his pocket. It had only arrived the day before. And it was breathtaking! Fit for a princess. He'd faxed the family jeweller over a week ago, listing his requirements. 18ct white gold set with a finest quality diamond. Maybe 1.5 or 1.6cts—he left it to them—thinking a 2ct central stone would be too big for Francesca's small, elegant hand. The central diamond was to be flanked by something different. Rare pink diamonds? Perhaps pear-shaped? He drew a sketch of what he wanted, the cost coming in as a secondary consideration. His gift to her had to be just right. The ring was to be exquisite. As flowerlike as Francesca herself.

The jeweller lost no time at all sending a return fax with two detailed sketches featuring a classic central stone, one oval, one round, flanked by the finest quality Argyle pink diamonds. In the second sketch the pink diamonds were pave set. He knew immediately which one he wanted. It all but fitted his own design except for the oval-shaped central stone, which looked better than his own idea of a round cut, the flanking pink diamonds set like leaves. He felt charged to the hilt, desperate to slide it on her finger.

"Rebecca has asked me to stay to lunch," he told her as they watched the charter flight lift into the peacock-blue sky. "After that I have to get back to Opal to supervise a maintenance check." He lowered his head, his eyes beneath the wide brim of his akubra, glittering like gemstones. "What if we take a quick run out to Myora? I want to show you something."

She looked at him with pleasure. "That will be lovely! I've been meaning and meaning to show you my sketchbooks but with all the rush of the filming there hasn't been much time. Fee kept them hard at it. She wanted it all over before the book launch. And you haven't really answered the question. Are you coming?"

"I insist on coming," he said dryly. "What with Richards still acting loverlike. Who said he could press kisses into your hand?"

"Didn't mean a thing," she teased.

"I hope so, I'm amazed by his cheek."

Ten minutes out on their cross-country drive they stopped to watch a pair of roaming emus, one of the world's largest birds, conducting a comic mating dance. The male was acting up so crazily, kicking up its long legs, crossing them, lifting itself off the ground, Francesca couldn't stop laughing. The female on the other hand was displaying a considerable hauteur that could have passed as indifference, stalking about the male or preening her mass of feathers, the assumed indifference as it turned out far from the case.

"Just giving him the run-around." Grant grinned. "Emus are remarkable creatures and not only for their speed. They can find a living in the most arid parts of the run but they seek shelter in thick scrub when they're nesting. The eggs are huge as you know. They require more than two months incubation."

"That's a long time for poor Mum."

"Poor dad don't you mean? The male undertakes that task."

"Well, good for him. Mother kangaroo at least carries her little ones in her pouch. They're just adorable, the joeys. It's absolutely fascinating watching a herd of kangaroos bounding across open country on their long hind legs yet when they walk slowly they use their forefeet and their tail to steady them rather like a tripod, as the hind legs come forward."

"You've made quite a study of them." He didn't tell her he had seen her wonderful sketchbooks. Not yet. She had the eye of the artist. The capacity for acute observation.

When they arrived at the site for his proposed homestead, they could see in the distance a large herd of cattle feeding on the purple flowering succulent, the parakeelya, peculiar to the sandhills. The stock could live on this or other succulents for months without water.

"Rafe and Ally will be home soon," Grant said quietly, still sitting behind the wheel of the Jeep.

"They're disappointed they're going to miss Mamma's party," Francesca said, "but she put the launch off long enough to fit in with filming."

"*And* her marriage," Grant drawled.

"She and David don't want to tie the knot without Ally present." Francesca gave him a quick smile. "Mamma and Ally are very close."

"Does it bother you?" he asked gently, relieved when she shook her head.

"Not really, I love them both. Mamma understands Ally better than she does me. I'll have to get married to convince her I've grown up."

"As long as you don't make it *three* times." Grant had a wry joke at Fee's expense. "Let's get out." He moved swiftly around the vehicle to help her, taking her hand, loving the way she twined her fingers through his. In front of them Myora glowed a fiery red under the hot sun, the breeze that seemed to have sprung up out of nowhere causing a strange sighing sound to emanate from its hollowed out cavities and caves.

"Voice of the spirits," Grant said, looking down at her. "Are you scared?"

"Why wouldn't there be spirits," she said. "This is an old old land, full of Dreamtime significance."

It was time to tell her. Here in this place so close to their hearts.

"I saw your sketchbooks."

She lifted her head, blue eyes surprised. "Why didn't you tell me?"

"I think I was too moved by them," he answered simply. "I didn't want anyone else to look at them. Or your sketches of *our* homestead. That's something uniquely ours."

"You liked them?" She stared back at him steadily.

"I loved them, Francesca," he said, his dark voice deep. "As I love you. I can't possibly draw like you but you read my mind. Your sketchbooks finally convinced me you truly love this country. The flowers and the animals you've drawn so accurately. Your idea of an oasis in isolation proves how closely our minds work."

She touched his golden face tenderly, in absolute love. "It means everything to me, Grant, you feel like that."

"I do." His strong arms encircled her. "Forgive me for ever doubting you couldn't adapt to a strange land. It isn't strange at all. It's part of the richness of your inheritance. And now I have something for you." He cast his eyes around, settling on a large boulder, mainly rust-red in colouring but with thick yellow ochre veins. "Come sit over here."

"What is this all about?" She let him lead her, feeling unbelievably precious to him. It was wonderful. Intoxicating. As necessary to her as the air she breathed.

"You'll see," he promised.

When she was seated he went down theatrically on one knee before her, flashing her his brilliant smile. "Lady Francesca de Lyle I beg you to marry me. I adore every hair of your Titian head. I'm even prepared to beard your father, the earl, in his den. I want his consent for us to marry. I want his blessing. I want everything that's going to make you happy. We can be married in England if that's what you want. I know you'll want your father to give you away. I'm certain it would please him. I'm equally sure he'll want it that way. I'll risk the grey skies and the cold of your winter. I'll risk everything if only you'll marry me. And just so you won't keep me on my knees too much longer I'd be honoured if, in the meantime, you'd wear my ring." He took a small navy case from his pocket, opened it and withdrew the ring. "Your hand, my lady." His smile deepened as he registered the joyous anticipation on her lovely face.

"Take it," she breathed, feeling her hand nerveless.

He did so, slipping the diamond engagement ring down over the satiny skin of her finger. "Not bad! A perfect fit. I love you, Francesca. I'll love you always."

"Oh, Grant!" she whispered, extending her hand to the sun, watching all the brilliant flashing lights. *Pink* diamonds! So beautiful.

"You're not going to cry, dear love?" Grant asked very tenderly, feeling extraordinarily emotional himself.

"Of course I'm going to cry. It's obligatory on these occasions. Tears of joy!" She flung herself forward, against his chest, his arms closing around her before he lost his balance. They both rolled on the pure clean sand that was covered in parts by a broad-leafed vine.

Now she was gurgling with laughter.

"Stay still. I want to kiss you." He arched over her.

"I haven't told you if I'm going to marry you yet."

"Tell me *after*." He moved with big cat grace, bringing his hands in tightly to hold her body captive, riveted by its *female* suppleness. Then he lowered his head.

"Ah, Grant...."

The laughter died. There was such burning desire in his voice and in his eyes she felt an answering flame lick her veins.

He kissed her into breathless submission, pressing the length of his body against hers. "Anyway I'm not going to take no for an answer." His fingers tripped the pearly buttons of her shirt and slipped inside, shaping and caressing her naked breast. He was utterly sure of her, the dominant male, but she loved it. Her arms slid around his neck, her fingers digging into the tawny hair that curved thickly into his nape. He was a beautiful man. Beautiful!

"I love you."

"I thought you did," he said passionately.

"I can't wait to marry you."

"I can't wait to marry *you*," he groaned, falling back on the sand beside her. "We have to see your father. We have to make him delighted with our news. A wedding has to be arranged. How the hell am I going to be able to manage all that without ravishing you?"

"But I *want* you to." Her voice choked on emotion. She ached for him to take her.

"And I going to." He was breathing harshly, his handsome, high cheek-boned face taut and hungry but with a strength that confounded her. "But not like this, my love. The first time we're together is going to be very, very, precious. The first time I lower myself into your body. The time and place will be right. No hurry."

"You're too sure of yourself, Grant Cameron."

He turned and kissed her again, brushing back the hair that fell about her face in wild disarray. "I have some news for you that you will like," he told her as they eventually lay back entwined. A small grin crooked the corners of his shapely mouth. "I'm having that architect I saw come out here to walk over the site. It's all organised. We'll show him your sketches. Let him work with them. I'll order it so we can have a three-month honeymoon. Anywhere in the world you want to go. Fiji, Patagonia, Antarctica, the Swiss Alps. By the time we get back, our dream home will be built."

EPILOGUE

THE CAMERON-DE LYLE wedding took place in England in June of the following year. The ceremony was held in the centuries-old village church of St. Thomas, adjoining the bride's father, the earl of Moray's splendid country estate in the rolling hills of Hampshire; the reception for two hundred people held in giant white marquees erected in the grounds of Ormond Hall the de Lyle ancestral seat, which at that time of the year were breathtakingly beautiful, a landscape gardener's dream and inspiration. The wedding said to be one of the most beautiful of the decade was covered by *Tatler, Harpers & Queen* and the *Australian Woman's Weekly,* so there were plenty of photographs for those who followed the social pages and weren't fortunate enough to get an invitation.

A marvellous shot of bride and groom looking gloriously happy appeared on the cover of the Australian magazine. Although the bride Lady Francesca de Lyle, dubbed by the Australian press, "The English Bride," was indeed English on her illustrious father's side, her mother was the internationally known Australian born actress Fiona Kinross who had had a brilliant career on the London stage, spanning some thirty years. Fiona Kinross, Mrs. David Westbury, was a member of the prominent landed Kinross family, daughter of the late Sir

Andrew Kinross, a legendary Australian cattle king, whose forebears had pioneered the industry in colonial days.

There were colour photographs of the bride on her own, looking exquisitely romantic in delustred duchess satin, the sweetheart neckline and bodice decorated with beautiful corded lace that ran down the full skirt. On her head she wore a flaring waist-length tulle veil held in place by a delicately beautiful family tiara of diamonds and pearls. Pearls with a diamond pendant at her throat, a small posy of beautiful white roses in her hands.

There were photographs of the bride with her two small flower girls, an enchanting shot; the bride with her attendants, the stunning Alison Cameron, nee Kinross, matron of honour, first cousin to the bride on the mother's side, Lady Georgina Lamb and Miss Serena Strickland, the bride's friends from childhood, all in harmonious shades of pink silk. There were photographs of the groom with his attendants, the best man, elder brother, Rafe, master of the Australian historic cattle station, Opal Downs, their close friend and recent brother-in-law by virtue of Rafe's marriage to the stunning matron of honour, and *her* brother, Broderick, master of the equally famous Kimbara Station. Mr. Kinross's beautiful wife, Rebecca, was clearly from the photographs some months pregnant but radiant in a simple, elegant blue dress with a gorgeous blue hat.

There was a lovely photograph of the bride with her father, the earl of Moray, both beaming with delight. A photograph of Mr. and Mrs. David Westbury, Mrs. Westbury wearing the most fabulous emerald hat and silk two-piece suit, shoes and handbag precisely matched. No photographs of the bride's father and mother together. But one of the earl with his present countess, Holly. Some photographs of people the English side of the family didn't know at all. Among them Miss Lainie Rhodes from Victoria Springs, a cascade of blonde hair and an irresistible big smile wore an elegant white-and-navy suit with a rather wonderful confection in navy with a huge navy-and-white bow on her head. "It's wonderful! The best fun!" Miss Rhodes went on record as saying. Seated beside her, a rakish grin on his mouth, a strikingly handsome young man who bore a decided resemblance to the tawny haired groom and his "golden" brother. Family, of course—Mr. Rory Cameron, world traveller.

The honeymoon, which included a flight over Antarctica said to be "truly awesome" in the true sense of the word, would take the happy couple to places as far away as Scandinavia and Canada where the groom wanted to look up members of the Cameron clan who had migrated there in the early days.

It was the perfect day for a perfect wedding, all three magazines reported. Sky-blue and golden the sun pushing its way through a few early-morning clouds to shine down on the happy couple. Everyone who was there and those who devoured the magazine photographs afterwards, agreed it was plainly a love match.

Wasn't that just wonderful!

* * * * *

Keep reading for an excerpt of
The Bull Rider's Baby Bombshell
by Amanda Renee.
Find it in the
Claiming The Texan's Heart anthology,
out now!

Chapter 1

Call Jade.
I can't do this.
Please forgive me.

Jade Scott read her sister's note for the tenth time since arriving in Saddle Ridge. Almost an entire day had passed since Liv had vanished, leaving behind her month-and-a-half-old triplets. Jade would've arrived sooner if there had been more flights out of Los Angeles to the middle-of-nowhere Montana. She'd ditched the godforsaken town eleven years ago and had sworn never to return. But her sister's children had annihilated that plan. Especially since Jade had been partially responsible for their existence.

"I didn't call the police like you asked, but now that you're here, I think we should."

"No!" Jade spun to face Maddie Winters, her sister's best friend and the woman who had taken care of the children for the past twenty hours. "As soon as we do, Liv's labeled a bad parent and those girls go in the system."

"Nobody will take them away with you here." Maddie

checked to see if there were any new messages on her phone. "I'm really worried about her."

Jade scanned the small living room. A month ago, it looked like a baby—or three—lived there. Today it looked cold and sterile, devoid of any signs of the triplets. The crocheted baby blankets and baskets of pastel yarn were gone from the corner. Once covered with stacks of photo albums her sister couldn't wait to fill, the coffee table now sat bare. Embroidered pillows with their cute mommy and baby sayings no longer littered the couch. Her sister had even removed the framed pictures of the girls along with their plaster hand- and footprints from the mantel. Except for the video baby monitor, nothing baby related remained in sight. Why? She knew Liv's desire for order was strong thanks to their chaotic upbringing, but she'd never thought her sister would wipe away all visible traces of her children.

"I'm worried too. We don't need to involve the police though. She wasn't kidnapped." Liv was a chronic planner and everything about the situation felt deliberate. "She made a conscious decision to walk away. She wrote a note, she called you to babysit and then left on her own accord. If we call the police, the girls go into the system. Hell will freeze over before I let that happen."

Jade knew all about the system. She and Liv had spent fourteen years in foster care, bounced from place to place until Liv had been old enough to become her guardian. Being two teenage girls on their own had forced them to grow up fast. Too fast.

Jade's phone rang inside her bag jarring her back to the present. It wasn't her sister's ringtone, but she reached for it to be safe. It was her office in Los Angeles. She answered, praying Liv had called there by mistake instead of her cell and they were patching the call over to her. "Yes."

"I'm sorry to bother you," Tomás, her British assistant, began. "I just wanted to let you know the Wittingfords have finally decided on their venue for their summer opener."

Jade's heart sank. Tomás's call was great news, just not the news she wanted to hear at that moment. The Wittingfords were the most extravagant clients her event planning company had seen to date. And their showstopping party guaranteed to outshine all the celebrity weddings she'd produced this year.

"I'm glad to hear it. I just wish I was there to oversee it." Jade tugged her laptop out of her bag and opened it on the dining room table. "Email me the contract and I'll review it. I want you to look it over first. Flag anything you question. I need you to be my extra set of eyes while I'm away. And please call my clients and tell them I've had a family emergency. Give them your contact info and make sure they understand I haven't abandoned them. But they need to phone you with any issues or changes and you can fill me in later."

"I'll get on it, straightaway. Any news about your sister?"

"Nothing yet." Jade lifted her gaze to see Maddie glaring at her from the living room. "I need to go. We'll talk later."

"I can't believe you're putting work first." Maddie picked up the baby monitor from the coffee table and checked the screen.

"I'm sorry you don't approve of my multitasking." Jade turned on the computer. "I know my sister. She doesn't do crazy. Wherever she is, I'm sure she's safe. While I try to figure out what's going on with her and where she ran off to, I still have a business to maintain."

"And walking out on your newborn triplets isn't crazy?"

Not unless you knew the whole situation. "All right, tell me again. What time did you come over yesterday afternoon?"

"A little after three. Liv sounded frazzled when she called. I asked what was wrong, but she kept doing that answer a question with a question thing that drives me up a wall. I got nothing out of her." Maddie ran both hands through her hair, on the verge of tears. "I tried to talk to her, but she took off the second I walked in. I found the note taped to the nursery room door a few minutes after that."

"When did she remove the baby things from in here?"

"I don't know." Maddie shook her head wildly. "I'm trying to remember the last time I came over."

"What do you mean? You're her best friend and you didn't check on her? When I left, you assured me you would. You only live next door."

"She insisted on space so she could learn how to take care of the girls on her own. I guess it's been a little over a week since I've been here. I'll be honest, her abrupt dismissal hurt. I had been staying in the guest room after you left. I should have noticed something was wrong."

Uneasiness grew deep within Jade's chest. "I keep thinking the same thing. I missed our video chat on Sunday night because I was too busy with work." Many of Jade's ex-boyfriends had accused her of putting her career before anyone else. Had she selfishly done the same with her sister? Jade scanned her inbox, hoping to find an email from Liv. Nothing. "I'll check her office. Are you able to stay for a little while longer?"

"For however long you need."

Jade continued to walk around the old farmhouse. Her sister had set up three bassinets in the room next to her office in addition to an equal number of cribs in the former master bedroom, now the nursery. Liv had been prepared. Some may even say overprepared. She'd read every parenting book and magazine she found. Took infant care classes and had insisted Jade learn infant CPR too. From researching the best laundry detergents and baby shampoos to memorizing the symptoms of childhood illnesses and diseases, she'd planned for every contingency. It didn't make sense why she left. Outside of neither of them not knowing what good parenting was.

Their father had been a drifter and their mother had been behind bars on and off since Jade was two. They'd seen the inside of more foster homes than they could count. Some good, some bad. Whenever they had made it into a decent one, their mother had gotten out of jail, claimed to be ready to raise them again after completing her therapy and halfway house program only to fail miserably weeks later and wind up right back in jail. Her mother had always wanted what she couldn't have. That included Liv and Jade. Once in her care, she'd discovered they were too much work to support. Besides, her drugs were more important. She wanted those more than anything. More than her children.

The court system had reached a point where they said no more, and Jade and Liv had mixed emotions the day they learned they wouldn't have to live with their mother ever again. Liv had handled it better than she had. Jade had been angry. All the time. It hadn't helped that kids had picked on her constantly at school. One kid had been the ringleader. The one she had trusted, and then he betrayed her. And she had never forgotten him. Wes Slade.

Jade opened the bottom filing cabinet drawer and scanned the hanging folder tabs. The last one had *BABY* scrawled on it. The generic word surprised her. At the very least, she'd expected all three girls' names to be written on the label, if not three separate files. She removed the thick folder, laid it on the desk and began looking through it. On top was the first ultrasound picture of the triplets. Jade ran her fingers over the black-and-white image. She could still see her sister holding up the photo to the screen during their video chat. Liv had been shocked, but thrilled just the same. She was finally getting the family she had always wanted. And it had been a long time coming.

Liv had battled fertility issues for years. Married at twenty-three, she and her husband had tried everything to get pregnant. There was just enough wrong with each of them to prevent a successful pregnancy. Kevin had wanted to adopt, but it had been important to Liv to carry her children and have a physical connection to them. He'd refused the donor idea and their constant baby battles wound up destroying their marriage.

Jade sat in Liv's ultralux, oversize perfect-for-pregnancy office chair and glanced around the room. Her sister had always been neat and organized. Not a pen or paperclip out of place.

She peered inside Liv's desk drawers hoping to find a clue to her whereabouts. Everything related to her job as a financial planner. Liv still had another two months of maternity leave until she had to return to work full-time. Working from home would help the transition although Liv had considered hiring a nanny during the day so she could talk to clients without interruption.

Her sister had a plan. A definitive plan on how her life would run smoothly as a single mom of three children. Walking away was completely out of character.

Jade continued to flip through the contents of the folder. The only item left was Jade's egg donation contract giving her sister the biological link to the babies she wanted. She just hadn't expected Liv to use all the embryos at once. Because of her sister's long infertility battle, the doctor had believed her best chance for a successful pregnancy was to implant them all in hopes one would survive. The surprise had been universal.

"Dammit, Liv, where are you?"

She stood to put the folder back in the drawer when she noticed another one lying on the bottom of the cabinet. Sliding the other files forward, she removed the thin, unmarked and probably empty folder. She flipped it open to double-check and saw another donor contract. Why? Jade had been the only donor. Liv had used a fertility clinic for the father.

She began to read the document:

This agreement is made this 22 day of July 2017, by and between Olivia Scott, hereafter RECIPIENT, and Weston Slade, hereafter DONOR.

"No, no, no!" Jade's heart pounded in her chest. "Liv couldn't have." She continued to read the contract. But she had. Wes Slade was the donor and the father of Jade's biological children. Her sister had fertilized Jade's eggs with the man she despised more than anyone.

* * *

A few hours later, Jade stood in front of the check-in clerk at the Silver Bells Ranch lodge. The woman whispered into the phone. "One of Wes's fans is here to see him."

"Excuse me. I am no fan of his."

The clerk cupped the mouthpiece and whispered, "She may be an ex-girlfriend."

"Are you kidding me?" Jade reached over the counter and snatched the phone. "This is Jade Scott. I need to speak to Wes concerning my sister, Liv. It's…um…an emergency of sorts."

Still reeling from her discovery, Jade needed absolute confirmation Wes was the triplets' father. She prayed he had backed out or that Liv had changed her mind at the last second. Anything…just not this.

"Oh hey, Jade. It's Garrett, Wes's brother. It's been what, ten years or more? I saw your sister and the triplets last week. They sure are beautiful. Reminded me of my two when they were born."

You have no idea. Jade swallowed hard. "I'm staying with the kids for a few days while Liv is—is away on business. She's unreachable today and I have a problem at the house. Since she and Wes are friends, I'm thinking he might have some ideas." At least Jade assumed they were friends. Who would ask a casual acquaintance to father their children?

"He's out with our guests on a trail ride. He should be back soon. You're welcome to wait or maybe I can help you."

"Uh, um. No. I appreciate the offer, but I need Wes. I don't mind waiting." Yeah, she did. The longer she waited, the more questions churned in her brain. "Where's the best place I can catch him?"

"The stables." Garrett paused. "Do you have the girls with you? I'm sure my daughter would love to me—"

"They're with the sitter." The last thing Jade needed was to introduce the triplets to their cousin.

The entire time Liv had been pregnant, Jade kept her part in the process tucked neatly away in the dark recesses of her brain. Surprisingly, Liv had carried to almost thirty-seven weeks. The day of her sister's scheduled cesarean, Jade had been by her side in the operating room, cheering her on. But the moment Jade had held those tiny bundles of perfection and stared into their blue eyes, reality hit. She was the biological mother of three little girls and she had wrestled with it during the rest of her stay in town. They were Liv's children. Not hers. It wasn't until she was on a plane flying back to LA three weeks later that she finally breathed easier. Once she had returned to her normal routine, any lingering thoughts of being their mother faded and she gladly slipped into the role of auntie.

Until today.

She needed to find Liv…fast.

Garrett took the reins as Wes dismounted. "Thanks for helping out."

"No problem." Wes didn't mind filling in for other employees while he was visiting the ranch, considering they had covered for him plenty during his last few months of employment on Silver Bells. It had been an unbearable period in his life and he'd wanted nothing more than to get away from Saddle Ridge. And he had. He'd moved to Texas and escaped the drama he once called home.

"Oh, I almost forgot." Garrett snapped his fingers. "You have a visitor. Do you remember Jade Scott?"

Wes damn near tripped at the mention of her name. Even though he couldn't think of one person he despised more than Jade, it was her sister he didn't want to think about.

"What is she doing here?"

"I guess she's babysitting the triplets while her sister's away on business. She has some emergency at Liv's house. I offered to help, but she insisted on talking to you."

"Keep your distance from the Scotts." Wes swallowed hard. This was exactly why he hadn't wanted to come home for his brother Dylan's wedding and his niece and nephew's christenings. "They can call someone else. I have no business with Liv or Jade."

"What's with the attitude?" Garrett asked. "I thought you and Liv were good friends. Besides, it's too late. Jade's about ten steps behind you."

Wes turned to see her weaving through the ranch guests walking back to the lodge. His stomach somersaulted at the sight of her and he wasn't sure if it was because of their past or how much she had transformed since high school. The mean girl who had once made his life miserable had gone from a rough, chip-on-her-shoulder teen to a California knockout.

Sleek, rich mahogany waves replaced the frizzy curls she used to have. But that body and those curves…good Lord Almighty! Her black polka-dot chiffon blouse revealed just enough of her ample cleavage to make any man look twice, and her tailored black pants hugged her hips in perfection. She exuded an edginess combined with old Hollywood glamour and if she had been any other woman on the planet, he would have moved in for the kill. Their past made her off-limits and his connection to her sister sealed that deal.

"Wes." Deep blue eyes held his gaze before traveling the length of him and back.

Transfixed upon her matte ruby-red lips, it took every ounce of strength he had left to respond. "Jade."

"Hey, kids. A conversation requires more than that." Garrett laughed. "Try hello, how are you." He nudged his brother in Jade's direction before walking away.

"What do you want?" Wes hadn't meant his tone to be as harsh as it sounded.

"It's about Liv. Is there someplace private we can talk?"

Wes stiffened. "I have work to do." He turned to tend to his horse, but it wasn't there. Silently, he cursed his brother.

"I thought you were on vacation from your job in Texas."

He reeled to face her. "Who told you that?"

"The rodeo school where you work." She stepped toward him and wobbled in her ranch-inappropriate four-inch heels. He reached for her arm to steady her and instantly regretted the contact. "I looked you up online. I need your help."

Wes released her and rubbed his palm, wanting to erase all traces of her from his body. "On second thought, I don't care what your reasons are. I'm asking you as politely as possible to leave."

"Wes, please." A half-foot shorter, even in those ridiculous heels, she stared up at him.

"What could you possibly need my help with?"

"Tell me I can trust you first."

"No. You can't trust me, so let's end this now. Goodbye, Jade." The intoxicating scent of her perfume wasn't enough to entice him to hear more.

"I know."

It wasn't so much the words, but the firm way she said them that stopped him in his tracks. "Do you care to expand on that?" He prayed it wasn't what he thought.

"I found the contract today at my sister's house," Jade whispered. "Before I go into details, promise me everything I tell you will stay between us."

Wes wanted to argue and deny his role in Liv's daughters' paternity, but the worry etched into Jade's face gave him pause. "Okay, you have my attention. And yes, you can trust me."

Jade assessed him sharply, making him more uncomfortable than he already was. She had no reason to take him at his word considering their past had thrived on a mutual loathing of one another after their brief high school romance. Her shoulders sagged as she closed her eyes momentarily, shielding him from the pain that reflected in them.

"Liv left the triplets with Maddie yesterday and hasn't returned."

"That doesn't sound like Liv." Wes's heart dropped into his stomach. "Have you called the police? Or checked the hospitals?"

"I called every hospital within a two-hundred-mile radius while I waited for my flight last night. I don't want to involve the police. This isn't a case of her getting in a car accident. She left a note saying she was leaving. Do you have any idea where she might've gone? Has she ever mentioned a place she enjoyed going to when she was under a lot of stress or anywhere she always wanted to visit?"

"Not offhand. I can't believe she left the girls." Wes propped a booted foot up on the fence rail and stared into the corral. "I was afraid this would be too much for her."

"Wait a minute." Jade grabbed him by the arm and forced him to look at her. "You suspected she was in trouble?"

"That's not what I'm saying." Wes checked over his shoulder to make sure they were still alone. "I was long gone before those babies were born. And for the record, this wasn't an easy decision on my part. There was never anything romantic or sexual between your sister and me. We were good friends. She was there for me during the darkest time of my life."

"So how did you get from point A to point B?" Her face soured. "She told me she used an anonymous donor."

"Liv hated the thought of a stranger fathering her children. I had initially said no, then I realized she wanted this more than anything and relented. I felt I owed her for being there for me over the years. But that's where it ended. I couldn't continue our friendship, knowing she was carrying my—" Wes shook his head. "They are not my children. I refuse to say they are."

"I'm not asking you to raise them." Thick sarcasm laced her assurance. "Just tell me what happened."

Wes hesitated before answering, not wanting to sound callous. "Liv and I went our separate ways. She called me once I was in Texas and told me she was having triplets. I'll admit, I had my concerns and asked if she could handle that many babies. She said she was a little overwhelmed by the news, but even more excited. I could hear it in her voice. She also had you and her friends. So, I continued on with my life."

"Turns out she was more overwhelmed than we both thought." Jade's phone rang. She removed it from her bag, checked the screen and then rejected the call. "No matter how long it takes to find her, I'm not abandoning those babies. You can't, either."

"I am not getting involved. I did my part and then got out of town for a reason. Many reasons. They are not my responsibility. She should have gone with an anonymous donor like she had with the eggs."

"She didn't use an anonymous egg donor."

"Then whose were they?"

"Mine. You and I are those girls' biological parents."